RING OF FIRE

Crashed in the bush the safari car lay on its roof with the wheels in the air. Three bodies lay neatly beside it in a row, the director, the starlet and the white hunter. All clear and tidy—an accident—except that the hunter's head had been most untidily blown off with his own shotgun.

Ashe and McNally agreed that the Kenya Police could handle it. Gareth Ashe wanted to take a break in Uganda anyway and Tom McNally had things to see to back home in America. It all might have ended just like that but Ashe somehow got himself tangled up with the murderous Smith and his grotesquely faced accomplice who still had some clearing up to do after the accident—and it included Ashe. Then there was McNally's memory of a dead man in wartime Germany—and a defector with an interest in nuclear warheads. Ashe and MacNally began to realise that there were ominous implications and they alone seemed to care.

Suddenly what started with an accident on a hunting safari exploded into grisly murder, bombing, maniacal fanaticism, international intrigue and a threat of worse to come. Trapped in a ring of fire that was about to catch, Ashe and McNally wondered if the world had gone crazy and just how long it could last before a final madness put an end to all reason and sanity.

RING OF FIRE

Bernard Gavin

W. H. ALLEN · LONDON
A Howard & Wyndham Company
1977

Printed and bound in Great Britain by
Butler & Tanner Ltd, Frome and London

For the Publishers, W. H. Allen & Co Ltd
44 Hill Street, London W1X 8LB

ISBN 0 491 02190 9

To Joyce, without whose help
this novel would have been
finished much sooner!

CHAPTER ONE

The big Boeing crawled like a blind insect towards the main block of the airport, and slewed around to turn a baleful, sightless look towards the balcony where I stood. The late afternoon sun in Nairobi was still fiercely hot but there was a hint of high altitude chill in the light breeze. That's the moment I remember best as a starting point because it was then that I knew I had made a mistake. I watched the main filming unit of Constellation disembark in a sickeningly shallow performance of posing and posturing which reinforced my realisation that I'd been wrong to accept the contract they'd given me. You can get pretty tangled up with life sometimes and in the middle of it all you stop and ask yourself how the hell you'd got involved anyway. There must be a point where you have some choice to make, and if you make the wrong one you just get carried along without there being much you can do about it. That point for me was when I accepted the job with Constellation. But then, the money was good and my prospects were far from healthy—and perhaps the most attractive thing about the job was that it was a chance to go back to Africa.

I had been recruited from the film company's London office; it would have been pretty difficult to have found the right sort of person, with a knowledge of the country and the language, in America. Sent ahead of the main party, I worked with the location manager to spot out the sites and generally negotiate the arrangements for filming rights in game reserves and tribal areas which needed special government permission. So for about a month everything was fine—I enjoyed the work, the night life in Nairobi was pleasantly 'different' and the money just rolled in. But it was all too good to last, I suppose. It's one thing to smooth out the rough places when you're working with sensible, intelligent craftsmen, but quite something else again when you have to do the same thing for self-centred, self-infatuated, spoilt and temperamental 'artistes'. I do use the word most loosely here. At the end of the day I was sometimes left wondering just who was supposed to be the primitive and who the sophisticated. Between the mud-plastered Masai moran and the mud-plastered star moron there was often no line to draw. I kept telling myself that I just couldn't take any more, but somehow I turned up again each morning either because I was fascinated by the bizarre or because I had been brain-washed by too many films during my childhood. The fact of the matter is that in Europe I would have probably accepted it all and thought it quite normal, even exciting maybe, to be so close to all the action in what was scheduled to be big box-office production. But Africa is not like that. There is some majestic timelessness about it which makes the advertising and mass media values all shallow and worthless, something which makes you re-evaluate yourself, restating the basic human necessities in raw and primitive beauty. It takes a world-shattering event to make any impact on Africa and although Constellation could, and did, shake its own tottering continent with a souless manipulation of the public, it failed to produce even a tremor there in Africa. The temporary prosperity that it handed out as bribes and dues to a few local chiefs and safari companies would be soon dissipated, and old Africa, having brushed the fly from her nose, could settle down to sleep again. Her sleep will not last long now, I know. Her dreams are troubled and she may yet wake screaming from some terrifying nightmare.

Perhaps if it had been left to me to make the decision I would have seen the thing through and hated myself for the rest of my life for selling myself short on the very few principles that I have left. As it turned out though, the decision was taken out of my hands by a pair of coincidences that were to prove as tragic as they were remarkable.

About a week before the filming deadline with only a few more scenes left to be shot, most of the acting staff were told to take some time out while the greater part of the camera units went up to Uganda for some background and continuity shots around the region of the Ruwenzori mountains near the Zaire border. Most of the lead characters, with an assortment of directors and the big producer himself, organised a hunting safari to kill time during the lull. Looking at them I realised that that was all they were likely to kill. I was left with the unpleasant task of procuring the game licences. It came as a bit of a shock and surprise to learn that I was included in the arrangements—and in fact had been assigned to the small group that was accompanying P. J. Hines, the producer. I'm no great hunter myself, but I had seen enough during the previous weeks to get pretty sick at the idea of that lot going out to shoot. There were a number of professional hunters engaged to guide—and I suppose kill off any maimed and wounded animals—but even so it was only my bank overdraft that induced me to accompany the group. With a month's salary due, and P.J. thundering about a breach of contract, I thought it best once more to swallow my principles.

I knew what to expect because during the past few weeks I'd seen what havoc Constellation had inflicted on the ecology of its locations. Most scenes involving the shooting of animals had had to be done many times, each time using a new animal. The last one, excelling the performance of the rest, received the same payment of course with a Mannlicher, fifteen feet from the camera. When you work out just how much game was seen to be shot during the film and reason that most of it had to be done three or four times at least, we don't seem to have moved very far from the days of Ancient Rome. The only development is the elimination of uncertainty for no dangerous animal performed for Constellation Inc. and lived to tell the tale.

We were to drive about eighty miles from where the unit had set up its base. 'Lion country' was the phrase used to romanticise the venture. I don't suppose I blame Pete Thomlinson really— he was the white hunter who was to accompany us and I suppose he had a living to make too, and was not above doing a bit of dramatic production himself. He was a lean, sombre-looking man who did nothing to maintain the image of his profession in appearance, but he had a reputation as a cool and accurate shot. I'd known him for a number of years in a casual sort of way. He was a native Kenyan, but lacked the flair and imagination of most of his compatriots. Except for the deep walnut sun tan, one could have taken him for a disillusioned Civil Servant, lined, bitter and glum, with all the anxiety of the white man in Africa, facing the end of a way of life with puzzlement and a sense of despair about the way events were proceeding.

Our particular party consisted of five Europeans, including Pete, and the usual assortment of Africans to act in the time-honoured tradition as cooks, gun-bearers and stewards. These latter were mostly Wakamba and they looked as cheerful and trustworthy as they could for the occasion, with a fine sense of human psychology in knowing what was wanted of them. We 'hunters' travelled in a big safari car and the servants followed behind in a Bedford lorry, loaded high with the equipment.

Thomlinson drove our vehicle and seated with him in the front was the great P. J. Hines, producer and chief director of the film we were making. He was a big florid man with a large hooked nose and close-cropped iron-grey hair. He had a world-wide reputation as a film-maker, and as a bon viveur—a man who could get just anything he wanted. Proof of this sat between him and the driver: Tela Parre, who had a small walk-on part in the film, but who appeared to be playing a larger rôle in Hines's personal life.

She was one of Hines's discoveries and he seemed to be still in the process of exploration. She was a tall, musky girl, all woman and all knowing, with the most fantastic pair of tits I'd ever seen in my life—they seemed to arrive in focus long before the rest of the personality and remain as a retinal image long after she'd gone by. I don't normally have much sympathy for anyone who describes a woman in terms of her tits, but in Tela's case you'd just have to excuse them. Her spoken vocabulary was confined to a few drawling interjections and comments, and yet what the rest of her said would fill volumes—all of them pornographic. She had a vague Indian look about her, with her hair severely drawn away from her face. She gave an impression of innocence joined to experience that was very disturbing and erotic.

There was nothing strange in this thing that P.J. had going. Ask anyone who's ever been around a film set and they'll tell you that it's open season from start to finish with all the casual banging a man could wish for, but that was the very thing that made it so odd, different and strangely immoral. Everyone in the business knew what was going on, but I think that they were both unaware of this. They carried on as if they were making monkeys out of all the rest of the people. P.J. was well and truly married, having had three wives, the first in Europe during the early forties, and then two others in America. The latest marriage was still viable, and rumour had it that one more dose of alimony and settlement would ruin him. So perhaps he was being circumspect. Me, I think he was just being kinky about the innocence bit. Like a lot of men his age he was hedging against the occasional failure to get it up by playing up the avuncular bit.

4

The hunting trip was just a front, it seemed to me, and I suppose that was the main reason for me being told to join the party. I was just one of the props, and I wasn't fooled for a minute when P.J. had insisted on having my local expertise at his elbow. But the reason for Lee Conway's presence was a bit of a mystery. He sat beside me in the back seat, silent and morose; he seemed to have no interest in the proceedings at all. There was some talk linking him with Tela, but I could see there was nothing in that. Perhaps P.J. had dragged him along as a red herring. A romance between these two, even if only hinted at, would be good publicity for the picture and also serve the double purpose of putting the present Mrs Hines off the alimony scent.

Lee Conway was a bit younger than P.J.—an actor who had worked his way up in the business, never really getting to the top but having a reputation for reliable and creditable performance that gave tone to a production. He was a big man, with a look of solid and powerful strength in spite of a thickening about the waist. I'd heard on the set that he had started in films as a stunt-man and extra. He still had that relaxed way of sitting that denotes the co-ordinated, active man who has spent a lifetime keeping himself in shape.

In the next few weeks, I often took my mind back to that morning, driving out into the wild open spaces with those two men. P.J. and Conway had known each other for about ten years, I suppose—and neither had ever had an inkling of the strange way in which their lives had touched each other many years before.

Eighty miles might be little more than an hour's drive on the main tarmac roads of Kenya but away from those, travelling as we were, one could only expect to average about thirty miles an hour. The sun beat down on everything and a lazy heat haze shimmered on the road ahead of us. The whole countryside was dominated by the red murram brown of the soil which showed everywhere through the sparse grass. The whole view looked like a gigantic autumn leaf shaded haphazardly with yellow, green and brown. The rust red of the roads stretched out like the veins of the leaf, twisted in death.

Behind our vehicle the dust swirled about and our slow speed was barely sufficient to keep ahead of it. Gradually everything and everyone began to get a light powdering of what looked like No. 9 Leichner. The inevitable shaking and bumping along the rutted roads, together with the still, relentless air began to show on the strained eye-screwed expressions of the passengers. The first hour had gone by quite quickly—there was buoyant conversation, a holiday atmosphere and the newness of the situation to lighten the boredom. Even though the company was not all it might have been, the very enthusiasm of Tela and P.J. was infectious and for a while it was possible to see everything again through new eyes as Pete pointed out and identified small groups of game. But soon it all began to pall and we settled down into a desultory drowsiness.

The only amusement—if you could call it that—was watching Tela play a complicated game of kneesy, or more accurately titsy, as the vehicle swayed from side to side. I found myself wondering just how far the game could go. I could imagine P.J.'s response there in front of me, secretive, furtive and therefore pleasant. Pete's on the other hand would be more philosophical: 'Take what's offered—the chance is always worth the game.' Of Tela's attitude I could only vaguely guess. She was a type that was difficult to weigh up, a type that evoked sensuality without being sensuous. I supposed that when it came to the point she would not be able to let herself get too involved. Perhaps like many of her sisters the world over, the whole point was the sublime duality of never letting your left tit know what your right tit is doing. I can't really understand this myself, but perhaps if I had secondary appendages to experiment with, life might hold all sorts of interesting diversions!

When we eventually arrived at the place that Pete had picked out for a base, he immediately sent out some trackers to look for spoor while the remainder of the boys set about making camp. They were experts at the job so that in a very short time after arriving we were sitting under a shady awning with cool drinks in our hands while P.J. stalked about doing his Hemingway/Ruark bit. Lee Conway seemed set on making a day of it for within seconds he was calling for another drink. He looked sour and mean, and yet, in his way, unhappy too. Something very deep was worrying him and he seemed set on taking it out on small sodas and very large whiskies. P.J. on the other hand was in a broad and expansive mood and he seemed to ignore the way in which his conversation was ignored by Conway. To Tela he was formal and polite, calling her Miss Parre and talking for all the world like the perfect gentleman who knows where he's sowed his oats and when the time for reaping will be due. But his eyes belied his words for they roamed all over her.

It was a most welcome relief when the trackers returned shortly after lunch, all excited with some news of '*simba nkubwa sana*'. They had come across the very fresh spoor of a big lion some miles away to the north. As I watched their gestures and saw their faces, I had the feeling that they had been watching too many Daktari films in Nairobi and were hamming it up a bit much, but Hines went for it all in a big way.

'Come on, Lee boy. Let's go get him.' He dashed off to the car shouting for his gun boy. Lee boy was not very impressed.

'What are we waiting for? Let's get moving!'

Pete had been listening to the boys, getting the details of their report. 'Now wait a moment, Mr Hines, don't let's go off at half cock. There's plenty of time. This one won't be going anywhere in a hurry; he's well fed and holed up to sleep it off.'

Pete was responsible for the safety of the expedition and he had a whole lot of organising to do before anyone went off 'shooting'. The guns had to be sighted in before leaving, but as far as P.J. was concerned all this was not necessary. Pete walked off to get things moving, leaving the producer fuming with impatience.

He glared at us. 'Now remember you two, this one's going to be mine,' he said. Lee Conway got to his feet.

'No need to worry about me,' he said thickly. 'I won't be coming along this trip.'

I expected that P.J. would have been annoyed but instead he shot a sly glance at Tela and much of his impatience evaporated.

'Well now that's all right, Lee boy. I guess we'll get along without you just this once.' He looked steadily at me a while. 'What about you?'

For a moment a devil in me prompted me to stick it out and insist on going, but then the thought of playing gooseberry to Tela and a lion convinced me.

'Not for me today, P.J. My knee's acting up a bit and I'd just slow you all down.'

'Well now, that just leaves the two of us, Miss Parre, unless you back down, too, that is.'

Tela shook her head quite coyly. 'I think I'd like to come along with you, Mr Hines,' she said. 'Perhaps I can get some pictures of you in action.'

'That'll be great,' he said. 'I always did want to get into the movies. Never thought they'd be blue though!' He guffawed loudy and went off to find Pete to tell him the news.

About half an hour later the safari car drove off, Pete at the wheel, looking anything but pleased with life, and P.J. and Tela in the rear seat, heads together, sharing some joke. We waved them off and then sat down again facing each other while the dust trail of the car disappeared over the low horizon. I had seen Conway around a lot during the past few weeks, but now I studied him carefully to try to see what there really was in him. With P.J. gone, much of the tenseness had left him. He sat there easily in his chair, a well-proportioned man with cool grey eyes. He was going a little to seed and his fingers showed a podginess that comes from idle living. I had hardly spoken to him since we met for he was always surrounded by a court of publicity men, managers, dressers and hangers-on. So now I saw him for the first time stripped of all his glamour. I suppose that my distaste of him must have shown because he returned a hostile look, determined not to be outfaced. For the first time I thought that there might be something in him after all. I felt an urge to try a little further. 'Why didn't you go with them?' I asked. 'Run out of lines, or are you afraid of being out-roared in the scene?'

He jumped from his chair. 'Look, I don't have to take that from you or anyone else.' His face was flushed and his hands were clenched by his side. I looked at him inquiringly.

'I know the lines,' I said, 'but I'm afraid I've forgotten just what picture they come from.'

I must have touched him on a raw spot. I don't quite know what happened next but I felt myself being lifted on to my feet and was dimly aware of his right fist drawing back. I just had time to jerk my head out of line as I felt it go past like an express train. So it's business, I thought, and brought my two hands up sharply to break his grip on my shirt. He fell back slightly and as I moved in he came back at me, both arms out like a bear. I sensed that if he got them around me I'd be finished so I went in with two crisp ones, one to the soft overfed belly and the other arcing over to the point of his jaw. I knew as I made contact that my timing had been faultless. Usually that's enough but he didn't go down. He swayed for a second and then shook his head and came on again. There was a wild light in his eye then. I think he was hurt, but it just hadn't got through to him. He suddenly hurled himself at me again and before I could think I was down beneath him trying to protect my head from his wild punches. We struggled together for a few seconds. I realised that things were a bit out of hand and might require some drastic action, then suddenly he went quite limp as if all the fight had gone out of him. It had. He got up slowly and looked down at my leg.

About five years earlier, during a riot in Jordan, I'd lost most of the bone and muscle of my left knee-cap in a grenade explosion and although the doctors in the Military Hospital in Lydda had done a first-class job on it, there was no doubt that it was gammy. It had left me with a marked limp and only with great difficulty would it bend at all.

All the rage had left his face and he looked awkward and apologetic, mumbling something that sounded as if he were sorry. It was my turn then. I felt an absolute fool for having riled him and for being responsible for his discomfort and misery.

'Look,' I said, 'this doesn't matter a damn, forget about it.'

He looked straight at me and then without any malice said, 'My public should have seen me today. I couldn't even take a ten-stone cripple.'

Not only did I weigh considerably more than that, I didn't like his choice of words. He must have seen this in my expression.

'Oh! damn, I've done it again,' he said, and as if to make up a little, he helped me back to my chair and offered me a cigarette. I shook my head and reached into my pocket for my pipe. My hand came out with the broken pieces of a Meerschaum. 'That's some fall you gave me,' I said. 'These things are supposed to take any sort of punishment.'

He offered me the pack again and I took a cigarette. We both lit up and looked at each other panting a bit and then we both saw the humour in it all and started to laugh. 'Come on,' he said, 'this calls for a drink—and that's not a line from a film either, just a plain statement of fact.'

We got up and made for the tree that stood service as a bar and pulled out a couple of beers from the bar box. As I drank I looked around and for the first time noticed the few men who were left in camp standing around grinning. One cracked his face in a wide toothy grin and expressed the panacea for all trouble in that part of the world: '*Mazuri saana Bwana!*'

The fact of the matter was that we were both tensed up till then and as it turned out it was more or less over the same thing. We sat in the shade drinking beer for a couple of hours, I suppose, swopping stories and experiences. There's something about the open air which lends itself to this sort of thing—how else could you imagine a man like Conway telling me that his real name was the improbable Thomas Poseidon McNally! By the time we'd had three or four bottles of Whitecap the metamorphosis seemed complete and Lee Conway was an identity that he had shed like a snake sloughing off an old skin—and the result was really an improvement. I found myself quite liking the man.

I responded to his anecdotes about his early career as a stuntman with a brief account of my own activities since leaving the Diplomatic Service. I told him nothing of the explosion that had crippled me—nothing of the terrible feeling of guilt and inadequacy that still haunted the edges of my mind whenever I thought of it. And I told him nothing of my dearest Fona who had died just because I had chosen that split second for a wrangle between my conscience and the dealer of death. I kept the story in my memory together with the everlasting image I shall have of the mud-stained, blood-streaked face of the terrorist as he threw the grenade.

Instead, I told him about the small one-horse business that I had set up since then: PIPIRAS, Pied Piper Representative Agencies—a fanciful title! But after my dismissal I had a reaction against the formality of the service and took on work that had taken me back to most of the countries of Europe, the Middle East and Africa. The work had ranged from the sublime intrigue to the ridiculous suburban. My way of life up till then had had little to recommend it. So after the affair in Jordon I was not really very sorry to have earned the extreme displeasure of Her Majesty's Government. I found myself a free man again with a small gratuity, a gift for languages, a few contacts all over the place and nothing else. I wanted to do something different from the ordinary run-of-the-mill jobs, so I blew the gratuity on the lease of a small office in Cardiff and advertised in the national press. It was a gamble that just had to pay off or I'd end up being a school teacher or something equally boring.

Within a week I got my first assignment, handling a rather delicate sewage problem in an immigration centre some twenty miles away. It was that which gave my idea its name of Pied Piper, for the rats I met that week were just nobody's business. After that things went fairly well, all things considered. Within two years I was making a steady income and leading an interesting life. I left suburbia and its problems behind and concentrated on the bigger stuff. I saw no reason to change the name of the agency for, one way or another, the rats still seemed to show up, though by now they were the two-legged kind and sweet music just doesn't work on them. I had struck an unusually slack period when the offer from Constellation turned up. I could have held out for a time but in the hope that one thing would lead to another I took a job with them, interpreting and generally oiling the wheels between them and the local people. The price was good and, as I constantly told myself, I needed the cash.

The saying goes that the grass is always greener on the other fellow's grave. By the time I had related a few of my exploits to McNally, he was fascinated. He proved to be very knowledgeable with a great deal more common sense than his publicity gave him credit for. The questions that he asked me were pointed and showed that he had a keen analytical mind. In no time at all I had taken him on his personal value and forgotten about the Lee Conway that used to be.

He told me about his life in Hollywood and how the whole set-up sickened him. His contract expired after this film anyway and he'd had enough. He had decided to get out. I sympathised with him. For a while he said nothing, but selected and lit a cigarette thoughtfully. When he eventually spoke, it was in an almost embarrassed way.

'Look, I've got maybe two weeks longer tied to this crap machine, I've had offers for renewal from Constellation and quite a few from other companies, but I tell you, Gareth, my craw is full. I just couldn't take any more of it for any price. I guess that this acting business just isn't in my blood. Now I reckon that I've made enough during these gravy days to last me for the rest of my life, but what I need is something to do! I've thought it over a hell of a lot during the past couple of weeks and given the go-by to dozens of ideas and schemes. They all seemed to lack that certain kick that I'm after. I thought of going to Canada and getting into lumber or Fleet fishing but Hell! Gareth, business is as bad as filming from what I can see of it, all cut-throat competition and worry! But this thing you've been talking about sounds more like it. We could make it go, boy, we could make it swing.'

'You mean that you want to join Pied Piper?' I asked.

'Just that,' he replied. 'Strictly on a business level of course, I'd be prepared to invest for a third up to twenty thousand dollars.'

I thought this over steadily. I liked the man and, no doubt about it, Pipiras could do with a financial kick in the agency. He'd over-valued the investment but that would do no harm.

'Come on, what do you say, Ashe? I'll bring my own pipe.'

'I've got to warn you that Pipiras is far from a healthy risk. You may be throwing your money away.'

'I'll risk all that. Come on.'

He held out his hand. I only hesitated a moment, then I took it and we shook on the deal. He had a firm and steady grip and I realised that life still had lots of mistakes for me to make, but I would never look back and count that as one of them.

The afternoon wore on steadily as we talked over details of our new partnership, of the contacts that he had in America, and the impact we could make when we got going there. We were still talking when we saw the dust cloud of the car returning. It was about a mile away, churning up the dry earth road like a tank. The boys saw it too and the whole camp, which had slunk away to sleep through the hot hours of the afternoon, began to bustle with activity as they prepared to welcome the hunters home. Tom looked at the car growing larger every second. He chuckled and said, 'Just wait till you hear me tell old P.J. about this. He'll throw a fit.'

However, as it turned out, P.J. had thrown his last fit and balmed his last ulcer. When the car came into our compound we saw that it was not the Safari car but a battered Land-Rover that belonged to some government department. In it sat a pale, thin man dressed in heavy khaki drill and incongruous-looking mosquito boots. He stepped out of the car and I could see the signs of quite a strain on his face. He leaned heavily against the side of the vehicle and spoke in a thick emotional voice.

'I think there's been a nasty accident down the road a few miles.' His face turned a ghastly pale hue and he turned to be violently sick on the ground beside his car.

CHAPTER TWO

There is something very strange about the Englishman abroad. He has the notion that every occasion in life requires an introduction, as if social convention must be kept at all cost, so together with the details he gave to us, we had to be told, and register, the fact that his name was Williams. He recovered quickly from his vomiting and set off ahead of us in his Land-Rover. We took whatever first aid kit we could lay our hands on and set off to follow him in the lorry. His hurried explanations had been almost valueless and we still did not know quite what had happened. There was an uneasy feeling in the pit of my stomach. I always get it, even when I only think of a motor accident.

Just over two miles from the camp, where the road took the crest of the hill rather steeply, Williams stopped. We could see the wreckage of the Safari car about a hundred yards below us. The scene looked ridiculously quiet and peaceful and I remember vaguely wondering where the lions were. Tom brought the lorry to a stop and we both got out and looked for a way down. Eventually Tom went down the slope alone and I sat on the wing of the lorry. Williams drove off on a detour through the bush that he said would bring him to the scene of the accident. I looked around me and back along the road. It was dangerous all right but I wondered how the car could have left the road so suddenly. Steering failure? The tracks showed that it had curved suddenly and definitely over the side with no sign of braking or skid. I could see the way it had cut through the brush down into the valley below.

In less time than I thought likely Tom came back. His face was blanched and serious despite the steep climb that he had just made. When he spoke, his voice was low and quite hoarse.

‘God, Ashe, they’re all dead. I didn’t like them, not any of them, but they deserved a better deal than that.’

I looked at the first aid box that he carried under his arm.

'Are you sure?'

'Too damn sure,' he murmured. 'Come, take a look for yourself.'

The way down was not easy and my knee gave me plenty of trouble, but we finally got there. The car lay on its roof, wheels in the air. I looked in. It was a twisted mass of metal and upholstery and some pathetic fragments of possessions which had meant so much to their owners such a short time ago: a handbag with its contents strewn about, some field-glasses and cameras. I looked up and asked, 'Where are they?'

Tom walked over to a thick clump of elephant grass and parted the stems. The first thing I noticed was the delicately shod feet of Tela Parre and then gradually the whole horrid scene forced itself on my eyes and I saw the three of them sprawled on the ground. They were dead, as only the dead can look, especially Pete Thomlinson, for his head had been blown in with a shotgun at what must have been point-blank range. We checked again, carefully going to each one in turn, but there was no sign of life.

Tom said something but I did not hear him. My eyes were fixed on the dashboard of the car, trying to visualise what could have happened. I got a disturbed feeling about it all but I could not say what had caused it. The lowering sun flashed momentarily on the bright chrome fittings of the dashboard. I think Tom must have seen it, too, but before either of us spoke, we heard the Land-Rover come crashing through the low thorn scrub. Williams got out.

'Anything I can do?' he asked. 'There's only about an hour's daylight left and we can't leave them here all night or the jackals will make very short work of it all.' He gestured vaguely and then shuddered.

We sat down to think it over and then collected all that we could of value or significance and loaded the bodies into the Land-Rover. Williams started off back to camp with his grisly load, while Tom and I laboured up the slope to where we had left the lorry. We got in silently. The long sunset rays gave the place a very eerie glow and the shadows lengthened stealthily as we turned the vehicle and headed back to camp.

'It doesn't look right to me, Gareth,' he said. 'It looks too neat and tidy.'

I pictured them all lying there together, about fifteen yards from the upturned car. It suddenly seemed very odd to me too. 'You didn't move them?' I asked.

'Not an inch,' he replied, 'and neither did Williams; he reckoned he saw it all from above.'

'No, I don't think he did actually. He was pretty confused I know, but I'm sure that I recall him saying that he had already been down before coming to camp.'

'I'm damned if I remember,' said Tom. 'Let's wait till we get back and then we can check it out.'

We drove on in silence for the remainder of the journey back to camp. The picture of them came to my mind again. They were all roughly side by side and lying on their backs. I know that accident presupposes a lot of random chance, but the odds of three people being thrown from a crashing car and all landing up dead side by side in the same place seemed long indeed.

Back at camp, Williams had already arrived. He was waiting for us with a very stiff peg of whisky in his hand. He looked better than I had seen him earlier. The boys had already rigged the mosquito netting and, stopping only to follow his example with the whisky, we joined him. Settling down in the canvas chairs, we were all silent, each with his own thoughts. We lit cigarettes and for a brief instant in the flare of flame, the African dusk shrank back, only to close in more intensely a moment later. A cook fire burned some way off but I don't think any of us had any thought of eating dinner that night.

McNally broke the silence first. 'Let's hear your story again, Mr Williams, I don't think that I got it quite right last time you told it and I'd like to hear it over. How did you find them in the first place?' Williams looked at us both over the glow of his cigarette, took another short pull at it and then started.

'I was up there on the hill, above the road where they were, I mean where they got killed. I'm on Tse-Tse control you know, I heard the car coming up the hill, it was making rather heavy going of it. From where I was I couldn't see the road, it lay somewhere below me. I wondered who it might be—we don't get many visitors in this area. I thought at first it was the police patrol. I'm pretty chummy with the police inspector and I was about to go back a bit to the crest of that hill and meet him there. Just as I turned I heard a sudden shot and I thought I heard a scream. Mind you, it could have been anything. The next thing I got a ringside view of the whole show, saw the car go down the other side at breakneck speed, bumping along until I lost sight of it. I headed down round the hill and up the valley until I found them.

It was terrible I can tell you. It isn't every day that one runs into this sort of thing. I was expecting a nasty crash—you know even someone killed—but when I saw them all like that . . . Ugh!—I wonder how it happened?'

Tom appeared to be in a sort of daze, but when Williams had finished speaking, he opened his eyes wide. 'You didn't see the car overturn or move them at all?' he asked deliberately. I looked into Williams's face—already there was a heavy air of suspicion in the mood of us all. I could feel that Tom had something on his mind.

'No, it's just as I said,' Williams replied cautiously. 'Everything just as I said.'

'About how long did it take you to get to the car?' I asked.

Williams rubbed his chin reflectively. 'About ten minutes, maybe fifteen, it's hard to say.'

Tom suddenly interrupted my line of thought. He nodded his head in the direction of the tent where the bodies had been placed.

'Well what are we going to do about it? We'll have to notify the police straight away.'

'The nearest police post is about fifteen miles from here, down the road,' said Williams.

'There's a telephone much closer,' I cut in, 'I noticed a line going off over the hill. There's a European-type house there, I think.'

'Much better get to the police post immediately,' said Williams. 'The house is empty anyway and the phone will be cut off. Anyway, we can't go buzzing off up the road in the dark leaving everything here, anything could happen—jackals, hyaenas and what not, you know the score.'

'We'll get up to the house,' said Tom. 'The boys will look after things here.'

'But I say . . .' began Williams.

Tom cut him off with a shout for Musa the head boy. For a long time there was no answer and then we noticed that the fire had gone down and the place was in silence, except for the occasional raucous cry of some night predator. We shouted and called again but it was pretty obvious that someone had told the tale, and the whole lot had deserted or gone to seek more lively company in a nearby village.

There was nothing for it then. We packed up as best we could and, loading the bodies into the lorry, set off for the police post, fifteen gruesome murram miles away, with our ghastly cargo behind us. Williams followed in his own vehicle. The few possessions of the three dead lay on the floor at my feet: two rifles, a shotgun, three pairs of field-glasses, an assortment of personal articles, Miss Parre's movie camera, which was very badly damaged, and the white shoulder bag that held the usual assortment of make-up and odds and ends. I broke open each of the guns. One barrel of the shotgun still held a cartridge, the other was empty and had been fired quite recently. The magazine of Pete's Express was three rounds short, and it, too, had the smell of being used recently. Everything else appeared to be in order, the safety catches were on both rifles but off the shotgun, so it seemed that they had met with some game, got three shots at it and probably failed to kill. They may have been giving chase or just scouting around when someone, probably P.J., had fooled around with the shotgun. It had accidently gone off killing Pete who was in the front of the car driving. They had all plunged over the side as the car got out of control.

'It all seems to fit,' I mused, 'even to Tela's scream.'

Tom kept his eyes on the road and for a while said nothing. When he finally did speak it was quite off the point—or seemed to be.

'Did you ever shoot craps, Gareth?'

It sounded vaguely familiar. 'I don't understand,' I said.

'Craps, ivories, you know—dice, for God's sake!'

'Oh! Yes, we used to play with them when we were children, ludo, snakes and ladders and things like that.'

He looked disgusted, noticed the grin on my face and smiled. 'Look, what do you think the chances are of throwing three sixes?'

I made a calculation in my mind. 'Quite long,' I said, 'but possible. Why?'

'Those three lying as they were fifteen feet from the car all side by ·side and right way up. What do you calculate the chances are of that happening?'

'How do you mean?' I asked.

'Well, just think of this. This hunter guy gets shot up on the road there with enough force to blow him out of the car. Okay, he wasn't. The car goes over the top. P.J. and Tela would be hanging on like hell, either way if the car turned over he would have been thrown out first.'

'Tom,' I said, 'there's just no way of knowing what might have happened. He could have been jammed in, the others might have held on to him, just anything might have happened.'

He looked annoyed at having his theory torn apart. 'Do you believe it was an accident, then?'

'No,' I answered quickly.

'Well, what makes you so damn sure?'

'Because the key was not in the ignition.'

For a moment he looked surprised. 'It could have easily dropped out.' This time Tom looked pleased to be demolishing my theories. 'It could be anywhere from the road down.'

'But it isn't,' I said. 'It's here, inside the film magazine of Tela's camera.'

It was true. In a small leather cylinder that she used for carrying spare reels of cine film my fingers had come across it. By the light of the dash I read the small plastic name tag that was attached to it—THOMLINSON. SAFARI CO., NAIROBI. KRF. 722.

'That's the number of the car?' asked Tom.

I nodded and we drove on for a while in silence. The only sound was the whine of the engine and the plopping of insects against the windscreen as they were lured to their death by our headlights. Just occasionally, there was an ominous thump from the back as our cargo shifted a little on the bumpy road.

A few minutes later Tom noticed that the lights of Williams's car were no longer behind us. With much cursing and impatience, he got the lorry reversed in the narrow road and drove slowly back, peering anxiously ahead. We had gone back about a mile when our lights picked up the Land-Rover with its bonnet raised and the thin figure of Williams beneath it. We climbed down stiffly. He was working by the light of a powerful torch and seemed to be having carburettor trouble.

'I'm afraid that I'm stuck for a while,' he said. We looked into the engine. Myself, I have no enthusiasm for carburettors and at that time of the night, neither did Tom. However, surprisingly enough Williams seemed to have everything under control. 'About half an hour should do it, chaps.' We walked to the side of the road and sat down heavily. He came over. 'Look it's damn decent of you chaps to come back like this and wait for me but really there is no need. Everything's under control. I know this old bus inside out, she's a bitch but she knows her master. You push on to the station, you can't miss it as I said and I'll be along right behind you.'

We gave the usual half-hearted protest, trying to convey that this was where we thought the scene was, but indeed we were both very tired and so we went on, leaving a cheerful Williams behind us.

The Police Post was small, consisting of about five constables, a sergeant and an inspector. Far from showing annoyance at being disturbed, the inspector seemed pleased to see us. He didn't often have company dropping in for this was a fairly lonely post with only a few scattered farmers and prospectors for neighbours. It wasn't until he learned that the company also included three corpses that his friendly air disappeared and the official in him took over. After an hour of being closeted with him in his office we emerged, having told him the whole story. Williams had still not turned up and I began to be a little worried about him and told the inspector so.

'I think he'll be all right. Driving in Africa is like that, you've got to be prepared for anything. Anyway, I'll send a constable back along the road to give him a hand and a bit of moral support.' He called the sergeant to him and in a little while we heard the roar of a motor-cycle leaving the compound. The day had seemed endless and now there seemed nothing to do but wait. I felt tired and jaded after the day's events so that when the policeman invited us over to his bungalow to clean up and have a bite to eat, it seemed wonderful.

After a meal of roast francolin and a most wonderfully refreshing shower, we felt better fitted to face the world and anything that it might send. Tom still had a worried look and often through dinner seemed to be listening for the sound of Williams's car or a motor-bike. When it did arrive we were half way through our second coffee, having talked of this and that for almost an hour. We went out on to the verandah to meet the constable. He came smartly to the salute and delivered his report to the inspector in a brusque Swahili. He had been all the way along the road and back and had seen nothing in either direction of Williams's car! The inspector was not unduly worried. He reckoned that this Williams knew some of the local people and had pulled in for the night somewhere. I looked at him. Something had suddenly occurred to me.

'Is that hill within your patrol area?' I asked.

'Of course,' he answered. 'I get up that way about once a week.'

'Well then, you must be the inspector that he spoke of being chummy with.'

For a while a frown crossed the face of the policeman. 'Williams, did you say? No, can't say I know him. I do know a Williams out that way—a good pal of mine, but he's on sick leave and has been for the last eighteen months, poor blighter.'

'Well, who the hell is this one we've been talking to?' said Tom.

'Not to worry, sir, there's been quite a lot of activity going on for some time up there. Quite a lot of departments seem to be coming and going. I expect this Williams is one of them.'

I could see that Tom was as curious as I was, but the policeman would say no more about the subject and he skilfully guided us away from it and eventually showed us to our room, leaving us with the promise that everything would be taken care of in the morning. For about ten minutes I thought sleep would never come. The bed and the room were comfortable and the night was cool and quiet. We had talked for a while over the strange events of the day, but I think that we were both tired out and seemingly, within seconds of thinking that I would never get to sleep, I awoke with the sun streaming in through the window and a police orderly knocking on the door to bring us our morning tea.

CHAPTER THREE

For years now there has been something in my mind which I can say is positively anti-American. It's nothing political or personal and is probably no stronger than anyone else's in the world. However, there it is. When I awoke that morning, this feeling came through very strongly as I watched Tom. He was up and dressed, shaved and spruce, looking a picture of fitness. I myself felt all bleary-eyed, gummy and every day of my thirty-five years. I replied to his efficient, clean-cut approach to the morning with nothing more than a surly grunt about how uncivilised his whole bloody tribe was.

The morning hours are not my best, and I never even think of activity until my breakfast is safely tucked away and the first pipe of the day is drawing well. So, rather agedly, I crept off to the bathroom leaving him in the middle of some fatuous remark about Kenya being a 'Man's' country. I tried to find peace and restore that sense of well being that a good night's sleep had robbed me of by having a brisk cold shower.

There was a long, mould-stained mirror in the bathroom. I looked at the reflection critically—me, Gareth Ashe, thirty-five years, five foot ten, lean, no belly yet in spite of a liking for beer. A rather dark face leered back, coolly estimating the me that stood there. The tousled dark curly hair stood well up despite the water from the shower—and the deep brown eyes seemed cynical and slightly disapproving. The small beard added a rather worldly look to what would otherwise be an innocent face.

I turned side on to the mirror and remembered the five ages of man depicted by the vertically extended fingers of an open hand. What was it? The angle of rictus, the thumb for the twenty-year-old, the index finger for the thirty-year-old—and so on. Well, I reckoned I would still get it up like a thirty-year-old. Oh, bugger it all anyway, I thought, and towelled myself vigorously, suppressing the first early morning horny feeling that always seemed to betray my feelings of morning depression. How the bloody hell could my rod be so perky when I was feeling so grotty. I went through the rest of the morning ritual muttering and swearing to myself as fluently as a preacher in full *hwyl*.

Breakfast did nothing to improve my mood. It consisted of nothing more substantial than coffee and toast. I can remember that morning quite well, thinking to myself as I spread the butter on to the toast that it was going to be another of those days. When breakfast was over, we sat on the verandah and took stock of the situation. There was much to do. Tom was going in to Nairobi later on to break the unfortunate news to the company and to contact the Embassy people about the matter. He was only waiting for the return of the inspector, who had gone to the scene of the accident very early that morning.

'This inspector guy is very efficient,' he remarked. 'Right on the ball there first thing this morning. I guess I was wrong about him. I never thought he'd get up there himself. I'd figured him as one of the famous chairbound division.'

I smiled, remembering just how efficient some of these chaps could be when they wanted to. Tom's expression grew a little worried. 'This is serious business, Gareth. It gives me the shivers to think that but for a small chance, I'd be with them right now, stone cold dead, but what is worse, stone cold dead because somebody wanted it that way. I wonder what this police guy will make of it!'

We didn't have long to wait to find out, for shortly afterwards the inspector drove up. It was about eleven thirty and already the sun was high overhead and beating down. He took his cap off and eased himself into one of the chairs beside us. Silently, an orderly arrived with a tall cool-looking drink and put it down at his elbow. He wiped his brow with the back of his hand and screwed up his eyes against the glare of the sun. The drink slid down without touching the sides.

'Well,' said Tom.

We both looked at him expectantly. 'Pretty nasty,' he said. 'I'll have to file a report on the whole business. I took a lot of films on the spot. I suppose there will be an inquest.'

Tom stared at him with open mouth. 'What do you mean—are you quite satisfied then?'

The inspector looked perturbed and not a little annoyed. 'Look, Mr Conway, I don't like the implication you are making. This is real life. There's no director or producer who can shout "cut" and the script writer is in a world of his own, and what's more there's no room in it for . . . for . . .' His voice trailed away into a vapour and then suddenly exploded. 'Oh, damn!'

He got up and curtly stated, 'I would like a written statement from both of you concerning the accident, which I shall attach to my own report. Please try to be as accurate and as factual as possible, no theories please. I don't want to find any parts that do not coincide. I can tell you now that I have received a written report from Mr Williams.'

'Williams!' I echoed.

'Yes, it was brought in by hand this morning, together with an explanation for his non-appearance.'

'Well, I'll be damned,' exploded Tom. 'If you want to know what I think, I'll tell you right now——'

'Thank you, Mr Conway,' cut in the policeman. 'Just a factual report, please, without any dramatics.'

He turned away and disappeared into his office. The askari at the door saluted smartly and, in reply to a quiet order, closed the door and placed himself between it and us, very pointedly. Tom looked like a eunuch that had just lost a game of marbles. 'And to think I called the bugger efficient only an hour ago. I sure did misjudge him.'

I was torn between concern for our suspicions and amusement at the sight of Mr Lee Conway being put in his place for the second time in as many days. 'Cheer up, Tom,' I said, 'you'd have got it worse if you hadn't been the great Lee Conway!'

'Okay, so I did ride him a bit. They're all the same in the end anyway so who'd be a cop if he had any brains. Come on, let's get on with these "factual reports" so we can get the hell out of here.'

What we produced in those reports was just what was asked for and the dry accounts of the happenings of the previous day lacked all the tingle of excitement and suspicion that we had felt earlier. About one o'clock, Tom left with the police inspector and several askaris in the safari lorry, still laden with its gory contents, bound for Nairobi and all the official duties that had to be done regarding the accident.

I say 'accident' again here because at this stage, after a cooler discussion, we did decide to leave it like that, and as for the key, as the inspector pointed out, it could well have been a duplicate that Pete had entrusted to Tela's care. The original might well have been switched off and dislodged by the falling body. As the policeman said, the only thing in any doubt was whether the gun had gone off by accident or not, but that would be for his superiors in the city to decide. He doubted if we would be troubled any further. So it looked trite and rather slick, but who knows—it was Africa and God alone knows what wheels turn what wheels there.

I did not feel like going to Nairobi or returning to my job with Constellation. I worked it out that I could take a short holiday, fly back to London and still break even with what I'd earned already. I'd been able to borrow a Fiat from the police and now I planned to drive to the location, pick up my salary and a few possessions and then drive off in my own car up to Uganda, thrash around there a bit and then sell the car before flying back to London. Uganda would be hot that time of the year I knew, but I counted on getting around a bit in the few weeks that I planned to stay.

Tom planned to 'tear all hell loose' in Nairobi before flying home to the States to wind up his film career. He was, as he put it, 'through'. This he reckoned would take him all of two months, so we parted on the understanding that we would get in touch in the following year. I was sorry to see him go. We'd been good company for the past twenty-four hours and I was finding it harder and harder to describe anyone as good company.

As our ways parted I saw Tom and the policeman wave from the cab of the lorry. I raised my hand back to them, feeling a bit nostalgic.

At the location everything was in turmoil. The radio phone at the police post had called in to Nairobi and the police there had lost no time in informing Constellation. Even the people from the camera units had begun to dribble back in. A top-level meeting was being held on the fate of the picture, and everyone was speculating. Believe me, speculation itself is a rat race in a set-up like that. Everyone was milling about and jockeying for an advantage. Every little group I met seemed to be remembering something spicy from the lives of the dead producer and actress, either separately or in conjunction. So I collected my cheque and, having given my account of the incident to the big three now in charge of the production, I left Constellation Inc., and took none of their dust on my shoes. Nevertheless, I felt contaminated somehow and longed to take a few long lonely days away from it all. It was this desire to get away from people that made me decide to abandon my original plan and spend a few days bushing it, to blow the cobwebs away.

I left the Fiat at the local police post near the location. As I left there I ran into Cornwallis who was Pete Thomlinson's partner in the small safari company that they operated. He was on his way into the post as I was leaving. He offered me a lift back to the location after he was finished so I sat in his car and waited for him. After about half an hour he came out again. He looked thoughtful and serious.

'They asked me a lot of questions about Pete and particularly about the car he got it in.'

I was curious. 'Did they ask you anything about the ignition key?'

'Why, yes.' His forehead creased into a frown. 'Now what was all that in aid of anyway?'

I told him about the key I had found among Tela's belongings.

'Oh! yes, it's as I told them. Pete had two keys for the car all right—you see he had this thing about keys when he was hunting. He never would carry anything in his pockets that might make the slightest noise. About a week ago, I remember his losing the key for one of his vehicles but I can't really say which, it was quite the usual thing for him to misplace keys and things, so I didn't pay much attention at the time.'

After he dropped me off, I walked over to the park where the film unit kept its transport, collected my car, stowed my baggage in it and headed for the nearest township where I might pick up the few items that I needed.

I enjoyed the comfortable feeling of driving my Ford again. It was the estate type and I had all my gear in the back which included the basic necessities for roughing it for a few days in the bush, and a small calibre magazine rifle that might be handy for a bit of small game shooting. I took the old ·38 that I'm very sentimental about too. I stopped at the first likely looking dduka in the township, filled up with petrol and added some tinned goods and water to my supplies and then I was away. The tarmac of the town was soon left behind and I was leaving clouds of red dust behind me and bucking every bump on the road, but I was happy for there wasn't a soul in sight. Even the rondavels away in the distance seemed deserted, and for a while I felt that all Africa lay at my feet.

What it was that took me that way again, I can't say for certain. It might have been an off chance, or maybe something in my mind was not satisfied with the situation, but after two days of wandering about and sleeping where I found myself, I realised that I was within five miles of the spot where the accident had occurred. Across the plain I could see what must have been the house that Williams had mentioned. Surrounded by flowering shrubs and Jacaranda trees, it stood out in the wilderness of acacia scrub.

I took my field-glasses and climbed to the top of a rise. I lay down in the harsh dry grass and studied the area. I could just make out where the brown snake of road went up one side of the hill. I lay there lazily in the late afternoon sunshine letting my thoughts wander. I brought the field of vision around once more to the house. Even from that distance it had an air of emptiness. There is something very sensitive about a house. It is as if emptiness is a disease of houses, they fall sick with it, they pine with loneliness and will die.

My attention was jerked back to reality very abruptly—something had caught my eye, I saw it again. Deep in the shadow beneath some shrubbery I had seen the unmistakable flash of sun on the windscreen of a car. I knew that the house was supposed to be empty. Although part of my mind kept supplying all sorts of logical reasons for the car being there, I determined to get closer and see who it was that was visiting.

There were perhaps two hours of daylight left. It would take one to get back to my camp so I realised that I could not get to the house before dark. I explored the ground with my glasses and plotted a rough route across country to the foot of the hill where I could pick up the road. I took some bearings and picked out some landmarks which I might follow even when it became dark.

On the way back to camp, walking with the setting sun in my face, I began to think about the whole business again, going over what bothered me. How could it possibly have been done and, perhaps more of a mystery, why? I realised that the answer to the 'how' required a lot of special information, such as what a coroner's findings might be and what post mortem examinations might reveal. I had none of this so I fixed my mind on the 'why'. Three people had died. There was a distinct possibility that they had died other than by accident. Now, excluding an act of insanity, no one would kill without reason and indeed it must have been a most desperate reason that would necessitate the deaths of three persons. A hundred ideas came into my head as I walked along, but by the time I'd reached camp I had things sorted out a little. This is how I saw it then.

It could have been a murder for robbery. This was difficult to believe for so many articles of value were left behind at the spot. It could have been a killing of hate. It was not so many years since the whole of that countryside was seething over the Mau-Mau revolt and there were still many people about with old scores of vengeance to settle. The only thing against that idea was that this did not have the marks of African violence. The attempt to fake an accident was too subtle and unnecessary.

I could think of no other reason if the victims were unknown to the killers. On the other hand, if I assumed the contrary it was simply a question of thinking of someone who had a strong motive. Someone could have wanted to get rid of one of the victims, and had included the other two in order to divert any suspicion from himself. If that was the reason then the motive must be sticking out like a sore thumb! While I packed up my camp and prepared for the journey in the dark, I went over in my mind what I knew of the murdered people.

First there was P. J. Hines, the producer and director. One of Hollywood's top men in the business, worth, it was rumoured, all of ten million dollars. Filming is a cut-throat game and he must have made many enemies. As a matter of fact, he had one right here in Africa, his own brother, William Hines. They had both fled from Europe in the mid-forties and restarted life in America. They met with phenomenal success there, and were very soon known as the most profitable partnership in the whole business. But there was a skeleton in the family cupboard. Popular gossip hinted at collaboration on the part of P.J. with the Nazi party just at the time when his race was going through its worst persecution in history. They were indeed a strange pair, almost unique in the business world, for never was there such dislike between two men who worked so well together. You could feel the loathing in the air, and yet their combined efforts produced some of the best films of the time.

Then there was Thomlinson the White Hunter. He had a first-class reputation in his job and, generally speaking, was well liked wherever he went. I knew very little of him really except what one hears in the clubs and bars. With the exception of a few years of national service abroad, he had spent all his life in East Africa. He was the son of the famous Justice Thomlinson, who was the great Mau-Mau judge. It was public knowledge that, towards the end of the troubles, two of his sisters had been most brutally murdered and no secret was made of the fact that it had been done in retribution for some of the sentences the father had handed out. The old man did not live much longer after that. Pete had been very upset at the time. He had disappeared for a while and some very wild rumours had been in circulation about his doings. When the terrorism did finally come to an end, he had returned to his old haunts and resumed his work with a Tea Company. He never managed to settle again in his old job though and eventually threw it all up and went into partnership with Old Rosy Cornwallis, the veteran White Hunter. If it was enemies that I was looking for, Pete had them in plenty among the Kikuyu people.

Finally there was Tela Parre. Except for P.J.'s patronage and the rumours that linked them together and all the social gossip, there was nothing significant that I knew of her. I was indeed in a poor position to speculate without getting to know a lot more about everything and everybody concerned. Part of the trouble of my life was that I could never keep my nose out of any affair that looked interesting. If I'd had any sense I would have packed up there and then and got well away from the district.

By the time I was ready to move off the sun had already gone over the edge of the world, twilight passing briefly. In Africa, the moment is hardly noticed, the pulse of life and death never pauses. You can feel it beating throughout the whole continent remorselessly. Everywhere nature tunes to it and turns it to a note of death. In the drama played on the game plains of Africa, there is no end of scene at sunset—no curtain—no interval. It is a pageant that flows by constantly—killers of the day are replaced by killers of the night, not a bit less violent, not a bit less obedient to the demand to kill in the mad sanity of survival.

It is a short period of unease for people like me—indeed for most strangers in Africa. We seek each other's company and huddle our minds together. I suppose that's what the sundowner is all about. The mutual drink, the sounds of the splash of liquid and the chink of ice against the background of voices that are just a little too high-pitched and tense to be happy.

I set off towards the house. There was no moon but the stars blazed in the sky, giving the whole landscape an unreal and ghostly appearance. By the time I reached the hill I could see the outline of the house standing out against the night sky, smudged here and there with the wispy outlines of rain clouds, warnings of the monsoon rains that would soon deluge the country. Miles away, the sky would suddenly light up with a soundless sheet of lightning, as a violent electric storm played across the surface of a distant lake.

I left my car about four hundred yards from the house and went the rest of the way cautiously on foot. As I entered the grounds of the house, it looked so obviously empty that I began to see the whole venture as a folly and yet there persisted a vague feeling in the back of my mind that the place wasn't empty. This feeling comes to me quite often. The type of work I do encourages it, I suppose. Many, many times it has proved wrong but there is the odd time that I can remember when it has saved my life.

A faint breeze stirred through the jacaranda trees and a huge borassus palm crackled its fronds. I could feel the pasparam grass of the lawn under my feet and felt glad that it would cushion any noise I might make. As I got close to the house itself, I stopped and watched for a long time. The car had been at the rear of the house over to the left when I had seen it earlier. I made my way carefully round to the back.

Suddenly my foot crunched on loose gravel. The noise seemed to split the silence. Cursing my clumsiness, I forced myself to remain still and silent for a full two minutes, until I had assured myself that I had not been heard. It might seem odd and perhaps over-dramatic to be so careful but it was a habit of years. I had found that in my business, assuming yourself to be alone could sometimes be a big mistake. The dim shape of an outhouse loomed up ahead of me. I walked towards it. The door was heavily pad-locked, naturally enough, but what surprised me was that by the light of the small pencil torch I carried, I could see that the lock and hasps were surprisingly new. The door was made of steel. It was close fitting and far more efficient then the usual type of door that people had fitted to garages. I walked around the building to see if there were any windows but the only break in the walls was provided by a number of grilles set high against the eaves, along one side.

There was something about all this that did not appear right to me. If the house was vacant why was this building so obviously in use? I decided to return during daylight to get a better look around. If there was anyone there then I could always think up some excuse to explain my presence. But I still wanted to avoid making any noise so I shone my torch momentarily ahead of me to avoid the gravel. There, in a three-inch pool of light, was an expended shotgun cartridge—a common enough sight I suppose in any garden in that part of the world, but it was not the thing itself but the very newness of it that made me stop.

If you drop anything on the ground, after a while it seems to become a part of the ground. This cartridge case had not yet had time to become one with its surroundings, the grass had not grown around it and, when I lifted it, there was no impression in the grass as there would have been had it been lying there for any length of time. This in itself was nothing, but seeing it there started my mind working and something that had been niggling there for days came up sharp and clear. How stupid I had been not to have thought of it before. I was right all the time! If P.J. had accidently shot off the gun in the car, and the car had immediately plunged off the road, then surely the empty cartridge would still have been in the breech of the gun. My mind flashed to the time when we were riding back from the scene of the crash, as I made a brief examination of the few things that we had brought from there. I distinctly remembered seeing the empty chamber in the shotgun and observing that it had been recently fired.

Thoughtfully, I slipped the cartridge case into my pocket and turned away. There was a sudden blinding flash of light in my head and I was briefly aware of a cold searing pain at the base of my skull and then complete blackness.

CHAPTER FOUR

I don't know how long I was unconscious but when I did come round, my lifelong habit of not waking with a start stood me in good stead. I just lay where I was, trying to collect my fuddled wits through a haze of pain from my head. Gradually the events of the evening came back to me. Without moving, I began to take in impressions from my surroundings. I was lying on a cement floor, I felt certain. I kept my eyes closed, but was aware of a light. I slowly realised that I was not alone, for I heard the rasp of a match and then the contented exhalation of someone lighting a cigarette. After a moment I could even smell the smoke.

I was lying face down on the floor with one cheek against it. I risked opening one eye slowly and fractionally. As I became used to the light I could see the three-quarter profile of Williams. He was sitting on a roughly made chair. His whole posture was tense and watchful, and before long he got up and began pacing the room. Each time his feet passed within inches of my head and I was just working up to floor him when I heard the door open. It lay somewhere behind me, so I didn't see the newcomer, but I saw the look change on the face of Williams. It was as if the personality were all drained out of him and only a shell remained, his face became almost a death mask and I felt myself go inwardly cold for some unknown reason. My legs began to feel cramped and I felt that I had to move.

'Is he dead?' The voice was deep with a harsh timbre. Williams's voice sounded pathetically thin following it.

'No, he's all right, I think; he'll be conscious in a while.'

'Get rid of him, and completely this time. No more of this accident business, it's too risky. We can't have any more interruption here. Take him well away to do it. This place must not be connected with any more accidents. My dear Williams, I am not blaming you for the last mess-up. In fact you did well, all things considered. The whole affair was written up in today's press as a most tragic and untimely accident. It was fortunate that the local police were, let us say, understanding.'

I could hear Williams breathing in the ensuing silence. I even heard him swallow hard before he said, 'I can't do anything like that again, this is not what I came here for. No, I couldn't.'

The voice rasped at him. 'Do you think I'd trust you to? I'm sending Kopft with you, he can do the job, you drive the car.'

I heard the door close as he left the room. Although he had spoken to Williams in English, the man was not a natural speaker of the language. There was just a shade in his phrasing, an intonation that betrayed the fact.

I felt in no immediate danger from Williams. The horror that I had felt at hearing my own death sentence had subsided a little as the stranger left the room. I made a moan, easily enough, and went through the elaborate act of a person returning to con-sciousness. I sat up carefullly and my head absolutely pounded. I lifted my eyes to find Williams behind a short Smith and Wesson ·45. I touched my head gingerly. I decided that it would be best to try to bluff my way out.

'What happened?' I asked.

'You were coshed for snooping around. That's what happened.' He waved the revolver towards the chair that he had been sitting in. 'Now sit down and don't try anything foolish. I won't hesitate to use this if you make me.'

'But I don't understand,' I said, easing myself gently down into the chair.

'You've been a damn fool, Ashe, coming back here like this. Now don't try the innocent act with me—you've been followed and watched ever since early this evening.'

This statement dealt a blow to my ego worse than the wallop on the head. I thought that I had been so clever—and I'd been completely outsmarted. I could have kicked myself for thinking that during the late hours of the afternoon, against the setting sun, I would have been invisible from the house. Why, I hadn't even taken the precaution of checking that I was not alone or not being followed.

When I spoke it was with a great deal more confidence than I felt. 'Well, what do you intend doing about it? You can't keep me here for ever. I don't know what you're up to, but if you take my advice, you'll stop the dramatics and let me get out of here.'

Williams's eyes held mine for a moment and then they faltered.

'You'll find out what's going to be done soon enough. In the meantime, just sit down and shut up or it will be the worse for you.'

I didn't doubt then that Williams fully intended carrying out the orders that he had been given. We sat there facing each other for about ten minutes. Occasionally I heard the sound of voices in the house itself, and regularly the sound of someone walking up and down outside the room, beyond the window. I felt very sure that we were still in the house on the hill for, although the window was heavily curtained, I could hear the borassus palms rustling in the wind. The room was lit by a low-powered oil lamp that gave very poor light beyond the circle that it cast around us. I made the decision that if I was to die that night it would be in making an attempt to escape. I did not think that there was much sense in making the attempt then, it was too dangerous, and besides, Williams had the answers to a lot of questions that I wanted to know about. He would not talk then, he was too agitated. He kept a suspicious watch on me but I was far more interested in what was going on outside than in him.

Just then I heard the sound of a car approaching the house. For one moment I felt a sense of relief, and then I realised that it was my own car. I'd have known the sound of it anywhere. Shortly afterwards, the door opened and a big man stood in the shadows. I could not see his face. I was only aware of an unusually large man framed in the doorway. But the voice was the same as I had heard earlier.

'He's awake? Good. Everything is ready, Kopft is waiting outside. Get him into the car and do as I told you. Get well away from here first. At least fifty miles, you understand?'

Williams nodded his head and roughly gripped my shoulder, jamming his gun into my ribs as he did so.

'Come on, Ashe, this way.'

The rest of the house was in darkness. The only guide I had was the moonlight coming through the open door. There was a bright three-quarter moon low down in the sky. As I left the door I saw that my guess had been right. It was the same house. Outside of the front door, my Ford was standing. It had been brought up from where I had left it, about a quarter of a mile from the house. I was bundled into the front passenger seat and as I sat down I felt the cold relentless pressure of a gun barrel stab into the back of my neck. A coarse harsh voice grated into my ear, and I smelled a whiff of breath so overpowering that it seemed the owner must be rotting away inside.

'You just fart too loud, mister. You dam dead.'

This I gathered was Kopft.

Williams got into the driver's seat beside me and I had no chance to see more of the house or the man who had sentenced me as we drove down the hill and out on to the road where all this had started. Not for an instant did the pressure of the gun relent from my neck, and, since the road was rough and ill-kept I started to sweat in a cold fear that each movement the road caused me would be my last. Williams sat silent and intent beside me.

About an hour later I felt the car settle down and run more smoothly as we joined the main tarmac road. I estimated that we must be about twenty or thirty miles from Nairobi on the Nakuru road, travelling through the Great Rift Valley. I could not see any means of escape, for although the pressure of the gun had eased from my neck, I had no doubt that it was still there. My mind raced over all the possible things that I might do, but nothing seemed feasible. My mouth felt dry and I needed a smoke badly. I asked Williams in a slow careful voice. 'Sure you can,' he said. 'Kopft!' Once again I felt the jab of the gun in my neck. Williams reached into his jacket pocket and handed me the packet, I opened it and took a cigarette.

'Light one for me,' said Williams, 'and please no tricks.'

I lit the two cigarettes and passed him one. He took it without moving his eyes off the road. There was hardly any traffic and we were travelling about sixty miles an hour.

'If you had minded your own business you wouldn't be here now,' he said.

'That doesn't help much now, does it,' I answered.

'Nothing can help you much now.'

'You're going to kill me?' I asked in as casual a way as I could.

'He is.' Williams pointed his thumb over his shoulder.

'It might as well be you pulling the trigger.'

'So what?' He sounded cold now as if taking a life meant nothing to him. I knew it was a lie.

'Look, Williams. Where do you fit in all of this? You don't seem the type to get mixed up with the likes of this chap here.'

He smiled sardonically. 'Well now, that's something isn't it, I don't look the part yet.' He started to laugh to himself but it was forced and unnatural, even a little hysterical. When he got control of himself again, I went on. 'It doesn't make much difference for me now, does it? Why were those three people killed?'

His answer surprised me. 'I don't know why. I think it was the fault of that man Hines. I think he recognised someone at the house.'

'So they did go there.'

'Oh yes, they were there all right. Why? I don't know, but around half past three that afternoon their car arrived at the house. They drove right up to the front of the house and walked smack into Smith.'

'Is that the man I saw back at the house?' I cut in.

'Yes, that's him. They stood facing each other for a moment. I don't know which of them was the more surprised. Smith was the first to recover. He called Kopft here and had them all taken around to the back of the house at gun point using the shotgun that the White Hunter chap was carrying. They had no chance to resist even if they had tried, I was given the job of covering them while Smith and Kopft went back to the house.

'They came back after a while. It was uncanny, Smith and Hines never stopped looking at each other. There was something between these two much deeper than hate. Hines was the first to speak, he asked Smith what he intended doing. When the reply came, it was only five words, but it struck absolute terror into Hines. He went all to pieces when he heard the words "repay my debt to you". He gibbered and crawled, practically licking Smith's shoes. He broke down completely babbling away in German. I think he'd have gone on all day if Smith hadn't kicked him in his upturned face. After that he just lay on the ground moaning, holding his face while the blood streamed through his fingers. The girl lost all control of herself then and started to scream. Kopft went into action and silenced her with a chopping blow to the side of her neck, then he lifted her head by the hair and hit her again across the front of the throat.'

Williams shuddered as he remembered it. 'I wanted to do something,' he looked pathetic, 'but I was afraid, I'd seen what they would do. Anyway I'm in with them now and it's too late for me to back out.'

I looked out of the window, partly to see where we were but mostly to avoid looking at Williams. We were passing through the town of Nakuru. It was deserted that time of night, and except for the lights it was no more helpful to me than being out in the bush. What I had heard of Kopft left me in no doubt of his ability to shoot to kill—even if we were in the middle of Kenyatta Avenue in broad daylight—if I made a wrong move. As if in tune with my thoughts he—and his gun—made me aware of their presence again.

We took the road for Eldoret out of town. Almost immediately on leaving the town the road began its long ascent off the floor of the Rift Valley into the Highlands. The car continued to run well and smoothly over the well-graded tarmac. It was obviously a stretch of very new road. It was then that a plan began to form in my mind. For the next few miles I had to keep Williams talking to lull any suspicion.

'What time will we get to Eldoret?' I asked, looking at my watch.

Kopft started laughing, a low chuckle without any humour. 'You'll no see any town again, mister. Stop the auto, Willy, we fix him here, now.'

Williams showed some spirit then. 'I've got my orders. Well away from the house remember. At least fifty miles.'

Kopft just grunted and I heard him ease back into the seat behind me.

'What about Pete Thomlinson?' I asked.

'Who?'

'The White Hunter.'

Williams thought for a while. I wondered if he was going to answer. 'I think the girl must have died with the first blow. When Kopft delivered the second blow, Thomlinson jumped me and managed to grab the shotgun. He turned it on the three of us and backed away. Kopft leaped straight at him though—he's afraid of nothing, except perhaps Smith. I heard the hammer of the gun fall. I expect it was a dud cartridge and before he had time for the other barrel Kopft was on him. He tore the gun away and in a moment had the poor man pinned beneath him. "Mister want to play guns?" he said, and the next moment he upended the shotgun, placed it behind Thomlinson's ear and pulled the other trigger.'

I heard Kopft chuckling behind me, enjoying the story. Williams continued, 'It all happened so quickly that the shock of seeing two people killed all in a moment left me quite numb. I stumbled away and was sick, and all I could hear was the laughing of Kopft and the pitiful moans of Hines as they finished him off with kicks and Gods knows what else.' Williams just stared ahead blindly and I said nothing, hoping he would continue in order to break the ominous silence of recrimination. After a few moments he took up his story again in a flat monotone.

'When it was all over, Smith had this accident idea. We took them back to their car and bundled them in, and then we couldn't find the ignition key. They started to panic then. The only way we could do it was to push the car, empty, out on to the hill road, let it freewheel down and then steer it over the side. Kopft and I came back then. We took the bodies in my Land-Rover down the valley road and threw them out near the wreck. It was easy really. The only care we had to take was to make sure there was no tell-tale mess lying about anywhere. The rest you know. I got the job of coming back to your camp with the story to keep anyone from snooping around the house. I knew just where to find the camp by the smoke but I was a bit shocked to find you and your friend there. I thought that I would only have to deal with the African servants and had hoped to get the bodies moved to the police post before any responsible person saw them.'

The coolness of it all horrified me. Williams had a flat dis-jointed way of talking which made it all sound so unreal. I wondered what hate Smith could have had for Hines and what secret from the past had caught up with them both on that afternoon.

'What about the shotgun?' I asked.

'That was Smith's own mistake. He only realised tonight that he had replaced the dud cartridge with one from the hunter's pocket and that he had expelled the used one, probably from force of habit, forgetting that it would have remained in the gun if it had been fired accidentally.'

'So three people had to die for something out of Hines's past.'

'And for what they might have seen,' said Williams. 'I can't think how they were even allowed to get that near to the house. It was just unfortunate.'

'Just what was it that they might have seen?' I asked. 'What's this all about anyway?'

Whether he would have told me then I don't know. He was in a talkative and thoughtful mood, but Kopft interrupted brusquely. 'Too much damn talk. Let's finish this mister and get back.'

I saw a road sign advertising a hotel in the Highlands flash by in the headlights. There were heaps of murram piled along the edge of the road. This was it . . . I just stared ahead through the wind-screen, my heart was hammering in my chest and I had a nervous flutter in my stomach. During the next few moments my life hung in the balance. I rested my elbow against the release catch of the door, tensed my feet against the floor and got ready. I seemed to be like that for an age. Then I saw it ahead in the lights and prayed that Williams had not noticed it and that he did not know about the local method of road repairing.

I was right! At full speed the car hit the murram again. It lurched wildly as it came off the edge of the tarmac, bounced down with a groan of the suspension and slewed as Williams struggled to regain control. We were thrown about inside but I was ready. As he applied the brakes, I pressed against the catch of the door and flung all my weight at it.

CHAPTER FIVE

I heard a shot cracking through the air as I hit the murram in a spinning dizzy abrasion and for a moment all the world seemed to revolve through a black nothingness of sensation Then reality came into sharp focus as an agonising pain seared up from my left knee which had taken the weight of my fall from the car. The pain brought me sharply to my senses and I scrambled, rolled and groped my way into the bushes that lined the roadside. There I got to my feet and ran with what seemed leaden, nightmare steps towards the darker shadows that indicated thicker bushes and the possibility of safety. There was a hammering of pulses in my head and it seemed that my pursuers could easily follow the thumping sound to find me.

On reaching what I felt to be the pool of deepest shadow in the fitful moonlight, I plunged in and the momentum carried me through thorns and branches that whipped across my face, but I felt nothing as I burrowed deeper in the densest undergrowth and then sank down crouching, and facing the line that they must approach from. I tried to remain dead still, and to quiet my laboured breathing and pounding heart. They were barely twenty seconds behind me, and I could actually see them both quite well in a patch of momentarily bright moonlight, as they passed each side of the bush where I had hidden myself.

I was calculating my chances of making a break again, realising that it would be impossible to do so quietly, when I heard them return—almost instantly—Kopft cursing away to himself, without anger or malice it seemed, but with a humour expressing that I had enriched his night. Williams's voice was high-pitched and excited though.

'He must be in there somewhere, Kopft. He could never have passed through that thorn back there.'

'The mister is here okay, Willie. We find—even till morning we waiting. Only one way out—same way in. You watch there, Willie. Belly shoot with this, I finish the bloody mister slow.'

'We'll have to get him, Kopft, we can't go back and say he escaped!' Williams sounded desperate and scared enough to shoot now, and I realised that I could no longer count on his squeamishness.

'Jus' stand there, Willie. When he come out, shout like I say. You miss, is okay, we got him now.'

I heard and dimly saw Williams move away from the bush and take up his position where he could get a good line of fire. I deeply regretted not having some weapon, and almost pictured my old ·38 in my briefcase in the car. It seemed that I had run myself into a cul de sac of bushes in the dense thorn scrub and the only way out was forward where Williams was standing some twenty feet away waiting.

Then began one of the most fearful experiences of my life. Kopft began to systematically search the bushes. The moon was fitfully bright as clouds went scudding along the early monsoon sky. It was frequently quite light enough to shoot by at close range—and alternatively so dark that you could not see a hand before your face.

I knew that crouching there helpless was a disadvantage to my morale, and as every moment passed I realised that I was that much closer to discovery. Each minute spent doing nothing weakened my resolve to try to escape—that is, until I got my first clear glimpse of Kopft's face.

He was a big man with a shaven head and long dangling arms— but the face! One side was relaxed into an idiotic expression from a scar that ran down the whole length of it, and the other was twisted into the paranoic grin of the sadistic killer. At one moment that horrible face passed within a few feet of mine and it was all I could do to keep myself still from shuddering with revulsion. If I had to die it was going to be as quick and clean as I could make it. At all costs, I was not going to fall into this one's hands—I knew the type quite well.

As soon as I felt he was further away from me again, I risked the noise of movement and groped about for a large stone near my feet. My hands grasped it gratefully, and then I waited, willing a dark patch of cloud across the face of the moon. It seemed endless and all the while Kopft kept murmuring promises of what he was going to do when he found me. The broken English did little to mitigate the reality of his threats. I could hear him poking about behind me, and then the first wispy threads of a cloud crossed the

40

moon and made fleeting shadows on the clear patch of moonlit ground between myself and Williams.

With great care not to betray my position, I threw the stone into some thick bush a few yards to my right.

'Ach, mister, so.'

Kopft passed close enough for me to touch, and I could just make out him bending down to the foot of the scrub where the stone had landed. I lifted my head, took my bearings and burst out as hard as I could go. Almost simultaneously, I saw the deepening of shadow that was Williams move from cover towards me—and heard Kopft's shot as I went bulling my way onwards, driven by fear and a blind urge to get away. My stomach muscles tensed, ready to receive the bullet from Williams, but he crumpled as I reached him and I thought I saw his expression, faintly puzzled and almost apologetic. He pitched headlong into the shrubs holding his belly lovingly. I ran on and heard the gloating voice of Kopft behind me.

'Come back, Willie, you bloody fool, I got him.'

I ran on as hard as I could, not daring to pause, and I reached the road before I realised what had happened. In the very dim light he had gunned Williams down, and now was thrashing about in the bushes looking for my body and shouting for Williams to come back! I gained the car before he discovered his error. It was slewed into the side of the road where it had been brought to a stop—and I blessed the nervous, tense Williams who had left the ignition still on. Within seconds, I was accelerating away with the lights off, as if the devil himself were after me. One nervous moment as an overheated coil made the engine falter and cause a bullet from Kopft to wham through the rear window—and then distance and the uncertain light made it impossible for him to do anymore than stand in the road raging.

I had gone a full two miles north before I felt the panic in me begin to subside. I slowed down and took a cigarette from the dash and lit it, feeling a delicious trembling as the tobacco eased off the tension in my knotted muscles. I realised that I'd won. With a feeling of elation, I noticed the left turn in the road that would take me on a detour through Londiani and then back on to the main road to Nakuru about ten miles south of my recent escape.

The clock in the car showed eleven thirty and I had roughly twenty miles to go to reach the town. As I drove then I began to feel a reaction. The cool tropical evening seemed cold and I felt that I could do with a drink. Every car that passed on the road sent a feeling of apprehension through me. Every moment, I expected to see Kopft's ugly face loom out of the darkness. I wondered about Williams, if he'd been badly hurt, and how they had planned to return after disposing of me. Even then I felt sorry for Williams. There was something so pathetically unvillainous about him!

It was with great relief that I finally got the car parked behind the Stag Hotel and limped in. The lounge was quite empty, except for the Asian night clerk. I went to the reception desk carrying a small bag that I had taken from the car and booked a room for the night. I must have looked in pretty poor shape, but this did not seem to bother the clerk. My knee felt terrible after the strain I had put on it and a long hot soak looked like the only remedy for my bruises and scratches.

As I lay in the water, blissfully comfortable for the first time in what seemed days, I tried to compose my mind and think things out a little. Gradually, the whole chaos of thought subsided and I began to think clearly of what I would do next. I did not like the way I'd been roughed up that night and was determined to even up the score a little with my new-found playmates.

I reasoned that Kopft would immediately try to get in touch with Smith. Again, the problem of how they had planned to return puzzled me. I began by considering what possibilities there were anyway. The thought crossed my mind that they might have a car waiting right here in Nakuru, but that seemed unlikely for Williams had selected his route quite at random. They would not have planned to use my own car, because the whole object of the exercise was to remove all trace of me and my belongings from the neighbourhood of the house. What then remained? Stealing a car? Hiring one? Williams was a fool in many ways but he was not the type that would have left his return unplanned.

When my bath became cold I got out and felt much better, not so tired but quite hungry, so I dressed again and went downstairs to see if I could get a beer and a sandwich. The bar was closed by that time, but the night clerk managed to dig up a few samosas and a beer. He was a lively looking character and, like most of his race, astute to the point where it actually showed on his face.

He looked so normal and predictable, and right then that was just what I needed. I listened rather vacantly while he chattered on about immigration vouchers and relatives in Wolverhampton, grateful for the way in which his talk precluded any need on my part to answer except in the vaguest of ways. The greater part of my mind was still struggling with the problem of how Williams and Kopft had planned to return but I was aware, too, of this man before me, with his anxieties and troubles in Africa where for several generations Asians had lived in the secure shadow of the British Empire. It certainly was an odd quirk of history that had brought them there during the days of the railway construction—a contrived migration one could say! And yet so natural, too, when one considered the teeming overcrowded millions of Asia and the thousands of square miles of undeveloped land and opportunity in East Africa. No dam could be constructed between the surging tide of humanity in Asia and the vast acres of East Africa that could be made to support hundreds of millions.

I was suddenly jolted out of my reverie by the memory of Williams collapsing in front of me. He was injured—quite badly for all I knew. Nakuru was the only place for miles and they would have to come here! They might even have arrived! Struggling with a wild panic that began to grow inside me, I asked the clerk as casually as I could, 'Has anyone else booked in since I came?'

'No, sir, just you this evening—a quiet time, sir. People are not having confidence as before—not wanting to travel. But if it's expecting you are for someone—well, there is one other first class hotel in Nakuru. Why not try ring there to ask? Telephone is here!' He indicated a small kiosk. I thought it worth a try and fumbled for some small change in my pocket. 'Not a paying telephone, sir, I am putting on your bill, just dial direct 20437—no sorry, sir, that's railway station—the other gentleman wanted that one—20548 that's it.'

I was suddenly curious. 'What other gentleman was that?'

The clerk looked slightly aloof, 'About half an hour ago but not British, sir, not really a gentleman, no manners, sir, he just walked in, asked for railway station number, used telephone and went out. No "thank you"—not even paying for his call.'

'Did he have a scar down along his face here?' I traced my finger along my cheek and the clerk's face lit up.

'Yes, yes, perhaps a friend of yours, you can pay his call then my book all square.'

I ignored this bit of business opportunism but could not help smiling. I had a debt to Kopft all right, but forty cents would not square it.

'You say he called the railway station?'

'Yes, sir, Nakuru 20437.'

'Is there a train to Nairobi tonight?'

'No, sir, first class train leaves here in the morning, coming from Uganda arriving Nairobi in the afternoon.'

'What about second class?'

He looked shocked, even hurt, to have such a thing mentioned. 'No second class trains, only second class compartments. All one train, you see.'

'What about goods trains?' I asked. This seemed to buck him up a bit. Apparently it was all right to discuss goods trains in his lounge, for they didn't have any class.

'Oh, very, very frequent, sir. Nakuru is a very busy goods place.'

I put in a call to the station master. He told me that a goods train had left the siding at a time which would have suited them very well. I imagined them riding the cars through the night and had the satisfaction of picturing their discomfort. After checking on the arrival time of that train in Nairobi, I put the phone down and told the night clerk to prepare my bill. I hurried upstairs again to pack and within a few minutes I was back at the car park. The train would arrive in the city at about five thirty in the early morning. I was determined to get to the house ahead of them. I glanced at my hotel bill before crumpling it up. Itemised on it were: one night's lodging, the refreshments that I'd had and *two* telephone calls! As I let out the clutch and turned on to the main road I made a mental note that Mr Kopft now owed me forty cents as well as everything else.

When I left Nakuru it was about one o'clock; within two hours I could reach the city. I reckoned on being able to get a few things done there with the police and also get the answer to some quesions back at the house, before Kopft and Williams got back home to their master.

The drive to Nairobi was strangely restful. Very little traffic passed me and save for the frequent U-bends where the road crossed the railway, I maintained a fairly brisk speed. I passed Lake Elementeita looking like a bright jewel in the moonlight set under the small escarpment near Gilgil. Even by day it has the same jewel-like charm, often mysteriously draped in vapour from the hot springs and tinged with a heavenly pink from the tens of thousands of flamingoes that feed on the rolifeis and algae, the only life that the bitter alkaline waters support. Always when I pass the spot, I get an eerie feeling of the unreality of time. There is evidence there of Neolithic habitation at Kariandusi and in my mind I think of these early people wandering along the edges of the steamy hot lake, with perhaps a primeval sense of innocence and awe at the phenomenon of the Great Rift Valley settling down after the earth-splitting cataclysm that must have accompanied its formation.

The city of Nairobi seemed quite dead at that time of the morning. I thought to make the Central Police Station my first call. A tired-looking desk sergeant sat in the outer office. The pale green walls and the strip lighting gave him a sickly looking complexion, in spite of his dark colouring. Some miscreant sat on a bench near the wall with his head in his hands, watched intently by an askari.

'I'd like to speak to the duty inspector,' I said.

The sergeant looked up from some papers on the desk in front of him. 'Very good, sir, if you'll just come this way,' he indicated a small side room, roughly furnished with a table and some chairs. 'We expect the inspector back in about ten minutes.'

I sat down to wait, going over in my mind the story that I had to tell. The time seemed to pass very slowly, and the only sound was a desultory conversation in Swahili between the two policemen in the next room. I heard the telephone ring in the outer office. At first I paid little or no attention to what was being said, but gradually the nature of the one-sided conversation infiltrated my mind. The sergeant was receiving a report from the Nakuru station about the death of someone. He had been found at the side of the road by a salesman returning from Eldoret about an hour earlier. Some details followed. He was as yet unidentified, but the circumstances of death suggested murder. A gun had been found near the body. The sergeant read back from the notes he'd been taking. I felt my heart miss a beat. It was my own revolver! Kopft had been using my gun with the intention of suggesting confusion when my body was found. He'd taken full advantage of the situation. He must have finished off Williams and dumped him at the side of the road, leaving my gun beside the body, knowing that it would be found and thus discredit anything I might have to say on the matter. Prompt police enquiries in Nakuru had produced a description of my car, a rough description of myself, probably from the hotel clerk, and the decision that my presence was required by the police to assist them in their investigations.

I knew then that I had to get out and try to think a bit, before the police started asking questions. If I waited I would surely be detained on suspicion and that would probably mean that the whole lot would get away from the house and that I'd have all hell trying to convince anyone of anything. It might be months before I was able to clear myself and by that time everything would have gone cold.

I walked out as casually as I could into the outer office. The sergeant looked up from the notes that he had just taken. I tried to look bored and disinterested.

'I'll just step outside a while and have a smoke while I'm waiting.' I spoke to the man in Swahili and he suspected nothing, for he nodded his head and looked back to his notes. My car was just outside the station, to start it now and drive away would look odd, but I decided that I had no time to weigh chances. I drove out of the yard as quietly as possible and as I passed through the gate I saw a police Peugeot just entering, driven by an askari with the inspector beside him. I brazened it out and lifted my hand knowingly. He returned the gesture involuntarily, barely noticing me. I guessed that within minutes the bored look would have vanished from his face, and I'd have half the Nairobi police searching the area for me. The first thing that I would have to do would be to get rid of my car.

I stopped at an all-night car park and looked around. It was well past three then and I had very little time to get hold of Kopft. Without him my story wouldn't be worth anything. I searched the park for a likely vehicle, looking for one that had been left unlocked. But this was not to be my lucky night for of the twenty odd vehicles parked there not one had been left unsecured. I decided to try somewhere else. It was only a couple of hundred yards to the New Stanley Hotel. I walked there, the car park was full of vehicles. I went around them casually trying the doors, and was rewarded on my fourth try. It was a Toyota Land Cruiser, covered with dirt and red murram dust. The owner must have arrived quite late that evening, for the attendants had not had time to wash it. I climbed in and got under the dash. After a few minutes' work I had the leads connected and was rewarded by seeing the red light glow on the panel. I exposed the two starter motor leads and then all was ready. Leaving the ignition connected, I left the car park and went round the front to the main lobby of the hotel. I had decided to put a bold face on it and enter the car park again from the hotel side, get in the car and drive away quite openly. I reckoned that it would not be unusual for a safari car to be leaving at that hour as the hotel was usually full of overseas visitors on holiday, and the best time to be at the game parks was daybreak, the animal life then being at its best and most abundant.

I walked up to the park attendant and even passed the time of day with him before climbing into the Toyota. I struck the wires together and the engine roared into life first time. I switched the headlights on and let the engine idle for a few moments. Everything sounded fine, so I started for the gate leading out on to the road. The attendant moved out into the road, looked up and down and then waved me out. Perfect! I swung the car out between a big Buick and a commercial van. Whoever had parked the Buick must have been a fool for there was hardly enough room to pass it. I slowed down and then something struck me about the big car. I was nearly out of the park before I had placed it. Of course! It was Tom McNally's. Where else would he be staying but the New Stanley! In a flash I had abandoned my plan to steal the Toyota. I slipped into reverse and went back into the park. I broke the ignition contact and got out.

The park attendant came over. 'It's very sick,' I said, 'a few miles and it would be dead.'

As I walked back to the hotel I began to regret my move. What if Tom had sold the car and was not there at all? Time was running out on me and as night moved to morning I felt tired to my very bones. All the fight was slipping away from me and I felt that the best thing would be to go back to the police and just let events take their course. After all, I had done nothing, I'd broken no laws.

I went up to the clerk and asked if Mr Lee Conway was registered. I can imagine all sorts of rebuffs that a disreputably dressed person could get from a receptionist in some other world-famous hotel but this was Nairobi; about the only place left where anybody could be anybody, where a king or a president could walk in unshaven and unkempt without anyone raising an eyebrow. Indeed the 'just-back-from-the-bush' look was often deliberately affected. Not for a single instant did the clerk's face show that he thought that I looked like a tramp with a hangover.

In a quiet respectful voice he said, 'Yes, sir, but Mr Conway has left instructions that he is not to be disturbed on any account.'

'What's his room number?' I asked.

'I'm sorry, sir.' A blank face. He proved unmovable. I looked up at the clock on the wall. Four o'clock. Time was going too quickly. I tried another line.

'I'd like a room for the night please.' The clerk looked like a monument of Eastern wisdom as he slowly shook his head.

'Nothing at all at the moment, sir, perhaps later in the morning.'

I went outside in a fluster. Something more direct was indicated. I looked around the building for a service entrance.

I went in along corridors and through rooms until I found myself face to face with a small wizened little man with heavy tribal markings on his face. He was the 'boots' of the floor and like his counterparts all over the world was a great observer of life around him. I gave him Lee Conway's name and description, but it was finally as the owner of the Buick that he identified him. Five shillings and three floors later I stood outside Tom's room and knocked at the door loudly and insistently. He must have been out to the world. Fully two minutes went by before I saw the light go on and then the door was opened by a tousle-headed, bleary-eyed bum who said, 'Aw hell, Gareth Bloody Ashe, it's you. This is no time to come calling, man. I've got big things going in here. Go on, get the hell out of here. Give me a ring about noon tomorrow or the next day—or sometime!'

He then noticed the state I was in and had me inside in a moment. I flopped down into a comfortable-looking chair. He went through into the bedroom of the suite, and pretty soon I could hear a muffled argument going on. The pitch of voices rose higher and higher, until one of the voices that had started low and sleepy and female and husky was suddenly raised into a strident harpy protest, cut off abruptly by a resounding thwack—unmistakably hard hand to soft female buttock—and 'When I say out, I mean out, woman. Now! Out!'

He reappeared looking a bit more presentable.

'I'm sure sorry about all this, boy, but, well—how the hell was I to know you'd be around so soon.'

He walked over to a supper trolley and from the bottles there poured a few fingers of Harper's. I nodded when he offered soda. 'Now come on—what gives?'

I listened to the sounds in the other room and took a gulp from the glass. She came out, ruffled but dignified and without so much as a look at either of us, she sauntered to the door then, opening it, turned back to face us.

'Now do have fun, boys, won't you, and, Lee darling, not so rough now. He doesn't look as if he can take it.'

The door slammed behind her, just in time to shield her from a jet of soda from the siphon that Tom still had in his hand.

'Will you look at that for gratitude—gets the best lay she ever had and then turns sour on me!'

I gave him the story as fully as I could of what had developed since I last saw him. By the time I was finished he was fully dressed and had already some sort of plan in his mind. 'Now this is what we're goin' to do!' I liked the way he included himself in the problem right from the start. 'You just sack up here for a couple of hours and I'll go get this guy and bring him back here. Then we take him and the whole story to the law and put it in their lap.'

I protested as strongly as I could and insisted that all I needed was a car. He would hear nothing of it.

'Look, Gareth, I've been thinking about this thing a lot. Now old P.J. was a bastard—anybody's bastard—but that don't mean I didn't like him some. He gave me my first break in films way back when I was still a soldier in Germany. I guess I was pissed off with life—you know, war and everything, the way it was. He gave me a new way of looking at things—and make no mistake about it, he knew his business. Oh! I guess he made his money on me but that doesn't mean I can just sit still and let some fat-arsed slob get away with killing him. I figure that my taking a hand in this will square up what I owed the old bugger—and besides, you and me we're just about partners, there's nobody goin' to push us around.'

I suppose that I was too tired to argue about it any longer, and he must have seen it in my face, for he brought a large scale road map over to me. 'Now give me a briefing on this and I'll be on my way.'

We sat down together at the writing desk and I showed him the location of the house and the road that I thought Kopft must take when he left the train. The house lay on the southeast slopes of Mount Suswa and the nearest point that the railway got to it was at the big bend where the railway turned east for Nairobi. We reckoned that Kikuyu Halt would be the nearest he could get and then he would have a ten-mile hike overland before reaching the house. If he were to be intercepted it would have to be somewhere on that stretch between the railway and the house. It was then about twenty-five past four and every minute was important. Tom bundled the map away and said, 'I'm on my way right now!'

He was half way to the door, when he turned, his face grave. 'Look, if all goes well I'll try to phone you here somewhere between six and seven. Then you'll be able to put your mind at rest.'

He left, closing the door gently behind him. I went to lie down and felt a little more like a human being. I was tired and a pleasant heavy-eyed feeling came over me quite suddenly.

CHAPTER SIX

I must have gone to sleep within minutes of Tom leaving the room. In my mind was the delicious thought that I could be certain of at least an hour and a half of solid sleep. He must have had the usual hotel arrangements for I was awakened, not by the telephone, but by an insistent knocking on the door. Waking was like coming through a thick fog. I stumbled to the door and opened it to the steward who brought the morning tea. As he put it down on the bedside table and departed, I gradually got my mind into focus again. I stared unbelievingly at the travelling clock on the table. Half past seven! If Tom had phoned I must have slept through the bell. Knowing how lightly I usually sleep, I checked with reception. There had been no call.

I went to have a shower and then made a very frugal breakfast of the tea and biscuits that had been brought. I rummaged about through Tom's clothes and eventually managed to make myself fairly presentable although the sizes were way too big for me.

I had a feeling of being hemmed in again and could not stand the thought of being cooped up in a hotel room. I was very worried about not hearing from Tom. He was the sort of chap who would phone if he said he was going to. I decided to get clear of the hotel and the city as soon as possible. Leaving the hotel would be no problem, but the other thing worried me a bit. The chances were that my car would have been spotted hours ago and the alarm would have gone out to all police. I doubted that I could go half a mile through the city without some policeman, with his eye on promotion, picking me up. They had a description of me, vague it's true, but how many bearded men do you see on any given stretch of road beats who walk with a marked limp? Being taken in was just what I wanted to avoid. Once inside, my chances of being believed were so scant that they were negligible.

I had very serious doubts on whether Tom had, in fact, succeeded. So I determined to risk it, and to try to get out to Kikuyu Halt and see what had happened to him. Once in a taxi, I thought that it would be very unlikely that I would be spotted. I left the hotel with no trouble at all. It was eight o'clock and everyone seemed occupied with his own affairs. Out on the street though and it was different. I felt that any moment I would walk slap into the arms of someone who wanted to arrest me. It was most unnerving. I was tense and anxious, so that is why, after a few hundred yards along the road I began to get the creepy sensation at the back of my neck that I was being followed. I tried to dismiss it, telling myself that it was all nerves, but try as I would, I could not get rid of the feeling.

I turned on to the main East African Highway. I had left the car the night before in a park at the foot of Nairobi Hill, near the Princess Elizabeth Hospital, and now I was making my way in the opposite direction, hoping to pick up a cruising taxi or get a lift out to Kikuyu Halt. I stopped to buy a newspaper at a stand outside the Railway Club, and then half turned to go before changing my mind about the paper. So it was then that I first saw him.

Tom had failed very badly indeed, for across the street from me, a little way back, Kopft was standing, trying to look as if he wasn't there and failing quite miserably. I gave no sign that I had seen him, and carried along up the road and went into a tobacconist's. I bought a packet of cigarettes and in leaving the shop stood in the doorway to light one. As casually as I could, I had a good look around. I just caught a glimpse of him disappearing into a shop on the opposite side of the road.

I had a plan. The main police headquarters of the city was about a quarter of a mile away, down a small street on the other side of the road. I crossed the road and walked briskly in that direction. Now if I could get Kopft to follow me down that side street I'd have him. For once there, with the central police station on one side of the road, and the headquarters on the other, I would start some sort of argument with him and hang on until the noise brought someone out to attend to it. Once inside the building, most of my troubles would be over. I reached the turning and carried on down the side street. I could hear his footsteps behind me. Two hundred yards more and I would turn to face him.

I began to feel my stomach tightening up as I walked. The street was deserted and the sound of his shoes echoed in my ears. I fancied that the footsteps were getting closer and I fought down the urge to run. In my mind's eye, I saw him as he had been the previous night, with the leering imbecile grin on his face and the look of lust when he spoke of killing. I was afraid of him with all the fear that the rational has for the abnormal, that the sane has for the demented. I remembered what Williams had said about the way he had killed Tela Parre: 'The strength of an ox and no fear at all'. This was the man I was about to involve in a fight any moment. If only there had been someone about, I'd have felt more game for it. Not for the help that I might receive, but for the moral courage it would give me.

Just then I was aware of the noise of a car coming along behind me. It provided just the support I needed, I turned to face him and as I did so I caught the blow that he had aimed at my head, on my upraised arm. Even so I staggered under it and felt that my arm had been shattered from the elbow down. But I was determined and went into him as hard as I could as I heard the car come to a stop. I aimed a blow for his head and in the fraction of a second that he took to throw up his guard to his face I kicked him with all the strength and timing that I could muster. I felt my instep strike home, just where it would hurt the present Mr Kopft the most, and just where any future little Kopfts in embryo would feel it too! It was quite a few years since I had kicked for touch in the Arms Park in Cardiff, but I don't think Kopft knew the difference. He doubled over and went down like a howling burst tyre.

I'd done it! I think that was the first time that I ever felt like gloating over someone in pain. I stood over him, waiting for the police and hoping that he would give me another opportunity to kick him before his howling brought out the whole force. In the corner of my eye I was aware of the man who had got out of the stopped car. I half turned towards him with an explanation but the words just froze. There were two very ominous objects facing me. One was an ugly looking face and the other was a still uglier looking automatic.

'Get in quick, no nonsense. Move!'

He was a short fat man dressed in a loud striped suit. The gun looked too small in his fat podgy hand, but I knew that it would make the same hole in me as one that looked bigger. With a last glance towards what I considered the deafest police station in the world, I was bundled into the large Peugeot family saloon. Some family we made! A driver, taciturn and efficient in the front on one side of me and the man in the striped suit on the other. A reproachful Smith and a moaning Kopft occupied the back seat. I recognised Smith by his voice, even though last time I had heard him he was speaking in English. The automatic was pressed very firmly into my side as I was searched for weapons. I made no protest. The only sound in the car was the muted moaning and muttering of the injured Kopft as we took the north road out of the city.

As the miles rolled by I began to suspect that we were going back to the house on the hill where all this had started. I could not help wondering morbidly if this would be so and whether it would be the last time.

My guess proved right for after what seemed an eternity of travelling we turned off the main road and once more took the west-bound earth road that now seemed to mean nothing but trouble for me.

The silence in the car began to get on my nerves. Kopft had recovered, and after being very strongly reprimanded by Smith, gave up the idea of tearing my head off with his bare hands, and joined his companions in maintaining an ominous silence. I tried a little conversation but the only response I got was an increase in the pressure of the gun in my ribs, and if that was to be the only partner I got in a *tête à tête*, I decided that I, too, could do without the small talk.

It was certain now that we were going to the house. I looked out and saw that we were very near, only two or three minutes away at the most. There was nothing I could do but wait. For all I knew these few minutes would be my last. The car drew up outside the house. The man with the gun got out first and bade me follow in no uncertain terms. As Smith got out I had my first really good look at him. He was the one I was going to have to bluff, so I tried to weigh up what I had to contend with.

He was a tall, heavily built man with a hard muscular face. His eyes, which were set very deeply, were a startling light blue, they seemed to stare right through what he was looking at. He might have been about fifty-five but he had an unaged look somehow. In spite of a stick which he leaned rather heavily on, he had a rigidity in him that one would expect in a much younger man. When he alighted from the car, his eyes roamed over the front of the house as if he were looking for something, and then he turned his eyes on me. I looked straight into his face.

There was the look of the fanatic in his face and eyes. His eyebrows arched steeply above them, and one had the feeling that there was nothing concealed in them, nothing but frankness. He had the look that you can sometimes see on the face of someone in deadly fear, wide and staring, with no attempt to conceal what lay within. In many cases this would be interpreted as honesty but not so with Smith. One could look into the uncurtained soul of him and see nothing. Not only were the fundamental expressions of the human being lacking, but also very humanity itself seemed absent. I felt a chill in my heart as I looked at him.

But if his looks were those of a fanatic his voice was quite the contrary. When he spoke it was in the well-modulated voice of an educated and cultured man. In almost perfect English he addressed me. 'I don't think there will be any mistake this time.' And then, turning to the gunman beside me, 'Put him there, and hurry back here at once, there are many things to be seen to.'

I was escorted to what appeared to be an outhouse a little way down the garden. I thought at first it was a summer house and wondered why anyone would have built such a thing here in Africa. But on closer inspection it proved to be an insulated cold store. About nine-tenths of the building was below ground. Admittance was gained through a small trap door in the roof. The fat man with the gun drew a key from his pocket and handed it to me. He pointed to the heavy padlock that secured the double doors. He growled his comment at me, 'Open the doors and put the key on the ground.' He stood back while I did so. Never once did the gun move from the line of my stomach. Up near the house I could see Kopft waiting. I got the impression that he was just praying that I would try to escape so he could have a go at me. He looked like a big hound that had been leashed while he was on the scent. There was nothing I could do. I raised the two doors up and out. They were heavily padded on the inside with layers of cotton and stout canvas. 'Get in.'

I could see that a flight of stone steps led downwards into the chamber below. It was dark and even from where I stood I could feel a damp dankness about the place that was almost chill. As I bent to enter I felt a sickening thud on the back of my head and the sensation of falling as I lost consciousness.

When I first regained my senses I felt a sudden panic for I thought that I was blind, and then things started to come back to me and I remembered grimly what had happened. I put an exploratory hand to the back of my head and touched the wet sticky place where I had been hit. I felt a surge of blind hate and frustration and swore savagely and fluently in the darkness to relieve my feelings. I was startled by a voice only inches from my face. Some of the hopeless feeling that had taken hold of me since my capture evaporated as I recognised Tom's voice, echoing through that cold, dark, empty place.

'Welcome to the party, Gary boy. I was hoping that you would turn up one way or another. I'm sure glad to see you even if I can't.'

I rummaged in my pocket for the matches that I had bought earlier. When they were satisfied that I had no weapon they had not taken anything else from me. I struck a match and after the first blinding glare of it, I saw Tom lying on the floor beside me, bound hand and foot. The remains of a mouth gag, chewed and wet, still clung to the lower part of his face. The match went out, and the darkness seemed even more intense. I fumbled for another match but Tom's voice stayed me.

'Save the matches, boy, and see what you can do to get me out of this rig they've put on me.'

Using the small pipe knife I had, I sawed away at his bonds. The knife was small and never intended for anything except novelty, but its edge was quite keen, so that in a very short time I could hear him stamping about trying to get the circulation flowing back into his cramped limbs.

'How did you get here?' I asked at last, for it seemed that he was not going to volunteer anything. 'I didn't see your car anywhere on the way.'

'I got a lift with our friend Sloeder,' he replied cheerfully.

'And who the hell is he?' I asked somewhat testily, for I was in no mood for the cheerful manner that Tom displayed.

'I suppose you know him better as Smith,' Tom said.

I struck another match. In spite of our grim position, a wide grin split his face, and he looked very knowing and secretive. I continued to look at him until the match burned my fingers. I swore angrily. 'Look man, if you know anything, stop acting like a coy virgin and let's have it.'

'Don't rush me, boy, this is my scene and I'm going to play it my way. Now let's start with a little story.'

I knew there would be nothing to gain by trying to do it any other way so I just sat there quietly. It was an effort at first but soon the story became fascinating and I listened.

'During the last months of the war, I was in Germany, a fairly raw soldier, just newly commissioned, and I was posted to Berlin on a special assignment with the Field Security Police.

'Myself and about ten other specially selected officers were given a few days' briefing on wet-nursing war criminals. We had been losing a lot of them through suicide. So each suspect was put in charge of three of us. We did eight-hour shifts so that they were never on their own for a second. I spoke no German, so that was probably the reason for assigning me to one who spoke very fluent English. His name was Sloeder. He was pretty big game I can tell you, with Field Rank and all the arrogance and bullshit that went with it.

'On the understanding that he was innocent until proven guilty, he had a fairly honourable captivity, and was treated with some respect as a prisoner of war. He was even allowed to keep his batman, a big surly individual with a face like a piece of decomposed granite. If all the tales that we heard were right, this Sloeder was in for the works. Even his name put the fear of God into the other Nazis that we had penned. According to all the scuttlebut that went around at the time, Dachau and Belsen even took second place to the little establishment that this guy used to run. It was a detention camp for opponents to the regime, and its reputation even had the boys in Munich quaking. It must have been living hell for all who went there, and there was not a single case of anyone who lived to tell about it.

'When the Allies had gone in to clean up the place, there was no one there except this bugger Sloeder and his bucket-faced bastard of a batman. They both surrendered with all the dignity that only the *Wehrmacht* Prussian can affect. It was assumed that the remainder of the staff of the place had made a run for it, and those two did nothing to dispel the illusion. Little wonder either, for the whole staff were found later, very dead and buried in a common grave, probably of their own making. Closer examination of the place showed that the most foul and horrible atrocities had been practised there. So it seemed that Sloeder's goose was really cooked.

'The early days of his trial were filled with the most horrible details of what had been discovered there. There were photographs and bits of apparatus that would make a pig sick. Oh! I guess we were all a bit abnormal during that time, there was war madness on us all but this——Ugh!

'Sloeder sat in that court and hardly said a word. He was indicted as being responsible for the crimes that had been committed there. He pleaded not guilty and reserved his defence, leaving the prosecutor a clear field—or so it seemed at the time. But, as it turned out, nothing could be actually pinned on him. He pleaded absence from the place whenever any crime was supposed to have taken place. Sloeder had a sort of roving commission that took him all over Germany and he never was in fact O.C. of the place at all. There was not a single shred of material evidence that could connect him with the events that took place there. There were no signed orders and not a soul could be found who could directly testify to his guilt. Apparently, he had received his orders right from the top, and there was no one in between who could put a finger on him.

'If retribution was what they were after they could have taken him out and hung him from the nearest lamp post, but such was our more enlightened form of justice that that solution was out of the question. There was not a soul who had anything to do with Sloeder who did not think him guilty, but nothing could be proved.

'It was on the last day of the trial that something happened to change all that. The judge was the most uncomfortable man I have ever seen doing his duty. It seemed that Sloeder was going to get off. The most they would get would be a term of imprisonment for the shooting of the staff, and even that seemed doubtful, for Sloeder's defence was that the garrison had mutinied and attempted desertion in the face of the enemy. Therefore, his conduct as senior officer was quite within the concept of correct military discipline.

'However, just before the verdict was to be considered, the Prosecuting Counsel received a message in the court, and he startled everyone by requesting an adjournment because some new evidence had come to light. When asked the nature of his evidence, he turned to face the prisoners—there was a deathly hush all over the room—and he said, "A piece of film will be presented to the court that will show beyond all doubt the guilt of the accused."

'All eyes turned towards the table where the prisoners sat, and as the judge, looking very relieved, ordered an adjournment, I'll swear that the sardonic look that Sloeder had worn all through the hearing faded and he became tight-lipped and pale as he turned to leave the court.

'Well, now, things being as they were I could have sworn that Sloeder had no contact with anyone that night, but it was not my spell of duty so I can't really say. One thing I do know, and that is that both Sloeder and his man got away from me next morning and escaped.

'We were on our way to the court in a closed car, the driver in the front, the two prisoners in the middle seats and myself and a sergeant M.P. in the rear. We were halted on the way by an army traffic cop, and when we looked out to see what the delay was, we found ourselves covered by four armed men in Canadian uniform. Four sten guns take a lot of arguing with, but I reckon we would have taken a chance had not the driver proved to be a phoney too. As it was, we were disarmed and ordered out of the car. There was not a soul to be seen anywhere, and I realised what a fool I'd been. We'd been driven way off our route and now we were somewhere in the suburbs of the city trapped in a narrow cul de sac.

'We were stood against the wall and I thought that the end had come, but for a reason I could never understand until today, we were spared. While we stood with our faces to the wall, the driver reversed the car. Each second I thought that a bullet would come thudding into me, and my back tensed up at the thought of it. As we heard the car accelerate away, we both dropped flat to avoid what we thought was surely coming. Nothing! In fact it was all over in seconds.

'As the car rounded the corner, we set off in pursuit, we commandeered a jeep and the four G.I.s in it and continued after them. As luck would have it, we picked up a glimpse of their escape car a few minutes later down near the railway marshalling yards. It was going flat out and seemed to be headed out of town. It was about a hundred yards ahead of us, and we'd hit a bad bit of rubble-strewn road, when it suddenly swerved into a side street. It was a dead end, which terminated in a sort of warehouse. As we came belting up, I distinctly saw Sloeder and his man leave the car and take refuge within, I even tried a few shots at them. We'd closed to about thirty yards by then but I missed rather badly. I immediately sent three men through the narrow alleyway at the side of the building to cover the rear. The remainder of us made a direct go for the front, but we were met with a burst of sten fire that sent us scuttling for cover behind the jeep. I guessed there were only a few of them in there, but it was impossible to move without a burst of fire being directed at us. During the ensuing stalemate, Sloeder gave me the benefit of his views on the efficiency of the U.S. army, but I wasn't done with him yet. At the back of the warehouse the situation was the same. I didn't think it was any time for heroics, so I called up a bit of help on the jeep's radio. Pretty soon the initiative was taken from us. A light patrol tank arrived with a platoon of infantry in support. A few shots from the artillery they packed must have put the fear of God into them. All resistance ceased and the infantry began to move in. Suddenly there was a terrific explosion which blew out all the windows of the building and in seconds the whole place was a raging inferno. I guess the place must have been packed with very inflammable material and one of the shells that had been fired had set the whole lot off. For a while we fell back and watched carefully at the front and back of the building, but after a few minutes no one had come out and after that no one could.

'Many hours later when the fire was eventually mastered, we discovered what little of them that remained, a few charred bones and some bits of metal, you know the sort of thing—medals, buttons, the pitiful remains of what, during life, had been a pair of the most absolute bastards that ever put on uniform. I think that the authorities were relieved. Fate had put a very clean and final end to the horror that had been Sloeder and Kopft!'

I had been listening spellbound but when he mentioned Kopft, I was startled into asking, 'Do you mean to say that the Kopft here is the same man and that Smith is Sloeder?'

Tom's voice was low and quiet in the darkness.

'I'm sure of it,' he said.

CHAPTER SEVEN

Tom's story explained a lot of things that had been troubling me during the past week. All the secrecy and the attempt to get rid of me now made some sort of sense. I could not help but marvel on the odd twist of fate that had thrown Tom and Smith together again after so many years. There was one thing that still troubled me though. Why had Smith, or Sloeder, as we now knew him, killed P. J. Hines? From what Williams had told me, I knew that Smith and Hines knew each other from the past. Was it just fear of betrayal? Or was it as Williams had suggested a deep hatred? I asked Tom what he thought about it. He knew Hines far better than I did, having worked with him for many years.

Tom's answer came as a revelation.

'I've got a theory about that. I've been thinking a lot about it while I was hog-tied here in the dark on my own. Do you know what I think it was? Hines was the one who offered to supply the bit of film that was going to incriminate Sloeder. He worked in Germany during the war, but his nationality was always a bit vague, I think he was an Austrian Jew. Even before the war his filming technique was beginning to catch the attention of the outside world. His documentary films were really works of art. There was no doubt about it, he was a first rate film-maker, and no doubt his talents were put to good use under the Nazi regime.

'After the war was over, I know that he came down hard on his former masters. He made a series of Allied propaganda films which really did inspire the people of the country back to peaceful co-operation with the occupying forces. This is where he gave me my start in pictures—I worked for him then, on loan from the army, and after I was demobilised, we just took up the business again in the States. One thing I do know—and that is that he left Europe in one hell of a hurry. I guess I can see why now. As a material witness against those top Nazis, his life must have been nothing but fear. Perhaps he just knew which side his bread was buttered. I don't know! But I figure that at some time or another he got hold of some film that was very compromising to a few of the high ups, and held on to it with the express purpose of using it in the event of Germany's defeat. He wouldn't be the only one who feathered two nests.'

'Have you any idea what the piece of film was?' I asked.

Tom fell silent for a while and I could hear him breathing heavily in the darkness beside me.

'I didn't **ever** actually get to see it,' he said. 'You see I was not quite cleared of "neglect of duty" at that time just after I let Sloeder get away from me, but I did hear something about it. It seems that he, Sloeder that is and a few of his companions, had been filmed at work in that little establishment of his during the early days of the war.

'That was a very exclusive place, you understand, none of your run-of-the-mill guests, only the very top brass who had failed to keep up with the party line from time to time. You see, Gareth, the way I figure it is this. A dictatorship like they had there could never last, practising the inhumanities that it did, unless the people were kept in a constant state of fear. How much more so for the leaders, then? They had to have something hanging over them that would help to steady their wavering faith. This detention camp was just that.

'Periodically, it seems, small groups of the leaders were forced to go there just to see what was going to happen to them if they were to fall into the error of deviation. Justice must not only be done, but it must be seen to have been done! And this was Sloeder's job in the whole rotten set-up. It was obviously impossible for all top-ranking military, the police and the political agents of the whole Reich to attend the camp. So this film was made, and when necessary a visit could be made to the Propaganda Department of the local party headquarters where a private viewing was arranged. The result of such viewing would be a steady allegiance for as long as the memory held.

'Fortunately for the W.C.C. many of the worst types of scoundrels were identified from such films and executed on the strength of them. Sloeder could have played the star role in one of these films, and might have thought that it had been completely destroyed, but friend Hines must have made himself a copy against the time when everything in the beer garden would not be so lovely. He must have offered or sold it to the occupying forces as a price of his own immunity, or as a sign of his new allegiance. You know, it's no wonder that Hines made such a success in America after the war, he jumped on the bandwagon of popular taste for realism and violence and the experience he had put him way, way ahead of the field.'

Tom fell silent again. I thought that he had reasoned it out fairly well. There was still something that I did not understand, though.

'If these two here are the same men, how did they get out of that warehouse and whose remains did you find?'

Tom dug into his pockets for cigarettes, handed me one in the darkness and we lit up. The little points of light were a great comfort in the Stygian blackness. After a few deep pulls, he answered. 'Well, now, it's like this. Remember I told you that I did not understand why I was never plugged that day Sloeder escaped, even though he hated my guts from the start. Well I think I know the answer now. The clever bastard wanted me alive so that I could follow them. I was all part of the plan.'

'What plan?' I asked.

'The plan for Sloeder to be taken for dead. The escape, the hot-headed young McNally who'd go off at half cock, the finding of them again, the warehouse, the fire—it was all part of a well figured-out plan. It occurred to no one at the time to doubt that those were the remains of Sloeder and Kopft. There were the medals and things belonging to them that had not been completely consumed by the fire, but now I know different. Those two held us off long enough to get an explosion rigged amid a lot of very inflammable material, and then must have ducked into a sewer or cellar until the whole show was over. It was all set up for them. Someone did get to them the previous night to arrange the whole thing. Those two bodies we found might have been anyone. Identification was planted on them just before the fire. God alone knows how easy it was to lay your hands on a couple of stiffs, in Berlin, during that time. Even if there were none available, they would have made a couple to measure without blinking.'

What he said made sense right enough, but as the full impact of it all came through to me I began to realise just what sort of man we were up against. If all Tom had surmised was true, this man Smith would think it nothing to dispose of us! A man who planned an escape like that and had the cool nerve to carry it out would make a very formidable enemy. No angry passion would force him to make a mistake over us as he had done over Hines.

We would be quietly, quickly, and, above all else, efficiently disposed of.

'Someone must have told who put the finger on him before he left the country,' mused Tom. 'I wonder where he did go afterwards and what he's been doing since.'

'We'll never find out if we hang around here,' I said. 'Strike another match and let's have a good look at the place.'

By the flickering light of the match we studied the room. It was solidly built of stone with a heavily timbered roof. Whatever ventilation there was in the place was indirect, for although the air continued to remain fresh, not a glimmer of light came in anywhere. Escape seemed hopeless and there was probably an armed guard outside anyway. Tom climbed to the top of the stone steps leading to the trap doors in the roof. I limped up painfully behind him. It seemed that for a long time now life had been handing me the knocks, and with the exception of my attempt to castrate Kopft with a kick, I'd had no chance to even up the score. I was beginning to get a red feeling of anger about it all. True, some of the mystery was resolved. We knew just how and why Hines and the others were killed and there was a great satisfaction in that. But small good that would do us now if we could not get out of this mess alive.

We listened near the doors. Tom put his back against them and levered from the stone steps, but the only thing that gave at all was the soft covering insulation of cotton and canvas. The framework itself did not budge, it didn't even creak. After a few exploratory heaves against the roof timbers, we crept back down to the floor of our prison. By the brief light of a match I could see that Tom did not look quite as cheerful, but when he spoke there was nothing in his tone to suggest this.

'What a set-up! Now if this were in a film, it would be time for the Marines to arrive.'

There was a rasping and creaking and suddenly bright light flooded down on us as the doors were thrown open. Even though we were momentarily blinded, we heard unmistakably the voice of Kopft as he ordered us out. We started to move forward. Tom didn't allow this to interrupt him. He went on in his bantering voice as we climbed the steps.

'What an artist this guy is. See the way he took that cue. He even looks like a Marine sergeant I once knew.'

I didn't feel like humour, but I admired the way he was taking it all. Me? I was busy thinking how Kopft was going to return the fast ball service that I'd delivered to him in town. That's the trouble with an active imagination, it gives you no peace at times like this. So, as I climbed out of the chamber over the top step, you might say I was expecting it, but that didn't make it any easier, for a boot is a boot any old time, and when you have it planted in your face, by someone of Kopft's size and temper, it hurts.

Thus the ball came back to me, fifteen all—fifteen thirty to Kopft as I took his knee into the pit of my stomach—fifteen forty to him as I got chopped down with a blow to the back of my neck and—game to him as I felt his huge ham fist splash on to my face, and a beautiful warm darkness came down blotting out everything. I learned afterwards that the match went on through quite a few more sets before he stopped, a satisfied victor. Tom watched it all through at the point of the fat man's automatic before being ordered to pick me up and carry me into the house.

When I came to, I found Tom bending over me in the same room as before. He was trying to clean up some of the mess on my face with a handkerchief. We were in one corner of the empty room, and sitting across from us was the fat man in the striped suit. It seemed that I had never seen him without the gun in his hand and wondered in a daze if he'd had it grafted on. Tom started to say something to me but we were silenced by the rasping voice across the room and ordered to lie on the floor and not to move or speak. To me this was no effort. I felt that I'd gone through a saw mill and come out the other side neatly cut up into pieces. For although everywhere ached abominably, no two pieces of me seemed connected. At that moment I couldn't have summoned up the co-ordination to wriggle, never mind give trouble to the guy. My lips were swollen and my nose seemed to be filling up my eyes. So we just lay there helpless and silent, hearing the sounds of our breathing and the occasional stirring of the man in the corner as he shifted position.

Somewhere in the house there was activity going on. We could hear the sounds of heavy things being moved about and the mumble of voices echoing through empty rooms. Somehow I was past caring, and yet the spark of resentment that had kindled in me earlier was now growing white hot inside. I could feel waves of hate and nausea passing over me. The door opened and in came Smith and Kopft. The noises about the house continued, so there were more people in the house than we had imagined.

'Sit up.' Smith's voice had the same impersonal quality as before, cold and well modulated. I struggled painfully to a sitting position.

What a contrast the two men made, standing there, each a foil to the other. Yet there was a similarity about them that was not difficult to identify. It is often easy to recognise clergymen of the same religion. That is what these had in common, a dominant faith, and deep satisfaction and conviction in their way of life. Remembering what I had been told of their past did nothing to quiet the feelings of fear that were growing in my mind. With a great deal of morbid satisfaction I noticed that Kopft still moved favouring his lower abdomen, and walked with great discomfort. Looking back on it now I can see that it was this very feeling that united them in evil which saved us that day. For had it not been for their desire to gloat and taunt, and engage in their favourite passion of inflicting human misery, we would have been killed outright much earlier. As it was we were, as one might say, saved for the last like some titbit of experience they wanted to savour before leaving.

Smith's voice cut through the growing silence, as we studied each other. 'Lieutenant McNally, you are a fool, a great blabbering idiot. I have always thought fate was very kind to me when I was given into your charge. I might have had one of the less stupid Americans. That would have made my escape just that little bit more difficult. And then this morning. Now, are not the fates on my side? How can you doubt it? Just think of it! It is the most amusing thing I have encountered since coming to this hell-hole of a place.' He moved to the centre of the room, and took up a dramatic pose. 'I am awakened this morning. My little Kopft telephones that he is in Kikuyu Halt. He is waiting for me, having made a mess, I fear, of the little task I gave him. I go to meet him. I am angry. What do I find in Kikuyu Halt. No Kopft but a slow-witted American who asks me where the nearest telephone is, and who babbles on about having a wanted criminal tied up in his car. I am asked by this American imbecile to assist him and keep a watch on his prisoner while he phones his poor friend at the New Stanley to put his mind at rest.

'I am overjoyed to help. It is the duty of every citizen to behave so, and I fervently wish that there were more public-spirited men of his ilk in the world. Over the barrel of my gun I invite this imbecile to join me in my car. Such company is rare after all, and not to be cast aside lightly. I release my poor mistreated Kopft and we return. I give my guest accommodation, but I feel he might be lonely so I go all the way into Nairobi to invite a friend for him. And now you are two!'

I looked over to Tom. His face was a picture of misery.

'It was all like he said, Gareth, if anything worse. Of all the stupid horse-arsed, big-mouthed morons, I'm the worst. There I was on top of the world, congratulating myself on being God's gift to the "clear-Gareth-Ashe" campaign and I have to go and shoot my big mouth to this creep. It was not until he had me behind the gun that I recognised him. I'm sorry, boy, I just couldn't get round to telling you it was my big mouth that landed you back in this heap of crap.'

I felt angry at him for a moment. All the pent-up frustration that I had been feeling was focused on him, and then I relented. 'What the hell, Tom, I'd have come anyway. They could have saved themselves a trip.'

Smith resumed his former position in the room. The situation seemed to amuse him. When he spoke again it was still with a heavy sarcasm.

'You gentlemen seem to enjoy our company, especially you— Mr Ashe, isn't it?' He indicated me pointedly with his stick. 'So let us see what amusements we can think up for you. Kopft here is very good at party games.'

I didn't look forward to a further demonstration of Kopft's talents. I tried as best I could to put an uninterested expression on my face. I must have failed miserably, for my face was no longer lending itself to expression of any sort. Tom on the other hand tried a different approach.

'Now, look here, Sloeder, or whatever you call yourself, you can't get away with this. Times have changed and we're not in Nazi Germany now. Your type of work isn't thought much of around here, and if you'll take my advice . . .'

Whatever his advice was we never got to know for Smith had started to laugh, though hardly a line moved on his face. It was a cold heartless laugh that sent a chill over the whole room. He thumped Kopft on the back, and spoke to him in German. Kopft joined in, his huge face gradually slitting to show his long blackened teeth.

'So, the big fat American lieutenant wants to advise me,' he said. 'From what I remember of you and have seen today, I would think that advice would be the very last thing you could afford to offer. Now as for my "type of work" not being thought very much of around here, I will want to know more about that shortly and indeed, whilst you are telling me more of your thoughts in this matter, you might come to change your mind and express a very healthy respect for it. Ah! McNally, do you remember how we tricked you? Ridiculously easy! Why, even in the post-war Germany, which grows softer every day, you would not be a lieutenant of boyscouts!'

Tom let out a low bellow of rage and charged straight at Smith. But with perfect timing and ease Smith avoided him, and tripped him with his stick, sending him crashing to the corner, a tangled, undignified heap of frustrated anger. A sharp business-like click, and a wicked nine inches or so of steel flicked out of the end of the stick in Smith's hand. In a second he was above Tom with the needle-point blade at his throat. A bright bead of blood grew there even as Tom strained away from its relentless gentle pressure.

Smith's voice was as sharp as the steel when he spoke.

'Look at Kopft! Do you see that scar?'

I looked where the ugly, badly healed scar ran down the side of Kopft's face. 'Once, only once, many years ago, this man tried something equally stupid, but he is a good man and I left him with a little reminder of his folly. You would seem to require the agony of personal mutilation as a similar momento, but you do not have time for mementos—no!'

I'm sure that if Tom had moved then or shown the slightest sign of fear Smith would have carried out his intention. As it was he did not move a muscle, and far from showing any sign of fear, returned his gaze steadily, as he would have in a poker game with a few pennies for stake. Eventually Smith seemed to make up his mind. The same sharp click and the blade disappeared. He was smiling strangely as he turned to include me in a wave of his stick.

'Take them to the back room and wait for me there. There is about an hour before we leave here, and we must entertain our guests. It's a pity that we cannot afford them more time, for McNally here promises to have all the characteristics of a very fine playmate.'

The fat man ordered me through the door with a wave of his automatic. A similar gesture from Kopft with his weapon and we were all leading out in single file. The room opened out into a hallway from which several other doors led off, left and right. At the extreme end two of them were open facing opposite each other. I felt the barrel of the gun jab into my back.

'Get going, last door on the left.'

I glanced behind me as I started to move towards it. Out of the corner of my eye I saw Tom behind my captor and then Kopft bringing up the rear. My heart started thumping and I prayed that my swollen lips would be able to pronounce the words clearly when I spoke and that Tom would be able to guess my intention.

'I hope you have something to eat. What I could do to a fat sandwich now is nobody's business.'

I got prodded in the back for my pains and I heard Kopft chuckle, but better still, Tom's voice cut in.

'You and me both, brother, we'll have it between us.'

As soon as I got to the open door, I went into action. I dropped suddenly to my knees. The fat man came crashing over me, tumbled into the room, and I was up and on him pinning him below me and grappling for his gun. Tom, meanwhile, had watched for the move and immediately I started he had backed Kopft hard against the wall, jabbed backwards with his elbow and then came hurtling in after us. I heard the door slamming with the sound of bolts being shot home and the roar of Kopft's gun all in one split second of time as I gained possession of the fat man's gun. He stumbled awkwardly to his feet and backed away from me to the door. Tom spun him around and levelled him with a punch that would do credit to a boilermaker.

We had barely cleared back from the door to the corners of the room when a series of shots thudded through the woodwork. From our position in the corners we looked about us. There was only one window in the room. Kopft gave up shooting and started to charge his way at the door. Luckily, it was stout enough to hold a while and the bolts, which must have been fitted long ago, during the Emergency, looked very formidable indeed. Still it could only be a matter of minutes before something stronger than a human shoulder were brought against it.

Thinking about how provident these terrorist precautions were, I looked again at the window. It was heavily reinforced on the inside with expanded steel mesh and as well as this, two very stout shutters lay hinged back against the inner walls. I soon got one secured while Tom dealt with the other. The lights was cut out so that the room was only lit by the dim sunlight that filtered in through the chinks in the shutters. The battering at the door had ceased now, and as our eyes got used to the gloom, we looked around.

The room contained very little in the way of furniture. A desk with books and papers and a stout table with a few chairs made up the whole lot. Except for those, a large wooden packing case, some odds and ends of tools and two lamps, the room was empty.

'Come on, boy, what are we waiting for? Let's dig in.'

Time was short so we started dragging the desk and other furniture against the door. The wooden packing case we pulled over against the window. It, too, was heavy and seemed to contain a number of metal appliances carefully packed in straw.

All this seemed to have taken an eternity but in fact it was all done in feverish haste and it had only been moments from the 'sandwich' to our taking up position at each side of the door waiting for what was to come.

We sat on the floor and looked across at each other. A sorry pair we looked indeed. Although we held the advantage at the moment, a few more minutes might see the whole situation changed. I looked at the automatic, and spent a moment opening the magazine and counting the shells. It went back with a satisfying click. At least we could give some account of ourselves now.

'Look, Tom, we've got to get out of here, this place is too active for me.'

'Just lead the way, son, I'm right behind you.'

I racked my brain trying to think of ways of getting out of there. I looked all around the room trying to work something out. Then suddenly it struck us simultaneously. We both looked up at the soft-board ceiling that was nailed to the roof joists with strips of batting. In a bungalow such as this one, that way would give access to the space under the steeply pitched roof.

'Go to it, Gareth. I'll create a diversion.' He took the pistol from me and angled a few shots into the top panel of the door.

A sudden burst of cursing and heavy scrambling footsteps was the result. I quickly climbed on to the table and started hacking away with fist and fingers. I tore out great lumps of the softboard with my hands until there was a hole close to the beam through which we could pass. I clambered down again, and took a look at the recumbent form of the fat man on the floor. He was still a long way past caring, and seemed unlikely to interrupt us for quite some time.

Suddenly there was a rending crash against the window frame. The sound of glass shattering was like a hailstorm, and the shutters bent in for a second then held. We heard the deep powerful throb of a diesel engine.

'Get up and out quick, Gareth, they're ramming us with the back of a truck!' There was no time for heroics I know, but the thought of him holding the rear didn't go down very well with me. 'After you,' I said.

We stood facing each other for a brief moment and then the truck hit again. This time plaster came showering down from the frame and cracks appeared round it. Were it not for the steel mesh, it would have given. We could expect no more than one or two attempts before it gave way.

I started pulling out the straw packing from the case, and drenched the whole thing with the contents of one of the lamps. The other I dashed against the doorway with its pile of furniture. The engine of the truck ground into forward again. I seized a handful of the straw and lit it, and set fire to both the piles. The paraffin made it leap into a blaze instantly. Everything was tinder dry. The truck came in again and this time a shower of masonry came down around the window, but it still held.

'Come on, let's go, you first and then you can hand me up.'

Tom was up in an instant, giving me a hand to take the weight off my knee. The whole place was a blazing inferno now, fanned by the breeze from the breached wall.

There are moments when time seems to stand still. As I had clambered to reach the hole and Tom's arms waiting above, I had seen a leather folder become exposed on the burning desk. I risked precious seconds for who knows what and reached down to pick it up and stuff it into my shirt.

I eventually got my elbows over the beam with the flames actually licking at my feet. Thick smoke filled the air and it was hardly possible to breathe as we made our way gingerly across the roof beams towards the far end of the building. The slats of light between some of the ill-fitting tiles guided us.

Through the crackle of the fire we heard the engine of the truck as it raced in once more. Looking back, we felt a sickening jar as, amid a chaos of sound and rubble, part of the wall of the house gave way. They were in. But in achieving their end the situation was only made worse. The extra ventilation caused by the great hole they made could be heard sucking towards the fire. Within seconds the whole ceiling and roof exploded into flame over the spot where we had just passed through. I stood watching, fascinated by the sight of the flames creeping slowly towards us. I was jolted out of it with a hard slap on the back, and I turned to follow Tom's example, levering at the tiles low down near the eave. They were the loose interlocking type, hung on battens transverse to the main roofing timbers. It was a simple matter to remove them. After taking out about six, Tom swung a double-footed kick at the remainder. He grasped a beam above his head and tried again. With his second attempt, the battens gave way, leaving a hole large enough to pass through.

I went out feet first, slid to the edge, and after a momentary pause to look down, dropped into the thick shrubbery growing near the house. Even before I hit it I saw Tom coming through the hole. He came out in a sort of forward roll that took him over the edge of the roof to land on his feet beside me. I'd barely got to my feet when he took me by the arm and we were running head down for the cover of the bushes as if the devil and all hell was after us. We dived in and came around smartly to face whatever there was.

I could taste acrid fumes in the back of my throat and bile in my mouth as we knelt there panting and gasping greedily, Quite unexpectedly, I began to feel a delicious sense of relief flowing all through me. It was like a quiet unhurried orgasm touching every nerve and fibre of my body. I knew before Tom's incredulous whisper—we'd done it, we had got away without being noticed.

From where we were we could see nothing of the side of the house where the wall was breached, nor of the front. The house itself was a complete write-off, all of the roof was ablaze and it was collapsing lazily before our eyes. Well back from the house in the cover of the bushes, we made our way round to the front. The truck had been driven away from the house and a number of men were fanning out to cordon the blazing building, urged on by a swearing Kopft and a tight-lipped Smith. They all faced inwards at a safe distance, each armed with some weapon or other. They were six Europeans and three short slightly built men of vaguely Oriental appearance. It was only then as I counted them that I thought of the fat man we had left in the building. I whispered this to Tom. 'He had it coming,' he murmured in return, and in the ensuing silence we watched a while, looking at the men who were waiting for the unlikely chance of our escape from the inferno so that they might shoot us down.

Tom turned to look at me and a broad grin covered his face, giving his craggy grimy features the look of a gloating villain in a melodrama. He winked slowly and pointed his thumb over his shoulder. Even if we had made any noise it would not have been noticed in the confusion of sound round the burning house, but I don't think we did anyway as we slunk away quietly down the hillside, avoiding the driveway and the road. About a mile from the road we turned around and saw a thick cloud of smoke rising on the wind.

CHAPTER EIGHT

After walking about five miles we were lucky enough to get a lift across the country roads in a maize lorry bound for Naivasha. Although it took us well off our way back to Nariobi, I think the time was well spent for we were both pretty worn out after the day's events, and the fitful sleep that we fell into on top of the maize sacks left us feeling a little better as we drove in to the town. By common consent neither of us said a word about what had happened. We had a bath at the town hotel and then an enormous meal, which somewhat surprised the management for it was only then drawing on towards evening. As a last chore, Tom did some phoning to Kikuyu Halt and managed to get the local garage to send out his car with a driver.

While we were waiting for it we sat in the lounge with a couple of tall beers and smoked, and let the excitement and tiredness of the day flow out of us. We were alone in the room, seated in a pair of deep armchairs, our legs stretched out lazily in front of us. The events of the day seemed strangely unreal in my mind. Not so Tom. He took a long pull at a cigar, letting the smoke curl lazily upwards in the way some smokers have of preferring to move the head rather than blow away the smoke cloud. He moved slightly to beckon the waiter who returned presently with two more beers.

'Well, what's to be our next move? It appears to be one of two alternatives. First, we could dump the whole mess into the lap of the police. Secondly, we can get to hell out of here and forget all about it, seeing that it's not our business to meddle with this sort of thing. Now I don't know about you, but I can't do that, and even the first alternative seems a bit tame after what we've been through today. I reckon we've had a bad deal from these guys, and I'd like to even the score up a bit on my own account.'

He looked serious and I felt my lethargy and indifference slipping away a bit as the beer began to establish a glow deep down inside me.

'Now hold on. We can't just go bursting into them again like that without knowing a bit more about what's going on,' I said. I couldn't see things in quite the same straight-forward manner as he did—I thought that it would need a lot more planning before we did anything. 'You are forgetting about the death of Williams and the fact that I might find it damned difficult to prove I didn't kill him.'

Tom waved his hand impatiently. 'With the record those two have got they wouldn't stand a chance of pinning something like that on you. Besides, what reason would you have for knocking Williams off?'

I ground out the butt of the cigar in the ashtray at my elbow.

'There is another thing. Granted we know why P.J. was killed, assuming your theory about the film to be correct, and we know why and how the other two were killed, from what Williams told me, but there is one question still unanswered.'

'That is?'

'What were Smith and that bunch doing out there anyway? What was the work that they had just wound up today, miles out in the bush in an empty house?'

Tom looked thoughtful for a moment and then he started laughing, helplessly. Perhaps the events of the day had been too much for him, I thought. His mirth gradually subsided.

'Sorry about that, boy, but what you said got me to thinking about that house and how it was the last time we saw it.'

'Well, what was so funny?' I asked, a little irritated.

'Well now, if that don't beat all! Sloeder and Kopft standing outside that burning building waiting for me to come out! Don't you see? That's just how they left me in Berlin that time, right behind the eight ball. This time it's them thinking of me getting burned up.'

He went off into another long chuckle of laughter and this time I joined him for the whole situation was so ironic.

We both realised that they were due to leave the place quite urgently, their truck had been all but loaded. Their urgency would have been increased by the fire, for the house, standing as it was on a hillside, would have showed for miles around as a burning invitation to every curious person in the area. And this, as we very well knew, was the last thing that they wanted—public knowledge of their presence.

They could hardly hang around and wait for it to cool down just to make certain that we had perished. They would probably have waited just long enough to ensure that life would be impossible inside and then gone. That left us with a very distinct advantage. I'm sure that we were all written off in Smith's practical, Prussian mind, yet there we were very much alive, trying to work out a surprise for our would-be executioners.

For the next hour we kicked the thing around and then came to a decision. As soon as the car arrived, we'd drive back to the city and get the whole thing straightened out with the police there and then watch from the side-lines for a chance to get back in when the opportunity presented itself, for who could tell where Smith and Company would be by the time we got back.

The Buick was a really first-class job, custom-built, and a good mover. The tyres hummed along the road as we ate up the fifty-odd miles that separated us from the city. It was quite dark by then and we sat in the back seat, leaving the worries of night-driving to the driver who had brought out the car. We were looking through the folder that I had rescued from the house. It held three bulky enclosures. The leather was old and supple, having an ornate H.S. tooled on the front in a decorative gothic script. There was very little that we could gain from the papers.

The first was a large folding survey map of East Africa on which someone had drawn a series of short parallel lines and dots and circles in red and green and black ink. Except for the fact that one of the small circles indicated the place where the house had been, there was nothing else significant about it. We put it aside for a more detailed study later. The second document looked far more interesting. It was a cross-section of what appeared to be a well boring, indicating types of rock and soil at different levels of the operation. This was annotated in a neat script, indicating dates in English. It was easy to read and appeared to be straight-forward. I read it aloud and as I went on some of the eagerness left Tom's face. The thing was obviously no more that what it appeared to be. The third bundle was equally disappointing and crashed any hopes we had of learning something from the folder. There was a printed heading on the top:

THE EAST AFRICAN ARTESIAN CO., P.O. BOX 4166, NAIROBI.
Area Manager. Harold Smith.

The papers contained a list of sites where boring operations had taken place, which varied considerably in degree and location, scattered all over Kenya, with results which seemed to range from dismal failure to abundant success. A glance back at the survey map showed that many of the sites were the ones which were indicated on it with circles. What the green parallel lines meant was anyone's guess.

The last page of the headed stationery was a mass of figures which seemed to calculate pressures at varying depths. I showed it to Tom. He looked at it for a moment and then shook his head. I repacked the papers and stuffed the folder and its contents into a pocket in the upholstery of the car.

There it was then, all neat and tidy. Director and area manager Harold Smith was obviously our Herman Sloeder in the innocent business of water-seeking in a country where it was obviously very badly needed. He even appeared quite efficient at it, too, judging by the folder. I must confess that we both felt rather deflated as the car toiled up the escarpment and tackled the last rolling miles. Tom as much as myself wanted there to be something more in this thing that would allow us to take some part in the final account that they would pay. Now it looked as if it were to be a routine police job in apprehending them and bringing them to account for their crimes. There was some satisfaction in realising that but for our persistence in the matter they would have got clean away with murdering three innocent people. It seemed we would have to be content with that.

By ten o'clock that night we were closeted with a superintendent of police relating the whole story. He sat thoughtfully behind his desk stroking his long moustache. His uniform was immaculate and he held himself with a soldier-like bearing. At the table near a curtained window a stenographer took down the whole story. His infrequent interruptions were mostly concerned with certifying times and places. By the time we had finished what we had to tell he had stopped stroking his moustache and was giving us his undivided attention.

'And what makes you think that this man Sloeder has any connection with Harold Smith and the artesian company?'

We had agreed to make no mention of taking the folder for to do so seemed trifling and I wanted to look at it more closely at leisure. To have mentioned it would have meant handing it in. I answered before Tom had a chance to reply.

'It's just guesswork, superintendent, based on some headed notepaper I saw on the desk in that room before the fire. It would be well worth checking anyway.'

77

He nodded his head briefly and got to his feet.

'Well, I think that will do for now. I will of course require you to sign these statements in the morning.' He indicated the stenographer at work. 'In the meantime I suggest that you get a good night's sleep at your hotel. I will be in touch with you when you are required.'

'You mean I'm quite free to go?' I asked. 'I mean, about Williams's murder.'

The superintendent allowed a faint grin to come to his face. 'Just how naïve do you think the police are, Mr Ashe?'

I had to be satisfied with this vague remark. We shook hands briefly. It was my private opinion that naïvety was a strong part of any police system, but I did not press the point. I knew that in spite of what we said the whole system of police operation would take days to defeat its own inertia and get moving. The wheels of justice grind exceedingly slow. We were ushered out by the inspector. At the desk in the outer office he stopped and handed me a piece of paper.

'You can pick up your car tomorrow, Mr Ashe, we should be finished with it by then.'

It was an official receipt. We started down the steps towards the Buick.

'Gentlemen, I am instructed to inform you that the only mention that will be made to the press will be issued from this office. This is not the time for sensationalism and it would be very much regretted if there were anything of your story to appear in the newspapers at this time. Do I make myself clear?'

We nodded assent and proceeded on our way to the car. Tom got into the driving seat and I beside him. It had started to rain lightly and the pavements gleamed beneath the street lighting. I felt cold in the clothes that I wore and thoroughly depressed by the attitude of the police. I knew of course that as they proceeded they would come to the same conclusion as we had, but why waste so much time when with what we had told them they could have sailed right into the problem. It had been a tough day for both of us and Tom looked just as clapped out as I felt. It was about eleven-thirty before I got myself settled into the hotel. By midnight I was fast asleep.

CHAPTER NINE

The morning was clear and all signs of the night's rain were gone from the sky. I joined Tom at breakfast as early as I could for I had lots of things to do before returning to the police station. He had some cables to send concerning his contract with Constellation, so, after we had a final cup of coffee and the first cigarette of the morning, we parted, agreeing to meet back at eleven-thirty at the Thorn Tree.

After the early-morning rush, the streets of the city were relatively quiet. Later the main streets would be crowded with the babble and confusion that would make even a London traffic policeman swear. Some people would give you Lagos for the worst driving in Africa, myself I'd say Nairobi without doubt.

I used the lull to get most of what I wanted done. I had my beard trimmed, and a shave from a Pakistani barber, and then shed my badly fitting and crumpled clothes for a suit of dove-grey gabardine which was serviceable without looking cheap, then I was ready to do something about my bruises and bumps. I went along to a local doctor who did a sound enough job on me and pronounced me fit if somewhat battered.

I felt better after all that and made my way to the central post office to send a few telegrams to London.

There is a large Georgian house in a quiet forgotten street that leads off the Great West Road in Paddington. The house itself had been converted into a number of office-cum-flat units. Room number twenty-two is the home of Pipiras. I keep whatever files I have there and do whatever organising there is to be done to keep the business end running from this office. Next door, in room twenty-three, Mari has a typing agency. We have a long-standing agreement. While I'm away she looks after anything that might crop up and keeps me informed about any changes that she thinks I might be interested in. When I want to get in touch with her for anything urgently, I use telegrams in a weird sort of code, partly for economy which is a considerable factor, and partly just for the hell of it. We did a lot of things like that together—I mean, just for the hell of it.

Mari is a great girl in many ways, efficient and cool when needed, but quite something else again at other times. It was the efficient, cool side of Mari that I wanted to make use of that morning but I began to get the feeling that I could do with her there in Nairobi to iron out some other sorts of tensions that were growing up inside of me.

I sat down in the post office and settled to composing some telegrams to convey the message I wanted to send. It took quite a lot of ingenuity to tell her about the other need, and I could just picture the charming way she had of flushing slightly as her mind went off the business side of our relationship to the more personal one.

When I handed in the filled blanks to the clerk, he looked a bit puzzled and then, with a wave of his hand that dismissed all Europeans as mad, totalled up the cost. I had about an hour left before meeting Tom. I suppose it was sitting there thinking of the office in London and then of Mari that made me aware of normal life again. I began to plan an evening for myself. A quiet dinner with an attractive woman, a little dancing, a few drinks—that was what I needed for a start, then I'd see what the night would bring. Danusha would be just right. It was over a week since I had seen her and I had promised to call her when I got back. She was the daughter of a Polish expatriate who had settled in Kenya after the war. He ran a business on Kenyatta Avenue, a successful and very select shop that dealt with curios and had a fine reputation for Makonde carvings and wood sculpture.

I reached for the telephone directory on the desk beside me and thumbed through the pages, looking for East African Arts, the name of the shop. I knew that Danusha helped her father there in the mornings and since it was still early she would not be too busy. I found the entry in the directory in quite bold type, and just above it, quite insignificantly in smaller print, East African Artesian Company. It suddenly leaped into prominence! The address was given in the River Road area of the town. Not the best side of town but certainly not as bad now as it used to be.

I decided that no harm could come from taking a look. So I left all thought of Danusha for the moment and made my way through the crowded backstreets of the town until I came to the place. I stood across the street from the address and looked at a single-storeyed, unimposing building. It had a concrete façade painted in a faded yellow, with blistered lettering across its length, which informed that it had once been the commercial hope of one 'Mohammed Valani, dealer in piece goods and fine quality merchandise, also bicycles. Step in for sizing.' Now the plate-glass windows had been half painted a dark green and bore the title of its new owners or tenants, East African Artesian Company.

I couldn't just stand there looking, for nothing is more likely to attract attention on a busy thoroughfare than the sight of a person standing doing nothing. I walked down the street about ten yards and took a seat for a shoeshine. The morning sun was quite strong by this time, and I found it pleasant just sitting there and watching the shop front across the street. The front door was closed and an expanding metal grille was drawn across the front. A very tidily dressed African waited outside, leaning on the grille and reading a newspaper. A battery of pens and pencils in his top pocket proclaimed his calling to all. The place was evidently not open for business.

I paid for the shine and was about to go when I saw a woman crossing the street from my side and going directly towards the building. It was possible that she could be going there, I thought, although, in truth, it was not so much that as the gorgeous sight she provided that made me stop to watch her. The short sit that I had had in the sun had done nothing to dispel that earlier feeling of animal indolence and indulgence that had been growing in me and I found the sight of her very provoking. So I watched her a while. She did go up to the shop and stood a while talking with the clerk while she fumbled the grille open and then led the way in through the door. That I supposed was the office staff of East African Artesian Company. Fair enough! The events of the past few days might not be such a dead loss as I imagined, and there was still that dinner date that I had done nothing yet to fill. Besides there was something about her that struck a faint chord in my memory.

Oh, I know it's a long-standing joke and all, but I really felt like asking her if we had met somewhere before. You know how it is sometimes—there is a certain something about people that makes you suddenly aware of them in the midst of hundreds. It was like that with her. I could swear that I had seen her recently. I passed it around in my mind for a while trying to remember just where it was that I had seen her face, and then I realised that I hadn't had a very clear look at her face—there was something familiar about her total look somehow.

I was half way across the street without even thinking of a reasonable excuse for entering the office. So I started to marshal some sort of story that might sound plausible while I got a closer look at her.

The shop had been partitioned into two offices. The outer one held a desk, some filing cabinets and a few large-scale maps of East Africa pinned up on the wall. The African clerk was busy emptying the contents of the filing cabinets into a large cardboard box and for a few moments did not notice my arrival. I looked around again. There were sounds of activity behind the door of the partition. In a prominent part of the door across the upper panel was a plastic strip carrying the name Miss A. Anselm. The name meant nothing to me. I put on a casual attitude, walked up to the clerk and asked for Miss Anselm. He half turned, pointed with his lips to the other office and then carried on with his work. I knocked lightly on the door and opened it.

The view I'd had of her from some distance had provoked a little ripple deep down where everything seems to happen. Close to, it was like a tidal wave down there. She really was something. When she looked up, I felt as if her eyes were pulling me into a whirlpool.

A thick knot of ash blonde hair was drawn back severely from her face showing the clean curving line of her throat as it dipped away into the upflowing lines of the rest of her body. I immediately felt the sensation of being engulfed by this upsurge of her. It seemed to be her whole personality. She looked up with one eyebrow slightly raised in that inquiringly defiant look that would seem to be the hallmark of the well-groomed, well-trained personal secretary everywhere.

Her eyes were a violet hue of blue, cold at first glance, but showing a deep glowing warmth beneath. There were faint traces of tired lines at the corners of her mouth and it was drawn a shade too tightly to complete a picture of careless aloofness. Hers was a studied and deliberate aloofness.

This was a situation that needed playing carefully, and I felt the cool, poised 'I've got the situation well in hand' feeling come over me as our eyes met and part of my mind gave up the idea of trying to find an excuse for being there. She broke off first and her eyes dropped down to the desk. Her hand went straying for the non-existent strand of hair out of place, a gesture that always betokens an awakening awareness on the part of a woman.

'Can I help you?'

The voice started well down and came out precisely with an accuracy that could serve as a model for radio broadcasters. I let her words hang on the air for a second or two and allowed her interpretation of my look and her own imagination to answer the question for her.

Just when it seemed that irritation would get the better of her I spoke, rattling out the story without even trying.

'My name is Ashe, from Gilchrist and Partners. My firm has an interest in acquiring the lease of this property, and I've been asked to take a look in and take a few notes about internal renovation. I did call earlier but there seemed to be no one answering the phone so I thought I'd come by anyway.' I let the words pour out smoothly and watched the initial look of irritation become replaced with efficiency again. She was poised and sure of herself once more. She put a few searching questions that were beginning to embarrass me in my new-found occupation of architect when I had the inspiration to cut across her grilling.

'I believe that our Mr Gilchrist had already dealt with all this with your Mr Smith. Perhaps you might like to check with him?' I leaned over and lifted her phone from its cradle and offered it to her as casually as I could.

'That will not be necessary, I think, but do excuse me now, I have very much to do. Please try to be quick.'

The ice was turned on now and I was dismissed as she redirected her attention to a pile of typewritten work before her. She sat so prettily, with a balance and distribution of charm that was quite upsetting. Occasionally, as I looked around the room with what I hoped was a professional eye, I glanced at her. A frown was growing from some little lines above the bridge of her nose, and the tired lines around her eyes were more noticeable. There was, too, a certain grim determination about her whole posture.

I left her room quietly, mumbling something about the outer office. Once the door was closed, reality came back to me and I looked around the outer office with an eye to anything that might provide some background information to Mr Smith and his associates.

The office was much as it had been when I first came in, except that now the contents of the cabinets and all the furniture were being loaded into a blue van which was parked just outside the door. Three very black men in khaki dungarees were moving back and forth with a miscellany of cardboard boxes and files, in the shuffling gait that, in Africa, passes as haste. They paid me no attention whatsoever and carried on their task with only an occasional comment from the clerk. I went across to one of the maps which still hung on the wall. On the floor lay a scattering of blue-headed pins. The random perforations were the only thing that made it different from any other map. Then perhaps it was the well-established training of my earlier years that made me look for some legend or title to it. If there had been one, all that remained of it now was a neatly cut line.

It was a map of East Africa, with the structure indicated in great detail. There were no words or titling on the map. It was only by the colouring that one could guess its purpose. The chief differentiation was between the mountains and plains of tertiary and quaternary volcanics, and the indication of scarp-forming faults.

My study was rather unceremoniously interrupted by a curt '*Tafadali, Bwana*' and a long, snaky brown arm reached up and unpinned the map from the wall. The last of the boxes was loaded. The doors slammed shut, and with a brief rasping cough of the starter motor, the blue van moved off, carrying the men and boxes with it.

I turned around to the desk, and saw the clerk empty a tray of paper clips into his pocket. Straightening his very straight tie, he knocked on the door of Miss Anselm's office and entered, closing the door very discreetly behind him. I began to feel rather foolish, just standing there. The office was stripped clean, and there did not seem to be much point in standing around any longer. The idea of coffee came into my mind and I remembered my appointment with Tom. But I thought that another look at Miss A. would not be amiss. I did not have to wait long. The door opened and the clerk came out smugly pocketing a cheque. With the briefest of nods, and a curt '*Kwahere*', he was out through the street door, and pausing only to wipe the toe caps of his already impeccable shoes against the legs of his trousers, he strode off jauntily towards the Thika Road, straightening his tie once more as he went.

'Will you be finished soon?' The voice, silky and smooth, came from an elegantly poised Miss Anselm. She stood framed in the doorway of the inner office. Under her arm she held a very bulky parcel, tied neatly with string and bearing a boldly written label and a pattern of angry red blobs of sealing wax. She was very obviously ready to go, and had a small bunch of keys dangling idly in her fingers.

'I'm all finished here,' I said and tried to smile. It worked a little and I saw the hint of a thaw in the touch-me-not aura that surrounded her. Maybe it was that slight relaxing that caused it, but quite suddenly the colour visibly drained from her face and she leaned heavily against the door frame. I moved forward quickly and steadied her arm, taking the parcel from her.

'I'm sorry,' she murmured. 'I don't know what came over me then.'

I led her unresisting to the desk and she gratefully flopped into the chair.

'Feel better now?' I asked. She really looked all in, but even so her hand went out to take the parcel back from me.

'I'll be all right in a few moments. It's just that I'm tired I think, and I've rushed things a bit on an empty stomach. I wonder, would you mind helping a little? I feel that I just couldn't manage driving and I must get this away.' She indicated the parcel.

'I'm terribly sorry, but I don't have a car with me right now.'

'We can use mine.' She offered me the car keys. 'It's the little yellow Fiat 850 just up the road near the corner.'

Even as I left the office I could see the car, parked about fifty yards up the road. In a few minutes I was back again. As I drew up to the office, she came out of the door, closing it behind her. She still looked pale and drawn, and somehow very attractive because of it. I got out to help her. She declined my offer to close and lock the grille, saying that she had to return in the afternoon anyway to finally lock up and dispose of some last-minute things. That seemed reasonable. I looked at the address on her parcel and noted the destination as Kampala. I got into the driving seat of the Fiat and leaned across to open the passenger door. She got in with a flash of smooth brown thighs. She straightened her skirt down with a brief smile to herself, and settled into the little bucket seat. I started off and completing a U-turn in the road, headed back up the hill, towards the centre of the city, making for the General Post Office on Kenyatta Avenue.

As we crossed Government Road and filtered into the main

stream of the traffic, she kept up a sort of shallow patter of conversation, politeness seeming to be her only interest.

'It really is very kind of you to help me like this. Isn't Nairobi beautiful in the morning? Have you been here long? Just imagine someone driving like that in London—I do love to see all the people moving about in the morning . . .'

None of this seemed to require an answer or comment so I just concentrated on the traffic and let her voice ramble on, only giving an occasional 'Mm' or nod as the sound of her voice seemed to indicate.

It was not until I moved into a different lane at the traffic lights to turn right that her voice became anything like positive again. 'Straight on, please.' I automatically made the necessary adjustment, and carried on when the lights changed green. 'Just about a half mile further on.'

I supposed that there was a sub-post office somewhere and she would be using that as the morning rush was in full swing in the city centre.

'If you would just pull in here.' She indicated a well-developed driveway into a block of office buildings set about twenty yards back from the road.

Again a flash of warm brown as she opened the door and got out nimbly, the parcel under her arm. Any idea I might have had of going with her was cut off half formed with a 'Shan't be a moment!' thrown over her shoulder.

She went into the neatly appointed building, through the glass door decorated with the motif I.A.A.S. surmounting a wing. Internal African Air Services was a small charter company that operated a fleet of about six light planes and was mainly concerned with the movement of tourists and business executives between the chief airports and landing areas of the three East African countries.

I sat waiting in the car under the freckled shade of a bottle palm and let my mind focus on the niggling worry I had that I had come across the very beautiful Miss Anselm before. But it was as elusive as a word on the tip of the tongue, and even as I watched her come out again, I was no nearer to remembering. I opened the car door. There was a marked change in her now. All the tenseness seemed to have drained away and when she spoke, it was lightly and for the first time warmly.

'Just wait a moment.'

I had started the engine, but at the light touch of her hand on my arm I disengaged the clutch and enjoyed the momentary contact. She continued to look at the building she had just left and then from round the back of it came the sound of a revving engine. A small Roho, emblazoned with the crest of I.A.A.S., spurted across the loose gravel, halted momentarily at the entrance, and then roared away down the road. I heard her breath release and felt a thrilling pressure of her fingertips.

'There now, that's finished. I want you to know how much I appreciate your help Mister . . .? I'm sorry, I didn't really take much notice in the office.'

'Ashe,' I said. 'Gareth Ashe. And you're Miss Anselm, but the initial?'

'A for Anne,' she said and smiled.

We turned back towards the city more comfortable in each other's company. Everything seemed to be clearer. The colours were brighter and there were many more smiling faces. I knew that as well as the parcel she had delivered, many worries would fly out of Wilson Airport within the hour.

The Thorn Tree was fairly busy with its usual mixture of people soaking up the usual variety of pre-lunch drinks. The sunlight was beating down from almost overhead, and the patches of shade thrown from the umbrellas and the Tree itself looked twice as deep and twice as welcome in contrast to the eye-tightening glare from the street outside. Several times as we sat there I had been on the point of asking her about the conviction I had of having met her before, but each time the idea died as I tried to frame the question so that it would not sound facile.

As it turned out I had not long to wait. She was telling me about something that she had got the day before. The New Stanley is a must for tourists and there are vendors selling every conceivable sort of money-catching souvenir that you can imagine, but Anne fancied she had really made a 'buy' and was enthusing warmly over it. A newspaper seller came up to the table where we were sitting and pushed a copy of *The Standard* in front of us—as only a Nairobi paper-seller can. I waved him aside impatiently, and he started to move to another table, but not before Anne had caught a glimpse of the front page.

'Please, may I have a paper.' She almost snatched it from the boy's hand and spread it out before her on the table while I fumbled about for the necessary small change.

Even upside down I recognised the picture and read the caption. It was a picture of Williams, with the legend: 'Body found at Timboroa'.

She was on her feet and grabbing the car keys from the table. The newspaper was grasped so tightly in her hand that the knuckles showed white. She let out a half-choked sob, 'Oh, Bill! Bill!' and then fled in a sharply faltering run towards the street.

I had half risen with her but resumed my seat. Perhaps it was seeing her in a state of distress that had finally jolted my memory. I knew then where it was I had seen that expression before, and why the features were so familiar. She had an unmistakable family resemblance to Williams. I bought another newspaper. Even the rather poorly reproduced driving permit photograph showed it quite clearly.

CHAPTER TEN

'Well I'll be damned if that don't beat all!' Tom sat in a chair that had just recently been filled in a much pleasanter way. His legs were stretched out in front of him, and the tall glass of lager was emptying rapidly as he took punctuating sips between his remarks.

He had arrived just in time to see Anne leave, and had listened keenly while I told him about the morning's events up to the time of her abrupt departure.

'If what you say is right and that this woman is a relative of Williams, then there's a chance to follow this thing up a bit.'

'In what way?' I asked.

'Well, don't you see? If she knows anything at all about this set-up then she's bound to try to get in touch with Smith, or someone else about Williams's death.'

I nodded agreement but began to be a bit uneasy about what he might have in mind.

'All we have to do is find her again and follow her until she leads us back to them. And boy, things will be a little bit different next time, I'll tell you.' He patted the pocket of his linen jacket, where it bulged significantly. 'I'm all for equality in matters like this, and believe me this is the sweetest little equaliser!'

In spite of his optimism I was not as confident as he seemed to be. When I faced up to the reason, it was simply that I did not relish seeing myself or Anne in the situation that he dreamed up for us. I told him so. He looked at me with an odd twisted smile and then said, 'Right, Gary boy, we don't do that. So what do we do?'

I had to admit that I could think of no other line to follow. We sat there for a while and let it mature and then decided that we would have lunch.

It was still early and the dining room within the hotel was only half full. I tackled a trout *meunière* rather indifferently, while Tom did excellent justice to a black pepper steak, done rare, a speciality of the place. We were each rather occupied with our own thoughts when a commotion near the doorway caused us to look up. A group of people were milling around and the sudden flashes of cameras announced the arrival of someone out of the ordinary. There was a brief continuation of this at the doorway and then the pressmen departed.

A rather pale man was left to make his entrance into the dining room. He crossed the room confidently to join another man who was already seated at a table for two.

'Now I wonder who that one is,' I said.

'Well that is what I call a man,' replied Tom, 'a real man. His name's Clarke—Murray Clarke.'

The name meant nothing to me and I shrugged.

'Just broken the London to Jo'burg record. That, sir, is the only way to travel . . .'

He went rambling on about the joys of solo flying, where the feeling through the seat of your pants was the only reliable navigation aid, when a thought occurred to me. I waited until there was a pause in his eulogy and jumped in.

'How long would it take to fly from here to Kampala in these light aircraft that one sees about?'

'Now that depends on what you mean by light aircraft, it's a pretty wide term, you know.'

'Well, you know, the sort of thing that I.A.A.S. might use.'

'I.A.A.S.,' said Tom thoughtfully. 'Well, now, I know their set-up, seen them out at Wilson Field many times. They've got a couple of beat-up Canadian Otters and two spanking new Cessnas from the States. Now if you put those babies on the run to Kampala, let's see now . . . how far'd you say it is?'

I made a rapid calculation. 'Four hundred-plus road miles.'

'Then it could be anything between two and a half hours for a really good run and up to four at the slowest, not taking into account the unpredictables—weather, take-off delays, and of course the pilot himself. You can bet that whichever one I flew, I could coax a better speed than the next guy.'

I looked at him. The idea I had in my mind became more and more plausible as I listened to him.

'You can fly then?' My question was hardly necessary.

'Got in two hundred hours already,' he said rather smugly.

'Listen, Tom, you just said that the trail of Smith was dead unless we could follow Anne. Now, what about the brown paper package she sent off? What if we could follow that? I'm sure it was taken from Nairobi this morning, and my guess is that it is already airborne, somewhere between here and Kampala.'

'You mean fly up there after it?' His eyes were already agleam with the idea.

'The only thing against the idea is cost,' I added ruefully.

'Hell the cost.' He was on his feet. 'Let's go!'

Fifteen minutes later I was behind the wheel of the Buick and nosing out of the traffic on to the main coast road that ran south towards the two airports of Nairobi. There was the main International Airport that served the world's airlines and Wilson Field, which dealt with most of the internal traffic. While Tom had gone to his room to pack, I had telephoned for the fastest machine on the field to be on standby for immediate take-off as soon as we could get there. I learnt from the call that the only flight of I.A.A.S. that had left that morning was the departure of an Otter at half-past twelve. With any luck Tom should be away by half-past two—two hours behind. A lot of leeway to make up but not an impossible task.

As we drove towards the field we spent the last ten minutes making arrangements for contact. We decided that a timed telephone call the next afternoon to the hotel would be the best plan, and that after the call, if needed, I would make a booking to travel up to Kampala by train the following afternoon.

We came in through the Aero Club entrance to the field. There was a desultory atmosphere about the place. One or two small planes stood outside near the hangars, with the cowlings off. A few mixed sounds, human and mechanical, floated about in the afternoon silence making it, if anything, more blanket-like. Standing alone out on the strip like some disdainful queen, was a twin-engined 310P Cessna. The gleaming red and white finish shone like a still pool of light, deep and beautiful.

A man came out of the clubhouse dressed in a short pair of shorts and a very long pair of moustaches. He approached with an outstretched hand. 'Mr Conway? Well, there she is—all tuned up and ready to go. Just a few formalities of course—documents, licence, cash, things like that.'

He took in both of us with a wide grin and led Tom, fraternally looping one arm round his shoulder, back to the clubhouse where he had a small office. Whatever it was that flying men had for each other the world over was established between them, and they walked away together going through the spoken rubrics of their religion, like priest and acolyte reciting a litany.

I watched the plane take off a short time later into a slight cross wind, and waved again as it faultlessly gained height. Already the sound of its engines was dying away as I climbed back into the Buick, feeling a bit like a caterpillar must feel as it watches a butterfly—a bit sad, but a bit safe too. I had my plans roughly sketched out in my mind and my list of things had two top priorities: one, to go back to the office of the Artesian Company, and, two, to see Anne again. I looked at the clock on the dash—quarter to three. I could manage both with a bit of luck, assuming that Anne was still around.

I rejoined the dual carriageway and turned back towards town. There is something quite indefinable about the afternoon light on the East African Plateau. The wind blows hot and strong sometimes with a sigh that makes one think of the endless miles of scrubland that it blows across. The great wild Africa that is Kenya comes up almost to the edge of the city and only reluctantly gives way to the suburban gardens and zones of acacias and palms that line the highways.

I went to the hotel, had a quick shower and changed into some fresh linen. Leaving the car parked in a sideroad, I walked the remaining hundred yards or so back to the office where I had first met Anne. I don't know what I hoped to find but it occurred to me that at least there was a chance I might see her there.

I could see from some way off that the office was locked and I blessed the providence that had made me include my key blanks as I came out. As I approached I selected the suitable blanks that might fit the Viro on the grille and the Yale on the door. The grille lock responded to my attempts quite quickly, and this was in my favour, for it might have looked suspicious to a passer-by if they had seen me fumbling. The Yale on the door proved to be a bit more stubborn, but after a few more attempts it, too, was opened and I was inside, closing the door quietly behind me. The place was just as I had seen it earlier and completely empty. The outer office was of no further interest to me so I went into the other one.

I knew when I saw the grille locked that she had been back and one glance at her desk confirmed this. The drawers gaped open and the top of the desk itself was impeccably bare. I started to look at the room very carefully. I tried to see everything because I was looking for nothing in particular. A flimsy door led off into a small cloakroom. The room held a low-flush toilet and a miniscule hand basin surmounted by a small cupboard. In the cupboard there was an opened packet of paper towels and a small packet of soap such as is issued in hotels and on airlines. It was still wrapped, and in addition to the brand name, it carried the very generous information that it had been specially prepared, packed and presented, for the sole use of the guests of the Hotel Capricorn. The name sounded vaguely familiar and I placed it somewhere in the Museum Road area. I thought then that this was at least something. It was quite likely that Anne had brought the soap in and it was therefore possible that she would be staying at that hotel. Being one of those people that can't resist a free tablet of soap, I dropped it into my pocket and then idly flushed the toilet.

I went back into the office. The telephone was still there as I had seen it in the morning, but it was only then that I noticed it was an internal extension set. I followed the wire up and found that it led out through the outer office and through the wall near the window to the rear of the building. I left the office and closed the doors, making sure the locks were as I had found them, and walked round to the rear of the building. At the back there was a warehouse-type structure, known locally as a 'godown', built on a high concrete ramp. I noticed the Estate Agent's signboard in the corner of the plot: 'Valuable Godown Space to Let.' Contact Manurbhai Patel . . . etc. So, it seemed that I was too late anyway. I walked on and at the next plot engaged the gateman in a bit of polite and casual conversation. I learnt that the evacuation had taken place only the previous day. They had cleared out, kit and caboodle, and he was very glad anyway, for no one had spoken to him the whole time they had been there and they even had a European gateman! He laughed long and loud as I walked on, saying how foolish that last bit of folly was, for everyone knew how lazy the Wazungu were at everything except ordering others to work!

Tea was being served in the Hotel Capricorn by the time I had located it. I sat down in a plastic chair that looked like a flower pot and ordered tea from the steward. I had chosen a place where I could get a good view of the reception desk and the comings and goings of people through the lounge. I hoped that I might find Anne without having to make any enquiries.

I was thumbing through a magazine when I felt that faintest of auras that herald a change in a hotel lounge. Anne had arrived. She was a very beautiful woman and there is always something about the entrance of a beautiful woman that makes itself felt. It's the time when men's hands move to their ties and women take comfort by touching their hair. She came straight across the room to where I was sitting as if she had known that I would be there.

'You don't look surprised to see me,' I said.

With a beautiful economy of movement, she sat down opposite, looking straight at me all the while.

'There is no firm of Gilchrist and Partners in the city. I tried to contact you this afternoon, and I found out that much.'

'Why did you want to find me?' I asked.

'First tell me why you came to the office this morning, and what you were doing there—does it have something to do with Bill's death?'

Until she asked about Williams, I was all ready with a story that was beginning to form in my mind that might have satisfied her in any other circumstances, an appeal to her feminine vanity, a story of simple attraction, my reason for being there being simply that she was there. But now with that frank distressed look in her eyes and with the obvious shock she had suffered apparent in her face, I was convinced that such a story would be useless. She would have listened, perhaps believed and then coolly left— uninterested. Somehow it did not seem the right place to be talking of the thing at all, and indeed I needed more time to think out just what I would tell her and how much, for I had no way of knowing to what degree she was implicated.

'Look, I'd like to help. I really would, but it's a rather long and complicated thing, and there are many things that I want to know myself, things you might have the answers to. Why don't we talk it all out over a drink tonight? Perhaps we could have dinner together and then get it all straightened out.'

I think she would have liked to decline, but the promise of some enlightenment made her ignore her doubts. We agreed to meet at The Shazan at half-past seven and after a few moments I went on my way, leaving her to the tea which had just arrived.

I drove to the railway station after that and booked a berth on the next day's train for Kampala. It was a long train journey— some twenty-four hours. It could be driven in about a third of the time by road, but somehow the thought of the drive put me off.

The relaxation that the train journey would provide was very attractive, for East African Railways are second to none for comfort and service. The very nature of the route, rising as it does through thousands of feet at Timboroa and then descending across the Uasin Gishu and down towards the land of the lakes, makes it a slow journey, but it is one, once undertaken, never forgotten. So I decided to leave the car at a garage in the town. Turning to go, I remembered the leather folder so took it out and carried it back to the hotel with me, walking through the city in the afternoon sunshine. My thoughts went into a sort of blank haze. The events of the last few days just slipped away from me. I was looking forward to the journey for its own sake, and went into a bookshop to get some reading material. I took my books and walked on through the town towards the hotel. Quite suddenly I felt very tired, my knee ached dully and I began to get the feeling low down in my stomach that perhaps life was a bit too fast and hectic for me. Although Kopft's attentions to my face had been most expertly delivered, my face was not too bad, but there was still an unfamiliar puffy feeling about it that made reality even more remote.

Back in my room I went straight to the bath. I let it fill and wandered round the room stripping off my clothes and kicking them all over the place. I slid into the scalding water and felt it creep up my body, inch by delicious inch, and numb away much of the ache and pain. At last I was all in up to the neck and gave myself up to relaxation with a deep contented sigh. I felt drowsy and mellow about life and Sloeder, Kopft and Williams faded away into unreality. Only Anne remained—a blurry-edged fantasy of lithe limbs and high breasts. . . .

I must have slept. The water was cool and the square of frosted glass window had turned quite dark. I stood up, quickly soaped all over and then stepped into the shower cubicle, letting the cold water lance all over me for a few minutes. I felt reality creep back to my mind. There was something odd about the East African Artesian Company and although their activities seemed above board they could be a cover for some less legitimate business. Then there was the question of Anne herself. Where did she fit into all this?

I dressed carefully and left the hotel with half an hour to walk to the restaurant. The night air was cool and refreshing, and I put a bit of life into my pace as I walked and wondered what the hell had got into me earlier when I had felt so low. Neon lights gleamed here and there, throwing unrealistic pools of colour on to the pavements. Small groups of African and Asian youths stood about in groups, outside restaurants and cinemas, wearing very modern, far-out clothes with a kind of self-conscious air at once charming and ridiculous. Nairobi is like that—in its short life as a city there has not been enough time for it to become really urban and dignified. It is like an adolescent, brash and unsure of itself.

I arrived at The Shazan with ten minutes to spare. The restaurant was not large, perhaps twenty tables in all, but had a well-earned reputation for a distinctive oriental cuisine, sensitively served. It consisted of an outside verandah of about eight tables, each pooled in intimate shadow, and an inside dining room with a well-stocked bar running along its length. There is, I suppose, a right drink for the right place at the right time. For me in East Africa this has to be warm lager beer. One of the better aspects of colonialism in Africa was the introduction of lager beer. I think the first brewers to set up business were Germans. Whatever happened to them, their beer remains, and it is probably the finest outside of Pils. All this, taken with the sensitivity of palate to drink it warm, makes a very fine first drink for anybody's evening.

Well down through the first bottle Anne arrived, looking surprisingly unsophisticated. I would have thought that she would have arrived rather as she did in the hotel lounge that afternoon. She looked good but I felt a little peeved, thinking that perhaps she had not bothered too much since it was only me she was meeting.

I smiled a welcome and indicated the stool beside me. 'Would you like a drink?'

There was a small amount of indecision before she replied, 'Gin and tonic, please.'

The barman busied himself with the order. A waiter hovered near with a menu which she took and studied a little blankly. 'Would you order for me?' she asked.

I scanned the menu quickly and suggested Avocado Pear Vinaigrette followed by Lobster Thermidor. She agreed without much enthusiasm. I could see that this might turn out a difficult meal to get through. Much of my earlier enthusiasm began to evaporate. She sipped her drink thoughtfully and I refilled my tall glass from a fresh bottle of Whitecap.

'You're very quiet,' I observed, just for the sake of breaking the silence. The only response was a faint smile and a murmured apology.

'Look, it's no good being like this—we have the whole evening before us. Let's at least enjoy this part of it. We can get to the serious part later and then we'll see—we might even enjoy that!'

'I know. It's just that . . . I'm sorry, I just can't help thinking about poor Bill being dead.'

'He was a relative of yours?' I ventured.

'My brother.' She looked down and fumbled about in her evening bag, changed her mind, and finished off her drink quickly. 'May I have another, please?'

I nodded to the bartender. 'Would you like to tell me about it?' I asked.

'Look, Mr Ashe . . . Gareth. I don't know how much you know about all this or how it concerns you. It does concern you, doesn't it?'

I nodded.

'How?'

'Well, I'm not really sure yet. I met Bill twice, the last time a few nights ago, the night he died in fact, but it was in a way that is very difficult to explain until I know more about it.'

'You mean that you were not working with him? You're not one of those people?'

'No, I did not work with him and I'm not one of those people.'

She looked at me intently for a while.

'I'm going to believe you because I want to.'

'There's no reason why you shouldn't. Up until a few days ago, I worked for Constellation Films, on location here in Kenya, just a contract job of liaison. I met Bill—he introduced himself as a Mr Williams then, by the way—whilst we were on a hunting safari. It was all by pure chance.'

I saw that she had become visibly more relaxed, whether from the effect of the drink or from the reassurance that I had given her I didn't know, but much of the tension had left her.

'Look,' I said, 'let me tell you something about myself, and then you might feel more like talking to me; there are some things that I would dearly like to know about.' I gave her an account of the less serious side of my work, highlighting some of the more amusing aspects, and was rewarded by her response. She smiled and chuckled.

'You're Welsh, aren't you? For a while I couldn't place the accent and then when you started talking at length, I got it.'

'From South Wales,' I said. 'Right on the coast.'

'Do you know Branddu Castle?' she asked eagerly.

I nodded. 'It's demolished now.'

'What a terrible shame that was. It was such a beautiful place. We all had a holiday there once together, my father, Bill and I. It was so long ago though, when I was quite small. Bill often used to talk about it when we were older, my memories of it are probably more his than mine.'

Branddu 'castle' was a large Georgian house, built almost on the coast between two of the more popular resorts on that stretch of shore, in a spot progress had passed by. It had been quite difficult to get to and thus all the more rewarding for me as an adventurous young boy. I had very pleasant memories of the place too. Death duties and other expenses had made the running of the place too expensive, and after a few attempts to do something with it, it had finally been abandoned and eventually sold to some contractor who stripped it of any valuable building material and then demolished it. I wondered what possible reasons had taken Anne and her family there.

It turned out that her father had been a business associate of the last owner, Cartland-Howes, the great coal and steel magnate, who had held an interest in practically all the development in the area before the days of nationalisation. Yet the name Anselm meant nothing to me.

We were called to dinner and sat at a little table for two on the outside verandah. Nothing was lost of the friendliness that had grown between us at the bar, and we continued through the meal with light casual conversation.

Anne was thoroughly relaxed now and her eyes glowed with life and response as she chatted about her childhood and early adult years. The tenseness in her body had all relaxed, to be replaced by an easy and graceful control of herself and the consequent desirable appeal that this produces. It made her a very attractive person. As we talked on I felt a warmth grow between us that relied little on the actual content of our words. I'm sure it must have registered that I was interested in her in a way which had little to do with what we were saying, and indeed I felt that she was feeling much the same.

So far I had gathered some objective facts about her. I guessed her to be around twenty-seven. She had grown up in a comfortable financial background, had received a good public school education and taken an honours degree in modern languages, specialising in French and Spanish. I guessed that she did not have to work for a living, but she had spent her latter years working at home in the Diplomatic Service in a secretarial capacity. All this was very satisfying—it gave me facts which could be verified later. Often as we had exchanged information, her brother Bill was mentioned. By then it did not seem to worry her so much to talk about him. One of my few talents is being able to talk, and I have the ability to be a good listener, too, which had paid dividends. I almost regretted having to stop her, and I knew that my next question would, but time was running out for me and there was still much which she might be able to tell me.

When I did ask her, I knew that she, too, had been toying with the idea of putting in a braking question. So there were still things that she wanted to know. As clever as I thought I was, thinking I was the one directing the flow of conversation, I realised that this was so only because she wanted it that way. I began to get the distinct impression that it was she who was in control of the whole exchange.

I had asked her how long she had been in Kenya. I think there was mutual agreement that the time had now arrived to clear the air a bit and stop circling about the point.

'Just six months.'

'What made you decide to throw up your job at home and come here?'

'I came to look for Bill.'

We sat over coffee and lit cigarettes.

'Was he lost?'

She showed a little irritation at what she took to be a facile remark.

'Gareth, I'm going to tell you about Bill even though I think you know. I'm going to tell you because I trust you now, and I want you to trust me, in the same way. You are suspicious of me, aren't you?'

'It's not suspicion, Anne. It's just that I'm confused about everything. I think you are right, though. Tell me about Bill, it may clarify lots of things.'

She looked at me for a moment without saying anything, and when she did start to speak it was in a much lower tone than before, and much quicker, as if she were repeating a story and she wanted to convince herself of the truth of it.

'Bill was never a bad man, no matter what you may think of him. He was always a bit wild and unorthodox, and often got into scrapes with authority wherever it lay. When he went up to Oxford we all thought that at last he would settle down. He'd had three years in the army and it seemed to have made him more mature. He did very well up at Oxford and had a fine career ahead of him, by all accounts. Daddy got him into the Civil Service at quite a high level of responsibility with the Ministry of Defence—not that he wouldn't have made it on his own in due course anyway, but that's the way Daddy was. Bill had been working in Whitehall for about two years when he met Tali. She was a writer, sensitive, very sincere, and her work, while full of poetry, was aimed at making an impact on whole areas of what she thought of as social injustice.

'Well, briefly, they lived in what one can only call a state of disastrous hostility, punctuated with moments of understanding and tenderness, for about six months, then one day she just walked out on him. Bill suffered terribly—I think that he really did love her—but he never did understand her, nor she him. Each one tried to see the other as counterparts of themselves. I think that Bill would have liked to settle down in some quiet, suburban area, but Tali had other ideas. They had a flat in town which attracted a constant stream of visitors, dissatisfied and disgruntled people who all wanted to put the world to rights and yet who did not have the ability to put their own lives in order. Tali walked out just after they'd had a terrible row following a police visit to the flat. They were never charged with anything themselves, but lots of those who had been regular visitors were taken in for questioning—you know, the usual routine, protests, drugs and all that.

'Before this time Bill and I had all but lost contact with each other, and Daddy wouldn't have him near the house. They quarrelled a lot, chiefly over Bill's rather way-out political views. I suppose he was what one might term a theoretical communist. I don't know. So it was quite a surprise for us to learn of his disappearance, about a year after Tali had left him. The first we knew of it was when the police came to make enquiries about him. All too soon the exact nature of his disappearance became public knowledge, for Bill had defected to the East and the last that had been heard of him was from East Germany, where he had been seen in the company of some high-ranking ministers from that country. Apparently, there had been a leak of classified information for quite some time, and Bill's defection coincided with the disappearance of some very valuable documents from his particular department—you may remember the fuss that was made in all the papers at the time.'

I did remember something vaguely about this so I nodded. She had paused to light a fresh cigarette. I called the waiter and ordered a fresh pot of coffee with two glasses of Glayva. I did not want to interrupt her story so hesitated to break the silence, but then seeing that she remained mute I thought it best to urge her gently with a question.

'Was it all true, all that in the papers?' I asked, although indeed I had only the slightest notion of what she was talking.

'Largely, yes. In fact eventually we did receive word from him through some of Daddy's business contacts in Eastern Europe. Just that he was well and sent his love to us both. Daddy was a tough old soul and I don't think that this business of Bill had anything to do with it, but shortly after that he died, quite suddenly. I don't suppose it all helped though.

'That was all of five years ago now, and then, last year, I heard of Bill again, not from him. A very old and dear friend of mine was out here visiting her uncle in Nyeri. She wrote to me saying that she was sure that she had seen Bill one day at a filling station in Nanyuki. He was driving a pick-up belonging to the East African Artesian Company. She'd had no opportunity to speak to him. He'd driven off in a great hurry, and although she had made enquiries all around there was no one who knew anything of him. But she was convinced that it had been him.

'It was only a very slim chance I know but I decided to give it a try. I applied for a passport and, using my mother's maiden name, came to Kenya on a holiday visit. After I had been here a few weeks a vacancy was advertised in *The Standard* for an Office Secretary who could deal with the normal run of office routine with minimum supervision. It was with the East African Artesian Company. I managed to fiddle a temporary employment pass through the influence of some friends here. So I applied for, and got, the job.

'Well, that's about all there is to it. I never did see Bill again. I could never directly ask about him, for I knew that whatever he was doing would be under an alias and I did not want to prejudice his chances of making a new life for himself. I just hoped that chance would bring him to the Nairobi Office one day, and that I would see him again. Of course, I kept my eyes and ears open for mention of anyone like him, but the situation with that firm was very strange, sometimes I even wondered if anyone worked for it at all! The work I had to do was minimal—just dull routine typing of endless figures and lists. After being employed I was given my instructions by a very taciturn Asian sort of man and, from then on, received most of my directions either by phone from him or by post. I suppose that by the time I got here I was too late and that Bill had moved on somewhere else. It's certainly too late now!'

She lapsed into silence, with her head down, idly drawing patterns in the spilt cigarette ash with a match-stick—I felt sorry for her sitting there looking so alone and dejected. 'I know this is hardly the time, but what about identification of his body and all the other formalities; can I help in any way?' She sighed deeply and then went on.

'As far as I know he was identified as John Williams by his driving permit issued in Dar Es Salaam. I don't want to stir it all up again, and I'm sure someone will do that soon enough once enquiries are started. For my part now I just want to forget about it and let poor Bill have some peace. His life must have been terrible since those days in London.'

I stood up and took her hand, longing to comfort her, but I knew that any word of sympathy then would have been the wrong thing to say. The way she had looked at me a moment ago when she said 'someone will do that soon enough' made me realise that she thought that I had some sort of official interest in Bill's death and was silently asking me to be as discreet as I possibly could over it. She had not believed a bit of my story about Pied Piper and had just played along in order to get her side of things stated before the official juggernaut of justice crushed all humanity out of it.

'I think it's time we went,' I said.

I settled the bill while she went to the ladies' room. I waited for her just outside the restaurant. When she did eventually come out, her eyes looked a bit puffy and I think that she had been having a quiet little weep.

'I'm sorry,' I said. She smiled bravely, linking her arm in mine. We walked to her car, hip to hip.

'You never told me about your knee,' she said.

'That's another long story for another long night. What you need now is a good night's rest. You've had a very hard day.'

'But what about your—— Oh Gareth! I must know, what about your meeting with Bill? Can you tell me . . . anything?'

We drove back to her hotel. She drove well and skilfully in spite of the wine and the emotional upset that she must have gone through during the evening.

'Come on up and I'll give you a last nightcap while you tell me about it.'

Her bedsitter suite was on the second floor of the hotel. She busied herself for a few moments taking off her shoes and preparing two long whisky and sodas. We sat facing each other from the two corners of a long, well-upholstered settee. I lifted my glass and looked at the light diffusing softly through the pale amber of the whisky, fractured and splintered by the cut-glass patterns.

I told her the whole story right from the time when I had first met Williams up to the departure of Tom that afternoon for Kampala. I wanted to reassure her and I believed her story implicitly. My account was punctuated with several refills of whisky, but at last it was over and we sat watching two cups of very milky instant coffee, both smoking thoughtfully.

It was quite late. My watch said one thirty, and the whole world seemed to be asleep around us.

'Gareth, you know I thought you were from some organisation at home, investigating a reported appearance of William Langley.'

For a moment it did not register, perhaps it was the late hour and the whisky . . . then . . .

'You mean Bill was William Langley! But you gave the impression that he was just an also-ran in some minor defection. My God! that was big stuff! It was his disappearance that caused all that fuss.'

There is a time in every conversation when words degenerate into empty symbols of thoughts and the rattling of them becomes pointless and irritating. I could see that Anne had had enough, and in truth I had too. We were both tired and under a strain. Her eyes were full and eloquent as she looked at me. I reached out my hand to her, meaning to apologise and somehow comfort her, and suddenly she came to me, holding me tightly with her head buried deeply in my shoulder. I held her close, trying to be the comfort she desired.

Her long hair lay fragrantly against my cheek, and the soft

pressure of her body against mine was at once comforting and disturbing. There was something so beautiful in that moment, a pulsating warmth held us together and a great feeling of out-growing began to swell within me. It was as if I must hold strongly to her in case the moment would slip away. Then inevitably the moment did go by as she lifted her face to me. I kissed her gently. Her lips were soft and warm, docile and yet responsive with tenderness. For a moment she looked at me with a faintly quizzical expression and then cradled herself into my left arm and sighed deeply, stretching her whole body upward.

I buried my face in her hair and kissed her arched neck. Even in the subdued light, I could see a warm flush spreading at her throat, and losing itself in the deep shadow at her breasts, which were provokingly visible at her loose, deep-cut neckline. I moved my hand to her breasts and cupped one easily—it was small, yet full and beautifully contoured. As I touched her, she moved again, turning her head to kiss me, and skilfully placed the whole deli-cate weight to my hand, her nipple blossoming to erectile nubility beneath my fingers. As she lay cradled against me I looked down the length of her body. Her long cotton wrap-around skirt did nothing to conceal the curves of her thighs nor every line of her body as she strained against me. What had begun as a spontaneous gesture of tenderness in me was slowly replaced with a hard stiff stirring low down. I felt myself break through the control of semi-tumescence suddenly, into the hard rigid urgency of full pole-hard erection—and then my hands were only blind servants to it. I shivered with the power of it and felt the woman beside me answer the age-old call.

My mouth wandered over her face, sometimes drawn to her throat but always returning to the hungry sucking fragrance of her lips, while my right hand moved from her breasts to her long bare thighs. I threw back the long skirt, like opening curtains to the morning sunshine, and my hand slid cunningly beneath the brief lacy cover of her pants to writhe rhythmically against the warm furry wetness of her. She came to this one with a small flurry of breath and a brief shudder of her whole body and then again with that thick warm flow of juicy need that has only one way of fulfilment. There was a brief standing up when we undressed each other.

We went back together and I could swear that before her back touched anything solid I was into her—right up her full—thrusting hard and finally spurting everything that ever was Gareth

Ashe, then nothing mattered except that we were man and woman in the eternal quest for peace and contentment in the mad world around us and the world obligingly tilted so that we might slip off into the exhausted, filled, drained, swollen abyss of nothingness.

Looking back now, it is strange to remember such an experience as nothingness. But I know that no feeling can be built, that means anything, on the shallow, false foundation of social intercourse. It is as if all the posturing and meaningless utterances have to be cauterised away in an abandoned selfish, selfless orgasm before the more lasting beauty of love can blossom where once it was only possible to have liking, respect or lust.

We had rolled to the floor, and I awoke feeling cold. Anne stirred with me and we very silently walked into the bedroom, arms about each other murmuring huskily, and found the bed, to lie in each other's arms deeply asleep, until the sun streaming through the window awoke me.

105

CHAPTER ELEVEN

I looked out of the window again. The whole length of the train was visible as it took a sharp left-hand bend over an embankment. The low setting sun flashed on the windows, making ruby eyes on the long iridescent millipede of a train that crawled its way north-west across the great scarp edge of the Rift Valley, tenuously feeling for a way to descend on to the safe flat floor below.

Nairobi was over two hours behind. The journey had begun during a torrential downpour of rain. I was glad, for it seemed fitting, like a bitter baptism that leaves old ways behind and prepares for a new life ahead. I was glad, too, of the long lonely hours ahead, where I could be silent and think, conversation not being exerted beyond simple requests to the stewards on the train.

I was the sole occupant of the double-berth compartment and hoped that it would remain so for the rest of the journey. I was travelling fairly light, having only a small grip and a briefcase. The compartment was roomy and comfortable. The steward would be around soon to make up the bed for the night so I walked forward along the corridor, through the second class portion of the train, to the dining room, and ordered myself a large beer to wait for dinner. By the time that was well down, the train had descended by some very tortuous bends to the floor of the Rift Valley, and was now running easily through the thorny, acacia-dotted countryside. A very brief twilight was giving way to darkness, and through the window at my elbow I could see my own reflection growing clearer every minute.

I thought of Anne. The image of her smooth brown body came to mind, with the soft tendrils of long blonde hair curling seductively around her breasts. She had wanted to come too, but I had argued about the danger, since she would be known through working for the Artesian Company. I was not convinced by my arguments myself, so it was hardly surprising that she was not either. When we parted in the morning, in spite of all that I could say, she was convinced that she was being dropped—indeed she might well have been right. Her whole attitude of happiness and settled contentment after we had made love again in the early hours of the morning was frightening in its completeness and had made me shy away from any further involvement.

There was such an unspoken depth to our feelings that it made me feel trapped. I loved her, I knew, from the moment I had seen her wake in the morning—but then, I had loved before, and knew the other side of it too.

I forced my mind away from her and thought instead about the events of the day. I had left the hotel, her hotel, about ten-thirty without even an arrangement for meeting her for lunch. I think she was crying and it took all my will to walk out like that. Even as I thought about it I felt a self-loathing. Why the hell was I made like that anyway, why couldn't I have been cast in the mould of the average man. I should have been in Nairobi now, enjoying the most sublime experience a man could possibly desire, the company and love of a woman who loves him. Instead I was stuck on some damn awful tortoise of a train headed god knows where, chasing an illusion of life which even at its best could only faintly make up for what I would lose by leaving her.

But then, the mould of the average man was not for me any-more. I had loved women before, I suppose, more or less normally, from the first heart-bursting fullness of adolescence, which is a strange mixture of romantic imagery and conscience-stricken horniness, right through the vain, cock-strutting, cock-wielding years of youth. And then Fona who made everything else seem a shadowy prelude. For over a year we had been together, and all the while the world had seemed to stand still, allowing us to love, denying us nothing and letting us explore and delight in each other endlessly. Endlessly? No, hardly that, she had died. I just think of it like that, not really having the courage to face the reality of it all. And her memory stood between me and Anne then in a way that I could never have explained to anyone. Fona had died because I could not kill. She had not only died instead of me, but because of me. The details were consciously blurred in my mind, but that one glaring fact faced me with startling clarity—that I had sacrificed her to my squeamish conscience.

I'd had to wait at my hotel all through the early afternoon for I was expecting a call from Tom, but it was in fact only half-past two when he did ring, so I decided to see her again and at least say good-bye properly. But I got to her hotel to find that she had already

checked out. No forwarding address. That was that. I had no one
to blame but myself. I asked if there were any message left for me.
Nothing!

Tom's call had come as I was lying on my bed after lunch. It
turned out that he had arrived only thirty minutes behind the
Otter, a remarkable performance made possible, he said, by the
rains and the better climbing power of his machine. He had taken
the airport bus into the city of Kampala and had managed to trace
the man carrying the package, to a small hotel called the Horns.
He himself had a room at the Grant and had managed to keep
something of a watch on the man, by eating large quantities of
Chinese food in the restaurant that was opposite the Horns.

I promised him that I would be in Kampala the next day and
arranged that he meet the train. I whetted his appetite by telling
him that I had a lot to tell him from my end too.

After I had returned from my futile visit to Anne's hotel, there
had been a message waiting at my own place asking me to get in
touch with the police. Time was running short if I were to catch
the train that afternoon, so I hurried over there and asked to see
the superintendent, and was shown into his office almost immediately.

'Mr Ashe, I have some news that might do much to reassure
you, although it gives us an extra headache. Four men left Nairobi
this morning on a flight bound for Cairo by way of Khartoum with
a booking to Beirut. Although they travelled on passports and
immigration documents that bore no name even remotely connected with the names Smith and Kopft that you gave us, two of them
undoubtedly answer to the descriptions that we have. Unfortunately, they have given us the slip for the time being. Oh, we've
made the necessary applications and requests, but things being
what they are in the Middle East just now we don't have a lot of
hope. Still, we'll keep trying and alert all the usual channels, to
try to keep them in sight anyway.'

I don't know whether relief or disappointment came uppermost
in my thoughts. I thanked him anyway and asked him if I could
get hold of the rest of my gear. That was all in order, so I then asked
if a trip to Kampala would be all right.

'If you keep us informed from time to time of your movements,
there is no reason why you shouldn't go where you like. If we could
get an extradition put into effect we would require you for
identification.'

I gave him my contact address in Kampala.

'Grant Hotel,' he repeated. 'A grand pub—stayed there often myself.'

As I left I remembered Williams's words about the shortness of time they had. They had certainly wasted none. It was a relief anyway to realise that if the four men had been the ones in the house, they were the only ones who had seen us, so there was no one in Kampala that could recognise either Tom or myself.

In the time remaining, I had stored away my car, sorted through my things and packed a grip for my journey. I organised my brief-case, putting in the Smith folder and, on a last-minute impulse, bought an O.S. map of the Rift Valley area coinciding with the maps that were in the folder. Whilst I was turning out my pockets for packing, I had come across the tablet of soap that I had picked up the day before. I'm not all that sentimental usually, but I weighed it in my hand thoughtfully for a moment. It's funny, so much can happen between people with so little consequence to their lives. A piece of soap was all I had of her—I suppose she had even less of me. Anyway, I had dropped it into my grip. I would keep it for a while!

The musical dinner gong on the train sounded time so I swallowed up the last of my beer and walked into the dining car, thinking to have dinner early, and make an early night of it. But it was not to be, for halfway through my '*Tilapia Tartare*', I looked up to see a middle-aged man enter the car. He looked around a while and then came up to my table, rather shyly.

'I say, would you mind if I sat here, place is a bit full, isn't it?' I nodded assent. He was a rather puffy-faced individual with a high colouring, around fifty, a bit flaccid in the belly and finicky in his movements. His accent, when he spoke, betrayed nothing save that he was a bland man from the bland South of England where, by some odd cultural custom, people deliberately macerate their voices and character to conform to some remotely grasped idea of social acceptability.

Through the meal we conversed lightly about topical things: the journey, the weather, the train. It was his first visit to East Africa. He had retired from the Civil Service in Britain and had been appointed to some commission to report on the feasability of setting up a market research project on behalf of the O.D.M. He was on his way to confer with his opposite number in Kampala, a Norwegian, whose country had a share in the project.

I exchanged a few noncommittal details about myself, as a tourist who had already been there before. I was about to excuse myself and return to my berth when I got an idea. I wondered if he remembered anything about the defection of Anne's brother. It would save a lot of time if I could get some fill-in on it, no matter how ill-informed. I looked at him then for the first time with anything like interest, to weigh up the possibilities of drawing him out on what I wanted to talk about. It would take time, patience and a lot of sympathetic listening. However, it was early and I had the whole evening before me.

He was just finishing his coffee. 'Would you care for a drink?' 'That's frightfully decent of you. Yes, I think I would. Whisky, please.' We sat smoking over the drinks, my offer had led to another from him, and there we were on the third round, warming up to the subject a little. He was not such a bad fellow really. It was just that a lifetime of unimaginative office work had crippled his own imagination. The whisky did much to warm him and pretty soon he was declaring how glad he was that we had run into each other and confessing that he had expected the journey to be a 'bloody awful bore'.

The upshot of it all was a fairly late night, during which he gave me some stories from his life, war reminiscences and anecdotes from the pale listless world of Civil Service Britain, with its cracked tea cups and rolled umbrellas. It was easy then to lead him on through Burgess and Maclean, Griffin and Knighton, to William Langley.

'What was that one about, anyway?'

'Why, don't you remember, old chap? Papers were full of it at the time. Did a bunk with very highly classified stuff. Then there was that popsy of his, wasn't there something about her too? Damned if I can remember now!'

'Thing that always surprises me is how easy it all is. You read all this fiction about espionage and all the intrigue they get up to, yet along comes a chap like this who quietly walks off with the lot.'

'Not that easy all the same, old chap, believe me. There's pretty tight security on stuff like that.'

'What sort of stuff was it?'

'Well, it's no secret now, I suppose—all out of date I should think, things move pretty quickly in that line of business. I don't know an awful lot about it, but I rather think that it was to do with transport.'

'Transport?' I echoed.

'What? Oh, I see. No, old boy, not that sort of transport. Jolly good that, what? Just imagine it, old Langley selling the secrets of the Green Line bus company to the Reds. Reds . . . get it?'

I grinned politely.

'No, not that sort of thing at all. It was a kind of new delivery system for nuclear warheads. New then, that is. Perhaps you won't remember, but there was a terrific fuss going on at that time about whether Britain should or should not get into the nuclear weapon race. A whole election was poised on the issue, and a lot of rash words were being flung about by either side. Right in the middle of all the fuss, this chap Langley takes advantage of a chaotic situation at ministerial level, when no one wanted to be caught holding the can, and was able to get access to material that he'd normally never have got a smell of.'

'What sort of material was that?'

'Not the faintest notion, old fella, but one thing's sure. As a result of it, twenty nuclear warheads just disappeared, and of course there was a further result as well. The issue as to whether Britain was to be a nuclear power or not was suddenly dropped from the attention of the public. No wonder, either. Too bloody ashamed of themselves to go on with it. I mean to say! Twenty nuclear warheads!'

I could not sleep that night for hours. I kept going over in my mind what we had talked about. If Williams—or Langley, had been responsible for the loss of those warheads, where did they go? What reason was there for their theft and what had it all to do with East Africa anyway? South of the Sahara there wasn't a single state or power that could make any military use of them, never mind coping with the logistics of handling them. Of course there was always the idea of it all being unrelated anyway and that Williams had, as Anne had said, been trying to make a fresh start in life. But there was nothing fresh about the company he was keeping, and there was no doubt about his implication in the deaths of three people, or his willingness to take a hand in mine! I was impatient to get to Kampala and see what new developments had occurred there.

Somehow, I must have dropped off to sleep eventually. When I was woken next morning at half-past six by the steward with the morning tea, my head ached dully from the lack of sleep and the whisky that I had drunk during the evening. Irritable at that early hour waking—bloody barbaric custom!—I could do little. I was awake and the day had started, even though the sky was only a pink pearly grey, and all sensibly evolved animals were still asleep. Man, the apex of it all, was abroad drinking his tea.

I nicked my face with a razor as the train ground over the points in Turbo, spilled coffee over my shirt at Tororo, and went back from the dining car convinced that this was going to be one of those days and that it would be better to just sit reading for the rest of the journey. I passed my companion of the previous evening in the corridor. Luckily, his English reserve was my salvation and all I had to do was nod. I will say this for the English, they stay in their place once they're put there. I went into my compartment convinced that I would not be disturbed by him again that day.

And then, his head poked around the door.

'I say, old chap, you don't look too bright. How about a hair of the old dog?'

'No, I'm all right really, just something I picked up somewhere. I seem to have these spots. I don't suppose it's anything catching. A drink you said—well, why not? I. . .'

'Spots, eh? Well then perhaps you'd better not, old chap, never know, do you?'

His head retracted back around the door, and he was gone . . . to gargle I supposed.

I got out the folder and let my fingers trace over the embossed monogram. The gilt was only just visible, and the leather had that fine patina of age and being cared for. Objects like that one seem to have the ability to soak in time and register something of its passing. Organic materials have a deep meaning within the life-time of a man, and a deep relevance to living. Metals don't seem able to do this. I remember being surprised, looking at bits and pieces of gold and jewellery that had been found at Knossos. It was almost as if they had been made that very week and bought in a tourist gift shop that very day! Cold inorganic metal is too slow to register the ephemeral impact of human activity. The only thing that affects it is the exposure to the grinding aeons of in-human time.

The folder held three enclosures. I drew out the map and spread it on the folding table below the window. The last time that I had looked at it was briefly beneath the poor light of a car driving from Naivasha. It was more properly a map of Kenya with the bordering countries shown in outline only. The scale was about 10 miles to the inch, so it was quite large when spread out flat. It was not what one would really term an O.S. map but it was detailed enough to show minor roads and settlements, even when the latter were only isolated farms and houses. In fact it was just an ordinary map which could be purchased by anyone. The only thing that was different was the drawing and annotation that had been done by hand. This was obviously the work of a professional. It consisted of a number of dots and circles in green, red and black ink and a series of short parallel lines.

I began to make a study of what appeared to be a random patterning, reasoning that there must be a meaning in it somewhere. I took some sheets of paper from my briefcase and the new map which I had bought in Nairobi.

After half an hour I had considered these marks from various points of view, settlement, land utilisation, natural vegetation, structure, topography. I rejected them all but the latter, and decided that, like the map that I had seen on the wall of the office in Nairobi, they related to the areas of activity in which the Artesian Company had operated.

I noticed that the house where we had been held captive was ringed neatly in green, and that there were three other places indicated in the same manner. It was interesting to note that in all cases they represented abandoned sites: the empty house, and three old diatomite workings.

The red circles were all on locations where one would be least likely to find or even search for water, along the eastern and western edges of scarp-forming faults. They were drawn, sometimes singly and occasionally double, from a line roughly level with Lake Baringo in the north to the latitude of Lake Magadi in the south, and concentrated most thickly along the Mau Escarpment. There was one feature that was easy to identify. There were a number of black circles that were quite obviously associated with some of the larger estate farms located on the floor of the valley. These could well be water-boring sites, but, except for this, I had to admit defeat at the end of an hour, no nearer to a solution than I had been when I started. I made a sketch map of the area and tabulated my meagre findings then turned my attention to the other contents of the folder. I rang for the steward and ordered lunch to be served in the compartment.

Over a ham salad, I read through one of the other papers. It was a list of the sites where boring operations had taken place. A careful check with my own map verified the conclusion that I had arrived at earlier. Operations had been undertaken in connection with the supplying of water to estate farms and ranching schemes —but there was also a considerable amount of time and energy devoted to the boring and search for water in places that even an amateur like myself could see were fruitless. And further, even if water had been found in such places, what possible use could be made of it far away from any human settlement or developable terrain?

We crossed the rail bridge which spans the narrow neck of Lake Victoria at Jinja, just above the spot where Speke had first identified the source of the Nile. It was about half-past two in the afternoon. We were well into Uganda by then, having crossed the border some hours earlier. I began to think again of Tom and what he might have turned up in Kampala. Then I turned my attention again to the papers.

The third in the folder was a well-drawn diagrammatic section through a well boring. This again was puzzling for, although at first glance I had taken it to be just that, I now noticed that it was different in as much as there was no impermeable water-holding basin at the bottom of the bore! In fact, it stopped right bang in the middle of the basement system after penetrating the sandy soils and volcanics that overlaid it.

The diagram was amply annotated in a fine written script. There was a lot of geological data, dealing for the most part with the pre-Cambrian systems of Western Kenya, chiefly the Kavirondian unfossiliferous sediments. There was, however, a considerable note devoted to the Duruma Sandstones of the sedimentary series near the Kenya Coast and the relationship of these to the basement system bounding them inland, and the overlying Jurassic rocks to the east. On the back of the diagram, the writer had put an account of Pleistocene land movements evidenced on the coast through raised beaches and coral reefs. Although this had at one time been a great interest of mine—geology, I mean—I could make nothing of it at all, except that whoever had written it had had a more than average interest in his daily work. Whatever connection all this had with Smith was beyond me. It just got curiouser and curiouser!

I put all the papers away and went for a wash, and then sat reading until the familiar sights of the industrial area of Kampala came into view. The train ground its way slowly over the crossings and points and drew into the station with a long sigh, as if it were mortally tired after the long four-hundred-mile journey.

It was about half-past four in the afternoon, a bright hot afternoon, and the station was crowded as it usually is on the arrival of the train. A connection here in Kampala could take one, if one so wished, right on westwards as far as Kasese and the Mountains of the Moon. People bustled everywhere, and it was especially noticeable that Swahili, the *lingua franca* of the whole of East Africa, was not to be heard so much, even in this place, which was a melting pot for all the tribes of Uganda. The softer, slower Luganda was more prominent, spoken with the easy courtesy that is so typical of the kingdom of Buganda. The kingdom itself does not exist now of course. It died with the last King Mutesa II, and is now only a region of the Republic of Uganda, but the people remain the same in most respects.

One of the most striking features of Buganda is the difference that it displays in the dress of its women. The *busuti*, or *bordingi*, is a sort of Empire style that was introduced by the early missionaries, and it took the place of an equally graceful garment of bark cloth that had been worn before. Its popularity lies in the fact that it enhances the standards of Kiganda beauty so beloved by the Baganda men—heavy, padded, swaying hips and full soft shoulders, swelling into ample, generous breasts that always seem to need tucking back into the free square neckline, like pairs of snub-nosed naughty puppies. The women have this statuesque beauty. They wear the *busuti* gaily, and proudly, like multi-coloured sailing ships at sea in a gentle swell. The men, too, unlike so many of the peoples of East Africa, have a roundness of features that makes them look bland, and perhaps this is the explanation of the apparent politeness with which everyone seems to address each other.

I saw Tom's huge frame above the heads of the milling crowd and soon he was pumping my hand and leading me through the crowded car park in front of the station where he had a hired Peugeot waiting. He eased his way out of the traffic and headed up through the town. The car was hot after having stood in the afternoon sun and I wound the window down quickly. The heat in Kampala was different to that in Nairobi. The city was a couple of thousand feet lower, and being on the edge of Lake Victoria, it had a muggy sort of feel about the air not unlike some of the coastal towns at certain times of the year.

115

The new facelift that the Grant Hotel had received since my last visit to Kampala had not altered the inside very much, and it remained the quiet, cool, restful place that it had always been, in spite of the road development and building that had gone on around it.

Tom saw me settled in a comfortable room with a small verandah, with a view across the park, and then left me to unwind a bit. He arranged to call for me for dinner quite early at half-past seven. I kicked off my shoes, stripped to my undershorts and flopped on the bed, watching a light breeze stirring the tops of the jacaranda trees in the park across the road.

I lay there a while, thinking of nothing, and presently picked up my book and continued reading, until the darkening sky and the distant call of a hornbill told me that the short tropical evening was over. I took a cool shower and dressed less warmly than had it been Nairobi, settling for a cool Trevira suit that looked formal and yet had the grace and lightness that made it very comfortable to wear. Clothes do much to create a mood, so by the time Tom called I felt up to anything that the night might bring. He was dressed in what was known there as a Kaunda suit, a high collarless jacket that needed no tie or even shirt beneath.

We went downstairs to dinner, and over a very pleasant and spicy Chicken Masala, Tom brought me up to date on events as they had developed in Kampala, while I gave him a résumé of what had occurred in Nairobi. I deliberately avoided mention of the personal side of my meeting with Anne, and made it appear that all the details that I knew of Williams were supplied by the man that I had met on the train.

'Well, what about this sister of Williams, then?'

'Who?' I asked.

'Who be damned. You know damned well who—that popsy who worked for the East African Artesian.'

'Oh, her. Yes, well, what about her, then?'

'Come on, boy, what gives? You're not coming through. What you holding out for? Give!'

There was something about the twinkle in his eye that gave the lie to the suspicious tone in his voice.

'Well, yes, as a matter of fact I did have a word with her, later the day you left, about her brother. It was she who filled in some of the details about her brother—it was just that it had slipped my mind, that's all. It didn't make a lot of impression at the time, see?'

'You just sort of happened to run into her again, I guess.'

'Yes, that's it, funny isn't it. Small world, I mean.'

The only answer I got was a long look and a comment in what I suppose he meant to be a British accent.

'It bloody is an' all!'

We finished dinner with a long leisurely smoke over a brandy and coffee. Then he got up and said, 'Come on, then, let's take a walk to settle the meal. Just up the road a way. The Hotel Splendide, it's got a good bar at the top end—the Copper Bar—with air conditioning. This heat is killing me!' We walked through the cool evening air. I chided him a bit about air conditioning and teased him about the American way of life. He responded in the surprising way he had of suddenly becoming quite serious. He delivered a little homily to me, quoting from McLuan on the extended personality of man. This was not the first time during our short acquaintance that he had pulled me up short, as if to remind me that he was not all the bluff, convivial hearty that his appearance led one to believe. He had a fine thinking brain, and his personal interpretation of McLuan once again showed that he had a philosophical leaning that was quite refreshing. Since he had set a serious note, I asked him further about the package and the man who had brought it to Uganda.

'He's checked out,' said Tom cryptically.

'I wonder where to.'

'I flushed him, I reckon,' he said and I looked askance at him. 'You see, I took the liberty of having a look around his room while he was out for lunch yesterday. I'd followed him and waited until he'd settled down with his bib and tucker on, and then dashed back to the Horns to see what I could see. After all, I figured that he had nothing to do with whatever we were after and was only acting as a sort of courier. Well, I bribed my way into his room on the pretext that he was a friend of mine and that I wanted to surprise him on his return. I was pretty careful about everything, 'cause I didn't want him to get spooked or anything. I didn't find a thing, but obviously I wasn't careful enough. Or maybe it was that he had handed over the package and was through here. I don't know, it could even be that he'd noticed that I'd moved his wrapper.'

'His wrapper!' I echoed.

'Sure,' said Tom, 'an old paper wrapper with a bit of map on it. It was in the pocket of his jacket, behind the door of his room.'

'What was it a map of?'

'Western Uganda, I guess, 'cause Fort Portal was shown on it anyway. Say, you remember that map that we got from the folder —the one with all the circles and lines and stuff like that? Well, it was a bit like that but it was on the back of a bit of old paper. A wrapper, just like I said.'

'Why didn't you bring it?'

'Well, now, that's just it. There was a noise outside the door of his room, and I panicked a bit and made a dash through the french windows, over a low roof and away through the garden. I stuffed the wrapper back, more as a reflex than anything, before I blew. But even I could have spotted that it had been moved, wrong pocket for a start and then, not neatly folded as it had been. I guess that I'm not cut out for that kind of stuff.'

'Can't you remember anything about it at all?'

'Not a damn thing, except that it was of the West of Uganda, it had lots of dots and circles and stuff like that, and that it smelled pretty!'

We were at the door of the Copper Bar by this time, and I pushed it open to let him pass in ahead of me. We crossed to the horseshoe-shaped bar and ordered two beers. It was still quite early in the evening, but the steady water-holers had already left for supper and home, and the post-dinner drinkers had not yet turned up. A few scattered knots of people stood about talking, not yet with the high-spirited, well-oiled confidence of a few drinks, nor yet with the subdued discretion of the abstemious.

Tom took a long pull at his beer. The air conditioning hummed with an unhealthy draught of smoke-ridden air. The bartender wound the cash into an automatic register, looked about vaguely for a moment with his finger to a nostril, and then resumed a low-toned conversation with two African girls at the end of the bar. I thought that they might be Banyoro, but they were so western-ised that it was difficult to be sure. It was paradoxical, the way they were westernised—they wore long Africana wigs of some dark shiny black modern fibre, and were dressed in long African-type skirts that must surely have been the product of Lancashire. When I caught the glance of one of them she used the long absorbed look that passes with her sisterhood the world over for awakening sexual interest when, in truth, there was probably nothing more interesting going on in her thoughts than how to recover the cost of the drink that she and her friend had to buy to make their presence there legitimate.

Tom eased himself off the stool. 'Gareth,' he said, 'I'll be away for a few minutes. There's a friend of mine staying at this place that I ran into yesterday. I think you'd get on well together.' He moved towards the inner door that led into the remainder of the hotel. As he reached there he turned back. 'And don't drink my beer!'

He habitually drank ice-cold beer. It was a peculiar American habit that made me wince. I turned away from the doors in mock disgust. Tom was very familiar with my opinions about cold beer and cold beer-drinkers.

I looked around the room again. The level of conversation was rising again. The outside door swung open and another of the 'girls' came in. She went over to join the other two. Just near the hotel section of Kampala there is a long winding road that follows the contour around Nakasero Hill. It is called Regina Road, and has traditionally been associated with the 'girls' ever since I could remember. Perhaps it was because it was in the centre of town at one end and then ran along into the quieter suburban area, or maybe it was because it was so near to the larger hotels of the town and therefore had better pickings. Theirs was essentially a car pick-up trade. They stood near the street lights offering a bewildering choice of variety. The most successful would often pop into the bar to rest awhile between assignments.

I looked at this one and she returned my gaze with that age-old expression in her eyes. I began to wonder about her. Age-wise she lay in the no man's land between virginal and raddled, indeterminate. One might say that she was at the height of her career. Even though she was dressed neatly and with a very fashionable outfit including long boots, she had probably grown up in a village, duly fetching water and hoeing in the gardens of her father till some trouble at home or the stories of an elder sister had led her to the city where she would undergo the hard schooling of her chosen profession. And her end? Who could say? There hasn't been time yet to see because all of this is new urban life, amidst the vast rural feudalism of Africa.

The voices had risen with the growing confidence that comes with a few drinks and I listened to the conversation of two people who sat on stools a little further along. One man with a pronounced Yorkshire accent was telling a story to his companion. But the listener had only half his mind on the story. The other few grammes of awareness were ranging freely between the long plastic boots and the dark brown thighs of the girl who had just come in. As if aware of this and of my attention, the chap with the broad accent included me into his story with his eyes.

'There was this white Father, see, who was down in Kampala from an up-country mission and it was his first time to be alone in the town. Well, he left the shopping a bit late so it was just getting dark as he started off for home, so he took the Regina Road out of town. As he went along he saw all the girls waiting, and as he went past them they all hissed at him and said, "Five bob for a quick bash!" By the time he'd got out of town he was really curious about this, so seeing that it was girls that had offered this thing called a quick bash, he decided to ask the Reverend Mother of the little convent they had at the Mission, 'cause he was new in the country and wanted to learn all he could about the place. So next morning he went up to her and said, "Reverend Mother, what would a quick bash be?"

' "Five bob—same as in town!" '

'You're dreaming, boy!' Tom's voice saved me the trouble of a laugh. 'I'd like you to meet a friend of mine.'

I turned. He was grinning like a big ape.

'Gareth—Anne.'

CHAPTER TWELVE

I had always thought that I could handle occasions like that but seeing her really threw me off balance and I stood there completely taken aback. It must have shown on my face. She only smiled faintly and said, 'I didn't expect to see you again quite so soon, Gareth.'

She did though, for her eyes never left mine for an instant and there was that trace of a smile all the time. Tom thumped me heartily on the back.

'Well, don't just stand there like a stuck pig, say something even if it's only goodbye as you disappear into the ground.'

'Tom—I . . . look you say something and give me a chance to recover . . . How did . . . I never expected . . .'

'Well okay, I reckon we'll let you off the hook. It's like this. At breakfast this morning there was a little note written in the prettiest little hand, addressed to yours truly, and in it? A mysterious message suggesting that I meet the writer at the Uganda Coffee Shop later in the morning.'

'You told me where he was,' said Anne, 'so I sleuthed around to find where it was and duly arrived.'

'How did you recognise each other?' I asked. I was beginning to recover from my surprise and was feeling a bit more poised in spite of the feeling that as well as humour in her eyes there was a hurt and hostility too, perhaps recrimination.

'Once seen, never forgotten,' said Tom. 'Do you think I could forget such a pretty face and all this,' his eyes did a quick roving tour, 'in a couple of days? Boy, I tell you they don't happen like this every day.'

I asked her what she would like to drink. She hesitated a while. 'Try the local gin, it's quite passable and everyone here seems to like it. Goes down well with a tonic or lime. It's called "waragi" and made here right in Kampala from a banana or cane-sugar mash.'

She agreed to try so I ordered a waragi and tonic and two more beers. We carried these to an alcove table near the wall and sat talking in an easy comfortable way for a while, but inevitably the topic of her visit had to be mentioned.

'Why did you come here, Anne?' I asked.

'I've already explained that to Tom, and anyway I don't want to go into all that again. Besides, I've a perfect right to be here just like any of you!' She looked vexed and the little tell-tale frown in the centre of her forehead was quite marked. 'And what difference does it make to you, anyway?'

This came as a surprise. I know that I should have expected it, but seeing her again had evoked a memory of the night we had spent together. There was a smouldering deep inside of me at the memory and a growing desire to repeat and enlarge the memory. But as I looked askance at her question, I could see that there was a wall between us and that it would take a great deal of time and effort on my part to remove it.

'Like it or not, Gareth, the girl is here. So drink up, boy, the night is young, and we're so beautiful!'

His gay air did much to ease the tension that had grown between us. At one time when he was away for a moment I tried once more to talk to her.

'Look, Gareth, Tom's right, let's leave this thing between us for now. Perhaps sometime we can talk it out but not now.'

'When is sometime?' I asked; and then, 'Later tonight?'

'No.' Her answer was not cold, her tone was not bitter or resentful, it was just a cool statement of fact. Tom came back, and soon the conversation got going again, and we were on our way to a good evening.

More drinks, and then somehow we all became involved with another group of people, regular Kampala residents who were working under contract to the Ugandan government. We all swopped stories and teased and chided and got very owlish by about midnight. The world's problems were solved and everyone began to see it as one great happy family. The centre of the group was a chap called Fletcher. He had been in Uganda for about fourteen years and was never lost for a story, which he would recount in a pleasant mixture of accent that had all the forthright bluntness of the North of England softened by a slight Irish lilt. He was mercurial and charming, and very witty, anticipating his own humour about a second before anyone else, and shaking with a mirth that was impossible to resist.

122

Brief snatches of song began to break up the unity of the conversation. In some part of my mind I was aware that Anne was drinking quite a lot, but then so was everyone else. By the strange common consent that these evenings have, the party began to break up. We three were invited to lunch the next day. Fletcher made a little sketch on the back of a cigarette packet, so that we could find the way to his house, and then gave it to Anne for safe keeping. She was the first to go. She passed through the glass doors, quite steadily I thought. I watched her smooth shapely legs with some regret, and then thought, 'So what? What can you do with it afterwards anyway!' Beer is a great aid to bar room philosophy, but not to bedroom action!

Outside the bar the air was hot and humid, but quite fresh after the sour, circulated air inside. There were a lot of loud and oft-repeated goodnights, and the sounds of cars starting up and roaring away. Tom and I walked back to the Grant lightly and somewhat unsteadily. The street lights were a greenish hue and we stopped to watch the groups of people that were milling about beneath them. It was the season of the *ensenene*—the large green grasshoppers which were swarming like, well, locusts I suppose! They were a local delicacy. During the beginning of the rain season they were attracted by the street lighting, and practically every street lamp was a pool of opportunity as the people waited for them to beat themselves against the lamps and then fall senseless to the ground, where they could be hastily snatched up into tins or anything else that would hold them to provide a tasty protein-rich sauce for the next day's meal. Watching their whirring bodies made me feel a little sad. If there is any dim awareness in the thing that is a grasshopper, surely we can find ground for understanding, I thought. In my beer-bemused state, I was back to philosophy but finding that it had lost its couldn't-care-less slant. Insects as thinking units of life—yes, that was it! All rather ridiculous afterwards.

The whole lightness of the evening began to evaporate, leaving my head spinning, my eyes slightly out of focus and my senses dulled to the edge of imagined sharpness. I felt cool, calm and absolutely in control of myself. I could not understand why the hell Tom should find it necessary to support me! I began to feel that these small mundane things were unimportant, my mind was centred on higher things, passing as a flotsam in the tide of my awakened wisdom. I was alive. I was aware! I was close to the hub of the universe. I was about to release the grip of the iron hand of time on the world when suddenly it all went out. I fell on to my bed. The only thing I remember was the dizzy spinning of the bed, and a sickening, falling sensation as it descended to whatever depths beds go to when they move like that. Then later came the great movement as it came back from the bottom. It was as if someone had lifted it up and shook me out of it. The great iron hand of time re-establishing itself!

In the grey-green, head-splitting light of senseless dawn, I awoke feeling cold, lying on the floor. I crawled back into bed, drained a carafe of water, and felt it hammer solidly around my temples. I pulled the blankets over my head and shut out the blinding, flashing chink in the curtains where the pale tone of daybreak shone weakly.

Later, about half-past nine, Tom woke me, banging as loud as he could bear on the door. He eased himself gently to the foot of the bed, holding his head in his hands. 'Let's get out of here and get some coffee, I feel like I've been kicked in the head by a mule wearing his best Sunday boots! That was one hell of a thrash. What do they put in the beer up here, anyway? I've drunk beer all over the world, but I've never had it get up and fight me in the middle of the night before.'

I grunted. A shower, cold, long and punitive, would be the answer.

I went into the bathroom and groped about for the necessary gear. I felt bad tempered enough, but discovering that there was no soap was about all I could take. I turned the water on hard and fast and then got under and let the world know what I felt about it. Some people fancy themselves as a bathroom baritone—me, I'm one of the world's best bathroom blasphemers! I contented myself with just letting the water stream over me for a few minutes, and then got out gingerly, for to move still had the effect of making my head thump. I fumbled about in my grip for the tablet of soap that I knew was there somewhere, the one I had taken from Anne's office, thinking, well, it's an ill wind that blows no good! I found it and zombied my way back to the bathroom to get a wash and shave. Tom had flopped out on the bed.

'Have you got an aspirin or Seltzer or something?' I heard him murmur.

'In here—bring the glass with you.'

I handed him the bottle of tablets that were in the cabinet above the wash basin. He shook out two and let them dissolve slowly in the glass, nursing it gently in his big fist. He sat himself down on the only available seat and presented a picture of absolute dejection reflected in the mirror before me. I was shaving carefully when he let out a yelp that made me nick my top lip.

'Damn, man, did you have to do that!' I splashed the remaining soap from my face, and dabbed at my bleeding lip. When I eventually turned, it was to see him still sitting there, gazing intently at the soap wrapper I had discarded. He picked it up and sniffed at it deeply.

'This is it,' he said, 'or one very like it anyway.'

'What is it?'

'It's the wrapper I found in that guy's pocket the other day.'

'Impossible, I've just taken it off a new tablet of soap, it's been with me all the time. That's just a wrapper from a tablet of soap.'

'Then what's all this then?'

He held the wrapper for me to see. Sure enough, inside facing me there was a map printed with the now very familiar coloured dots, circles and lines.

'Let me see that,' I said, taking it from him and moving back to the bedroom. I went over to the window and spread it on the small table. Tom was looking over my shoulder.

'No, you're right, Gareth, that's not the one that I saw before, it's the same though. I remember noticing the Semliki Valley. That's where our people went for the game shots for the film.'

The map was of Western Uganda, that much I knew. I'd travelled over most of the country, and a few of the names were familiar to me. Finding out more about it would be fairly simple, it only needed comparing with a large-scale map of the area. I told Tom as much.

'Sure, that's fine, but where did you lay your hands on this?'

I began to dress hurriedly and put the wrapper away in my pocket.

'Come on, I'll tell you as we go. There's a little bit of explaining to be done by our Miss Anselm. Let's get across to her place, though I've a vague suspicion that we won't find her there!'

As we walked across I told him about the soap and the office in Nairobi. We went into the foyer and asked for a call to be put through to her room. Rather to my surprise she was still there and answered quite promptly. I let Tom do the talking on the phone as I thought that way the chances would be better of her seeing us. Soon we were on our way up. Room 212 on the second floor. We knocked and walked in.

She was still in bed, sitting up with a breakfast tray across her knees, reading the newspaper.

'Well now, this is no time of the day to come visiting. Especially after a night like last night. As if the drinks party were not enough and then all this on top of it.' She indicated the paper that she was reading.

'Look, Anne, never mind all that now. There's some questions that I'd like an answer to, and I don't think you've been quite straight about some things so far.'

'My, but you are intense this morning, Mr Ashe. I see that you've decided that being "straight" has some virtue. How wonderful it must be for you to have made that discovery!' Her eyes were quite cold and mocking. 'It really must be important. Well, go on . . . what can I do for you this fine disastrous morning?'

I pulled the wrapper from my pocket. 'Do you recognise this?' I passed it to her.

'Why, yes, as a matter of fact I do.'

'Can you explain it?'

'Explain it! What sort of explanation do you want, Mr Ashe? How does one go about explaining a piece of paper that was wrapped around a tablet of soap?'

'Now don't give me that, Anne, this particular one came from your office in Nairobi.'

'Yes, I gathered as much. Did you take it from there?'

'Yes, I did, but it's my turn to ask the questions.'

She inclined her head in assent, busied herself with some marmalade and toast, and poured some more coffee. The smell was very enticing and I wished that my head had been clearer.

'How did it get there?'

'I put it there.'

'For God's sake, Anne! Stop this fooling about and tell me what you can about it. It is very important, and probably has something to do with your brother's death.'

She looked suddenly crestfallen and rather pathetic. I wanted to hold her and comfort her. She put the tray down and made an effort to control herself.

'Look, honey,' Tom interrupted, 'Gareth here seems to have gone off at half cock, and I don't suppose the one we hung on last night is helping either. Let me explain.' He looked askance at me. I nodded in agreement, and went across to the window and looked down at the street below. Across the park I could see the sculpture of Maloba stretching up to the skyline above the trees, depicting the rise of independent Uganda as a woman in bonds, raising her child above her.

I thought to myself how stupid I had been to barge in like that. If I'd had any sense I would have done as Tom was now doing. He was seated beside her on the bed, holding her hand. It would have been better from all points of view. The beer-induced feelings of non-involvement were gone, and I was very aware of her as a woman and of the warm responsiveness that she was capable of.

I heard his soft drawling voice tell her in a matter of fact way about the discovery of the soap wrapper and its significance to us. He was quite circumspect, and yet carried enough conviction and warmth to make her feel more relaxed.

'All right, I'll tell you all I can about the wretched thing . . .'

I continued looking out of the window, listening to her, my eyes looking at nothing.

'When I took the job with the East African Artesian, they did insist that I lived at the Capricorn. I thought that it was because they had some sort of financial connection or that they had a long-standing arrangement for purpose of economy. It suited me okay, it was a bit far from the office, but then it was quite near the city centre and convenient for walking into town for shopping, so I moved in. Now, about this soap thing.

'About once every ten days or so, I had to despatch a sort of supply box to several of our field stations. The supplies were usually dropped into the office by the man I told you about, and then it was my job to pack them into steel boxes, which were picked up the same day. The thing is, though, that some of the contents were supplied by the Capricorn. The contents were what you might term luxuries for a field expedition, you know, toilet rolls, soap, toothpaste, sometimes items of food, tins and packets of soup, things like that. Well, it's just that one day, in the office, I thought that we could do with a few basic necessities ourselves, the clerk was always pinching my soap anyway, so I kept a tablet in my desk drawer. It was only the day I left that I put it in the washroom. I'd forgotten all about it and on impulse, as I was clearing out, I thought that I would leave it there—it would have been silly to take it back to the hotel, wouldn't it?'

127

'Were any of these boxes ever sent to Uganda?' asked Tom.

'Yes, as a matter of fact the last one that I sent came here. It was a couple of days before I met you, Gareth.'

I still did not turn from the window when she addressed me. Something in the street below had caught my eye. From the second storey, I looked down on a newsvendor, selling his papers on the street below. The headlines were upside down from me, I only made them out with difficulty. Tom went on.

'From Nairobi to Kampala is a long way to take a packet of soup and a bar of soap.'

I turned to Anne. There was an excited feeling knotting my stomach. I walked over to the bed and took up the newspaper that she had discarded.

'Do you remember where the supplies went to in Uganda?' I asked.

Anne thought for a moment. 'Yes, wait a moment, there was only one field operation going on here, it wasn't a big thing. I think that the name of the place was Busia or something like that.'

I spread the paper on the bed for her to see, with a feeling of triumph. There, blazoned across the front page, were the headlines that I had seen on the pavement below. . . .

EARTHQUAKE DEVASTATES TORO

At 3.40 a large area of Toro district was shaken by what is proving to be the worst tremors in that area during human memory. Reports of serious shaking have been received from as far away as Nsumbura and Juba. Slight damage has been reported in Kampala, where reports indicate that . . .

Suddenly the memory of the previous night came back to me, of the sensation of being picked up and thrown from the bed, and my waking up on the floor. Similar memories must have come back to Tom.

'Well, I'll be damned,' he said, 'and I thought it was the beer!' He started to read aloud from the paper. ' "Two areas have been identified as centres of the 'quake, one near the small trading centre of Busiira and the second, fortunately far from any centre of human habitation, near the Kiraki River." ' Tom dropped the paper. 'Let's see that wrapper again.'

He spread it out, smoothing it carefully with his strong brown fingers. 'But this is crazy, it can't be—it's got to be coincidence.' His finger was pointing to a red circle neatly labelled Busiira, and there was another, unnamed, but unmistakably near a small river which was called Kiraki R. One other double red circle completed a trio of these marks.

'That's no coincidence, Tom. This is it. All this has something to do with Smith and his friends, and this is where we get in on the action again! Come on!'

'It's all right for you, but what about me?' This from Anne as I was pushing Tom towards the door.

'We'll call for you later, about half-past twelve. We've got a luncheon date, remember?'

I had good cause to remember this myself, for one of the group that we had met the previous evening had been a Lands and Surveys man from the headquarters of the Department at Entebbe, and if my next idea didn't work, he'd be just the sort of chap who might be able to tell us something more about this earthquake business. I had a vague idea that he was staying the night with our host for lunch, Fletcher, and would probably be there for lunch. But just in case there was a call that I had to make.

'Where to?' asked Tom, when we were once more outside the hotel.

'Let's get the car,' I answered. 'We're both going back to school!'

CHAPTER THIRTEEN

Makerere University stands on a hill just over a mile from the City centre. We drove in through the main gates and up to the administrative block on the crest of the hill. I didn't know quite who to see or who to ask for. Then I noticed a name on the door of one of the offices that led off from the foyer, D. JENKINS, ASSISTANT REGISTRAR.

The name Jenkins abroad, and associated with Education, usually meant a Welshman. It was worth a try anyway. I walked across to the door, knocked and entered, followed by Tom. 'I'd like to see Mr Jenkins, please.' This to a bored-looking African typist who sat behind her machine, prodding at it in a way that seemed to suggest that she might have been hired on her connections rather than on her meagre ability. Her only response was a pursing of the lips, and then a most surprising demonstration of the African's power to point with the lips. She indicated the door leading to the inner office. As we went towards it I was wondering if this surprising labial control extended to the other labial areas of her body. The possibilities were astounding!

D. Jenkins was a small man, dark with the Silurian brow, so my first sight of him was encouraging. He had the features at once so common and varied in South Wales and typically of the Western Valleys. When he spoke it was with a well-controlled lilt that might escape unidentified in any group, but which I recognised immediately as the polished result of the heart-warming Rhondda idiom.

On an impulse, I tried him in Welsh. He answered immediately in the same language, and with shining eyes and a lively response that had been absent in our first greetings when I introduced myself and Tom to him. This one unifying factor of language, in what must be the most disunited race of people in the world, has the advantage of retaining cultural and sympathetic implications, that work like a tocsin. After a lengthy opening where we established birthplaces, religion and politics and the possibility of mutual relations, I reverted to English to include a very bewildered Tom and then explained the purpose of our visit. This was to get an introduction to some informed person, who could fill us in with some details about the previous night's earthquake. For some reason it was assumed in an earlier part of our conversation that we were journalists. I let this go, thinking that it would serve as well as any other reason to explain our curiosity.

'Old Pendlington would be the chap that you should see,' said Jenkins. 'With any luck, he'll be in the Senior Common Room now having coffee. Come on down, and I'll introduce you to him. You look as if you could do with a cup of coffee yourselves.'

On the way down to the Common Room, I told him about our night in the Copper Bar.

'I thought so,' he said. 'You hardened newspaper blokes all make the same mistake. You think all other beer in the world except British is not to be taken seriously. I made the same mistake myself when I came here first. Come to think of it, I make it regularly since, too. Yes, quite regularly.'

We were laughing together as we went into the long room full of low coffee tables and bright plastic chairs. It was fairly full of people, a babbling multi-coloured motley, earnestly aware somehow that it was incumbent on them to produce an academic atmosphere. We followed Jenkins to a corner of the room, and were introduced as a couple of old friends to Old Pendlington, who turned out to be quite a young man in his early thirties. Conversation was already on the topic of the earthquake, and for a while Tom and I sat gratefully sipping black coffee and listening to the few people who were already at the table discussing the report that was in the morning's edition of the *Uganda Argus*.

Details it seemed were lacking and until someone actually went up to Busiira, it was unlikely that more could be added. Most of the talk was the exchange of personal experiences felt here in Kampala—they ranged from complete ignorance of the event to trivial occurrences involving broken crockery. I ruefully remembered my own.

'What about Busiira itself?' I asked Pendlington. 'Is there likely to be much damage there?'

'Shouldn't think so. Busiira's nothing but a couple of ddukas and a few scattered houses. I doubt if there's one cement or brick building there. It's all baati and budongo.'

'What's that again?' said Tom.

'Well, baati is corrugated iron sheets and budongo is the local method of building—mud and wattle. Most of the houses wouldn't even have baati roofs, but would be grass-thatched. So I doubt if there'd be very many serious casualties—still, you never know.' He lapsed into a reflective mood.

'What would be the chances of getting up there to take a look—you know, pictures and interviews?' asked Tom.

'It's a hell of a road up there,' put in Jenkins. 'Tarmac for the first forty-five miles and after that—after Mityana, nothing but dust, potholes and dangerous bends for the next two hundred, with the chance of meeting a lorry or a taxi, head on, on any of them.'

'A taxi?'

'Well, that's what they call them, anyway. Pirate motor cars that serve the local population as transport. They get anything up to ten people into an ordinary saloon car, load up the roof rack and boot with chickens, bananas and bintu, and come thundering along the roads from all directions. And since time is money, they don't spare the petrol. It's first to the crown of the road and every man for himself on the bends. There is a train, of course, up to Kasese, that's about two hundred miles of the way, only it takes all of fifteen hours. Even a lot more sometimes. I remember there was this chap called Bowes, see. Well, one day he wanted to . . .'

Tom was smiling encouragingly at Jenkins as he went on with his story. I took the opportunity to move closer to Pendlington. 'Look,' I said, 'I've got to make some copy out of this. It's not often that one gets to be around just when an earthquake happens, and although I know it's not a big one that will make world headlines, I thought that I might be able to work it up into something better than the A.P. will hand out. It could do me a lot of good.'

'What sort of thing do you have in mind?'

'Well, I don't know really, but since we can't get up there today, I'd appreciate it very much if you could add anything to the general run of the mill type of stuff that I might get. Perhaps a look at some large-scale maps, some technical data, that sort of thing.'

'Yes, I think that I could help you in that sort of thing. But I've only got until twelve, though. Come along up to the department now and I'll see what I can dig up for you.'

Jenkins had finished his story and over Tom making the right noises, he caught the last of our conversation.

'Well done, Pen you old bugger, I knew you'd be the right bloke.'

We stood up and made our way to the door. We shook hands with Jenkins as he left us for his office.

'Come on up for a drink this evening, meet Pam. Houseful of bloody kids but never mind. That's what comes from marrying a Welsh girl i'n it—can't get enough, can they, boy?'

He went off on his business and we walked the few hundred yards to the Geography Department in Queen's Court. The sun was high overhead by then, and the light lanced into my eyeballs which started up the dull ache in my head again. Each jarring footstep jolted my spine and I was thankful to get into the relatively cool shade of the building. We were taken to a large demonstration lecture room. Dominating the centre was a very large three-dimensional relief map of Uganda, and the walls were draped with big scale maps of the same region, dealing with population, climate, vegetation, natural resources and structure.

'This is what we call the Uganda Room,' he said. 'Now where shall we start, let's locate the place first.'

He walked up to the large relief map and put his finger down on a spot. 'This is Busiira, near enough. We, by the way, are here.' He indicated a spot with his other hand. 'Busiira has been identified as the first centre of shock, and Kaluli on the Kiraki River as the second—not quite as severe, I believe.'

'Are there likely to be any more?' asked Tom.

'Who can say for sure? But I'd hazard an opinion and say no. Of course there is movement recorded all the time, but of this nature you mean? Well, no, I don't think so.'

'Is there any connection between the two centres?' I asked. 'Yes, there is, you see it's like this . . . now how can I explain it?' He paused for a moment and then his years of lecturing experience took over. 'Immense forces are continually at work within the earth. What goes on deep down in the earth is not such a mystery as it was. The continual stretching and compression can now be measured. Perhaps you didn't realise this, but just as the moon causes tides on the seas and oceans of the Earth, its gravitational pull also affects the land masses of the Earth and causes a rise and fall—only several inches it's true, but significant none the less. Even now after yesterday's 'quake there is still a vibration, too small to be experienced, but it can be recorded on a seismograph, which indicates primary, secondary and surface shock waves, so when it is read with a time scale it is possible to calculate the distance from the centre of the shock and also to locate it quite accurately. You see, any earthquake causes vibrations to travel through the whole earth, and these can be picked up by seismographs located all over the world.'

'What is it that actually happens at the centre, then?' asked Tom.

For answer, Pendlington turned to the desk at the front of the room, and came back with a flat wooden ruler. He held it down on the table with one hand so that more than half of it protruded over the edge. He then leaned on the piece that was sticking out.

'If I sustained pressure here it would snap, agreed?' We both nodded. 'I won't go that far but if I did the resulting snap would leave the broken pieces twanging, as it were.'

He released the pressure suddenly from the end overhanging the table, and it vibrated briskly.

'That, very simply stated of course, is what happens along a strata of rocks when a shock is recorded. It vibrates.'

'You mean that rocks bend and move that way?' asked Tom. 'That's very hard to imagine!'

'I suppose that an ant crawling along a steel girder would hardly be able to imagine that it could bend either, but as we know it can bend and whip quite a lot. It's all relative to size, isn't it? Remember now that the movement along a fault that causes a major earthquake can sometimes be as little as a few inches, but that is sufficient to set up vibrations that could bring a whole city down in ruins.'

'I see what you mean, this strata of rock could stretch for miles and miles.'

'Exactly,' said Pendlington. He looked pleased to have got his point across and, by way of emphasis, gave the pointer another twang. 'There are certain areas that have been identified with faults and pressure build-up deep down in the earth's crust. One can even predict an earthquake today from careful measurement and data recording. It's common knowledge now that Southern California is in for a big one fairly soon. The trouble is that there is no way of calculating the time when it will occur. It could happen any time from now.'

'Was this one here last night "expected" then?' I asked.

'Oh no, we're not that sophisticated here at the moment. We do have some recording going on at a few stations, but far too few instruments and trained personnel to give us anything like a significant idea of what's going on up there near the Mountains of the Moon. All we can say really is that it is a very active area volcanically—a violently disturbed fault complex and therefore likely to quake at any time. Of course, you must know that the area includes the Western Branch of the Great Rift Valley, and that, friend, is the largest fault system on the earth's crust. Here, let me show you.'

He walked across the room to a large wall map of the structure of East Africa, and pointed to the great valley running north and slightly east on the western side of Uganda, including Lake Edward, Lake Albert, and the big range of mountains called the Ruwenzori.

'That really must have been a sight when that lot slipped.'

'Probably not so dramatic as you imagine, but if you could telescope time, it would stand out as the most significant feature of the earth's changing shape . . . mm, fascinating, but look, you chaps, I'm sorry to rush you but I've got to get away now.'

'Of course,' I said. 'We do appreciate what you've already given us and in fact it's all a lot clearer now.' Certainly what I said was true but I'd felt as if I'd been back in the classroom. Once into his subject Pendlington became so typical of the academic. He probably had his wife wired to a seismograph to measure the strength of her orgasm.

We went outside again into the sunshine. Luckily, it had begun to cloud over a bit by then so the experience was not quite so painful. The coffee had worked wonders and I began to feel a little like a human being again. Since we had looked at the large relief map, an idea had begun to grow in my mind. I had remembered the soap wrapper, and the fact that a third area had been marked with a double red ring. It was a spot that I was determined to visit in the very near future. In the back of my mind was the idea, wild though it was, that the earthquake had been brought on by some human agency. But if I mentioned this to Pendlington he would have thought I was some kind of nut—maybe I was! I tried to think of a way of asking him without leaving this impression. We were nearing the main building again. Tom and he were walking slightly ahead of me. He turned as we reached it and held out his hand to say goodbye. I had a sudden inspiration. 'There is one final question I'd like to ask,' I said, and he looked at me. 'Well, it's in two parts really. The first is: What size force do you think is involved in an earthquake?'

'Well, that's pretty easy, it varies with the size of the eruption, but anyway, a major one expends more energy than the most potent of man-made explosions, thousands of megatons! You see, the forces shaping the earth's crust wind themselves up with tremendous potential energy and suddenly let go, in a tremendous burst of violence, like a clock spring suddenly breaking loose, only with the force of a couple of million tons of T.N.T. all going off together.'

'Some clock spring,' observed Tom. 'At what sort of depth does this happen?'

'The most devastating are those that are quite near the surface—a few miles deep, that is. Quite a number occur in the earth's mantle itself—that's about forty to a hundred and eighty miles deep. Occasionally, very deep ones are recorded all of four hundred miles deep, but those occur only in the major earthquake belts, around the Pacific Ocean, and through Southern Europe and Central Asia, the ring of fire, as it's called.'

By this time we had already reached the car, parked below the Main Building. Pendlington had his hand out once again, I shook it warmly. 'So it is possible to estimate how deep the centre of disturbance is—what would you say of this one in Busiira?'

He had turned to Tom who was already shaking him by the hand. 'This one? Well now, it was quite a small one as the world knows them, but I would say that it was quite near the surface for all that. And now I really must be gone.' And with a little flurried wave of his hand he scuttled up the steps to disappear through into the building.

We drove back to the town, tossing ideas around. There was a growing conviction in the two of us that the shock of the previous night had been a man-made thing, probably engineered by the East African Artesian Company. Tom came up with a thought about this, it related to the method that is now used for oil prospecting where small charges are detonated below ground so that, with the aid of a seismograph, the nature of the rock strata below can be known. But it was impossible to imagine that such an activity was responsible for all this. In this respect the charges that were used were quite harmless, and even my half-forgotten knowledge of geology told me that searching for oil on the edges of the rift valleys of East Africa would be nothing but folly. We were both very aware that the people we had met in connection with the E.A.A.C. were far removed from indulging in idle folly.

By the time that we reached the hotel again we were both convinced that we were right about the earthquake. Far too many coincidences were involved for it to have been a natural phenomenon. But there were two outstanding things that we could make no intelligent guess at, namely—How and Why.

'Remember what the guy said about the size of the force that was required? A cool couple of megatons!' said Tom.

'That's the size of the force that's released. I've been thinking about this one. Look, supposing that as he said it is possible with the right trained personnel and instruments to predict the likelihood of an earthquake. Don't you see, that the amount of force required is already there—it would just need triggering. Big triggers I know, but what about those missing warheads that Langley was mixed up with? That certainly might tie in.'

Tom just looked incredulous for a moment and then, as he began to realise the possibility, he let out a long low whistle. 'But why? What the hell is it all about? It can't be any legal activity, or else why all the secrecy? It can't be a business deal, because God only knows they're rough enough in that set-up. Why all this involvement with defected Civil Servants and wanted war criminals?'

We crossed over to Anne's hotel to pick her up for our lunch date. We were both agreed now that the only thing to do was to follow up the lead we had and get up to Western Uganda as soon as possible, and that would be when we could get a briefing from someone in the know who might be at Fletcher's for lunch. We all got into the car, Anne looking as cool and beautiful as if she had spent the previous couple of hours in a beauty salon. Tom was at the wheel of the Peugeot, and already moving off before it occurred to him to ask, 'Which way?'

'Damn, Tom, you've got the directions.'

'Me? Hell! You've got them. I gave the directions to you.'

'Not me,' I said irritably.

Anne leaned over from the rear seat and smiled sweetly. 'Me,' she said.

'Well,' said Tom, rather relieved, and grinning foolishly, 'in that case just shout them out as we go.' He put the car into gear again.

'There's just one thing, before we go, that I want to get clear.

You two are planning a quiet flit, unless I'm very much mistaken, just as soon as you can wangle some lunch and directions. I want to make it quite clear before we start that I don't intend being left behind to stew in this humid hell while you two get all the excitement. I'm not very clear what it's all about but I've got a right to know!'

'Aw, look, honey,' Tom put on his best Consolidated Films smile, 'there just isn't any excitement. Six hours of baking, bumping dusty road through the heat of the afternoon. Just think! You could be in that nice air-conditioned room of yours in the hotel, looking forward to a wonderful night, dinner under a tropical moon, soft music, a hint of romance in the air. Why, a beautiful woman like you could have yourself a ball, well I mean you could have a great time. Tell you what, now I . . .'

Anne did not look the least impressed. She turned to me; there was no appeal in her look, only frank enquiry.

'I don't really think so, Anne.'

She coloured in anger. As she spoke her eyes flashed beautifully and her breasts rose and fell most disturbingly.

'Mr Ashe, you do not improve with acquaintance, and as for you, you hulking great yes man!' she yelled at a very subdued-looking Tom. 'Don't you have any mind of your own? Do you have to agree with everything he says?'

'But honey,' he apologised, 'it was me that said it first. He agreed with me!'

'What do I care who said it first, it's all the same anyway. All right, so it's no go.' She calmed down quite quickly and I was glad she had accepted the position. 'Well let's get to this lunch, I'm starving!'

We both sighed with relief. Tom eased out the clutch.

'Which way out of the parking lot?'

'I haven't the faintest idea,' she said from the rear seat, 'but do get on with it, I'm starving, and dinner tonight under a tropical moon is such a long way off!'

'Now look here, Anne . . .' I began.

'Don't you look here me, Mr Bloody Ashe. I'll make it very easy for your little minds. No trip, no directions.'

She leaned back again in the seat, looking triumphant. I looked at Tom. He had an appreciative grin on his face. We both turned back to face her.

'Honey,' he said, laughing, 'you've got a deal!'

She looked towards me.

'A deal,' I repeated.

By the time we arrived at the house I felt unsure of her coming, though. The pleasure that the thought of her coming gave me was in the balance against the danger that she might be exposed to. The 'trump' card she held was of no real value, and she knew, as we both did, that, in her very distinct feminine way, she had charmed us into agreeing.

Fletcher's house stood in about a quarter acre of pleasant garden, laid out with a most bewildering variety of flowering shrubs. Although barely a quarter of a mile from the centre of the town, it still showed the leisured spaciousness that was once the pride of the colonial planners who had made the town half a century ago, never dreaming that it would one day grow and outrank the administrative capital, and become a city in its own right. The house itself, though roofed with iron sheets, was cool and airy inside, and the interior showed a tasteful combination of colonial style furnishings and modern bric a brac of pictures and wood sculpture. A fine tall piece of Makonde ancestor-carving dominated a corner of the room beneath which a temporary bar had already been set up.

There were about ten people in the room, including many of the group that we had met the previous evening. The french windows were open and the bright sunlight streamed in, toned with the deep green of the shrubbery. Our entrance was barely noticed, a momentary pause in the conversation, some nods of recognition, and then the hum of pre-lunch machinery was resumed. A tall, leggy, dark-haired woman detached herself from the group and came over to us. She was lithely attractive and moved with a full awareness of her body.

'I'm Mrs Fletcher, you must be the people that Dennis met last night.' Her voice had the distinct curly edge of the north country controlled with poise and self-possession. I could well imagine that under stress or provocation it could rise out above the control and become strident and strong Yorkshire. Tom moved smoothly to her and took her hand. He introduced himself and then Anne and me to her. We moved to the little bar and were soon engaged in the ritual of pre-lunch drinking. In spite of the easy relaxed atmosphere, I began to feel a little uneasy.

In moments, Tom's presence was recognised and he gradually

became the centre of a cluster of people. The conversation grew a lot more animated and Mrs Fletcher, who seemed anxious and nervous when we had come in, relaxed visibly as she realised that she had a 'lion' for lunch. Anne had also become the centre of a small group of men. She was an attractive woman in her own right and could have held her place anyway, but it seemed that the men were trying to make up in some way for the neglect they were getting from the women who had moved around Tom. At one moment I caught a glance from her and I could swear that there was something of triumph and smugness in it. Damn her, I thought! I looked about the room. Neither Fletcher himself nor his friend from the Lands and Surveys Department were present. I moved across to where Mrs Fletcher had gone to check a little anxiously on the cold buffet that was laid out in the far corner of the room. I tried what I thought was an engaging smile, and complimented her on the attractive and varied lay-out of the table. 'No sign of Dennis yet, I see.'

'Oh! I don't expect *it* yet for a while. It always makes straight for the Club after Saturday morning's work, and if it's got that Mike with him, well! It could be anytime.'

As if in direct contradiction to her words, there was a hearty and noisy laugh from the doorway, and the pitch of conversation went up a bit. Her face relaxed a bit even though her words belied it.

'Well, it's back, we are honoured. Club must have burned down or something!' We moved back to the corner near the bar.

'. . . God man, it's five bloody hours to Fort Portal on that road and a bloody sight longer through Mbarara. If you think that it's a joy ride or something you've another think coming . . . still I suppose that . . .'

Good for Tom, he had got down to the problem straight away. I had thought that he had been carried away a bit by the attention he had been getting, but I suppose he was well used to that and had used it to good advantage. He'd learned that Mike's wife was staying with the Fletchers while her husband went off to Fort Portal that afternoon and had got her to ask her husband for a lift for us as soon as he came in.

'. . . You could share the driving, I am a bit pissed and wouldn't mind getting my head down a bit. But look, I've got to be away from here by two at the latest, do you think you can be ready by then? I know what these bloody women are like.'

Tom looked at his watch and then at me inquiringly. 'What do you think, Gareth, twenty minutes?'

I downed the last of my beer. 'Come on! You get Anne and I'll go and make our apologies to Dennis and Mrs Fletcher.'

Moments later we were outside again in the Peugeot. We dropped Anne at her hotel entrance and then went on to our own. We had decided not to check out but just to put a few things together for a short visit. So by the time that Mike did arrive at the entrance to Anne's hotel we were all waiting for him on the steps. His Land-Rover was a battered grey model, but with very serviceable tyres and the engine sounded healthy too. We got in and put our bags behind us. I sat in the front seat and Tom and Anne got into the rear. Soon we were threading our way through the thinning traffic, and nosing along busy streets to the Fort Portal road. Just as we left the town, I looked at the tall clock tower on a traffic island—2.10!

Mike eased himself down behind the wheel, changed gear and said, 'Well, that's it then, that bloody town gives me the creeps on a Saturday morning, we've just got one stop to fill up and then you three can nestle down to the most boring bumpy ride of your lives. I've had some bumpy rides in my life, I can tell you. . . .' He lifted his eyes to the driving mirror to look at Anne as he said this and something in his thoughts made him grin slyly and crookedly. 'And some bloody smooth ones too—bloody smooth!'

He pulled into a roadside filling station, switched off the engine and walked over to a small cubicle office, leaving the pump attendant to make what he could of his Ki-Settler Swahili.

'Jaza kapisa, maji ne mafuta, tayari.'

Anne noticed a stand across the way that sold a variety of local titbits fried in sim-sim oil. 'You know, I'm still starving, and what's the use of all these inoculations and injections that we get before coming here if you can't put them to the test.'

We all walked over to the stand and bought a quantity of samuzas and golden spiced balls of fried flour, and walked back to the car munching happily. The samuzas were very heavily spiced and jazzed up with the addition of green pili pili peppers, but we agreed in our hunger that they were really something special.

The petrol station was quite busy, and we had to wait several minutes for a tyre pressure check. There was the usual assortment of cosmopolitan trade there, the usual conflict of tongues, and the usual collision of wills. The hasty brusque European clashed above the bird-like, volatile twitter of the Asian, and through it all, holding it together like a warp, the phlegmatic African murmured, as confident of his tomorrow as the others were fearful of theirs. I stood there in the sun and reflected on it all. If there was such a thing as Black Power, then this was the essence of it, the slow grinding patience, backed up with an almost sublime confidence in the future, a confidence that was considered by the western world to be groundless, primitive and unscientific, just as they had once considered the confidence of the Vandals and the Goths.

I was jolted back to reality by a nudge in the ribs from Anne. She was facing me and spoke softly.

'Do you see that big green car there?' Her head nodded slightly to the right. I looked over and saw a large green Toyota pulled in near the next line of pumps. In it were four men, youngish, European, and quite ordinary-looking.

'Yes,' I said.

'They're taking a lot of interest in us. They keep looking this way.'

I looked at her. Her very beautiful eyes were clouded most attractively with the suspicion of a frown. Her long blonde hair crowned her head like a halo and trapped the afternoon sun in a burst of light, and her lithe young body was alert with an excitement that was radiant. I smiled at her and winked at Tom who was listening.

'Honey,' he said, 'for any normal man there is only one place to look in this apology for a gas station, and that is what we are all doing, and from where I stand it sure looks good.'

'Anyway, they're leaving now,' I said. It amused me to see her with this air of intrigue, it made her look even more charming. The long green car moved slowly away into the stream of traffic coming out of the town. I saw the two rear seat passengers look back and then they were gone. It was as Tom had said—she was certainly worth a stare. Momentarily, I thought of her and the night we had spent in Nairobi, I looked back at her as we drove off, and I think that perhaps something of my thoughts were showing, for her eyes took on a different expression and the tip of her tongue showed briefly between her small square teeth.

'Watch the road, Mr Ashe, you do want to know where you are, don't you?'

The road out of Kampala was of modern surface for the first forty-five miles and the 'Rover just sped along. Banana plantations

flashed by one after the other with only occasional stretches of
virgin forest in the valley bottoms to relieve the monotony.
Everywhere the smell of wood smoke hung in the air. The afternoon sun was hot, and although all the windows were open, the
draught was warm, the air limpid. I half turned to see both of
them with their eyes closed in their respective corners, and almost
immediately felt my chin drop on to my chest with tiredness. I
gave in to it and fell into a light slumber, only just aware of the
hum of the tyres on the road, and the dry toneless sound of Mike
whistling to himself as he drove along.

I awoke to find that we were in a town of sorts, Mityana I
guessed. On both sides of the main road, façaded ddukas were
built. It was a miserable, dejected spectacle of urbanisation that
had earned itself the name of township because no one could
think of anything else to call it. It consisted of mud-coloured
pseudo-buildings, with mud-coloured pseudo-people. In the
bright emerald jewel of the countryside, it lay like a piece of tatty
old tinsel. There was something about the town that was very
familiar, it had the same look as the frontier towns of the old West
as depicted in films. But it had a sadness about it too, a feeling of no
future in its clapped-out rusty iron sheeting. It was an end, not a
beginning—a sorrowful failure to impose the Western ideal of
commercial enterprise on the bawdy, free-loving old whore that is
Africa.

We went slowly through the town. On its western edge, just
where the tarmac road gave way to the snaky, dusty red murram
track, we passed a small hand-operated petrol station. The green
Toyota was there. I recognised its four passengers as we went by.
They looked at us with great interest, and this time there was no
shapely Anne to cause their stares since she was huddled down out
of sight in the corner of her seat, fast asleep. I had a feeling of
uneasiness about it, a feeling of being alone and I realised for the
first time that although there was a point of view about all of this
from our side there was also most certainly a different one from the
other. I leaned over to give my sleeping partners a shake and,
more to hear my own voice than anything, asked Mike if he'd
like to take a spell off from the driving.

'Too bloody true I would, it's time you idle bastards started
earning your ride, and those lunch-time beers are catching up on
me.'

He pulled in to the side of the road, on a straight stretch, just where the swampy papyrus flats of Lake Wamala come right to the road edge. We all got out and made ourselves comfortable by wandering and stretching so that we could face the next part of the journey. A couple of curious looking hammerkofts perched on the telegraph wire above my head as I stopped to look out over the poisonous green of the swamp, deepening the waters imperceptibly the while. I got back into the driver's seat and waited for the others to get in. Anne was the last, and I was rather pleased to see that something of her composure was disturbed by the idea of having exposed her delicious rear to the very real threat of the snakes and insects that abounded in the lake. We moved off again, taking the crown of the road.

Looking in the driving mirror, I saw a swirling dust cloud that grew as I watched. And then the green car went by, blaring its horn and throwing up a choking cloud of dust.

'Bloody tourists!' This from Mike, huddling himself down in the rear seat. Tom must have felt himself to be included in this general term for, expressing a sensitivity that lots of transatlantic travellers have, he replied a bit acidly, 'More likely to be some of the local expatriate guys trying out their newest bit of phallic image!'

'Well, the number's not a local one anyway,' said Mike. 'It's a Tanzania one—Arusha I think . . .' He went on to give a rather boring account of the system of road number licensing until a general unresponsiveness from everyone shut him up. He yawned and eased himself down in the seat once more, tilting his battered bush hat over his eyes.

'Straight on for the next hundred miles, mate.' At this he laughed. 'Yes, straight on.'

Quite soon I realised what it was that had amused him. The earth road lost all appearance of directness, and began to twist and turn in all directions. Every few yards pot holes seemed to yawn like pits. Even the few straight stretches defied any speed for they were covered with corrugations and any attempt to go over forty miles an hour threw the old Land-Rover into a teeth-chattering judder. The steering wheel kicked and bucked about in my hands as if it were alive. The next hour passed in furious silence as I wrestled and sweated the old thing westwards.

Every now and again, just to make things interesting, a vehicle came down from the opposite direction—from behind a blind bend usually. All the drivers seemed to be addicted to the game of 'chicken': holding the crown of the narrow road as long as possible before moving over fractionally in order to pass. Someone in the Ministry of Works with a wry sense of humour had erected signs here and there that read: SLOW—DANGEROUS BENDS. The random with which such places were chosen was ironic. Very frequently along the roadside—although never in the signposted places—we passed the remains of cars, lorries and petrol tankers that had crashed. They lay overturned, gutted of everything useful, and abandoned to rust into the ground where they had fallen. They were far more grim and effective reminders than any of the road signs.

Red murram dust swirled into the car whenever anything passed us. In spite of the gay bandana that Anne had tied around her hair, she dramatically turned into a redhead. When we eventually stopped again for a change of drivers I took the back seat and Tom took over.

'Now I've always fancied entering the East African Safari, so let's just see what this old bitch of a British car can do,' he said.

Surprisingly enough he did a lot better.

'You've got it quick,' Mike said to him. He turned to me. 'You see, there's a certain speed that you've got to keep up, and then the bumps and corrugations aren't felt as much.'

I was holding on for dear life as he said this, and closed my eyes as another car passed us.

'Another thing,' he said cheerfully, 'that's why I don't get this old bus painted, another coat of paint and we'd have never got past then!'

By the time that we got to tarmac road again just outside of Fort Portal, Mike was back in the driving seat. The last of the sun was dipping down ahead of us as we pulled into a small neat compound, tidily laid out with gardens and flowering shrubs—the Mountains of the Moon Hotel. Hot water, a fine dinner and cool clean sheets seemed the height of our needs. There was just one uneasy thought in my head, the thought that had stayed with me all afternoon. What if the people we were searching for were aware of us and were already making some sort of plan to deal with the interruption that we would cause?

We all went to bed quite early that night, all that is except Mike who went off in search of some place that he referred to as the Glue Pot where, he said, we could have a good time and make up for the drinking that we had lost on the road. The three of us declined his offer, and after a good dinner we all went off to our rooms to catch up on our well-earned sleep. I personally thought that I would never drop off, but I must have, for I woke in the small hours of the morning with a feeling of chill in the air. I went to the window to close it a little. I drew back the curtains, and saw a beautiful bright three-quarter moon scudding along through the thickly piling rain clouds. Down below my window in the car park I caught a sight of the Land-Rover that we had travelled up in and next to it the same green car that we had seen twice in the afternoon—the one with the Arusha number plates. Still, the hotel had a public bar, and it was the only social meeting point for Europeans for miles, I mean, people like ourselves—travellers, tourists or fools!

CHAPTER FOURTEEN

Next morning dawned grey, cold and wet. After I had gone back to bed, I had been vaguely aware of the lashings of a thunderstorm on my window, but the worst of the rain was over by the time that I came down to breakfast. I entered the dining room and saw Anne, sitting alone at a table for four near the window. She was busy squeezing some lemon juice on to her paw-paw, and I thought that she hadn't noticed me. She didn't look up as I sat down opposite her, facing the window.

'Gareth, I've been wanting to talk to you alone for a while now . . .' still squeezing her lemon, '. . . but what with Tom and all the rushing about that we seem to be doing, there just hasn't been any opportunity.'

'Well then?' I waited for her to go on.

'It's about that night in Nairobi, I mean the night in Nairobi—why did you leave like that, I mean after, well—everything?'

I felt that I wanted to avoid the topic, the time was not right and I knew I was confused in my own mind still. There was a feeling of panic within me and a sense of being in a corner. I poured the milk on to my cornflakes, slowly and deliberately. I decided to hedge a bit.

'Would you have preferred that I had stayed then?'

There was no answer, so I looked up. Her face was slightly flushed and her eyes flashed in anger.

'Gareth Ashe, you are the most stupid and arrogant man that I have ever seen, I'm sorry that I brought the subject up.'

'But Anne, listen . . .' I could see that I had made a mistake in trying to be obtuse with her. 'It's not what you think. It's been on my mind ever since then. Thoughts of you come crowding in on me all the time, but I just can't let them . . . perhaps when all this is over . . .'

'It *is* all over as far as I'm concerned,' she flared.

'Oh, I don't mean that, Anne, I mean when all this trouble that we've got mixed up in is over.'

'Don't you think that you've got your priorities confused?' she asked icily, without any of the warmth that had marked the beginning of our conversation. In her cool *hauteur* she looked even more desirable.

'I don't know, Anne, I really don't know!'

'Then I think that you had better find out. For my part it is finished and I'm just putting all thoughts of you and that night right out of my mind. And I'm telling you here and now, that were it not for the connection with Bill I'd have done so ages ago. Now if you'll excuse me, I'll be up in my room when you are ready to go to wherever it is we are going. Ask reception to give me a call.'

She got up from the table and walked away coolly with an air of complete control.

Mike joined me at the table a few moments later.

'What the hell's wrong with the bird this morning then, I just passed her in the lobby, gave her my brightest little smile and what do I get—the big freeze off! I tell you there's no accounting for 'em. Pity too, seems a nice girl otherwise, but then, mate, that's the way they all are. Friend of mine used to say, "They're put together different—the same amount of brains as a man but half of it's in their cunts." Well, what's all this then, what's for this morning? Bit of a Sunday breakfast and away, is it? Where's this mate of yours, then? Held up? Can't get the top off his After Shave, I expect. Ah! here he is. Morning, Tom, good sleep then? That's it, come and have a bit of nosh and we'll get on our way....'

Mike rattled away about his plans through most of breakfast. They suited us well enough, as far as they went, and he was moving in the same general direction as we wanted to go, so we just agreed with what he suggested. He intended taking the road north to Hoima and Masindi to call in at Busiira and the Kiraki River area, each of which lay some ten miles from the main road to the west. All in all it would be a full morning's driving again.

We finished breakfast and went into the lobby. I asked the clerk to put a call through to Miss Anselm's room with a message that we should be leaving in fifteen minutes. I did not feel that I could talk to her then—I was all mixed up about her and wanted time to think things over.

My attention was caught by a large framed wall map on the wall near the desk. It was the usual Caltex map, showing the two National Parks, Queen Elizabeth and Murchison Falls. I called over to Tom and Mike who came and joined me. Mike drove a blunt index finger along the road that went north east from Fort Portal, he stopped at the village of Kitoma and then wandered west a little and stabbed, 'This here is bloody Busiira,' and then north a little, 'and this, gentlemen, is the arse end of the whole country, the Kiraki River, noted for elephant, pygmies and bugger all else.' The short lecture over, Mike soon gave up his topographical peregrinations. 'You two ready? Well, just hang on here for a minute. I've had my shave and shampoo, but there's the third item of my morning duty yet to be attended to, then I'll get the old bitch of a bus started and it's up and away!'

He disappeared through the door of the cloakroom, leaving his last words hanging on the air. I took the soap wrapper from my wallet and held it up against the large wall map.

'Where do you locate the third mark?' I asked Tom, indicating the double red ring.

'It's in the same general direction right enough. But there's nothing on the big map that's anywhere near it. It just seems to be two red circles around nothing. Let's ask our talkative friend when he gets through with his morning prayers. You know it really is eerie when you think of it.' He was looking at the small map again. 'Two earth tremor centres spot on prediction—a remarkable coincidence, or what?'

I shook my head. 'Whatever else, I think we can rule out coincidence, we'll just follow our noses until something turns up or we reach a dead end.'

Anne came into the lobby, carrying a small bag. She looked cool, crisp and efficient, dressed in a tailored skirt and jacket in brown denim, over a pale amber sweater. Her long hair was caught to one side and cascaded down the front of her shoulder, framing her breast most provocatively. I felt my inside turn over with wanting her. I had cupped her breasts in my hands, I had passed my fingers through her hair, and I had watched her nipples swell to life at my touch. I remembered her long contoured thighs, firm outside, and warm silky smooth within. As she turned, she tossed her head and, for a moment, our eyes met and held. It was still not too late. I felt that all this was wrong, that she should be turning away from me. Within, I called myself all sorts of fools. One word then, one gesture, could have remedied the whole ridiculous situation that had arisen over breakfast, but perverse, pig-headed Ashe let the moment pass and did his obtuse bit again, even though the wanting of her was swarming inside him with a sharp keen acuity that almost hurt.

We collected our bags from the reception desk and settled our accounts, then stood near the main door, waiting for Mike to appear. As we watched, the light drizzle of rain grew into a steady thrumming, probably the last spurt of the storm. Mike came along presently with a canvas holdall hung carelessly on his arm.

'What a bloody shower. Here, hang on to this and I'll bring the old bus up to the door, no sense in us all getting a soaking, is there?'

He opened the holdall and took out a thin plastic raincoat which he draped over his head and shoulders. Leaving his bag behind, he ran out into the rain towards the side of the hotel where he had parked the Land-Rover. We stood on the steps watching the rain and waiting for him to appear. We heard the wheezing of the engine as he coaxed it to fire. It caught and roared into life and we saw with a sharp focused clarity, I swear, the very raindrops on the leaves of the trees and the drips from the ends of the jacaranda flowers, as the Land-Rover drove into sight beneath them. Sheltering under the jacaranda tree, huddled from the rain, were two men who had a stall there, covered with a tarpaulin.

They flew into the air like flapping crows a split second before a blinding orange flame shot out to overtake them, and a near head-splitting, booming blast physically bowled us over the low wall at the side of the steps. Time stood still in a hung-up moment of realisation. In the front of my mind, I was aware of being thrown about like a leaf in the wind.

Reason clamoured for explanation and started sorting through causes in a whirr of suggestions and rejections. But, in a lazy, dreamlike way, I was hurled into another dimension of time, and I could see Fona's face, beloved yet horrible, dissolving before me, with an expression of . . . regret? remorse? accusation? The same loud brain-deadening sound of an explosion had accompanied her death—I felt the same helpless inadequacy as my body was hurled about and waves of percussion hammered through my head. I felt the same heart-sickening sense of loss and clawed and groped in my memory to bring her back. But the image of Fona was gone, leaving only dusty shadows of tears in that dark recess of my mind —and a return to consciousness in the other part.

Dazed and shaken, I rose to see a roaring inferno where the Land-Rover had been, and the heat of the flames came searing into my face against the cool splatter of raindrops. I could hear Anne sobbing beside me. 'Oh, my God, my God, my God! . . . .'

I remember being strangely attracted to the fire and stumbling towards it almost hypnotised when I felt the hand of Tom upon my arm, shaking me and heard his voice begin to make sense through the throbbing that was in my eardrums.

'Come on, Gareth! Come on! We've got to get away from here!'

We stumbled back up to the hotel steps against a press of people, who seemed to be coming from all directions. What had been a quiet Sunday morning had turned into a shouting, screaming turmoil of fascination and horror. No one paid the least bit of attention to us as they ran shouting towards the door.

'Tom, just a moment, let me go, the bags, we must get those, my things!' This from Anne who looked dazed and horrified. Our belongings were still near the door, pitifully askew. We picked them up and withdrew hastily into the hotel lounge. We sat down on a long settee near the window. An eerie orange light flickered on the ceiling. Anne was the first to speak. 'Mike,' she said. The word was a question, a hope, and in a way a recrimination that was mixed with relief.

'Not a hope! Wouldn't have known a thing about it, that much anyway, thank God!' I answered.

Tom was nodding slowly. His nod suddenly became a shake, as if he were clearing his head after a blow.

'That was meant for us you know; you do realise that, don't you?' he said. We let the idea hang in the air for a moment.

'You don't think it was an accident, the petrol tank or something?' asked Anne.

'The petrol tank and something that was explosive and thermal. I know, honey, I've dealt with enough of it during my life, lumbering and filming. It's all so simple really, all that's needed is the time, and whatever murdering swine did it he would have had all the time in the world—while we were asleep last night, I guess. A wad of plastic and a can of thermal, a minute time fuse to the ignition, and up goes the whole works.'

'But you do realise that if it hadn't been for that shower we'd have all been in the Land-Rover by then and . . . Oh, Gareth, when I think of it, and poor old Mike. What had he ever done. . . .' She started to cry in the dry tearless way that I remembered. I took her in my arms.

'Just don't think of it now. Try not to think of anything at all.'

151

Over her shoulder Tom was making gestures with his head towards the door. I nodded agreement to him.

The sound of confusion was growing steadily outside. The noise of running feet, the shouting and the yelling could be heard above the roar and the crackle of the flames. I eased Anne into a chair and went across the room to where Tom was standing. He spoke softly.

'I don't know whether you've thought about this, but anyone who is prepared to go this far is not going to stop now. He'll try again if he thinks that he's failed. I know that this will sound callous, and won't go down well with Anne, but Mike, poor chap, is beyond any help from us or anyone else. We've got to get away from here, and without trace if possible. We've got to dump these bags, separate, and then try to get into town. So take what you need and can carry from your belongings, and we'll try to meet again later.'

I nodded agreement although every instinct of decency revolted at the thought of just running out and leaving Mike like that, but I could see the sense in what he had said. We had no idea what we were up against or, in fact, at what moment another attempt would be made on our lives, or from where. As three people moving together we would be instantly recognised, but to go now, singly, while there was still a crowd and a confusion, was the most sensible thing to do.

Somehow or other our presence in Uganda was known, and there was very little doubt in my mind now that we had been followed up from Kampala. It was probably only uncertainty that had saved us from being killed the previous day on the road. When I thought of the bends in the road and the speed that we had sometimes reached, and the possible effect of a bullet in a front tyre, it made me quite sick. What really convinced me was the method with which the Land-Rover had been destroyed. No one travels about with plastic explosive and thermal material ready at hand to dispose of a chance enemy. It all requires decision and planning, and that meant organisation to a degree that we could not hope to match. They had all the advantage in knowing us, while we were unable to recognise our would-be killers even if they had walked right into the room that very moment.

'Explain to Anne while I take a careful look around,' I said, 'I'll find somewhere to hide the bags.' I suddenly got an idea. 'Tom, do you remember where Mike took over the driving yesterday before we came into town? We were near a large sign about ten miles out—I think the place was a tea estate, just across the road from a filling station.'

He nodded. 'Sure, I remember the place. I'll tell Anne and we'll try to meet up there. At what time do you reckon?'

I looked at my watch. Still only just after nine. 'What about noon?'

'Noon it is!'

While he went off to find Anne, I rummaged about in my bag and transferred a few articles to my pockets, and then had a good look round. Not a soul inside the building. There was just a chance that it might be assumed by whoever had tried to kill us that we had already perished in the explosion. I wanted to be sure that we would leave no trace behind so I went out of the rear door looking for a place where I could hide the bags. Across from the back door there was a patch of waste ground adjacent to some servant accommodation. I reasoned that the best way to make the cases disappear would be to have them found! Anyone coming across such a windfall, to all intents thrown away, would keep the secret carefully hidden and not go about advertising the fact. Without going any further, I heaved the bag into the weeds and then went back for the other two. Having disposed of those in the same way, I walked around the hotel to the front. A dense crowd had gathered at the grisly scene by this time, and a considerable amount of activity was going on among the other vehicles that were parked nearby. Anxious owners were getting their cars as far away as possible from the flames. I started to walk down the short drive that led from the hotel to the road. It was still raining lightly so I put my head down and turned up the collar of my jacket around my neck. I had a terrible feeling of vulnerability as I walked along, and although I had an urge to hurry or even run I kept my pace down to an ordinary walk and tried to look as if I wasn't expecting something to happen to me from behind. Near the gateway to the drive I saw a police car come tearing up the road, amber light flashing and siren blaring. I was grateful for its presence and moved off the road on to the verge to let it pass.

Suddenly I heard the squeal of brakes at my back. I turned to see a small pick-up stop just behind me, allowing the police car to pass also. I wanted to shout out something, but with the noise of the siren as it passed me I merely opened my mouth. The driver of the pick-up put his head out through the window. He had a small-featured, bearded face above a soutane which, although a puggy white, appeared startlingly clean because of the contrasting black rosary that hung about the neck and down the chest.

'Now that is quick for them. *Mon Dieu!*'

And then they had passed in a swirl of gravel, eyes intent on the column of dense black smoke that was rising through the air above the hotel.

The White Father offered me a lift and I accepted it gratefully. He was going into town, the opposite direction from where I wanted to go but I felt better and less exposed the further I got away from the place. He was a missionary priest, he explained in a heavy French accent. He had been saying mass in the hotel which acted as a mass centre once a month.

'I 'ad finished and was 'aving my coffee in the 'otel when BOOM! A very bad accident. *Mon dieu!* they are saying that there were four people in the car and not one escaped, it was so sudden. Three men and one girl, it is said. Europeans—American tourists who had stayed the night.'

We turned into the main street of the town and I asked him to drop me off there. He acknowledged my thanks with a wave of his hand and then was gone, probably to relate the events of the morning to his incredulous *confrères*. Just across the road there was a faded but clean-looking restaurant/bar. I walked in and ordered a cup of coffee and, for the first time in my life, a glass of brandy to take with it. My damp clothes felt chill, but I knew that the shivers that ran over me were more the result of shock and sustained tension. The coffee came hot and steaming. I drained the brandy in a gulp and then thankfully took some sips of the hot liquid. I got out a smoke and sat back to let the relief I had felt on hearing that we were assumed dead replace my anxiety. For a while at least we would be safe from any further attacks, and yet care was very necessary still. I sat there smoking a while and tried to sort out some ideas.

By the time that I left, the rain had stopped and I walked along the road to Alibhai's Motors where I had been informed in the restaurant I could hire a car. Although it was Sunday and the shop was closed, I could see through the window, between two rows of second-hand cars, what must have been Mr Alibhai balancing his books. I knocked and was soon sitting at the desk opposite him. We dickered a bit about the price and as a result I was given the benefit of a tear-jerking story about taxes and costs that made my heart bleed! I felt even more pained on coming outside to see his brand new shining Mercedes 220S which stood near the clapped-out old Zephyr that I was hiring for a price to make a horse trader blush.

I arrived at the place that we had agreed on well ahead of the other two. I was not worried about them now and felt quite confident that they would turn up all right. I spent some of the time talking to a man who had come for petrol. He was an engineer on the tea estate across the road. Luckily, he had been in that part of the country for many years and knew the place well from his shooting trips. I took the opportunity to ask him about the spot indicated on the map by the double red ring. I had nothing in mind very much except the thought of the trip back to Kampala, but I was curious about it and it was something to talk about. He was in no great hurry, so I referred him to the greasy Esso map that was hanging on the wall of the station and pointed as near as I could remember without consulting the wrapper that I had in my pocket.

'Nothing at all up there, not even to shoot, just barren rocky outcrops for miles and miles, just thorn scrub and acacia and aloes. There is a sort of road in there though, what the hell for I don't know. Wait a bit—yes, I do too, come to think of it. I remember the place now. Yes, that's it. We had an old Greek here years ago, tried his hand at everything, he had a mining concession there. He was looking for wolfram, or bismuth was it—I don't remember which. Anyway it never came to anything, the stuff was there all right but it just wasn't economical. He lost a pile of money. Went into tea after that, then papein, and then fishpacking down at the lake, but it never came to much either. He's dead now of course, but he must have been one of the craftiest bastards that ever was 'cause he left a small fortune to his son. Much good it did him either, come to think of it. . . . No, nothing up there, I don't suppose that even the road exists anymore. There's nobody up there to use it, no soil, no grazing, and if Old Pantelakis failed, there's no minerals either!'

He got into his car and drove off, but he had hardly gone a few yards when he reversed back to where I stood in the shade. 'I've remembered the name of the damn place now, came to me just like that! It's Kaluli. Hell of a place though, as I said.' And he was gone.

I sat back to wait for noon, beginning now to worry a little about Anne and how she had made out for herself, all alone. I needn't have! About eleven o'clock a car stopped on the road outside the station and then she appeared, waving cheerfully, and it went off again in a cloud of dust. I beckoned to her and she came over.

'No trouble?' I asked.

'None at all. I walked into town and was just having a cup of tea when these two nice boys offered to give me a lift, just like that! Do you know I think I could have gone anywhere with them, they were so polite and accommodating. Anyway, I was so pleased to see you standing there just now, even if I do think you're a rat. Oh yes, we passed Tom on the road about five miles back, I think he's walking here. He told me that it is best that we are not seen together so I didn't ask the boys to stop. He saw me though and looked right through me. So I suppose that I did the right thing by him. Although I must say that I can't really see the need for all this secrecy!'

'Look,' I said, 'there was an attempt on our lives back there, a serious and cold-blooded attempt to kill us. I agree with Tom all the way on this. We must be careful, and, Anne, while we're on the subject of being careful, I've got it all worked out, I want you to go back alone to Kampala. There is a bus this afternoon that will take you part of the way and then you can get through to Kampala for a hire car to pick you up. I think it would be much the safest thing to do. You can wait for us there and then . . .' I let my voice die. I didn't really know what to say to follow up the 'then'. We had failed and there was nothing else that could be done. But it didn't really matter, for she was shaking her head in a very determined way.

'Here I am, and here I stay, with you . . . both, that is.'

She sat herself down in the shade and looked fixed to stay so I pointed over, rather proudly, to the old Zephyr.

'If that's how it is, we'd better go and pick up Tom and then we'll be off—together!' I was pleased that she had refused to go, and I felt sure that the danger was past anyway. 'Will you have dinner with me tonight though, I mean, just the two of us— together?'

She smiled up at me, placed her hand in mine and we walked to the car. 'I'll think about it, Mr Ashe!'

By the time that we came across Tom we were laughing happily. He got in but was obviously not prepared to share our mood. He was scowling and muttering under his breath. The walk had obviously not put him in a good mood. I turned the car eastwards again.

'Well then, that's that, back to Kampala?'

'No! By Hell, that is not that, not for me anyway! No one's going to pull a thing like that on me and get away with it!'

I explained to him what the White Father had told me and how I thought that since we were safe for the time being it would be better to return to Kampala and put what we knew before the proper authorities.

'And what the hell do we know? That someone tried to blow us up! That we think it might have been some guys in a green Toyota which has probably disappeared by this time over the border into Rwanda! That we don't know why but that we think it's the same people who wrecked Busiira the other night with an earthquake! Because we've seen a map with some red rings on! They'd have you in the booby hatch before you got through half of it!'

He was right, of course, in a way. It would take a lot of careful thinking before we told our story to the authorities. That the car had been blown up by explosive would be very difficult to prove and might take laboratory techniques and equipment that were just not available. As I began to reflect on the police in Uganda and the way in which their rôle had become a purely political one, I realised that there was very little chance to get anything done with so little for them to go on.

'Look, Tom, all right—I agree with you. What you say is true, but it comes down to this: we either head for Kampala and try to forget about it, or we carry on with our original idea and get up to Busiira and down to the Kiraki River to see what we can find out. It's as simple as that. One or the other.'

The decision was made and we were driving along quite steadily on the Masindi road towards Busiira when I started to talk about an idea that had come to me. The road, though wet, was a lot steadier and straighter than the other, and it showed a greater variety, passing as it did through stretches of dapple-lit forest, and fording a number of swampy streams that had swollen with the rain. I told them about the engineer that I had spoken to that morning, and about the remote isolation of Kaluli. I explained to them why I thought that we should avoid Busiira and the Kiraki River.

'You see, whatever it was has happened already up there and by now must be a very cold trail, which would probably yield nothing anyway. We're not equipped for anything but the briefest of visits. Both those areas are populated, even though sparsely, but just think of the other. If any vehicles have gone in there any time during the last week, we'll be able to see and follow the tracks across the countryside, and then that would at least give us a positive approach. Anyway, Busiira and the Kiraki River will still be there, and we can tackle those places afterwards. Well? What do you think?'

We were all sitting in the front seat of the car. Anne gazed up expectantly at Tom. He looked thoughtful for a moment and then asked, 'Do you think that you can find this Kaluli place? If so, I think that you're right and I'm all for the idea. But I don't fancy spending the day horsing around in the middle of nowhere looking for a place that isn't there!'

'Well, as for finding the place, I think that I've got it fairly well bracketed, within a mile or so, from the small-scale maps that I've seen. When we stop next we'll take another look at the wrapper and decide then, all right?'

'May I have a word between you lords of my fate, please? Yes? Thank you both so much. No matter which direction we take or where we end up, we are going to need something like food and drink. Would you try to make your next stopping place a little more relevant to all our needs? All you two ever seem to want to stop for is to visit the trees. You're like a couple of dogs in a park!'

I think that neither of us could think of a word to say to this and we both sat there a little sheepish.

'You men are the most incompetent planners. Did you never hear that success in great ventures always hangs on small issues? I think this once you had better listen to the great female oracle, for to ignore me is doooom!' And she mischievously loomed over us, her fingers clutched into claws, her warning extended into a long witch's cackle.

Our tension evaporated in laughter and we all unwound to it, and went travelling along, suddenly high-spirited, singing and joking together, across miles and miles of African countryside. We passed the turn off for Busiira which was easily noticeable by the heavier traffic as people from every direction seemed to have arrived to view the spectacle of a village wrecked by an earthquake. Much later in the afternoon, Anne pointed to a signboard at the side of the road which read Kiraki River Forest Reserve and had a direction pointer that showed the place to be six miles away to the right. We left both of the turnings and carried straight along the road for we had decided that it was going to be Kaluli.

About an hour's driving past the Kiraki River, we came to a small trading station that was little more than a huddle of mud and wattle ddukas, but there was also a hand-cranked petrol pump outside one of them so we decided to make a stop there in order to fill up and try to buy some food. It was well on the way towards four in the afternoon, and we had not eaten since breakfast. In all the long miles that we had travelled we had passed nothing that would have provided us with food. This little place looked more hopeful. While Tom and I made a cursory check on the more obvious points of the car, Anne went off to shop in the most promising of the ddukas. She returned carrying a full paper bag and we left. We drove about a mile beyond the village and then looked for a place to have our meal. Beneath the shade of a tall palm we ate a late lunch of corned beef and crackers with some soft drinks to finish off.

There was a marked change in the terrain by this time, and the lush growth that we had travelled through had given way to a rolling grassland, dotted with tall palms and the ubiquitous termite heaps that stood out like sandstone citadels all over the plain. Over to the west, a long line of jagged hills appeared some ten miles away, curving nearer to the road ahead of us to lie right across our way before curving away to the east again. They were like a giant horseshoe dropped carelessly across our path. These were the Mbinga Hills, a ridge of barren rocky upthrust that lay between us and Lake Albert to the far west. Relying on the fact that the wrapper map had been produced with great care, we assumed that it could be relied on for accuracy too. So using the scale of distances that we had already covered, we calculated that the way to Kaluli must lie somewhere within the next ten miles. Therefore the road or track that would lead to it must show up on the left-hand side within the coming half-hour. So while Tom took over the driving, Anne and I both sat on the left side of the car to keep a look out for anything that could possibly be a way. We drove on. The road began to climb steadily and the surface became harder and more flinty. The vegetation became sparser and sparser until hardly a clump of grass was left or was visible amid the arid summits of the hills. The road ran on through a desolation of flinty-looking screes and boulders. We were all wrapped in our own thoughts and it was

Tom who eventually broke the silence that the whole place seemed to breathe.

'Well, as I figure it we should be about there so all eyes down and sing out if you spot a likely place.'

He dropped the car into a lower gear and we began to search intently for any sign of a track. It was not very difficult for at most places the road ran in a series of low cuttings that made getting off it an impossibility. The stone-scarred, eroded area precluded the possibility of the track being overgrown with concealing vegetation. At one time Tom shouted out, 'Possibility there, but the wrong side of the road.' We looked briefly where he indicated and then resumed concentration on our own side.

It soon became evident that we had drawn a blank. The road had risen to a high crest from which we could see below us the vast stretch of papyrus-choked river valley, snaking towards Lake Albert, that limited the area of our search. Tom turned the car in the narrow road.

'All over to the other side,' he said. 'We'll try again.'

'There's not much use really,' said Anne. 'I don't see where there could possibly be one. If it wasn't there when we passed the first time, how could it be there the next time?'

There was nothing else to do, however, so we set off once more. Anne proved to be quite right. After another slow and careful search, we could still find no sign of any track or path that led off towards the west. Because there was nowhere else, we returned to the spot where Tom had noticed the place on the east side of the road. Although there was no visible track it was possible—with difficulty—for a vehicle to leave the road. We got out and took a look round. The side where we were looking for something was bordered by a drop of about ten feet so we spread out on the other side. It was Tom who first found something of interest. He called and we went across to where he was bending down to look at what he had discovered. It proved to be an old weather-worn signboard partly buried in loose stones and sand. It was still possible to make out some of the letters. After a moment of brushing and scraping we guessed that it read: Danger No Through Road Beware Blasting, and the same message in Swahili below it.

'I reckon I can see what's happened here all right. The road has obviously been re-routed since the track was used, it used to lie over there.' He pointed, and sure enough, a vague redness in the stones might surely have indicated an old murram surface. We had missed the track because the new road had been levelled and no embankment had been thrown across it. A further look confirmed this. We thought about it for a moment and then decided to conceal the car as best we could off the level side of the road and, while the daylight lasted, to walk along what was left of the old track.

We walked for over an hour in a general westerly direction. After the long hours of driving it was a great pleasure to stretch the legs in the coolness of the late afternoon. Even though the area was virtually a desert, it had a dry, restrained beauty at that time of the day. It is one of those areas of Africa that means very little today now the great thirsts are no longer feared, but once they were areas of dread and fear for anyone who had to cross them. All the old stories of the Slave and Ivory routes are punctuated with disasters in areas such as this. For us though, it was no more than a pleasant evening's walk.

There was certainly a way which could have been used as a road many years ago, but no matter how we looked, it became increasingly obvious that no vehicle had passed that way in a very long time. There was no sign whatever of any human activity. So it was rather a dispirited group that we made as we sat to rest a while in the shadow lee of a large outcrop of rock. Then, very faintly at first, we heard the unmistakable chop sound of a helicopter. It grew stronger and then it appeared, high up in the sky. Surprisingly, it was difficult to spot against the lowering sun. Quite suddenly its engine cut.

'Quick, get down!' shouted Tom.

We dropped automatically and watched from a prone position as the dot grew larger and larger, the machine losing height. It seemed as though it were plunging slowly and remorselessly down towards us in its low, lazy curling movements. Its motor was turning, but so slowly and ungeared that it was quite visible.

'It's going to crash!' Anne almost screamed and had half risen when Tom pulled her back down.

'No, no wait, lie still!'

It seemed as though there was no hope for it as it dropped below our immediate limited horizon, when we heard the engine roar into life, sustain for only a few moments and then throttle back under control to stop.

'Well, I've seen some chopping done in my time, and I've done quite a bit myself, but that guy is the most. He's got it all ways. I wouldn't have believed that it was possible to make a down like that. The guy must have no nerves at all. Everyone that I ever knew that flew one of those things is in a constant state of prayer that the bloody thing will keep going! But to stall and drop like that—whew!'

'I'm sorry, do you think I was seen?' asked Anne.

'Not a chance in a million, I shouldn't think. Whoever was in that thing would have no time for looking around him, believe you me, he'd have his eyes glued to his instruments for dear life, and any spare thoughts that he might have had would have been on his last will and testament.'

'And anyway,' I added, 'we were in the shadow of this rock and the light's none too good either. How far do you think he came down?' I asked Tom.

'No more than half a mile. Just over the horizon there.'

We made our way cautiously to the crest of the ridge that had been our horizon, trying where possible to keep well apart and to stay in the lengthening shadows of the outcrops of rock that lay scattered over the whole area. On the top of the ridge we lay flat and looked down into a shallow basin perhaps two hundred yards across. The only thing to be seen was a very large tip of whitish rubble, and a few pathetic, twisted remains of what must have been the mining venture of many years past. All was still in the basin, nothing moved, there was no sign of life, nor of the helicopter.

'It must have come down behind that rubble tip,' I said. 'Come on, we'll make our way round to the other side.'

Fifteen or twenty minutes later, we'd made a complete circle around the lip of the depression and seen nothing in any direction.

'Well, I'll be damned!' I said.

'Crazy!' agreed Tom.

Anne just looked in astonishment. Nowhere in that whole basin could you have hidden a wheelbarrow without seeing it from our height advantage, but of the helicopter there was not the least sign.

CHAPTER FIFTEEN

At no time since this crazy business had started could I remember being so baffled and irritated. I felt tired out and exhausted, both physically and emotionally. I was quite prepared to believe then and there that I had not seen a helicopter a few hundred yards from where I stood. If either of the other two had only half indicated that we should go back to the car, I think I would have agreed without any argument. We had kept off the skyline so that anyone who might be watching would not see us. I sat down on the ground well below the lip of the depression. The other two joined me. Tom kept crawling back to the edge to peer over, but each time he reappeared with some variation of the same theme.

'I just don't believe it, I just don't, that's all!'

The last of the daylight was draining out of the sky. The shadows had blended into a grey-brown monotone in the last gleams of red light from the dipping sun. Anne produced the last of the crackers and beef from her shoulder bag, and we munched away silently, each dreading, yet waiting for someone to say, 'Well, what now?'

'We'll have to stay here for an hour at least and wait for the moon to rise,' I said. 'There's no use in trying to walk back through the dark till then.'

They nodded acquiescence.

Anne had fallen into a light sleep, I think, and all efforts at conversation had been abandoned, when Tom went up to the edge once more to look down. I heard his urgent whisper in the still dark night air.

'Gareth, up here quickly, don't make a sound.'

I joined him on the crest and could hear his heavy breathing as I lay beside him in the darkness. There was no need for him to say more. The mound itself was just an intense blackness against an already dark background, but the top of it was crowned with a ghostly green radiance. It looked like the cone of a stirring volcano on some remote planet where lava might flow green in the stygian blackness of everlasting night. I heard Anne come up beside me. Her hand reached out to touch mine. 'There,' she whispered. 'Not behind it but into it!'

I realised then that the mound of waste material had been most cleverly conceived as a circular barrier, within which might lie many of the answers to our questions. For surely no enterprise, however secret, would go to such lengths of concealment if it were lawful. The faint light represented an opening in the top, of that I felt sure, and as for the light, it was so dim that at a distance of only a hundred yards it would not be perceptible especially during the nights of bright tropical moonlight. If we had been looking a half-hour later I doubt if we would have noticed it, for there was already a lightness in the sky that heralded moonrise.

'How high is it, Gareth? How high is the mound?' Tom was peering intently into the darkness, and answered himself before I did. 'All of thirty feet I'd say. It's perfect except from the air perhaps. Whatever is in there is completely hidden. I was beginning to think there was nothing here, what with no road or track, nothing like it. Whatever transportation is needed is carried out with the chopper, and did you notice the direction it came from? Over Lake Albert from the Forest, I reckon—you could keep a whole army in there for a year and no one would be any the wiser.'

'That's why there are no guards or look-outs. Anyone trying to climb up the side of that mound would start a minor avalanche and would be heard from the inside, immediately,' I added. 'So what are we going to do?'

'Well, the first thing is to get down there and take a closer look. We'll certainly get nowhere sitting up here talking about it—come on! And for all hell's sake make no noise even if it takes an hour, we've got to get across that open ground without being discovered, we can't take any chances about guards.'

We moved painfully slowly across the hundred yards from the ridge to the mound, and stood there looking up at the sloping sides. It was genuine mine rubble all right, and not artificial, as I had imagined. It had been there some considerable time too, so therefore it was not so loosely bound as I had thought at first. It was mixed through with a clayey shale which did much to bind it.

'I think it will hold if we climb up,' I said, 'but what about you, Anne?'

'I wasn't brought up in a convent you know!'

164

'Right girl, let's go—Tom first, then you, Anne, and I'll bring up the rear.'

Tom set a pace that would have bored a tortoise. Foot by careful foot we climbed up, stopping every step to verify hand and foot holds. It must have taken all of a half-hour to climb the thirty feet, and Anne—bless her—was as solid and calm and careful as if she did this sort of thing every day.

The final three feet at the top was formed of the same stone and shale, but had been cunningly cemented to make a wall. Lying on this, we looked down into a saucer-shaped depression about twenty feet deep. The helicopter stood at the bottom. I guessed that it was probably painted in the same pattern and colour as the rubble, so that even from the air it would be well camouflaged. The faint green glow that we had seen emanated from a sort of round, manhole entrance that had been left open. We crept down towards it and noticed that the floor on the inside of the depression was quite firm and cemented, unlike the outer surface of the mound. When we got closer we saw that the round entrance was about six feet across, with iron rings that were set into the wall descending to the floor below, which I estimated must be about ground level outside the mound. The only sound that we could hear was the humming of machinery, perhaps a generator.

'Looks quiet enough,' said Tom. 'You two stay here while I take a look.' He lowered himself slowly, feet first, into the hole, then we saw his face looking up and his arm beckoning us to follow. I went first and Anne followed. We joined him to find ourselves at the end of a built tunnel which stretched ahead about twenty yards, sloping gently down away from us towards a solid looking steel door. The only illumination was from a single bulb about half way along which only barely lit the way. The only other feature of the tunnel was a short squat tractor, probably used for transporting the heavier items of supply that could be winched out of the helicopter. Tom moved over to this and then led the way forward, gripping a heavy spanner he'd picked up in his right hand.

We stopped at the door. It was the sliding type, set right into the face of the solid rock. I guessed that this was once the entrance to the mine. We stood for a few moments, undecided about our next move, when suddenly we heard, quite unmistakably, the sound of approaching footsteps on the other side of the door. I pointed for Tom to move to one side and pulled Anne to the other. We flattened ourselves against the rock face. The door slid aside, almost silently. I was only just aware of a booted leg coming through the opening before I saw Tom swing away from the wall and the flash of the spanner as it arced downwards. The man dropped to one knee with a grunt and in that instant I saw that he was wearing a helmet of sorts and realised that the blow, for all the force of its delivery, was not enough. He half rose again, with a puzzled and dazed look, to fold over the left hook that I put into his body—any other blow could have left him the use of his voice—and then I followed in closely with a fierce, hard chop to the base of his neck. He crumpled down like a sack and lay motionless. He was dressed in a type of uniform, blue overalls, black boots and a yellow fibre helmet. Slung over his left shoulder was an ugly-looking machine pistol. I passed it to Tom.

'Inside, quickly!' I said. 'Slide the door closed once we're all inside, Anne!' Tom went in first, pistol at the ready, and I followed, dragging the man by his armpits. Once we were all inside and clear of the doorway, I nodded to Anne, and she slid the door along its well-oiled channel. We still stood in semi-gloom but now in a large chamber.

Suddenly, bright fierce lights sprang to life all round the room. We froze, startled into a heart-thumping panic. Gradually it dawned on me that the lights were operated automatically with the closing and opening of the door. I relaxed and turned my attention to the unconscious form on the floor. A brief examination showed that he was out cold, but just to be on the safe side, Anne was detailed to keep an eye on him, a spanner poised ready over his bared head in case of trouble. We were all getting so used to the bizarre aspects of the whole business that, even though I noticed at the time the oriental cast of his features, I did not comment on it nor even reflect upon it until later.

The chamber seemed to be a store room of sorts, with a large variety of cases and wooden boxes stowed neatly along both sides. They mostly held machine parts and tools. There were also quite a large number of boxes of high explosive. Very significantly, these boxes were stencilled with the name that evoked a variety of mixed feelings in all of us, pain, fear, excitement and anger jumbled together. The East African Artesian Company. Proof enough that we were on the right track! Ironically, there was a box bearing the same legend which Anne touched rather wistfully, and I could see she was thinking that it might have been the one she had sent out from Nairobi when her brother was still alive.

Each of the four walls of the chamber had a door similar to the one that we had just come through. We tried them cautiously but the only one that seemed to be open was the one at the far end of the room, directly opposite to where we had entered. Motioning Anne to remain where she was, we went through into a long tunnel-like room.

It must have been all of ninety feet long, cut into the solid rock. The walls were unbroken, save for one more doorway that led off about half way along. Most of the floor was taken up by a long cat walk beside a cement trough that ran along the whole length of the tunnel. The trough was perhaps eighteen inches deep, and contained a long rod of fused quartz suspended on two metal piers.

Tom gave a long low whistle and whispered. 'Now what in all hell is this?'

He walked its length. At the far end, it terminated in a jumble of apparatus which was familiar from a long time ago when I had been interested in such things. It was a galvanometer, activated by an electromagnetic transducer. It appeared to be much more sophisticated and advanced than the old Benioff models that I was familiar with. It was of the capacitance bridge type, capable of recording even the faintest of earth movements.

'It's what you might call a strain meter,' I answered. 'This long quartz rod measures the expansion and contraction of the earth's crust. The apparatus on the end there magnifies and records the movement on a paper strip, see? It's the most sensitive and accurate instrument of its kind.'

The lower end of the tunnel was enlarged into a wider chamber and the whole made up a subterranean observatory. A bewildering array of instruments occupied both sides of the chamber. There were three seismometers, again of the electromagnetic type, based on the Golitsyn designs. They were arranged in the usual pattern: two horizontal, on an east–west, and north–south axis; and one vertical. Standing against the extreme end of the tunnel, there was a large working surface not unlike a draughtsman's table.

Perhaps we were pushing our luck by staying, but I signalled Tom to follow me, and went down to the table at the end of the tunnel. I began a systematic study of the schedules, charts and diagrams that lay there. Tom feigned interest for a while, and then said quietly, 'You stay here a while, I'll get back to Anne, but for

God's sake make it quick, will you. I've got a spooky feeling about this place. There must be more people here, and they're probably just beyond that door!' He jerked his thumb over his shoulder.

'All right, just give me a few more minutes here, and then I'll join you. I'm certain we're on to something here, but I must check out some details.'

He nodded and left me.

We were on to something all right! I felt my stomach knotting with excitement at the discovery, and the dawning realisation of how big it was made me want to shout out, but I contained the feeling and carried on with my examination of the material spread out on the table. Work of this sort has always been of great interest to me and, although my knowledge was rusty, I found it all returning in the effort that I was making. I began to see a pattern emerge from the chaos that had first beset my brain.

You see, shock is recorded on a seismograph in several waves. Those marked with an L on the charts in a familiar squiggle are the slowest, rather like the ripple waves on a pond, emanating out when a stone is thrown in. The other two, marked P and S, are the primary and secondary waves which drive straight into the body of the earth. Thus each earthquake leaves behind a signature, as it were, on a timed and dated chart. A series of the P waves, which are the quickest and therefore the first to arrive, followed by the S waves in their pattern, and, finally, the L waves. It is possible, by reading off the graph that they make, to estimate quite accurately how far away the disturbance is from the recording station.

Now in the case of the Busiira earthquake, whose profiles lay on the table, this distance would be negligible. Yet the chart was neatly labelled 'Kaluli Experiment 3rd Sept. E.T.A. P wave: 3.00.00 hrs. E.T.A. S wave: 3.00.08 hrs.' Thus the waves, travelling as they do at roughly seven miles per second, showed that eight seconds had elapsed between the P and S waves. That would be fifty-six miles, which was about right. Now at first, this fact did not register, I mean the fact that it was headed E.T.A. It was only when I saw the same abbreviation on another set of charts, that I realised. These said, 'Ladong Experiment. 10th Sept. E.T.A. P wave: 2.45.00 hrs. E.T.A. S wave: 2.46.13 hrs.'

I did a quick calculation and saw that Ladong must be about five hundred miles away. I was wondering whereabouts Ladong could be when it hit me! The 10th September was still over a week away, I thought, and then I got it. E.T.A. was Estimated Time of Arrival! An earthquake was actually predicted to an exact second of time the following week in a place called Ladong! And what was even more significant, according to the first set of charts, Kaluli had predicted the recent one in Busiira, too, for time, place and, of course, magnitude—for no one would remain underground fifty miles from an earthquake centre unless they knew it to be safe.

One further curious fact revealed itself from my examination of the information, and that was that at least two other observatory centres must exist somewhere else in East Africa. No accurate plot or record can be made from a solitary station because the number of directional points is almost infinite from one spot. If there are two stations the locations are reduced to two: the points where the plotted circumferences of two circles would intersect. But only with three stations can the centre be absolutely spotted as the three circumferences would intersect at one place only! I wished that I had brought the folder that belonged to Smith, for I was reasonably sure now that activities that passed as water drilling in Kenya were connected with the 'Ladong Experiment'. The fact that a third centre was required indicated that there was yet somewhere else involved, the whereabouts of which we did not as yet know. I guessed Tanzania, where the Rift Valley continued southwards. All of this left me in no doubt whatever that some method of induction had been devised which could trigger off an earthquake, that this had actually been done already in Busiira, and that it was about to be repeated at a place called Ladong in the following week. Whatever agency was involved in this, it was secret, illegal and, as we had reason to know, very dangerous.

I selected some of the data and charts, rolled them together and made my way back to join the other two. I had a moment of panic as I passed the doorway, wondering what lay beyond it. I carried on as quietly as I could towards them. Perhaps it was the undue caution or the panic that had risen in me, I don't know, but suddenly I knew that I was falling and I felt my legs go from beneath me, twisting on a turned ankle. I collapsed in a pain-seared heap into the trough that held the strain meter, near the galvanometer end. I made no sound as I fell although the pain in my knee was intense, and for a moment I thought all was well. Then I saw Tom moving towards me along the tunnel, and behind him, to my horror, the door that he had just come through sliding shut. I shouted then, realising that we had been discovered anyway.

'Quick, Tom! Behind you! The door!'

But it was already too late. It slid home with a decisive clunk. Tom hurried forward to help me to my feet. The lights in the tunnel began to flicker rhythmically, and a large red bulb flashed on and off in silent alarm, flooding the whole place with a baleful eerie glow.

I staggered, and Tom rushed back to the door, but it was of sheer steel, secured with the unmistakable firmness of an electric device.

'We're trapped, boy. Shall I try this?' He lifted the snout of the automatic level with the door.

'It would be a waste of time and bullets. Quick, let's get to the other door . . . it's our only chance now. If we remain here we're helpless. I only hope that Anne had enough time to make a bolt for it.'

Suddenly the red light stopped flashing and the other lights steadied. We hurried on, noticing that they were steadily increasing in brilliance. And then Tom spotted the reason. High on one side of the wall, the light reflected off a moving object. It was the elongated lens of a television camera, traversing slowly through the full arc of the room.

'Quick, get down,' he said, but hardly had he spoken when its movement stopped and it fixed on us like a gleaming, evil Cyclopean eye. 'We've been discovered and it looks like we're trapped, but I'll be damned if we're going to be spied on!' He swung the pistol into action. It chattered briefly, and then the camera shattered in a blue flash of short circuit.

'Well come on then, you bastards—let's have a look at you!' His words echoed in the eerie waves of silence that followed the shots, until all sound died away. The only disturbance was made by the tiny motes of dust, floating gently down from where the camera had been, and the occasional tick of an instrument far down the tunnel.

CHAPTER SIXTEEN

The lights gradually lost their brilliance, returning to a more normal glow. We crossed the long trough and took up our position behind it and facing the other door. I don't know what we expected. Coupled with the natural fear of the unknown there was the senseless disadvantage of being on unfamiliar territory. I tried to keep calm by thinking about the right of our position and the wrong of the people we were up against. I didn't know if there had been any loss of life at Busiira, but if there was none that was only luck. The wanton destruction of homes and property seemed to have been undertaken without any thought for the suffering this might entail. The fact that the other test at the Kiraki River had done no damage was entirely a matter of luck too. For I was convinced that if the geological formation had been right in some populated place the plan would just as lightly been carried out there.

Tom contented himself with muttering under his breath. 'Why don't they do something? Sonsabitches!' I looked at my watch. A whole fifteen minutes had elapsed since the alarm had been sounded. The waiting made me edgy. 'For God's sake, Tom, shut up and think instead of blathering on like that.' He looked long at me. I could see that he was just as tense as I was. 'Sorry,' I said.

'You're right, boy. What we need now is thinking, big thinking. Sometime, any minute now I expect, we'll be faced with whatever is coming. Let's try to get some sense into this thing.' He paused. 'Look, it's like this. There's only two things that we can do: throw it in, or make a fight of it. Our only advantage is half a magazine of slugs for this little thing—but hell! They don't even have to face that. They might have all the time in the world. They could starve us out for all we could do about it. Mind you, there's Anne, I've been wondering if all the doorways closed at the same time. If they did she'd be trapped in there too!'

'There's no way of knowing,' I replied. 'That door between us is all of eighteen inches thick, and insulated against all sound vibration. Some of these instruments are so sensitive that if you dropped a packing case on the floor out there it would show and perhaps ruin a profile. And anyway, even if Anne did get out, how far could she get? On foot and miles from anywhere, she'd be picked up easily. No, I don't think that we can put much hope on Anne.'

'I expect you're right, boy.' Tom took a handkerchief from his pocket, and mopped at his face that was beaded with sweat. On thinking about it, I realised that I was very warm too. The chill cold of surprise and shock was wearing off and I was beginning to feel uncomfortable and stuffy.

'Do you think there's a system for freshening the air in this place?' I asked.

We looked around. It was not easy. I was beginning to feel an apathy about everything. Tom pointed down the passage. 'There's a ventilator grille, and another at the other end!'

But any faint hopes that I had of using the grilles as a way of escape were soon dashed, for they were only about twelve or fourteen inches square. 'I expect that the lower one is for extraction and the upper one is for renewal,' I commented.

Tom began to chuckle, and oddly enough it did not seem out of place. But suddenly he pulled himself together. 'That's it,' he said. 'No wonder they can afford to wait. Come on!'

We climbed back over the trough and walked down to the ventilator, set about seven feet above the ground. He put his hand to it. 'Not a bloody thing!'

Just to be sure, I lit a match and held it against the grille. There was not a flicker of movement of the flame. We walked back quickly to try the other one which was set much lower in the wall. The look on Tom's face was enough to tell me the worst, but I put my hand to it just to make sure. There was air passing through this one all right, but it was moving out of our chamber! The increase in temperature and the feeling of apathy and discomfort were now explained.

I slipped my coat off, and pushed it against the grille. It was sucked on firmly, but at best it could only slow the procedure down for the cloth was not airtight. 'Let's look around for something that will block this thing more efficiently,' I said, 'anything will do. Plastic sheeting, a bit of polythene packing, even cardboard!'

'Look!' said Tom.

I saw my coat drop to the floor as the pressure drawing the air out was reduced.

'I bet all hell to a pinch of crap that they've switched the system round.' We hurried back to the first grating, Tom getting out of his jacket as we went. He reached up with it and it was sucked positively and somehow satisfyingly over the vent. For some reason I looked at it all with a sense of detachment. A dream-like unreality seemed to persist. I watched my chest rising and falling and was aware of a stupid grin on Tom's face as he started to laugh. 'God! it's like musical chairs!'

Awareness seemed to intensify and become more acute. The remark about musical chairs seemed so droll that I could not stop myself from laughing too, and the rushing and roaring in my ears was just an unimportant side effect. Only a dim, half-formed thought glowed somewhere in the thick, sweet pudding that was my mind. I tried to form the words 'oxygen starvation' with my lips, but all that came out was a drunken stammer. The rushing and roaring increased and swirled like a vortex, all around, and I went down the plughole of consciousness, with an ever-increasing speed, in a spiral of ever-diminishing circles, until I disappeared from myself and into myself with a puff of blue smoke—extinct!

What beautiful things legs are—long, sexy, female legs—more eloquent than words when they speak. That's the funny thing about legs, they definitely have something to say and when they say it, it is very significant. Now a woman's breasts are different. They have something to say as well, but it isn't significant, it's the old, comforting story that we learnt when we were incapable of learning anything else. Legs are not comforting—their message is always something new, strident, inviting and very compelling. I looked along the whole smooth length of them, golden in the light, and watched the latent power of movement in the muscles along the smooth pilgrims' way up the inside of the thighs. I ventured a hand, a mere gesture of compliance with the urgent appeal in them. My fingers ached with the splayed nerves of sensuality, trembled with a delicious sensitivity in anticipation of the velvety feel that was curiously hot and passive, and beautiful, like the petals of a flower. . . .

All the more agony then, as the thick composite sole of a boot came instead, crashing down into the back of my hand, crushing it against the floor and grinding it relentlessly against the concrete.

I let out a scream, not from the pain, but from the sense of being
deprived of something that would never be attainable again, and
from being thrust from the dark womb of unconsciousness out and
back to the cold reality of the senses. All five came on like a series
of tripped circuits. Pain from my hand. The harsh glare of an
electric bulb. A low mumble of voices. The taste of thick flannel
in my mouth, and the not too unpleasant smell of damp mustiness
that one associates with below ground. And then a sixth sense—
the heart knocking with fear. The crawling of the skin and other
wild alarms as the body clears for action.

I forced the panic down, and by concentrating on my damaged
hand, I gradually got in control of myself again. I sat up and
looked around me, blinking against the light. Awareness came
screaming back to the front of my head as I remembered the events
of my last few hours of consciousness. Tom was there in the
corner, already awake. Anne lay where I had been, out to the wide
I guessed, with her long, beautiful legs in a provocative disarray of
abandon.

We were in a room, quite small compared with the tunnel, yet
it had none of the austerity of a workroom. It was quite tastefully,
if simply, furnished. A number of good prints and pictures hung
on the walls. A practical-looking bookcase occupied one whole side
of the room. Behind the only table in the room sat a man, twirling
a long-stemmed wine glass thoughtfully in his fingers. It was his
shoes that convinced me he was not the only one in the room we
would have to deal with. He was not wearing the heavy-soled
boots that were responsible for my aching fingers. I half glanced
over my shoulder and saw the other two men, either of whose
feet might have done it. One I recognised as the guard we had
knocked out at the entrance. He had very firmly and convincingly
repossessed his weapon. The other was of the same nondescript
alien appearance, dressed in the same fashion but of much greater
size. He was further distinguished by the leering, hot look in his
eyes as he stared at Anne on the floor. He watched her with the
same intensity as the other watched me, who must have remembered my face from the time that I had hit him near the entrance.

I looked across to where Tom was sitting on the floor with a
dejected attitude. He looked back at me with eyebrows slightly
raised, and shrugged his shoulders vaguely.

'Stand up!' This from the man behind the desk. It was a well-
controlled and insistent voice that expected to be obeyed. 'Stand

together here.' He indicated a minute spot on the carpet, in front of the table. We occupied it, shuffling rather foolishly together.

For a long moment he looked us over, and as he did so I tried to assess what sort of man we were up against. Racially, I would have said that he was Eurasian, but his features included a high, hooked nose reminiscent of Persia. His cultured accent had been discernible even in the two short phrases that he had uttered. From him came an air of complete self-possession. He was a man of purpose, not easily panicked. There was something very easily recognisable about him, familiar and in a way reassuring. I wondered about it and then realised that he belonged to that large group of men who are attracted to a creed or a faith by their desire to follow the stern hard path of intellectual conviction.

Every movement, revolution and religion has two types of devotees: the emotionally convinced and the intellectually convinced. The latter are the continuation and strength of every innovation, they are the spring in the white-hot fire of idealism, tempered in the ice-cold waters of reason. The most formidable of all human metal.

He leaned back in his chair and spoke again. 'I am not going to waste a lot of time with pointless questions, gentlemen. I want you to answer promptly, and without evasion, all that I shall ask you. I do not intend to keep you here long. I am a very busy man with very, very much to do and I cannot afford the time. So listen, listen very carefully to what I have to say.

'You have either accidentally or intentionally stumbled across a project which, to say the least, requires a great deal of secrecy for its successful conclusion. I want you to know right from the start that it is of such magnitude that it affects the welfare of millions—even perhaps eventually the whole world. So, have no illusions about the value of your lives. They are worthless, expendable, one might even say—expended, except for one small thing, and that small thing is what I wish to know from you. That is, gentlemen, the extent of your knowledge concerning this affair of ours, and secondly the extent of your implication. You see, your presence here makes a difficulty for me. It is this. If you are here from curiosity or a sense of personal adventure, I can dispose of you without any consequences. If, on the other hand, you are here in, what shall we say, a representative capacity . . . then I can dispose of you. But I will be left with a sense of insecurity, inasmuch as I

will not know what to expect next from whomsoever you represent.
Clear?'

He spoke with such a drawling calm that I had difficulty in
adjusting his tone to his meaning. When he spoke of disposal, he
meant just that. It took some getting used to. I tried to think, but
there was still a vague cloudiness in my mind. Conway's brain
seemed to be functioning better, so that when he spoke I was
content to leave it to him.

'Do I read you clear, mister? Did I hear you say we'll be "disposed of", anyway? Then why the hell should we tell you anything.
We get nothing either way!'

'Why? Oh! perhaps I left this little bit out—do forgive me—who
knows, perhaps I imagined that you would not be truculent, I
should have known better. Yes, I see now. An heir to the great free
world of western democracy would be truculent.' His lilting tone
became crisper and icy. 'This little bit I left out now. It's this—
what you get out of it is quite simply the difference between a
quick, clean bullet in the back of the head and a much more
sustained and painful experience. Clear?'

For reply Tom raised his fingers in the time-honoured gesture
and growled, 'Up yours!'

A nod from the man behind the table caused the snub end of a
machine pistol to jab viciously into the small of Tom's back—
another time-honoured gesture and one that left Tom down on
one knee, his face grimacing with pain. A further nod caused a
heavy boot to swing into the other kidney, laying him out, writhing,
on the floor, soundless and blanched.

'Now, while your friend is reconsidering his position, perhaps
you would oblige . . .?' His look was one of polite inquiry. I felt
like a man poised on the brink of a pool on a cold, frosty morning.
I was tightening my resolve to join Tom in his little Serpentine
swim. I've never been able to decide since whether I was an
absolute coward or a devious Celt with a mind as tortuous and
twisted as any Mede or Persian. I took one more glance at Tom on
the floor, briefly looked at Anne to see if she were still unconscious,
and then decided—the water looked too cold.

'Yes, I'll tell you what you want to know—after all what difference can it make.'

I saw the faintest flicker of puzzlement come into his eyes. It was
comforting in a way to see that he hadn't expected my co-operation
so soon. I did not want to make it sound too easy because I wanted

time—I wanted time for us all. I was counting on his mind. It was my last hope and a last hope has got to be played and explored to its full extent. Every minute or moment we gained provided positive opportunity. Every kick, blow or insult was a negative decline in our chances.

'You see, it's Anne—the girl there. I don't think I could stand her being hurt, and you'd get round to that eventually I know, wouldn't you?'

'What a vivid imagination you must have. The quality of a sensitive mind, Mr . . .?' He paused and looked down at the table where a jumble of our personal possessions was piled. 'Ashe.' His faint accent hardened the sibilant. 'A strange name. I spent many years in Britain—no doubt you've guessed that. I would suggest that you might come from the country of long names and short tempers. That would help to explain it. You lack the hard-headed pragmatism of the Anglo Saxon, Mr Ashe. You are too sentimental to be involved in matters such as this. Now, returning to this matter of your presence—explain it!'

I swallowed nervously. Everything was in the balance, which was so heavily loaded against us. If I could gain only a slight advantage it would be a start. The slightest touch could start things swinging back in our favour.

'I will explain but I would feel freer if they were not here—my friends I mean.'

He thought this over, looking straight at me, and then pressed a button on his desk. The door opened across the room and an armed guard entered. Then he spoke briefly and curtly to the other two in a sing-song, throaty language that I failed to recognise. Tom was hustled to his feet and prodded, stumbling, through the door. I watched the other bend to pick up the recumbent Anne—his hands wandered lewdly over her whole body until a sharp word of command caused him to pick her up like a rag doll and follow the other two out through the door. I clenched my hands until I felt the nails in my palms; I felt wretched as I saw her limp form across his shoulders. My very vivid imagination was giving me hell as I thought of what might be in store for her.

'Don't worry, Mr Ashe, no harm will come to them yet. You see, I will need, what shall we say, corroboration of what you might have to tell me and therefore, in the circumstances, I think it would be wiser for you to be quite frank. Do you understand?'

With the others gone, we were left in the room with just one armed guard who stood against the far wall with a clear field of fire and me in the centre of it. So the pieces on the board had moved. I didn't think that the actual physical chances were any better, but we had gained something. In fact, two things. Firstly, the knowledge that we could still control a certain amount of movement; secondly, that this man before me had shown a chink in his very formidable armour. He was a vain and proud man possibly, or a very, very clever one. Either way it was a weakness.

'May I sit down?' I asked. He nodded to a chair.

'Draw it up here and make yourself quite comfortable, but do be careful. My man here is very nervous, and has orders to shoot you down at his own discretion. I would feel rather sorry to lose you so soon, you interest me, Mr Ashe. But you do see that you're hardly indispensable, don't you?'

I moved the chair carefully so that I sat where I had stood a moment before. I had determined that nothing less than the whole truth would do, so I began to relate the story just as it had happened, trying to leave nothing significant out. All the while I watched him carefully. Only when I mentioned Sloeder and Kopft did he raise his eyebrows enquiringly.

'And what did you make of Herr Sloeder, Mr Ashe?'

'I must admit that I don't see how he fits into all of this. His presence in Kenya was a great surprise to us, but I suppose were it not for him and his desire to avenge himself on Hines we would never have got here. I'll tell you what I make of Sloeder: I think he's a deadly, dangerous man, but that his danger is quite as bad for his associates as for his enemies.'

'Interesting. It is a conclusion that I—we, that is—have already reached. There are times, you see, when such men are useful, and then, the situation outgrows them. Perhaps later, as the evening develops, you might learn more about our friends, who knows?'

He offered no more than this so I had to go on, my curiosity unsatisfied.

The tension the guard had shown gradually became replaced with boredom. For him, it was probably just a continuous rattle in a foreign tongue.

I had got to the part of the story where we had experienced the shock waves in Kampala. He was smiling, self-satisfied and smug. He interrupted, 'If you could only imagine what that moment meant to me—to all of us. It was the proving point of years and years of exhausting research, the fruition of endless agony and frustration and the proof of the faith so many of us have held for so long—faith in our ideals, faith in our leader, faith in our future.

'Yes, you tell a good story, Mr Ashe—and what is more a convincing one! I am all but reassured that this is nothing but a misadventure for you—an unfortunate and, I'm sorry to say, a fatal one. For you must see that even several days ago you already knew too much. That in itself was no problem for, as the saying goes, "dead men tell no tales" but there was just this niggling fear and suspicion that you might have already been in touch with some authority. Not local, of course, that could be taken care of for we have sympathisers in very high places. It was suspected and feared that, shall we say, 'foreign' influences might be brought to bear.

'I did not agree with that clumsy attempt on your lives yesterday. The order came from—well, shall we say, above. You know it's ironic really, isn't it? If, instead of coming here, you had quietly gone about your business, I doubt if anything further would have been thought of you. The accident was reported as a complete success you see. You seem surprised, Mr Ashe—did you not know then? Surely now, I thought you would have guessed that that was an attempt on your lives!'

All this was said in such a cold, disinterested way that I felt the anger beginning to boil in me, but I had to hold on. Every moment showed the chink getting wider. I remained perfectly calm outwardly and asked, 'Why a success then—and did you say yesterday?'

'Of course—yesterday. You have all been, shall we say, held on ice, while I've had enquiries made. It is now, let me see, 18.00 hrs. Monday—a whole day lost in your life!' He chuckled quietly. 'Not that I think it matters now. Oh yes! why a success? You see, there were the remains of four bodies eventually recovered from the burned-out car, and you and your companions had disappeared completely. I'm afraid that the news of your most tragic deaths has already been sent to your various Embassies. I even believe that arrangements are in hand to have the remains transferred to Kampala. Oh, by the way, the car you hired has been returned to Fort Portal.'

'There were three bystanders when the car blew up—vendors, I think—poor devils!'

'There you go again, Mr Ashe; too sensitive—too, too sensitive. But you see it's not all bad, is it? Now, instead of just disappearing without trace, there will be three nice, neat, orderly funerals—

though from what I gather the cremations were practically completed outside the hotel. Comforting, isn't it, to know that there will be a corner of a foreign field that for ever will be yours—in name, anyway.'

He started to chuckle again, this time with genuine amusement. He got up and walked round the room, stopping here and there to touch a book or look at a picture. He turned to look at me again, rubbing his chin reflectively and then said, 'Would you like to have dinner with me, Mr Ashe?'

He said it casually without the least trace of sarcasm and as if nothing had happened between us. I must have looked astonished for he went on rapidly. 'You see I have enjoyed talking with you, you cannot imagine how I have missed talking with someone like yourself. I have a feeling that, in spite of the circumstances, you and I might have a lot in common. I want to hear the rest of your story, and I think—yes, I really think that I would like to clear up a few little points that seem to have escaped you. You see, curiosity seems to have been your motive in coming here, and it would be a neat conclusion to your adventure to have it satisfied before you die of it.'

CHAPTER SEVENTEEN

The water from the shower streamed down over me. I could not remember ever enjoying the feel of hot water so much in my life. Except for the presence of the guard, I could have given myself over to complete relaxation.

I was sure that the man we had just met was either unbalanced or intoxicated with a sense of power and achievement. Whatever the reason I was still alive, and I had moved again along the line that I had decided on—the principle of mobility and concession. In telling my story, I had gained more time, and had also triggered off some desire in him to play cat and mouse with me at an intellectual level. I had moved, and also gained the promise from him that Tom and Anne would have their immediate needs catered for —a promise that he had given, shaking his head rather sadly and saying, 'Sensitive again, Mr Ashe, too, too sensitive.'

I had no hope at all that his intentions had wavered. In some strange way, I was already dead to him. We were, all of us. I had been taken from the room where I was questioned and through a bedroom to the bathroom. At no time at all was I away from the direct view of the guard, but I was to all intents and purposes alone and this in itself was a relief. My mind toyed with the idea of making an attempt to overcome the man in the room. I reasoned that there might not be another chance of a one to one struggle, but I decided against it unless some very favourable condition arose. There was, even then with death staring us all in the face, a very strong urge to hear the answers and reasons for the mystery that surrounded the whole business. I had the feeling, too, that our position was improving—had improved from the time we were first captured—and I decided to let it ride a little longer. It was a desperate gamble I knew, with not only my life at stake but those of Tom and Anne as well.

I had expected the meal to be a simple affair, but to my surprise the table where we sat earlier was now set beautifully with a snowy-white cloth and gleaming silver. While we ate we were served by a manservant in a spotless white jacket. A gentle background of music was provided by a record player in the corner. It was only when I started to eat that I realised how hungry I was. It was as if he realised this for no attempt at anything but the most trivial of topics was made. It did seem strange to be sitting there so calmly talking of Prokofieff and eating a most delicious King Fish Portugaise with uncertainty and death only hours away.

When the last of the meal was over and cleared away, we sat at one side of the room in two comfortable chairs, coffee was brought in and I was offered an exotic, long, thin cigar. I lit it from the table lighter and inhaled the smoke gratefully. Despite the circumstances, I felt easy and relaxed. The guard had been replaced and the new man sat across the room. As a factor, this changed nothing; he had the same bored anonymity as his predecessor, the same efficient-looking weapon and, as I was told, the same order to shoot at his own discretion if he suspected anything.

'Now shall we resume?' he said. 'How shall we start? Let me begin by introducing myself to you. My name is Luay Firaz Pasha, citizen of the third world.' I looked enquiringly at him, he raised his eyebrows slightly, made a deprecating gesture with his hands and then walked across to a writing desk. He returned carrying something in his hands. He gave it to me. It was a lozenge of highly machined stainless steel, with a beautiful, tooled device in the centre representing a ring of fire surrounding the Roman numeral three.

'Yes, the third world, Mr Ashe, the hopes of millions, the dream of a few.' He seemed to sink into a reverie.

'But I thought the third world represented a political ideal, just an idea in the minds of non-aligned nations.'

'The title has caught the imaginations of such people, it is true, but that is far from what the third world really is. I will explain. I cannot go into too much detail, of course—I do realise that you don't have the time.' A wry smile turned up the corners of his mouth. 'An organisation exists, a powerful, well-knit organisation, with adherents and members all over the world, but mostly in what is termed the East. It was started strangely enough in Europe during the early fifties. Its aim is to establish a new order in the world, a new set of values, a new concept of society and government which will ultimately control and administer the whole world society. Our dream sprang from the defeated remnants of national socialism in Germany.

'Just after the war many of the great administrative and military brains of Europe were left to lie in the ferment of inactivity. Minds that had once controlled thousands, even millions of others, were suddenly relegated to the backwater of either a shallow victory or hopeless defeat. That was anticipated by our first leader. During the latter months of the war in Europe, risky contacts were made, meetings were organised which, had they been discovered, would have meant a charge of collaboration, treason and summary death. High-ranking soldiers and ministers from most of the belligerent countries of Europe were contacted and sounded out, tested, rejected or finally accepted until a council of twelve was formed. By a system of cell growth that twelve has now grown to millions. There is still a high council of twelve who meet regularly to administer the organisation.' He paused a moment.

'Do you mean to say that a world-wide organisation exists which numbers millions of people and that it's secret? That's almost impossible.'

'Yes, I agree. It would be impossible but for two very important facts. Firstly, what you might term the proletariat of the organisation do not know that they belong—I will explain this later—and secondly, the existence of the cadre is kept a secret, not from within but from without. The most important governments of the world know of our existence, but are held to secrecy by a threat to their own welfare, for to acknowledge our existence is to betray the use they make of us, and that in the dirty world of international politics is vast and fairly universal. They have, as the saying goes, a tiger by the tail and just dare not let go. The implications of one nation admitting of our existence to another would be shattering, literally shattering. If only one theatre of activity were exposed, let's say the Middle East, the immediate result would be a vicious breakdown of all cease-fire agreements and an escalation of involvement with all the major powers of the world. And you know what that would involve.

'Then there are all the other areas of our activity, any of which is a situation which could be very embarrassing if the facts were revealed. You see the whole system of espionage in the world has changed. Such fear exists between the major powers that they prefer to contract the work out. You might say that our organisation looks after the very nasty smells that arise out of international involvement, and human nature being what it is, no one power wants to admit to the other that it smells.

'A drink? I have a very fine malt whisky—Glenfiddich.'

I nodded, deep in thought, and wondered where on earth all this was leading. It seemed to grow more and more complicated by the minute. It crossed my mind that perhaps this Firaz was quite stone mad and that it was all a figment of a paranoic mind. I was still holding the plaque that he had given me. My fingers followed the cleanly incised lines of the flames. When he returned with the pale glowing spirit, I sipped and cleared my throat as the strong, smooth taste seemed to fill my head.

'A great whisky,' I said. 'My compliments on your taste.'

I wanted him to continue—there were a hundred questions crowding about in my head—but I knew that he would not be rushed. His weakness lay in his sense of power, words to him were life. He was the type of man who could either talk himself out of the grave or into it as fate dictated. At the moment he was playing with me, using his words like cats' paws, trying to nudge out some response with a velvety touch, but I knew that the claws were there, too, so I decided to play mouse again.

'Do you really expect me to believe that what is going on here— this earthquake business—is known about by the responsible authorities, and a blind eye is being turned to the fact that you have just engineered a disaster and plan to do the same next week at Ladong?'

A look of surprise crossed his face, but only for a moment did he lose the sardonic, wry expression on his face.

'Mr Ashe, I seem to have under-estimated your powers of perception. You have a quick brain—I would not have thought it possible for you to have gained that much information in the short time you spent in the observatory. You have some training in these things, I feel. Seismography? Geology? Espionage, Mr Ashe? Which?'

There was the beginning of a suppressed fury in his tone. I was wondering if I had gone too far. Mice should not try to be clever or the game gets too exciting for the cat.

I shrugged. 'Basic common sense, too much curiosity and, yes, I did study seismology years ago, but as for the spying bit, nothing there I'm afraid. Anyway, didn't you say that that sort of thing was contracted out now—to your organisation?'

'While it was an organisation, yes, but now, you see, we are a power in our own right, and a power must have policy and policy must maintain its secrets—at all costs.'

A quieter, more confident look had replaced the rising flush of anger on his face. My cigar had burned down steadily and the pale amber in the glass was barely a wetness in the bottom.

'One for the road, Mr Ashe?'

I nodded eagerly. Much as I appreciated the whisky, it was the time that I needed more. He knew this and it pleased his sardonic sense of humour to be able to give it to me. He returned with the glass generously full. He settled himself down opposite me again, placed the tips of his fingers together and spoke. 'Have you any idea of the size of this little operation here? Personnel-wise, I mean? We are a working strength of fifty men. Can you appreciate the logistics of this—supply, maintenance, disposal of waste?'

I made no reply. There was a feeling of prelude in this. The last act was about to start. He was performing. I was his audience, and now was the time for me to sit spell-bound while he set the pace. I wouldn't be required as an actor until the finale.

'This place was a mine once, worked out and abandoned long since. It was selected as a site for this operation because of its ideal geological situation and also because it fulfilled the necessary conditions of secrecy. It is remote yet accessible. Years were spent on its conversion for our purpose—slow, painstaking effort to create an underground observatory, living quarters and a system of perfect camouflage. This has been my project from start to finish. As you have guessed, similar bases of operation exist in two other places in East Africa. Ladong area now is quite differently conceived, being, as it is, quite a thriving and large coffee-ginning station—operative, perfectly functional as such, yet all the while the other work has progressed apace.

'Aringot in Tanzania is something quite different. To all intents and purposes, it is a project for the mechanisation of local agriculture. The ironic factor is that it was a world bank loan that financed its building—a centre for the assembly and distribution of agricultural machinery—and it was we who gained the tender for its construction. What dismay there would be in the halls of the United Nations if they realised that they had helped to finance the establishment of a seismological station that would contribute to the destruction of the very feeble power that they are still able to wield. We are almost ready, Mr Ashe. It is a moment of tremendous historical significance. Throughout time such moments have existed. Thresholds of change. Only a few have been aware.

The vast, teeming populations of the world have gone about their daily life, not knowing that the day was upon them.

'But I spoke of logistics, didn't I? My mind is wandering a little in the knowledge of power and the awareness of destiny. Disposal was one of the great problems of our secrecy. Our project here was at one time nearly abandoned, because there seemed no way to conceal the evidence of our presence. Consider the mole now, always discovered by the mounds of earth, trapped and destroyed by them. Even the most subtle and successful of human enemies, the virus, gives away the secret of its presence, by the detritus it leaves and the symptoms it causes—and how does all this affect you, my dear friend? Well, simply this. It's your disposal I'm thinking of—and your friends, of course.

'We solved it all quite simply in the end—the answer was lying right under our feet. The old mine shaft itself. Twelve feet in diameter cut down into the solid rock for a depth of three hundred and fifty feet. For years the excrement, rubbish and refuse of some fifty people has been deposited there. It has always been an efficient method. It is no time to be squeamish, Mr Ashe. The issues at stake are far too big to be influenced by the lives of a few worthless individuals.

'Consider now, I have here twenty guards, besides my professional staff. They are men chosen for their lack of sensitivity, for their complete devotion to the masters and the project, but even so, the years of confinement here have affected them. It is like a prison for them although all material comfort is provided. Once recruited here, there is no way out until the end of our project. It has been hard for some, impossible for others, some have died naturally here and some have been disposed of for one reason or other. Besides me, there are perhaps only five or six who have any contact with the outside world. What needs there are, are supplied from outside. I have women brought for my men. The tour of duty for the women is one month only, after that they are replaced. They are obtained quite easily locally, and then disposed of. An occasional dressing of quick lime and all is forgotten.'

Nothing of the horror of his words showed in his face. It was as if he were discussing the condition of his dogs.

'But I promised you a quick clean death and indeed you shall have it. You will suffer no indignity, you will all be killed cleanly before being thrown into the pit!'

He had already lost interest in me. I could see that his mind was beginning to move into different thought patterns. He glanced at the half-full glass in my hand as I stubbed out the end of the cigar in an ashtray. Like a perfect host informing a guest that the visit was over, he let a hiatus grow in the atmosphere between us. Years of response to this made me automatically drain my glass. I almost said the ritual words, 'Well I'm sorry but I really must be going,' but then the chill horror of what came next suddenly gripped me. Somehow or other I had let the small advantage I had gained slip from me and once again the game had gone back to the point where I had first met him. All I had really gained was a vague satisfaction to my curiosity and an hour or so of time. Well, that was all, but what had he gained? Nothing either.

Come what may, if that was to be the end he'd get nothing more out of me except trouble—even if the only trouble I could give him would be to mess up his beautiful Bokara carpet with my blood and guts as the guard cut me down with his nasty little automatic. I felt the painful thrill of anticipated action as I rose slowly to my feet. I looked round lazily, trying to conceal my intent. I was looking for a line of action, a gap in the line or a momentary falter somewhere in the opposition. I could hear the roar of the Arms Park in Cardiff. Minutes to the final whistle and two points down. Blood started to pound behind my eyes as I measured the distance between me and the guard. I looked at the pattern on the carpet between us. There was the line, there was the gap—where the hell was the ball? Come on! Pass, give it out, come on, you sweating, boneheaded buggers—heel! heel! heel!

I subsided back into the chair with my head between my hands.

'Now, that's better, Mr Ashe. For a moment there I thought you were going to be—ah—rash.'

I heard the voice remote and distant as if through a cloud. And then—in the idiom of my previous thoughts—an idea came crashing through. Extra time, the whistle was not yet blowing. Fall back, dig in and hold.

'Now surely you didn't think that I would—ah—let you go without achieving the object of this little *tête-à-tête*. To think of you dying for nothing would be too painful. I want you to know why you are dying. I would hate to think of you going, thinking that all it means is that you are a victim of international gangsterism. You will know, then you might die with pride, with regret, and with dignity in the knowledge that your death means something. Come, I will show you.'

He left the room with a nod to the guard who came behind me and prodded me gently with the barrel of his gun in the general direction of the door. I followed.

The room was of similar size to the one we had left, again cut from the solid rock. Where the former room had given evidence of the personal taste and comfort of its owner, this one epitomised another aspect of his character. It was economically equipped rather than furnished with a number of tables, wall charts and installed apparatus. I guessed it to be the very nerve centre of the operation which used instruments of remarkable sensitivity and resembled, in a humble way, the Large Aperture Seismic Array technique that was developed in the State of Montana when America woke up to the dangers of underground nuclear testing. I guessed that here, too, like the L.A.S.A. system there was a back-up service in compiling and computing. There was a great difference, of course; all this was not just for observation and monitoring, it was for action.

Odd bits of information came tumbling into focus in my mind as I looked around the room. I could have kicked myself for a blind fool as I remembered the significance of drilling and water pumping in relation to recent research in the control of earth-quakes. There was a half-formed question in the front of my mind. I was tempted to ask him if he had ever heard of the rather disastrous attempt that had been made by the U.S. army to dispose of contaminated water resulting from the production of nerve gases and insecticides at the Rocky Mountain Arsenal. They had tried to get rid of the stuff by dumping it down a two-mile deep well, and had got quite an unexpected result!

I took a look at his face and decided this was not the time to appear too smart. I knew that the slightest thing could change his mood and, as I said before, to cats, smart-arsed mice are expend-able. I turned away from him.

Closed circuit television screens flickered erratically, showing many different scenes. I even noticed the cold dejected black and white image of Tom and Anne sitting, hunched over, on a bench in a bare room. My heart went out to them. They looked so hopeless and defeated.

'This way.'

I joined him at a table where a large map of the Indian Ocean and Eastern Africa lay, permanently fixed. The pattern of markings was by now very familiar. 'There you see it, the home, the empire and the heart of the third world. No ideal in man can exist without its heartland, its *patria*. Men can live and die for an idea only when it is entrenched in the soil of their homeland. So this is what it is all about then—conquest and the establishment of a physical reality to our world.

'This is not the day of conquering armies, war and glory. That was the mistake of the latter nineteenth-century imperialists and the mistake of the scarcely different twentieth-century totalitarian ideologies. Conquest must be different. Military conquest has been tried over the ages and eventually negated by the sheer dead weight of its own shortcomings. Cultural conquest has succeeded in producing a bastard culture that inherits all the bad of both its parents. I think we agree about this. What then remains? A problem? Yes, but not insoluble. Total conquest is the only answer. We have two very good examples of total conquest. The United States of America achieved the total conquest of indigenous people—and, mark you, this was not a military conquest, although militarism played its rôle as it shall when our time comes. The United States exists by the total negation of anything significant in the ideas, customs and culture of the original inhabitants, by the reduction of everything to a myth, which can be manipulated until it means nothing more than a carved wooden Indian outside a cigar store. And the other example is, surprisingly enough, the other great ideology of the world, the pseudo-Marxism of Communism, which achieved and is achieving the same ends as its hated rivals by exactly the same means. Ironic, isn't it?

'Now both these miracles of conquest had something in their favour that we have not: territorial opportunity, inasmuch as they were there at the time; and minimal interference from outside powers. Just think, Mr Ashe, what the result of a mass movement by our people into East Africa would be. Interference from outside, prevention from inside and a screaming protest by all the peoples of the world, black, white, brown and yellow. Armed resistance to us, and the word injustice flung from every unjust seat of government in the world.

'So then, that is the dilemma that faced our organisation's planners. For many years the third world has existed in the minds and hearts of thousands of people and it exists in the dreams of millions of others. The millions of the world's desperate. At least five countries have agreed to the expatriation of these millions, provided those countries themselves are not involved in the conquest. Just think of the hypocrisy of it. They say, "Take our starving hopeless millions," but at the same time they say, "Don't let us know how, until it's done—and if we catch you doing it, we'll resist you to the death."

'Look at the map. Here is the answer! The greatest brains of the world have underlined the project in theory, data has been obtained from the world's most sophisticated computers and at last it is possible. Within two weeks it will be accomplished. Already in preparation is the greatest migration that was ever attempted by sea. The initial wave is already launched, fifty-thousand-strong. They wait in the Indian Ocean, under the cover of fishing and trading. Some are on observation vessels, some on luxury cruises, and they are organised, my friend, down to the last detail. This first wave are to be the administrators, the soldiers and the organisers of the new world. And when they have established their foothold, they will be followed by the hundreds of thousands of people who have nothing to lose in abandoning their hopeless existence in other lands, where over-population, apathy and ignorance chain them to a life no better than the most humble beast of the earth. From this clay we will build such eugenic stock as the world has never seen, a society that will mould the world, a power that will shake it and an organisation that will discipline it.'

He looked at me with a wide glazed stare. Hardly a sound could be heard when he stopped talking. A faint humming of instruments, and the steady rachet click of a chronometer made a bizarre background to the scene. He remained motionless awhile and then started to nod slowly, his eyes hooded with heavy lids, and when next he spoke it was almost in a whisper.

'And all this will be possible because of us; we who labour in the bowels of the earth. It is like the concentric rings that spread on a calm surface of a pool when a stone is dropped into it. The new society, the third world, will be the ring of completeness. So this then is how the stone will be dropped into the pool. Very soon now the centre at Ladong will conduct an experiment similar to ours here. There will be a controlled earthquake centred in two selected sites monitored from their station. Following that, Aringot will perform a similar operation, and if all these are as successful as I have been here, the data, information and technique will be computerised so that these three centres may move into the second phase of operation.

'These centres are not of random choice, each one has been

selected for its geological significance, they are the focal points of stress. They are like the three key logs in a jam—move them and a natural power will be released. Our years here have not only been spent in the creation of a seismological station, but in the patient ceaseless drilling and boring into the very heart of strata that have been patiently buckling and tensing for unknown time. And this second phase is ready, Mr Ashe. All three stations have reached critical depth. The setting and firing of the charges depends only on the completion of the Ladong and Aringot experiments. These major charges will be supplemented by well-calculated booster charges along the edges of the major Rift valley. It will be an upheaval of cataclysmic dimensions. Indeed it is impossible to predict the extent or duration of the shock waves, earthquakes and volcanic activity that will result. It will be a world disaster, predicted, timed and engineered to fit the will of man.

'Can you see it, Mr Ashe? Every valley shall be exalted, and every mountain and hill made low, the crooked straight and the rough places plain!'

His eyes glowed with a fanaticism, his voice had risen to a shriek. His whole body trembled with excitement. Yet, never once did his gaze leave my face—it was as if I was being scorched by its intensity. I was incredulous and dumbfounded. All the confusion and puzzlement of the last days began to resolve itself in my mind. At last I began to see it all clearly. This earth-shattering blow was to be dealt to East Africa; the count in dead and maimed might run to millions. Years of planning and work had gone on to make it possible. It was possible as the test at Busiira had shown, but this time cities would crumble and the whole region would suffer a mortal blow. Complete disruption of everything would follow; law, government and society would collapse.

'You have seen it. You have seen it now!' he shouted. 'You know it, you know it will succeed, and long before the effete societies of the world have recovered from the shock of this, the world's most potent disaster, help will be here, we will come organised and efficient. Almost overnight we will have gained control of the whole territory and all in a way which none can gainsay. It will be an act of mercy, and a sublime charity which conceals the greatest conquest the world has ever seen. Every harbour, airport and road will be under our control, every vestige of administration will be in our hands. And once this beachhead is established, nothing from the outside will come in, no one who does not belong will enter, and no one who does not sympathise will live. Our homeland will be established, and surrounded by this—the Ring of Fire—until the second ring is ready: the Ring of Control.'

I sat down on a stool near a table and looked at the map. It was as if it had already happened. I imagined the small coloured marks and dots erupting into a ring of fire that flamed and throbbed across the whole land. I visualised the invasion, cool, organised and efficient, destroying any feeble resistance that the completely demoralised African governments might offer, while at the same time fulfilling the function of mercy, feeding the starving, sheltering the homeless and comforting the distracted. It was indeed the most horrible face of evil—hypocrisy. Here would be the most horrible crime that man ever practised on man, and even if the cost were the decimation of the whole population, it would be demanded in full. The most horrifying part of it all was that I knew deep inside me that it would happen. Nothing I could think of, short of an act of God, could stop it once it had started. I knew it could not work for long—power and all ideology corrupts itself —but it could happen! It was happening!

The unmistakable prod of a gun in my back brought me back to the present with a shattering jolt. A few muttered words and a gesture later and I was on my way out. As I passed I looked into the face of Firaz. It was as if I no longer existed; he had already disposed of me. My execution was already a fact. I left the room as he bent to his work.

The next few minutes passed in a daze of unawareness. I walked ahead of the guard, my only directions being a series of grunts and prods along a dimly lit corridor, and then through a plain steel door into a cold bare room furnished only with a bench and crude table made from packing cases. My eyes had become used to the gloomy light of the passages but even so I saw the gleam of hope die in the eyes of my friends as I was pushed roughly into a room flooded with harsh glaring light.

CHAPTER EIGHTEEN

Anne's head lay cradled on my shoulder. I could smell the soft, animal fragrance of it. I think she was crying softly in the stark brightness of our cell. All that I had told them left no hope for us. They had both listened attentively while I had related the events of the past few hours. Tom, strangely enough, had accepted every word without protest or question, and now we sat side by side on the bench with a sense of futility and hopelessness descending over us. He was the first to break a long silence.

'Well, there's just nowhere to go but forward, is there? We sure as hell can't go back. As I see it, any moment now the sanitary squad will be around to dispose of the rubbish and there's just nothing to do but rush them. Nothing to lose—all odds against and any gain we make is something.'

I gestured to the closed circuit camera set high in the corner of the room.

'Every move we make is being watched,' I said. 'For all we know every word we say is overheard. We can't prepare or even plan anything.'

He stood up with his back to the camera, casually yet carefully so that his hand movements were hidden from it. He mimed the door opening, and crashed his fist silently into his palm, then carried the fist right on through. Whatever his intention was and what part we were supposed to play, I'll never know, for at that very moment the bolt on the door slammed back and it was flying open. His reactions must have been at a peak, for almost simultaneously with the door opening, I was aware of him flying at it in a blurr of movement as he flung himself at whatever or whoever might be coming through it. Unfortunately for him, and all of us, he was not the only one with quick reactions that night, for he ran straight into the clenched fingers of a beautifully timed karate jab which must have left him unconscious even before a second chop laid him, spreadeagled, flat on the floor.

Any ideas that might have occurred to my sluggish mind then

were quickly squashed as a booted guard stepped carelessly over him—an immense man, solid, pug ugly, with a deadly Biretta held in his right hand. He was followed into the room by two others in similar dress. One bent over Tom and tied his hands securely behind his back while the other did the same to me. Protest and struggle seemed pointless then, but a moment later I regretted my acquiescence.

Whatever form of despatch had been planned for Tom and myself, it became evident that Anne was going to suffer additionally. No attempt was made to tie her. Instead, she was picked up bodily by the big man as if she had been a child. When both Tom and I were secure, he put his gun away and slipped his free hand under her sweater. With a grunt of satisfaction, he moved out of the room carrying Anne on his left arm like a doll. She did not struggle. As I was pushed out of the room behind her, I saw the look in her eyes. It was one of cold blind fury and a determination to give nothing, not even the satisfaction that a struggle or protest might provide for him. I glanced behind me and saw that Tom was now on his feet, and stumbling along in our wake followed by a guard. I was glad that Anne was sensible enough to act that way and prayed that she would be able to continue showing such courage.

We came to a set of double steel doors. Very boldly painted in three languages in bright red colour were the words: 'Danger, unauthorised entry is forbidden.' Whatever the authority that was required for entry our guards had it for the biggest, who appeared to be in charge, placed a flat plate of metal momentarily against an electronic scanning device set in the wall, and the two doors slid back noiselessly on well-oiled rollers. He stood back with Anne while we were hustled in by our guards. Once inside we were made to sit on the floor, then my guard took another rope from his pocket and lashed my feet together. The rope bit into my ankles cruelly, but, like Anne, I had decided that dignity was all that was left, and I would show no reaction now whatever was done. Tom was being dealt with in the same way.

The room seemed to be roughly circular in shape. There was nothing much to be seen. The whole centre was occupied by a low dome of metal rather like a flattened version of an observatory dome. There were two parallel rib structures curving across the top of it which continued along the floor of the room like a pair of rails, set flush with the surface. These led away through the door we had just entered.

This then was the pit, with an opening device that seemed to be operated electronically, or by the presence of some sort of truck that would run on the rails. The section between the rib structures would slide open to reveal a sheer drop into a quick-limed oblivion! In my imagination I could visualise its yawning threat as it opened to receive our violently protesting bodies.

Somewhere nearby, there was a narrower, deadlier pit that had been drilled deep into the heart and bedrock of the region. This one was destined to receive a charge of nuclear violence that would cause thousands of violently protesting bodies to disappear into a fiery maw of gaping, heaving earth, ruptured to fulfil an insane plan of conquest.

Firaz had promised a quick clean death for us—a merciful bullet in the head before disposal in the pit—and I believe that he had ordered it so. He was not a man who would gain any personal satisfaction from violence for its own sake. His attitude to Smith's methods seemed to indicate this but I feared that this very fact, and his lack of further interest in us, would enable his henchmen to indulge their whims without fear of interference.

The slavering look of lust on the face of the big man and the grins of coarse humour that accompanied the remarks made me feel sick with apprehension for Anne. I watched, somehow fascinated, with a mixture of horror and strange detachment as she was untied and held between the two smaller guards. The big man gave a nod and the other two tightened their hold, locked her arms behind her, and thrust her forward towards him. He reached forward with a slow, deliberate movement, and tore the clothes from her body, pausing with a mock look of absorption, like a sculptor engrossed in a piece of work. He stopped sometimes to glance at me, as if for approval, as he went through a bizarre mime of artistry, sometimes adjusting a limb, sometimes fondling intimately. He was encouraged with roars of laughter and grunts of approval from his assistants, but Anne kept her eyes closed all the while, softly and gently shut as if she were striving for a complete detachment from the indignities they were forcing on her.

I felt a blind, baffling fury rise within me and knew then that passive submission had been a mistake. There was something about Anne in this situation which was beautiful despite all the ugliness, something vaguely vibrant in her passive rejection. I knew then that she accepted all that was happening to her because

she had also accepted the far graver certainty of her death. If Tom
had not been dazed and in a state of semi-consciousness, I'm sure
he would have resisted—this made me feel worse, and added self-
loathing to my anger. I saw him recover and could not meet his
eye as he gradually became aware of what was happening. He
recovered and muttered a baffled, angry cry to find himself bound
hand and foot. 'Of all the stinking, gut-rotted, lousy bastards.'
He aimed a kick with both tied feet towards the guard who stood
nearest him—one of those holding Anne. The lithe athletic
prowess that he had shown before was still with him. Even though
tied hand and foot his whole body arced through the air, pivoting
from the shoulders into the stomach of the nearest guard who was
lifted off his feet. He seemed to hang poised in mid-air for a moment
before he crashed back against the dome with a rattling in his
throat to slide senseless to the floor.

His companion released his hold on Anne's other arm and drew
his pistol. He moved purposefully towards Tom who had regained his feet and stood trying to find his balance. I expected to
see him shot down before my eyes but a curt order from the big
man stopped the guard. Instead of shooting, he merely kicked
Tom's legs from under him and added a few vicious kicks into the
small of his back. Then he went to a console where he pressed a
button which activated the sliding door on the dome. It slid back
noiselessly and revealed a dark, gaping slit of nothingness in the
clean polished surface. A faint, sweet, nauseous smell rose like a
miasma and filled the room. They spoke for a moment together in
a lilting Eastern accent that somehow seemed too gentle for their
purpose.

All the while Anne had said nothing. When Tom's attack had
caused them to release her she had slid to the floor and sat there
with her back to the dome, hunched over as if to soothe and hide
the violation to her body. But the big man was impatient and
wanted to get back to her. As they spoke together his eyes never
left her near-naked body. Were they arguing or merely working
out a priority of diversion? I couldn't tell. It seemed that the
intention was to throw Tom into the pit, alive as he was, but that
the smaller man didn't fancy the task. He kept glancing at his
unconscious companion who by now lay askew on the floor,
bleeding profusely from the nose and mouth and moaning faintly.
He wanted to shoot Tom first—just for safety! The big man wasn't
having that—I think that some perverted sense in him was getting

a big kick out of the idea of raping Anne right before our eyes. He wanted an audience and the more reaction we showed the better he liked it. I remembered what Firaz had said about the guards—disposal had become a ritual with them! I struggled to my feet carefully without haste and managed to edge myself over to the wall where Tom lay. I leaned against it. They didn't pay much attention to me. I was a broken spirit, a lame duck, no fight, a passive lamb who took slaughter without a bleat.

I caught Tom's eye and shook my head, willing him not to try again. But he was helpless now and he knew it. The chance that had brought him within striking distance would not be repeated. They were fifteen feet from us now and could not be taken by surprise again. We could only look on dumbly and shocked while they came to an agreement and proceeded with their ritual.

The horror of it became apparent all too soon. Anne was pulled to her feet. She did not struggle. It was as if she realised that a struggle would have incensed us further and brought on our death —that a struggle now would somehow take from us the only vestige of hope that we had. She was spreadeagled against the dome, half standing, half lying, and the last pathetic bits of clothing torn from her. Her head was turned to one side with her eyes closed gently; she lay just as she had been placed with her arms raised to about head height and her legs apart. With a curt order to the other, the big pug ugly turned to face us, watching intently. His friend began to undress, twittering away excitedly and laughing rather nervously. He was thin and lean and his nude body almost waxen pale, except where a black mass of pubic hair sprouted a dark erect penis. He took it in his right hand and walked jerkily over to Anne, with his left hand stretched out before him. He stood there near her feeling her body with his left hand and moving his right up and down rhythmically as he took over the task of watching us.

The bigger man undressed almost casually—he was absolutely confident. We were bound hand and foot and the guns lay on the floor close to the dome. He was right to be confident—we didn't have a chance. Whatever caused Anne to open her eyes at that moment I don't know but she looked over to the big man just as he turned towards her. Then, and only then, did she allow her fear to show. He was a big man indeed and now all his size and strength seemed to be concentrated in a terrifying angle of rictus that seemed capable of splitting any woman apart. I watched Anne tremble visibly as he approached her and saw the mixture of fear and fascination in her face. As if she were in a dream, she moved her hands slowly out in front of her to somehow lessen the force of him as he came up to her. In recognition of the inevitability of her fate, she grasped him and eased herself to him, hoping to lessen some of the indignity and violence—she closed her eyes as she did this. But suddenly, as if he realised the loss of initiative in this, he grunted wildly and thrust himself violently up and into her. I heard her gasp and cry out with a mixture of fear and pain and, as a man, I could not begin to guess what else.

The smaller man began to grope lewdly between them, crying out encouragement and delight, like some jackal at a lion's feast, nipping about and snatching at whatever obscene morsels he fancied. Anne was being violently raped with sickeningly powerful thrusts only feet away from the Stygian black slit of emptiness. Then the form of the ritual became apparent, as with rhythmic motion he lifted her body to him and then ground down into her each time moving nearer to the hole.

This then is what Firaz had meant. I couldn't help thinking how many of the local women must have disappeared this way when their allotted time was up. A last climax of emptiness as they hurtled to their deaths, each one a twitching, shivering mass of realisation. There on the edge of fear, the man could play out a gamble with death that would become a passion in itself. That last moment, when gravity effected a withdrawal that threatened to send him plunging into the orgasm of death, just as he reached the peak of his living, was his playing of the winning card. If Anne was aware of this, she did not show it. Now and then I could see her still face and it was expressionless in spite of the little gasps that she gave as he bore into her. I started to talk to her. I willed her to hear me. I kept my voice low and controlled so that she might hear. I spoke to her urgently and insistently so that she must hear. I threw my very soul into the quiet instructions I gave her. I felt Tom join me in the intense act of will that it took to get through to her. She was barely inches from the emptiness, and seconds from his groaning, mounting climax. He lifted her to him in a long, shuddering embrace, moved over the hole and released her with a long groan. She dropped from him as I acted.

The console was behind me under my fingers. I had my finger on the button, I pressed. The aperture slid noiselessly to a close and Anne slid to the floor at his feet. She had heard! I pressed again and launched myself forward in a long, heart-stopping leap, head first towards him. I felt my stomach contract as every ounce of effort I possessed drove me through the air head-first at the small of his back. I fell flat on my face with my head overhanging the hole—so I heard him screaming as he fell through the rotten, sweet smell to join his lovers. I wish that I could have seen him but the absolute blackness denied me this last sweet taste of revenge.

I knew that I should be up, I knew that the other would be on me and that I would be joining in the death dive with half my head shot away. I expected to go anyway. But I didn't. The other had dropped his gun near the clothes of the big man while he had assisted with the ritual. As I learned later, he had made a dive for it and gained it in his clutching fingers just as Tom's second hop broke his neck at the base of his skull.

But my face was buried in Anne's hair. I could feel the wetness of her tears now as she held me. All the restraint and self-possession that she had shown burst away from her and her body was wracked with the sobbing of violation, indignity and relief. It was a brief ecstatic moment of joy for me. I felt her arms about my neck and her hands in my hair as she stroked my neck to comfort me and I realised that our tears were mixed on her face and that I was sobbing too.

There was a moment of time, a hiatus, when all I could be aware of was the sounds of emotion and agony, the inarticulate murmuring of Anne, my own deep rasping breath, Tom nearby struggling to separate himself from the twisted tangle that had been one of the guards, and the rattling choking death agony as the other died, suffocated in his own blood as he lay helpless and unaided on the floor. And then a silence.

I broke the deep, sighing quiet, feeling that I was desecrating something with my voice, but knowing it had to be done. I tried to speak calmly and without haste and was rewarded as I felt Anne's hand go to my pocket and pull out the small knife I had there. In a moment I was chafing at my wrists to get the circulation moving again, while she went across to Tom and sawed at the rope that bound him.

In a strangely dignified way, without showing any of the revulsion that she felt, Anne pulled the big man's discarded tee shirt over her nakedness. I took off my jacket to put over her shoulders for she had started to shiver with reaction. I fumbled among the clothing and found what I was searching for—the flat metal plate that had been issued as a key to gain entrance. Tom was checking through the guns that he had removed from the bodies—I did the same with the Biretta that lay with the clothes and handed it to Anne. Then we were ready. In all of us I think there was a wild turmoil of panic that urged us to dash, and rush and escape, yet we forced ourselves to be cool and to think.

'When we go through this door,' I told them, 'we must be prepared for anything. If there is anyone outside we must be prepared to fight our way out of here. I don't think that there is any alarm yet, or we would have had the same treatment as we got in the strain meter room. The closed circuit television has not been active in here—Firaz was too squeamish, I fancy, to watch us being executed—but it might start at any moment, so let's move now before the situation changes. Once through the door, we move straight down to the left and then it's a question of getting out as soon and as quickly as possible. Anyone in the way has got to be hit first. This is no time to hang back. Anne, do you understand? You'll have to use that if necessary. Do you know how?'

'Yes, I think so—and I think I can, too.'

The door slid back noiselessly and we burst out into the passage-way to meet nothing but the eerie glow of the lights and the distant, steady hum of machinery. I don't know what sort of hours or working schedule were maintained there—it may have been the fact that it was late—but we reached the cell where we had been imprisoned, unmolested.

I took a moment to get my bearings and then led the way off down another corridor which ran back towards the rooms where Firaz had entertained me. I was hoping that there would be a way past, and that it would not be necessary to pass through his control rooms to get access to the outside. We were lucky—the lay-out of the passages gave a direct access between the various storerooms and the crater entrance gallery that we had come through on arrival. Only once did we take a wrong direction. Just past the entrance to the control rooms, there was a choice of two directions, straight on or sharply left, and I led the way left, out of desire to put as much distance between us and Firaz. It proved to be a wrong decision. We came to an open doorway through which we could make out what were obviously the living quarters of the majority of the workers and guards. We turned quickly, but not before an alarm was raised. From the first exclamation of surprise to the clattering of alarm signals and the flashing of red lights took only a few seconds and then we were being pursued by a disorganised rush of men from the quarters. I knelt and, putting the lever over to burst, pumped bullets into the mass of men coming through the door. There was a screaming and a hasty retreat in which at least two did not take part. I knew that it was only a moment's respite while they went back for arms.

'Go on,' I shouted. 'Take the other turning,' and moved to follow Tom and Anne. He led the way back and I occasionally sent a shot whamming behind us in the hope that it might give us more time. We rounded the angle and set off in the other direction just as a burst of firing directly ahead of us coincided in a deadly cross-fire with those who were behind.

Amidst the clanging of alarms and the flashing of lights there was an unmistakable hum of power as doors began to close automatically and cameras high on the walls panned back and forth like groping-eyed insects. As we ran down the corridor we saw that the doorway ahead of us was still open. It was locked back while a detail of men were moving some stores from the entrance gallery. There were three of them, and we couldn't tell if they were armed. I don't know what they thought for they went down beneath Tom's pistol like skittles as he burst into them, and then we were through just as the automatic safety system over-riding the manual lock-back went into operation and closed the sliding double doors.

We were in the gallery store by which we had originally entered. We turned to face the way we had come. Tom emptied the remainder of his magazine into the control panels beside the other three doors. There was a rewarding flash of sparks from each, but we could not be sure if the control mechanisms had fused with the doors in a locked position. We could only hope. At least now we had gained time and had only one doorway, the tunnel, and the manhole entrance to negotiate.

'Gareth, hold the door here while I take a look at the next one.'

I started dragging the heavy boxes of machine tools and spares against the door we had come through. Anne pitched in and for a few minutes we worked feverishly and then stood back to survey the handiwork. We could hold on here for a while anyway.

Tom joined us. 'It's hopeless. It's shut tighter than a turtle's arse, with nothing but flush steel to work on. Even the control panel's on the other side, I reckon.' He examined the barricade that we had hastily thrown up. 'Hell! you're not going to get behind that, are you? You'll be blown to hell and gone with the first shot!'

It was true. We had used the handiest size of the boxes for, even though small, they were effectively heavy. We had constructed a breast-high barrier of high explosive!

'But there sure is one thing more to try, and we may as well risk it as wait here to be picked off. You agree?' He had picked up a stick of dynamite and looking around for a fuse.

'But, Tom, with all this stuff around the lot might go up.'

As if in support to Tom's idea, the door which we had come through began to tremble under the impact from the other side.

'Nothing else to do I reckon. Get back as far as you can in that corner, we're goin' to have to try. It'll be all guesswork and gamble, but I've handled this stuff plenty! Go on!'

Anne and I huddled down in the furthest corner and watched him. He took two fused sticks and jammed them tightly into the channelling on top of the far doors. He shouted to us, 'Get down as close as you can to the floor and for God's sake cover your ears with everything that you can—use your clothes, your hands, everything.'

He was struggling out of his own jacket and sweater as he spoke. He lit the fuse and came back to us in a low dive and we all buried our heads under our arms with our hands clapped tightly over our ears. Even so, the head-shattering, nerve-jangling boom swept over us for an eternity. It seemed to reverberate around the chamber in an agony of repetition until I thought that I would go mad. But even before it was over I knew I was alive and I struggled to my feet to look through the smoke and dust to see that he had succeeded. A gaping hole above the doors had let them collapse outwards. Our way was clear. Tom was dragging Anne to her feet.

'Come on, honey. Let's get out of here, Gareth. Go on, get going! I'll be right behind you.'

I hustled Anne along and we made our way choking and stumbling through the ruined doorway and along the narrow tunnel. We edged past the small loading tractor that operated in the tunnel, and then we were below the manhole looking up at the stars. I pushed Anne towards the rungs. 'Go on, get up! Hurry!' She started to climb and I looked back to see Tom coming backwards through the blasted doorway. He called over his shoulder, 'Is the chopper there?' I shouted up to Anne who peered down through the opening. She nodded vigorously. 'Yes!'

'Well come back here, take this!'

I joined him to find that he was unreeling a small drum of electric cable. 'Take it, pay it out carefully—right out through the hole!'

I took it from him and moved slowly back towards the manhole. I could hear the sounds of the assault on the door and a wild unreasoning panic made me want to drop the cable and run. Tom had gone ahead of me and as I looked over my shoulder I saw him tearing at something on the tractor. I passed him and started the slow climb up the rungs, still paying out the wire. Anne reached down to help me from the manhole. I passed the cable to her. 'Take it to the helicopter.' I went back down to find Tom and heard the engine of the tractor roar into life. In the dim light I saw it begin to move. It trundled forward down the incline, slowly at first, and then as it gathered speed I saw him step off carefully, holding something in his arms. He came up to me and then turned to see the tractor as it hurtled down the slope and crashed into the blasted doorway.

'That'll hold 'em a while longer—come on!' He was carrying the tractor battery. In what seemed to be an eon of time we were all outside again. Anne was standing near the helicopter that lay crouched like a huge dragonfly under the moon. Tom handed me the battery as we got to it and climbed in. 'Pass me up the cable and the battery and then get in here on the double.' I came in behind Anne to find him fumbling with the controls.

'Pay out as much of that cable as you can and let it run outside. When you get to the ends, strip 'em.'

I worked in frantic haste, letting the reel run on the floor of the small deck. I could hear his voice as he talked away to himself. 'Come on, baby, come on for Uncle Tom, come on! You stupid, onery old bitch—give, you old bitch—give! damn you!' I had the end of the cable now between my teeth and felt the plastic strip from first the brown and then the blue. I knew what we were going to do now and I prayed that there was enough length to do it.

Suddenly, the motor coughed, once, twice and then stammered into life. Tom, with his hands on the controls, was grinning with a fiendish delight.

'Once we're over the lip of this crater, spark her off, son.' He inclined his head to the battery. I nodded understanding. We rose into the air with a sickening lurch that nearly wrenched the cable from my hands, but we were up and I still had it. In only a second or two I heard him shout, 'Now!' and saw the edge of the crater pass below us and felt the lurch in my stomach as we went down. I had an exposed end of wire in each hand and clutched a contact to the battery terminals simultaneously. Then all in a flash the cable scorched through my hands. The whole world split and in a roaring, flaming vortex we were thrown and propelled sideways and upwards like a leaf in a hurricane. In the bright moonlight we could make out the small crater below us. One moment it was there with a roaring orifice of flame where the manhole had been, and the next, it had sunk lazily and was collapsing inwards as if the whole underground complex had fallen in on itself. We heard nothing above the whamming, chattering blades of the helicopter. All we could do was imagine the ear-splitting chaos of sound as the secrets of Kaluli were swallowed and digested into the grinding, timeless maw of Africa.

CHAPTER NINETEEN

The dark smoked glass of the sky was fractured with a million pinpoints of light which grew brighter every moment as the setting moon dropped further towards the horizon. The stars leaped to brilliance as we turned in a general south-east line towards the main road to Kampala which Tom reckoned would be sufficient landmarking for him to pilot us back. A check on the fuel had shown that there was enough for about three hours' running. The journey, he said, should take about two. The flight deck was not very comfortable, for it seemed that the helicopter had been designed as a load carrier rather than for the transport of people. The instrument panel lights were the only illumination, and they shone into Tom's face, reflecting an eerie ghostly glow.

'Why don't you two try to get some rest?' he said. 'I can manage this little baby all alone and if I want anything I can holler.'

Anne leaned against me tiredly. She felt limp and cold with all the life gone out of her. I put my arm around her shoulders and she looked up. 'Gareth,' she said, 'we'll be too late for that dinner date,' and then she was asleep.

To think of sleep with my mind in such a state of excitement and turmoil was impossible. Images of the past day kept flitting before my mind. I did not want to talk, and obviously Tom was content with his concentration on handling the machine. Its rotors whacked above us with a regular monotonous pitch as he picked up the main road and swung roughly west to follow it, easing back on the throttles and tuning the pitch of his blades. We were flying quite high, determined that our way should cause the minimum of notice. But I suppose that I must have slept lightly, for it seemed no time at all before I felt a toe in my ribs as Tom stirred me awake. I looked out and saw Kampala ahead of us, about five miles away. The lights seemed to cling to the sides of the hills on which the city is built. The tallest of these, Kololo, was crowned by the steady red lights of the T.V. transmitter mast. I pointed these out to him.

'There's a flat area cut into the hillside there,' I said. 'It's used for celebrations and festivities now—you know, the usual old stuff, parades and tattoos to celebrate the latest coup or triumph or failure—but it was intended as an airstrip once. I've heard that the crosswinds are wicked there, but the helicopter should get in—they use them frequently there.'

'Okay, I'll circle it once to get the lie and then we'll go down. Now I want you to listen a moment. Leave nothing—but nothing —behind in this machine that can give any clue or lead to us. Even give everywhere you're likely to have handled a rub over. I've been thinking while chopping along; we're going to drop down there,' he indicated the Kololo airstrip, 'and then disappear. I don't want to make any explanations about this thing yet. I think we ought to get it done properly, if necessary, at Embassy level. I don't fancy ending up in any old hick town jail like that,' he thumbed down into the lustre that shone on the pearl of Africa, 'without benefit of a decent mouthpiece. What do you say?'

'I think you're right,' said Anne. 'I remember hearing lots of cases recently of people who've been imprisoned in some of these developing countries and have a devil of a job to get their cases heard in anything like decent time. Oh, I know it would all come out right in the end and justice would be done, but really, I don't want to spend the next few days in custody, looking like this, and feeling—well, after all we went through, I've had enough. I agree with Tom, let's just creep quietly back to the hotels and hope that nobody connects us with anything!'

'All right,' I said, 'let's do that, but I've got to warn you now that it won't be that easy; there's something I've forgotten to tell you—but let's leave it for now and just get the next step over with. Put her down, lad!'

The moon had set. Tom extinguished all lights and went down, as they say, by the seat of his pants. We landed with a lurching, sickening impact, but safely, and scrambled out. Straightaway, we headed down a steep bank and made for the lights of the club-house across the golf course. There was a faint sound of music coming from the club. It was probably some late local 'thrash' where the hard-core would still be at it. I looked at the time. It was nearly two-thirty in the morning. I realised that I didn't even have any idea what day it was. The others were no better—all sense of time seemed to have slipped away since we had first seen the helicopter come down on the Sunday evening.

In the gloomy starlight, I spotted a bench near one of the tees. We were near the long road that ran along the front of the course now and a walk of about a mile through the suburbs would bring us back to the hotels, but I wanted to talk to the others first. We were far enough away from the airstrip, so I thought that we could sit a while and catch up with ourselves.

We sat down gratefully. There was something so secure about the darkness that surrounded us and there was a strong feeling of companionship about it all that did much to make up for the feelings of hunger, thirst, and fatigue that we shared. But they had to be told.

'I don't think that we can go back to the hotel!' I could hear a pause in their breathing and a sort of exasperated sigh from Anne. 'Well, at least, not that easily. You see, we were presumed dead at that "accident" in the Mountains of the Moon Hotel in Fort Portal.'

I told them what Firaz had told me about the embassies being informed, and arrangements having been made for our 'remains' to be taken back to Kampala. 'For all we know there are bits of us lying around in the mortuary at Mulago right now! How can we just walk into our hotels and start living again as if nothing has happened?'

We thought for a while.

'Why not do just that,' said Tom. 'Walk in, collect our keys from the night clerk—don't forget there's none of us checked out—and just go off to bed. Chances are that nothing would be thought of it anyway. We'll see Anne through first and then pull the same thing in the joint we're staying at.'

I accepted that there was nothing else we could do. We were exhausted and just too tired to think. As it happened, things went smoothly. Anne's appearance aroused something in the night clerk, but it was not suspicion. She wore the sweat shirt like a nun's dress and after giving her hair a bit of attention, looked quite presentable if somewhat way-out. She looked very, very nubile.

I was too tired to bathe. I just flopped down on the bed as I was, making a mental effort to try to wake in time for the rendezvous that we had planned for nine the next morning. As early as we could we would check out and meet at the lobby of the International at nine, at nine . . . at nine. . . .

By ten the next morning we were all sitting together—cleaner, fuller and somewhat refreshed by the five hours' sleep. As if by common consent nothing had been said about the previous days. I think there was a deep-seated something in all of us that wanted to forget about those days—yes, days, for it was Tuesday morning —of suffering and fear. But there was the immediate future to attend to.

Anne made the first definite contribution to this when she said, 'I'm going today—I have a provisional reservation on the day flight from Entebbe to London. I rang this morning first thing. I just have a few bank things to do and then I shall report to the Air Terminal here at eleven in time for the B.A. flight at one o'clock.'

I felt a little disappointed with her decision. That she wanted to go just like that, I could understand, but to have decided so definitely without telling me was somehow hurtful. Then I looked at her face and saw the hurt was still there, that the injury she had received would be long in healing, that she needed the security, love and companionship of familiar things and she needed them badly now. I nodded approval and saw that Tom agreed with her decision too.

'Sure, honey, that's a great idea, that's just what you need to set you up again—get away from the whole damn mess. Really go to town, get some new gear and a hair-do. Rub shoulders with normal people for a while. But forget about that air terminal nonsense, you're not travelling on any airport bus. We'll drive you to Entebbe in time to get the plane. Get back here about quarter to twelve and that'll give us plenty of time to check in before the flight.'

Anne left to go to the bank with a little wave and a rather wistful smile.

'What about you and me, boy—what's next for us?'

'For me, Tom, I think that this is too big and too hot to handle any further. We either turn the whole thing over to the Ministry of Internal Affairs here—and my mind just boggles to think of the complications involved, not to mention the element of risk by personal implication—or we let it be done at diplomatic level from London. Put the whole story to someone in the Foreign Office and let them take it up from there, or do what the hell they like with it, without involving us at all. But one thing—we'll keep Anne out of the whole thing, I think she's had enough already, Tom, and raking it all up again won't do her a lot of good. So when she gets back here, we'll put it to her that she remains out of the whole story, right from the beginning, and this time—no arguments—right? And there's another thing, we must let her go alone today. If we can, we'll take a later flight. When it's all over we can meet up again and have a night on the town, but right now, she needs to be alone and wants time to forget. What do you think?'

'Well, that about Anne, yes—I guess you're right there, I'll leave that to your judgement. This London thing though, I think we should be careful there, you say we could find ourselves in a mess here with the government. Hell, do you think we'll be any better in Britain? That damned government you have there would sell out half the population if they thought they could shuck off the guilt complex by appeasing one of their former colonial possessions. Let's just get the hell out of it—send in the facts anonymously and then let them worry about it.'

For answer to this, I went over, point by point, the sequence of events that were going to lead to an earth-shattering cataclysm. I pointed to the city of Kampala, humming busily in the morning sunshine and asked him to imagine the consequence of a bit of anonymous information being ignored, or treated as the work of a crank.

'No, Tom, I've got to get to someone with this, and what's more, I've got to convince them—and that'll be hard enough to do personally, believe me.'

'I guess you're right at that and I reckon you can count on me for all the backing you want. Come on, let's see what the travel agent over there has got. No sense in going out in that heat.'

We walked across the hotel lounge, past a pathetic display of stuffed animals, into a small shopping arcade of tourist traps, baited with pseudo-Africana. Next to a dazzling display of butchered and flayed wildlife, cut up into key rings, tags and watch straps, there was a small branch of Equatorial Travel Agencies. There we secured seats on a 2.15 flight to London via Athens. It would get us in around nine at night, taking into account the time gain.

We stepped out into the cool damp drizzle that was London. Sheltered till now by the air conditioning in the terminal, the only difference I had noticed was in the plump pinkness of everyone, bulging with the confectionery of living and glazed over with their identical mass media look, but as soon as we went through the external doors I became sharply aware of the inadequacies of my thin tropical suit and then realised that Africa was behind me, away over the horizon of time and as remote as it ever had been.

We shared a taxi into town and then Tom got out at a favourite hotel of his, just dying, as he said, to get in touch with some Elsa who, if he was to be believed, was about to be screwed through her bedroom floor clear down to the cellar. 'I'll be by in the morning!' I had given him my address. 'But don't expect me early, daddy-o, because I've got a long, hard problem to solve and it might just take all night to get it down to size!'

I gave the driver the Paddington address and sat back watching the lights flash by with something like nostalgia for the long, sighing silences of the bush. I let myself into my rooms. Familiar things came rushing to meet me. I walked about, touching objects and seeing as if for the first time, the few good prints that I had on the walls. I selected *Eroica* from my records and went to my small kitchenette to put a tin of soup into a saucepan to heat. I walked about, letting the music wash over me and kicking off clothes as I went.

Mari, bless her, had everything in working order. My call to her from Athens had found her in. Central heating was on, cooker was working, but, damn, no hot water! I started muttering and cursing and came out from the bathroom to see her standing there just as she always did—cool, efficient and very lovely. She beckoned with her finger and I walked over to her. She led me to the kitchen, lifted my simmering soup from the plate and with a flourish poured it down the sink. She spoke with the same sweet sexy voice that she only seemed to use after five in the evening.

'I have supper ready, Gareth, across the passage in my place. I have a hot bath ready for you too—and, Gareth,' she slipped out of the door and looked back, 'I'm ready for you, too!' I made a grab for her, but she merely closed the door a little and said teasingly, 'I'll wait for you, Gareth, come when you're ready but please do put something on first—at least to start with!' and she was gone.

I looked down at myself—starkers as the saying is—and I realised that I, too, had a long hard problem to solve. And it might just take all night too!

The metamorphosis that Mari can undergo by morning is something of a miracle. I sat in my office and she brought in the things that she thought needed my attention. Outwardly, there was nothing in her small dark features that suggested anything but the most formal relationship. Yet, only hours before, she had been like a wild demented animal when we had been together. I could never quite understand her even when we made love. She would hold back, determined that she would reach her climax after I had. There was a stubborn streak of independence in her, even in passion. I never came from her without wondering who'd had whom! Still and all, she was a very lovely and refreshing person with a small, well-shaped body full of lithe grace. The game she played often gave me a chance to watch her coolly as she writhed and wriggled to reach the top moment only when she was sure that I already had. I would hold her tiny breasts in my hands and feel totally removed and isolated from the internal fires that consumed her. Afterwards she would lie still beside me and talk, deeply and with love, while her finger traced the hysterectomy scar that ran a vertical, angry weal into a jet-black, silky tuft of hair.

Nothing ever remained of this in the morning. She was all cool, remote efficiency—except perhaps in her eyes, hazel and heavy-lidded, I would detect a faint smile, just a hint of conspiracy as though we shared a deep, deep secret.

I dealt with the matters that seemed most urgent and scribbled off a number of letters that Mari would type for me. One was particularly ironic as it was a reply to a telegram sent from the British High Commission in Kampala regretting to inform of my death and requesting what arrangements would be required for my funeral! I wrote back suggesting that there had been a mistake and that a check with immigration would show that I had left, but not in the way that they thought! That would stir up something, but I was past caring.

I had just about got through with everything when Tom rang. He said he would be with me in an hour, so I started to make arrangements for the afternoon.

The first thing that I had to do was to ring a very old acquaint-ance of mine—Sir Gerald Manley Floud. We shared the same club in town and frequently met for lunch or a chess game after dinner when I had the time. He was a tall straight man of about sixty, a reserved and well-controlled man, whose friendship with me had grown steadily over a number of years. I had a great liking for him, for his judgement and for his sound common sense. I don't quite know what he got out of our friendship—there was such a contrast between us. I think it showed through in our chess games where, from his solid base of formal tactics, he found it stimulating to decimate the attacks I would make on him. And so it was with our conversation too. Now I wanted to meet him for lunch with Tom, to tell him all I knew of this plot, and to take advantage of his connections to get me to the top so that I could unload it all and feel free.

And that's just how it turned out. Sir Gerald was in, and when I stressed the urgency he cancelled an appointment he had and agreed to meet us for lunch at Cotts. Tom had come round, so after chatting together a while, Tom, Mari and I went off for a pre-lunch beer. I left them a while and put in a call to Anne at the number she had given me. I was told that she had left that morning for Chester and was not expected back for a week.

Lunch went rather as I expected. Mari had left us after her sandwich and returned to the office. Sir Gerald listened as I began the story and Tom supported it with confirmation. We did not wait for the customary after-lunch breather to relate it, but went straight in with the soup, through the Dover sole and on to the cheese board. By the time we were on the coffee and cigars, we had outlined the whole thing briefly and succinctly. I don't know what I expected from him—I don't know to this day what he thought deep down inside for, although he showed no particular enthusiasm, he did give me the benefit of long years of friendship and promised to arrange an interview for me that afternoon at the Foreign Office.

The day had turned from the bright, hopeful September morning in London to the dull grey hopelessness that is London on a wet autumn afternoon. Everything seemed grey: the buildings, the sky, the striped trousers adorning the elegantly crossed legs before me. And any bright hopes I had of being able to convince anyone with my story faded as I went over in my mind the improbable sequence of events.

But it began to look all so different in the austere but luxurious office of Douglas Barrett. There was something about his iron grey hair and deep blue eyes that suggested he might once have been a man of imagination, a man of action, one who was capable of seeing right into the heart of a problem and deciding on the line to take. But I found that the years of desk-bound administration had taken the edge from that side of his character. He listened to my story right from the beginning, stopping me now and again to check a detail, a time or an inconsequential point. We had, for reference, a fairly small map of East Africa before us and I tried to indicate the areas of our activity accurately. When I had finished and brought the story right up to date, he was thoughtful a while and then spoke, or shall I say delivered, his response and reaction.

'Mr Ashe, you will realise that all this is most interesting, and if I might say so, very well related, yes, indeed, most interesting. Now I can't really think why Sir Gerald wanted me to hear all this, but he is a man I have great respect for, his judgement has always been hitherto most sound, yes indeed, most sound. Now I am not going to ask you to make a transcription of this or anything like that. If you have been involved in any, shall we say, incidents that concern us here, then we will take up the matter in due course. I personally think, and mind you, this in no way reflects an official viewpoint, that if, and I say "if", you have, let us say, embarrassed the relations between government and another state, then it is beholden on you to follow a procedural . . .'

He went mooing on through twenty minutes. Sometimes he got up and looked thoughtfully through the window, but at no time would he let me have a further say. I had said my piece and now he was saying his.

And that's all it was. As I went down the stairs and surrendered my floor pass suitably stamped, franked and countersigned, I reflected that the whole business had been a complete mess-up from fiery, spluttering start to damp, fizzled ending. How could an administration of this size and significance be so stupid! Only twice in the whole story had I seen anything like life come to his eyes. All my fears and worries about the cataclysmic events that were to happen seemed to leave him unmoved. When Sloeder was mentioned, a flicker of interest lit his eyes, and when I told him of the ships in the Indian Ocean he interrupted and asked me to repeat it. But after it all, the whole gist of what he had to say was: 'You've blotted your copy book somewhere, old chap, and want to get government involved, but it won't wash, old chap. You get yourself out of any mess you might find yourself in. Try the old cock-and-bull somewhere else—we're just not interested.'

But he must have been a little bit interested or I had suddenly become very attractive in a funny sort of way for, as I left the building, I was sure that an unobtrusive-looking gentleman became my shadow and stayed with me for an hour or so. After that I could not be sure.

I met Tom back at my place as we had arranged and told him

rather bitterly about the way things had turned out. It was such an anti-climax that I felt really deflated—and it did nothing much for my ego either when he told me that he and Mari had a dinner date for the evening and that within a day or so he was off home anyway to get some of his affairs put in order.

'I suppose you're right, Tom, there doesn't seem much else left to do, anyway, but why so vague about going? What do you mean in a day or so?'

'Well now, boy, that's just it. I think I might get some action on this thing from my end. I'm going to give Washington a try anyway, and as for the day or so—well, now, that just depends on the way the cookie crumbles, and this Mari sure is some cookie, I tell you!'

He'd tell me! So that's how it was then. I decided, rather than be in the way, I'd go off for a bit of fishing for a few days to North Wales. I could start off in Clwyd near the Cheshire border. Well, Anne was up there and I might just go and look her up. But in the meantime there was the night. I had some thinking to do so I went off for a bit of a crawl round some of the old places I knew. And what with life being as it was I had a little too much beer through the night and, quite unsurprisingly, grew very uninteresting to anybody.

CHAPTER TWENTY

There was a dapple of green and yellow light on the slate grey of
the water. Sodden autumn leaves dripped from the trees above the
deep pool at Ysceifiog. There was a cold bite in the air that afternoon and it felt good to be away from London, even after being
there only a few days. It looked as if there would be a mist soon and
that meant my finned friend would get away. But there would be
time for a few more casts. I decided to try the 'butcher' again,
always good for this water. I reeled in and took off the 'Cochy-
bonddu'. This was a wily one all right and I'd had a couple of
glimpses of his silent shadow gliding where the water raced around
the boulders. A very light rain began to grow in the air, making
pearls of water on the tweed of my jacket and I knew that he'd
beaten me again for the day, but I was already planning for him
again as I walked up the slippery, muddy path back through the
woods towards the road.

By the time I reached it, the rain had begun in earnest, so I
walked briskly back the mile or so to Pentrefod and the spartan
comfort of the pub. I stayed at the Scyfarnog quite often and there
is something about its bare boarded, nineteenth-century look which
is very appealing on a fishing trip. There is none of the horse-brass,
ship-light, low-beam atmosphere that characterises so many of the
country pubs of the Welsh border counties. The Scyfarnog is a free
house and the owner gets quite effervescent whenever anyone
mentions coach and car trade!

So the day had not been bad—a good morning with the trout,
a packed picnic lunch and now the thought of tea in front of an
open fire, followed by a warm, cosy evening listening to the lilting
Welsh of Clwyd, and a few pints of draught Wrexham lager.
Indeed, life could be worse. I was disappointed about Anne. The
few hours spent in looking her up in Chester had been fruitless.
She had not even been there yet so I had left the address and telephone number of the pub on the offchance that she might ring
sometime in the evening.

But the call, when it came, was not from Anne. About ten in the evening, during a game of darts with '*dim ond ugain i gael*', I was called to the 'phone. After I had waited through a number of irritating clicks and buzzes, the voice came through quite clearly.

'Hello! Ashe—Barrett here. In London.—Yes, that's the one.—Yes, I can imagine. In fact I didn't expect to be in touch with you again either, but I take it you've heard the news.—Well, it had national coverage this evening, I thought you might have.—Not that it was a big affair or anything.—You didn't? Well, you see it seems as if there's been a bit of an earthquake at a place called Ladong, somewhere in Kenya, I gather. I was just wondering if you wouldn't care to come in again so that we might go over that little matter we were discussing a few days ago a bit more carefully.'

He did not say much after that. In reply to my suggestion that he might find it convenient to attempt some complicated biological experiment on himself, he became firm, even insistent, and then, throwing all pretence away, suggested that arrest pending extradition would be the alternative if I failed to appear the following day.

In spite of the tension that had built up over that telephone call the night before and, thinking of it coldly afterwards, I could see that my final remark to him had been a bit blue, he was in a surprisingly receptive state of mind when I sat down with him once more. We were not in the same room, nor even in the same part of the building. It was quite a different thing from the green leather chairs and the small atlas. The room was a functional operation centre that was obviously used for co-ordinating activities on a world-wide scale.

'Now, Mr Ashe, I suppose I should start with an apology, but I'm not going to. I think you will understand that we have to deal with quite a number of people who, to view them charitably, are a bit cracked and I think even you will see that your story sounded just like that. But there were one or two points that I was prepared to believe you on—or at least to check out—but the rest . . . Well!' He sighed deeply. 'So I've had you followed since you left—that is how I was able to get in touch with you so promptly last night. You've seen the newspapers about the Ladong thing by now?'

'There was a small account in today's *Telegraph*—nothing much though it seems—no casualties as far as they can make out. It'll be forgotten about in a few days' time.'

'Yes, that's precisely what's worrying me. Look, Mr Ashe, there's nothing for it now but for me to be perfectly frank with you. It is not easy now to do anything about this thing. Some years ago it might just have been possible to have intervened in this part of the world, and indeed it would be possible today—by invitation. But there's no need for me to tell you how unlikely it is that an independent government in any African country would invite us to send a military task force, however small, to their country. And then there is the further complication of a growing Arab interest in Uganda, and subsequent anti-Israel feelings, all of which are a keg of dynamite that could go up in an instant of misunderstanding.'

'But surely the United Nations Security Council would shoulder this responsibility. There are going to be hundreds of thousands of lives lost, and at least three member states face total collapse and conquest. If this is put in the balance against the possibility of stirring up trouble in the Middle East or offending some African military administration they must realise that they have got to act immediately!'

Douglas Barrett looked at me as if I were a child to whom he was trying to teach his A.B.C. 'There is possibly some effective purpose in the cultural and sociological side of the United Nations, Ashe, but their political and preventative side is literally valueless. I could point out to you a dismal record of failure if it were necessary. I'm sure you know all this already.

'Now I'm going to ask you to be very patient about this, and go through the whole story in great detail from start to finish. You might as well make yourself quite comfortable, it will be an all-night session. I've taken the liberty of bringing a few of your things from your flat in Paddington and arranged a room and bed for you here for the night. You might be needed at a moment's notice, and I'd like you to be on hand. I expect some high-powered company before the night is out and some very well-informed academic gentlemen who might wish to question you more closely on various aspects of your story!'

My first supposition about Barrett having been a man of action and imagination now seemed to be proved. The bored civil service mask had dropped and had been replaced with a keen and intelligent enthusiasm. He looked happy and I had the idea that the promise of some action had effected the change. All the sad feelings of disillusion that had followed my first meeting with him left me. His attitude was infectious and I found myself responding to him in a new way.

217

As the hours went by I experienced a tremendous feeling of relief that at last the terrible weight of responsibility was being taken from me.

At no time during that day or night do I remember feeling tired. Except for endless cups of coffee and sandwiches all idea of food was forgotten. A bewildering variety of people seemed to come and go. During the course of the evening I spoke with military personnel, with geologists and with seismographers—all had a serious business-like attitude which left no doubt in my mind that at last something was going to be done about the tangled and threatening situation that I left behind in East Africa.

A huge, illuminated wall map developed as the night wore on. First, those details of Sloeder's map which I could remember were put on. Every significant piece of information was added to it as time went by—even to the extent of plotted isotherms and isobars and estimated wind pressure systems, details of tidal changes and currents along the coast.

It must have been very early morning, about sunrise, when some developments occurred which seemed to bring everything together and change the situation from one of frantic information-gathering to one of dejected inactivity.

I was lying down in a small room, not sleeping but watching the aurora of the London sky blend into the velvety grey of very early dawn, when a courier knocked and came in. Douglas Barrett wanted to see me once more in the operations room. When I entered, he forced his attention from the pile of papers before him, and took me aside. He did look tired then, and there were also deep lines of worry drawing down the corners of his mouth. The grey stubble on his cheeks, and his soiled, crumpled shirt collar dispelled the illusion of calm confidence that he had shown earlier.

'There have been a few developments during the last hour, Ashe, and although from one point of view they're satisfactory inasmuch as they verify some of the details of your story, from another standpoint they evoke a new sense of urgency into what is still a very confused and complicated situation.

'The first is a telex confirmation from Nairobi. Williams was Langley, no doubt about that—it's required some very delicate handling at High Commission level, and an exhumation for orthodontic identification. Fortunately, when you first told it to me there were one or two parts of your story which interested me and I started enquiries immediately. The bit about Langley was one. The other was equally positive in result but rather more difficult to confirm, however. It seems that your Mr Smith and Mr Kopft did in fact arrive in Beirut and, it seems, left a week ago for Entebbe via Libya. This bit of information was rather more difficult to come by, but we have been fortunate that, although identities may be changed, a face like Kopft's is remembered everywhere!'

'Can't some form of extradition be put into effect?' I asked.

'Far too long a process I'm afraid, and one that would scarcely be worthwhile from our point of view. Still I'll get someone on to that.'

He walked back to his desk and spoke into one of a battery of telephones for a few minutes. I walked over to the wall map and looked at it again. All through the night the best brains of the service had wrestled with the problem and, judging by the serious gloomy atmosphere that hung in the room, had come to a confirmation of their worst fears.

Even then I felt like shouting at them, and at Barrett particularly, for the days that had been wasted. He must have sensed my feelings for he joined me almost apologetically. 'It's not only you I should apologise to, Ashe, but to those thousands I may have condemned to death.'

I turned to face him. All the anger drained away from me as I watched the heavy burden of responsibility weigh on him. 'No one could have done more than you already have, it's just a cock-eyed bloody world anyway!'

He smiled a little wistfully. 'Cock-eyed and bloody it certainly is, Ashe, but it's the only one we happen to have.'

'What about N.A.T.O.?' I began. 'Surely something . . .'

'According to our information, all N.A.T.O. forces have been put on emergency stand-by. Everyone is twitching, but no agreement can be reached on a line of action. It's the most terrible decision to have to make. Large scale intervention now could involve the world in a wholesale destructive war. Non-intervention could mean an oriental colonisation of Africa that would have equally disastrous results in the near future.'

'What about an appeal now to the East African Governments concerned to take the necessary action? Perhaps through the Organisation of African Unity. Surely they must see the seriousness of the situation . . .?'

'Three specially briefed courier missions are airborne right now, but it's a very, very tenuous hope. This is not something which can be shouted for all the world to hear.

'The last envoy we sent to Uganda a few months ago sat kicking his heels in Kampala for two weeks and then never even got near to the President. We thought that it might have been pique, or just calculated insult—now I'm not at all sure. When you were told about the influence in "high places" I'm sure that it was no idle boast. It's not the governments of those three countries, but the structure of authority which will block any efforts we might make. God! Ashe, when I think of it, even here in London, if anyone wanted to get through at high level urgently from even one of the friendly Commonwealth countries, I myself could hold him up for about a week if I were interested enough to do so. Don't you see, man? We're all but strangled with our own systems of safety.

'Unfortunately, this is the one aspect of European government that was so well taught in Africa that now the pupils excel their mentors, and when you complicate this situation with a few lessons that have been learned from the less democratic countries of the world plus a susceptibility to bribery, it's just ... just, well, impossible!'

Barrett stopped for a moment and when he continued, the feeling with which he had spoken was replaced by a tone of irritated frustration.

'Ashe, if you or I tried to fly an illicit pound of nails out of the the Middle East into Africa, we'd be checked, arrested and probably locked up for our trouble. Yet this man Smith, or Sloeder, manages to leave Beirut and fly through Libya to Entebbe accompanying a very significant load of "industrial equipment and spare parts". It went through customs without a hitch and was last seen by our man there leaving the airport with a military escort—destination uncertain!'

Barrett seemed to run down quite suddenly. He went back to his desk and sat looking into space with an air of puzzled defeat. I followed him, seeing his implication.

'You mean that those spare parts might have been the nuclear charges that will be used?'

'Almost one hundred per cent certain,' he replied. 'You remember the secret system of transportation that Langley was involved with? It fits perfectly to the description of Sloeder's merchandise. I have very little doubt but that right now preparations are well ahead for the arming of a number of deep drilled holes at all of these places.'

He got up to indicate the red circles and double circles along the scarp-forming faults on the eastern and western edges of the Great Rift Valley. In my mind I could visualise the massive fault, and picture the cataclysmic erupting, heaving, shuddering origeny, the like of which had never been experienced before in the history of man.

I checked my imagination before it became too vivid and encompassed the destruction of the cities, towns and settlements.

'Perhaps the preparations are even finished by now,' I said gloomily. 'Firaz was very confident about all being ready—perhaps that's what he meant: ready to receive the charges. But he did speak of two other experiments—Ladong and Aringot. There is a chance that the charges have not been placed yet, in fact . . . I wonder if we could get a professional opinion on this, because I have an idea that there was still a lot of calculation to be done in respect of the Busiira eruption. The data collected from each of the experiments would have to be correlated and interpreted—and final decision-making was not in the hands of the heads of the experimental stations. That decision would have to be made outside Africa.

'Judging by the amount of data, it will be a very big computerised task to process it all in terms of the other stations. So surely the final step of arming the sites will not have been taken yet. An error of a few miles could break the chain reaction which they hope to trigger and render the whole operation sterile!'

'That's it!' Barrett had brightened, even though it only meant a slender hope of delaying the inevitable. 'Come on, we'll get that professional opinion right here!' He started out of the room, once more walking with brisk purpose.

I had spoken at great length earlier that afternoon with Matt Spencer, a man of brilliance, with a world-wide reputation in his field of geophysics. I felt the usual trepidation of the amateur facing the professional while I tried to put my query to him. Barrett's hawk-like presence did nothing to make the task easier either, but Spencer was like the true professional in any field, completely at ease in his competence, without having the need to make others feel smaller in order that his own image should appear larger.

In answer to my questions relating to time and the compilation of data he merely shrugged his shoulders and said, 'All I can do is tell you the sort of time we'd take on it here—I mean, given a good team and men of my own choosing. I suppose if I were in their place I'd give it five days after the third monitored explosion. After that, it would be a matter of how long the other chaps would take over the setting of the charges—and I'm afraid on this one I just don't have a clue!'

'You mean to say that you're sure that the charges would not be placed until after the last calculations had been done?' Barrett almost willed him to agree. After only a moment's pause Spencer replied with a wide, open-eyed stare.

'Man, that's the very reason for the calculations! You see it's like this——' He looked at us both for a moment, and then visibly changed his mind. 'Yes, I'm sure!'

Barrett paused for a long moment in silence and then turned from him to face me. 'Ashe, this calls for a minor celebration and I think breakfast with a good pot of tea would be just the thing.'

Even now, I don't really understand the English mentality that looks to tea as the answer to every problem, but I went with him anyway.

'Hell,' I thought, 'this might be the time when I'll find out what this tea thing is all about!'

CHAPTER TWENTY-ONE

Barrett kept up the mood of optimism all through a breakfast that amazed me by its size and variety. His choice of tea left me with the impression that it had been brewed in an old tar barrel. He raved over its bouquet and body and flavour, but I remained unconvinced.

When it was all over, he looked round the small early morning café that was obviously a favourite place of his for such meals. He seemed to be well known by the proprietor and was favoured with very special attention, even more apparent, I suppose, because we were the only customers at that early hour.

'Now,' he said, easing himself back from the table with a deep sigh of satisfaction, 'I think we can talk quite safely here. I've been thinking a lot during the last hour and I've come up with something. I want you to listen and tell me what you think.'

I lit a cigarette and nodded agreement. There was something likeable about him, a naïve eagerness that contrasted sharply with first impressions. He began slowly and analytically.

'There were two big reasons for our earlier feeling that there was nothing we could do. The most important was the conviction that any interference we could have made at diplomatic level would have been held up or, what's worse, it might even have precipitated the very crisis we were trying to avoid. The other reason was the threat of escalation if direct action were taken by any outside force without official approval. These two factors are further complicated by a sense of urgency and the fear that there is insufficient time to put either into effect.

'I don't mind telling you, Ashe, that the high-level meeting we had prior to your being informed of the latest developments last night was grim, very grim. As well as the difficulties which faced us, there was a strong feeling in the meeting for no action at all! This feeling was expressed by some who had political capital to make by opposing anything. You know—"there'll-be-questions-in-the-House" type of thing; and it was also supported by others who, quite frankly, have had enough of our erstwhile colonial brethren and advocate the "stew-in-their-own-juice" line of approach. It was only with great difficulty that we managed to keep it open to action at all.

'We're scheduled to meet again at eleven this morning, so I have to come up with something good, not only effective, mark you, but good—good enough to satisfy even those who advocate no action.

'What I'm going to propose is this. That since Spencer is certain the charges are not yet placed, it must follow that the warheads themselves must either still be at the three control centres, or perhaps not even distributed yet. Do you agree?'

I thought about this for a moment then answered, 'Since the charges cannot be placed until after the calculations, I don't see where else. They certainly would not have enough charges to arm all the alternative "chain reaction sites" they've drilled, would they? They have to be selective and therefore have to wait until the data is available.'

'Precisely, so therefore it follows that if those charges were prevented from leaving or reaching the three centres, the threat would evaporate into thin air—or at best have to be postponed for a long time, and in this time, proper diplomatic contacts would be made and preventative measures could be effected against all the sites they have already prepared. In fact, any delay of reasonable length would increase our chances very favourably. Time, Ashe, that's what we need now. Too much time has gone into thinking and planning immediate destructive action, when we should have been planning on harassment to gain time. Do you see?'

I could see what he meant all right. He was not thinking of a complicated task force to meet strength with strength. Nor a great tactical plan to challenge their years of preparation and scheming.

A quotation came to my mind: 'An army's strength is its greatest weakness.' It is never closer to defeat than on the eve of victory! I quoted this to him and warmed to the idea.

'The organisation that Firaz represents must be just like that now. All its strength must be concentrated in this one venture and poised for success—that's the very moment to hit it. Right now, a small miscalculation or disruption should throw it right off balance, but that small thing has got to be in the right place. And the timing has got to be good, too—just like a good judo throw.'

He looked at me thoughtfully a moment then said, 'You know,

Ashe, I've been thinking about you! Our minds work alike, but you've got too much imagination, man. I could use you but not the imagination and sentiment that go with you. Yes, you might have made a good operator. Too late now, of course. A pity—I could have made a good man of you though, mind you, it would have taken training. My God it would, but I think you'd have come through!'

I let this sublime bit of complacency pass. I felt angry at the patronising attitude he was taking, but my curiosity right then was stronger and I wanted him to continue.

'But our work is cool, Ashe, even cold I would say. Too much imagination or emotion could wreck weeks of careful planning and endanger our whole set-up, a pity really. Still, you were saying?'

It crossed my mind to give him my experienced opinion of the unimaginative, bloody British Civil Service in action as I had experienced it in my years with the F.O., but I resisted the impulse.

'I was just thinking about the explosion we caused at the old mine in Kaluli. I suppose you would not call that a small distraction, but it was not in the right place—nor at the right time— so it was obviously ineffective because the recent "test" from Ladong went ahead as planned. Firaz might have lost a few men and a quantity of material, but that was all. The heart of the project, the strain meters and the deep shaft were untouched. If I'm any judge of calibre of these men, they will have learned their mistake at Kaluli and it would be damn difficult—even impossible —to gain access to one of these three critical sites again. The situation has changed now. They know that their project is no longer secret. It's obvious that they will ensure there are no further interruptions. Nothing short of a military operation could effect even a small change in the right place.'

Barrett looked triumphant—smug and complacent again. 'Now, you see, that's precisely what I mean when I say you have too much imagination. You just let your mind run wild, my dear chap. This has got to be simple. Listen, all I'm suggesting is this: these three sites must be blockaded so that nothing will get in or out of them. If the charges are at the three main centres, we can prevent them being distributed to the other smaller sites, and if they are not, we can prevent the arming of the three main sites. You see, simple as I said. We have it on very good authority that explosions at the three centres, terrible though they would be,

could not separately or together create the desired result. It is the
chain reaction which is important, the critical timing and triggering of the many, many smaller charges along the scarp edges—and
the resultant release of pent-up forces far in excess of the world's
total nuclear destructive output. That's the key to their success—
and it is also the weak link at which we must strike.' He paused
thoughtfully for a moment, running his fingers through his short
grey hair.

'God, if only we could pull this off—just think, all we need is
time and the luck. The first we've got, perhaps not as much as we
would wish for, but enough I think. The other, though, can only
be at best a fifty per cent chance. But the great thing is that it is
a chance—and by God we're going to take it! Even if it . . .'

'Look,' I interrupted, 'maybe it's being up half the night or
perhaps it's that bloody Lapsang Chou whatever-it-is tea that's
curdled my brains, but first you say you will not use any sort or
size of task force against these centres, and then in the next
breath you tell me you want to blockade all three tighter than the
proverbial duck's arse so that nothing can get in or out of them.
Just how many men do you think it would take to throw a cordon
around them? And what sort of reaction do you think there would
be from the Military? To make an effective blockade against these
places would take a couple of hundred men for perhaps a couple of
weeks or more. And you talk about my imagination being a draw-
back! Barrett, old friend, you are suffering just as badly from lack
of it!'

I could feel my face getting red. I was about to enlarge on my
theme when he started to get up. I stood up with him, face to face,
and noticed that the earlier warmth and frankness was now
obliterated from his expression as if it had never been there.

'Please, Mr Ashe, if you have to shout, would you mind not
doing it here. In fact would you mind not doing so at all!' He
lowered his voice slightly. 'Perhaps I should remind you of the
Official Secrets document that you signed yesterday and refer you
to the penalties for betrayal or disclosure of classified information.'

Nothing in the lowered tone disguised the seriousness of his
threat. The proprietor of the cafe, as if in answer to some dog
whistle, stood at his elbow.

'It's quite all right, Carter, I think Mr Ashe has finished now.'
He looked askance at me. I nodded and Carter withdrew to his
kitchen or kennel, depending on how you viewed him. Barrett

remained standing, he put out his hand. 'I'm sorry about all this, but you see we just can't afford to take any chances—can we?'

I considered a moment and while one side of my mind accepted the rationality of what he said, I still felt piqued. I was tired of carrying the weight of responsibility and wanted to get far away from it all. I decided I'd had enough. I answered as shortly as I could. 'Sorry, but I got a bit worked up there. Nothing further you want me for now, is there? Well then, I'll say goodbye.'

I took his hand, and met his gaze quite directly.

'Just as I said, Ashe, a pity—a great pity—you'd have done well for us. Before you do go, I think I owe you our deep thanks for the splendid co-operation yesterday, and for the valuable help and suggestions. There is one thing I'd like you to do for us. Would you mind?'

I nodded my acquiescence, feeling rather sheepish.

'Will you sit down and listen while I explain a bit more fully before you start indicating what you think is wrong with my idea? Perhaps we might have some more tea? No? Oh well, I don't suppose you'll mind if I do—I say, Carter!'

I hailed a taxi just outside the café and got in feeling a lot cooler after my outburst with Barrett. I sank back into the seat and gave the driver my Paddington address. The heating in the car was just a little too high for comfort, but I was thankful for the morning had the brisk cold of September and as usual I found myself not dressed to cope with the whims of the British climate. I felt irritated at myself for getting at Barrett that way, but there was something so bloody complacent about his typical Anglo-Saxon attitude.

As the taxi prodded its way through the early-morning shoppers and commuters, I began to wind down a bit more. An indifference induced by the heat came over me, and I began to see that Barrett, for all his faults, was right, and in fact his solution was the only one that could be used. I had felt a little foolish when he had gone into the details of his idea. He hadn't been able to suppress a smirk when he pointed out to me that the blockading of the three sites would not take anything like the number of men I had suggested. In fact, he had visualised only about six people for each, pointing out the remoteness of the places and the fact that, without exception, they were accessible by only one lonely ill-kempt road.

I thought that I might have deflated him when I reminded him that air transport in the form of helicopter was the method used in Kaluli, but he had obviously thought of this and had even counted on it in his outline plan saying, 'If they use helicopters, Ashe, it will, if anything, make the task easier and more certain. Each group will be accompanied by a ground-to-air missile, the design of which we owe to our "Black September" friends. They planned to use it here in London only a few months ago. They had it by courtesy of, let us say, a country that is known for its indiscriminate sale of such things and one which I fervently hope will suffer the results of its own indiscretion someday.'

He had openly shown his disgust then and I had no difficulty guessing the country he meant.

'Anyway, their recent bit of ingenuity just fits our requirements for this operation. It breaks down into a number of components which could be innocent and genuine tourist equipment, but when assembled it may be used against even the largest aircraft. Very small range of course—hardly eight hundred yards—but very effective.'

Before we finally parted he had outlined two other aspects of the plan which not only increased its chances of success but also simplified the whole operation. The first was the fact that the blockade would not have to be total because the 'pay load' when it was moved would be very easy to identify. The method of transporting the warheads was apparently still the same as that used at the time of the Langley scandal and it had been used recently by Smith to move them from the Middle East to Entebbe. It was quite easy to spot once one knew what to look for because it was so bulky a method that it could not be moved unobtrusively. It required loads some thirty feet long and six wide. The second factor was that the operation was to be undertaken by 'private agencies' who knew no more nor less than what they were told to do; that being to make sure those loads never arrived at their destinations. Each group would not know the reason nor of the existence of the others so that, in the event of their being discovered, nothing could be divulged to make international complications.

I had baulked a bit over the 'agencies' bit but he had assured me of their existence and their willingness to undertake such work. 'Rest assured on this—such "agencies" are available to our use, too, and that brings me to the one other thing I'm asking you to do for us.'

I had a moment of stomach-knotting panic. 'You're surely not suggesting Pipiras for this venture?'

'Oh no,' he replied. 'No, no, nothing like that. Do you really think that you . . . well, never mind now. No, Ashe, what I want you to do is make yourself available for a briefing with these groups—separately, and of course with the maximum security precautions which, I guarantee, will leave them unknown to you and you unknown to them. I want to get this scheduled for tomorrow at three different places and times. Could you make yourself available?'

I had agreed of course. What else when he had concluded our talk on such a serious note?

'This operation, as I said, might give us a fifty–fifty chance of success. It's our only chance and I don't have to tell you what failure will bring. Everything, even the slightest bit of information you can give these groups, particularly in response to their questions, will be of value and might just turn the thing our way. I've got a hard day ahead, Ashe, trying to convince others that this thing must be done. I'm confident I can do it, but it won't be easy, and the security will be one of the worst headaches we've had for years. It would be disastrous if any of this leaks to the public now. One irresponsible newspaper account would blow it all wide open to an international panic that no country can afford.'

We fixed a contact time for the following morning. Short of going back to Africa to help, I was prepared to do all I could. Hell! I was glad enough to be getting out of it all and, unlike Barrett, I've got faith in the ability of the human society to rise above the mad, bloody rat race they've been led into.

As the taxi dropped me off, I looked back along the crowded, frantic street leading to Paddington station and for a moment allowed myself the weakness of seeing just what it was that made men like Firaz believe that nothing short of a completely new start could solve the tangled, hopeless riddle which man had got himself into. They were not so wrong on theory—it was just their method that was so abominable!

I let myself into the office and cut short my musings with a few home truths: *Great stuff, Ashe! A bit more of this thinking and you'll convince yourself that Smith and Kopft are just a couple of frustrated idealists at heart. Their only concern is the eventual good of humanity! Balls, Ashe! Barrett is right—too much bloody imagination that's your trouble!*

Mari looked up as I entered. She was busy over a fat folio and had a 'not-at-home' look in her eyes. Two little creases between her brows clearly indicated a preoccupation with something that had nothing to do with me or my troubles. One of Barrett's sublime ignorant millions, I thought! I leaned down and peered into her face.

'Anything for me?'

A brief nod of recognition, a slight, whimsical twist of a smile and, 'Nothing you could use right now by the look of you!' And then she was back into her work, as if I didn't exist. I say as if because there was nothing she could do to conceal the fact that the two furry little bunnies that were her breasts suddenly developed pointed noses, but then perhaps it had been the cool draught of air from the door which I'd left open.

As if she was aware of my thoughts, without looking up, she added, 'Do please close the door, Gareth. As you go out!' The tone of voice convinced me that what I had taken for absorption with her work was in fact a studied indifference. The chill was not from the door, but from the icy reception that I was being given. I knew her well enough, and women in general, too, not to try to sound her out on it. She'd simmer for a while and then come storming through with whatever was on her mind. I could take it from there. But she must have been nearer to the boil than I figured because, as I walked to the door, I was informed by inference, tone and some carefully chosen words that the stupid American oaf I had introduced her to had called long distance the previous evening and would be calling again later in the morning and also that a rather seedy lady of perhaps 'middle age', grey or blonde—she couldn't remember which!—was waiting to see me in my office next door.

Even taking into account that Mari was feeling bitchy that morning over something, and obviously her getting to know Tom hadn't sweetened her any, I was hardly prepared for the sight that met me as I went into my office. When I first saw her I was so surprised that I must have stood for a moment, dumbfounded. Anne was dressed in a light woollen suit, a pale sagey-jade mixture that reflected the subtle light tones of her hair. She had turned to face me still holding something from my desk that she had been toying with. She looked a vision of poised, quiet comfort, in spite of the round splash of red costume jewellery on her right shoulder. She was cool, calm and confident with the suggestion of dramatic excitement like Hausner's Penelope—a woman involved with the small unstable items of life contrasted by the round red ball of perfect creation!

She did not get up. I hardly expected her to, so involved was I with my image of her, but it made me feel awkward and strangely embarrassed to try to suppress the urge to hold her lovingly in my arms. If she had moved then, or acted with some spontaneous impulse to meet my feelings half way, it would have made the meeting easier, but, as it was, all I could do was mumble something about how well she looked. Indeed, the tired strain that had marked her appearance during our last days in Uganda was not so apparent.

It was a very slow and gradual process to bring back any warmth into our relationship. I felt a stupid clod. Nothing I could say seemed to hang together and somehow I could stand outside myself and see that I was being obtuse. There was a tension in her too. For a while I had been too occupied with my own feelings to notice, but as we settled down and I told her what I could about the result of my interviews in London, I noticed a marked reluctance on her part to think of our recent experiences—and then felt a double fool for being so crass as to remind her of it.

She changed the subject rather pointedly and told me how she had spent the last week visiting the family and telling them of her brother's death. It must have been a very trying time for her.

This, following the traumatic shock she had undergone, was enough to subdue anyone—and yet there I was, silently rebuking her for lack of spontaneity on seeing me again!

The realisation of it all changed my whole attitude to her. I felt tender and wanted to protect her from her memories. I wanted to tell her I loved her, I wanted to hold her tightly and keep the whole ugly world from ever hurting her again. I could see then that it would be a long, long time before she would ever jump up spontaneously and leap into the arms of any man. I reached out and took her hand in mine.

'We never did make that dinner date, did we?' There was a momentary look of alarm in her eyes, I could almost feel the tension in her hand. 'Anne, Anne, look at me. Don't you see—I understand.' I felt almost choked with the emotion of trying to get through to her and then, gradually, warmly, she responded and I felt the tension drain from her.

'Yes, Gareth, I think you do.'

'I tried to find you in Chester,' I said.

'I never did intend going there. Oh Gareth, try to understand —I felt so terrible, I just wanted to be away from everyone and everything that could remind me, and then after a few days I felt so lonely in my misery. I tried looking up friends and things like that, but I kept thinking of you and missing you, and I realised that it's only you I want to be with now.'

I moved her closer to me and held her head against my shoulder, kissing the soft, fresh fragrance of her hair.

'I've loved you, Anne, ever since . . . oh, for years and years— since the day you fell down in the school yard and I bandaged your elbow with my handkerchief and spit!'

'Since I what?' Anne turned her head to look up at me, puzzlement and inquiry in her eyes.

'Well now, you were much younger then—different name, too, and, come to think of it, a bit skinnier and a shade darker, but what I mean is . . . You are everything I ever did love and you remind me of the young feelings of love—the total filling of my heart, the wanting and the not wanting, the pride in knowing you love me and the feeling of confusion when I think about it. That's been the trouble all along, I am afraid of this confusion, Anne, and afraid of the hurt it brings.'

'Loving can never bring hurt, Gareth—real love I mean. To think so is to go against the very meaning of the word. But you have been hurt, haven't you? I can see it now, I can understand that morning in Nairobi, and yes, I can see how love might bring hurt too.'

Then somehow I found the positions reversed. I had started out trying to comfort and protect her but suddenly felt comfort and protection in her arms. With that deep intuition that some women have she had guessed, not all the details but she was aware of that ruinous moment that at a stroke had ruined my career, crippled my body and twisted my mind away from the norms that allow men to settle, live in houses, have children and generally find a contentment in what for me is nothing but a living hell of frustration and bitterness. In that moment of violence so long ago really, but so close in time to my heart, I had seen my woman, my flesh, my heart and my soul, my most beautiful, lively, loving Fona become a nothingness of tattered flesh in a death that should have been mine.

I felt my tears in Anne's hair and heard her cry quietly with me and for me. She looked up through stranded hair and eyes that were sad with tears.

'I should have guessed before, my poor dear Gary. Do you want to tell me about it?' I heard her through the pain-filled memories that I had managed to shut out from my mind for so long and answered her as gently as I could.

'Not now, but sometime I will.'

I struggled with the trembling feelings that made me feel so weak and vulnerable and, holding her away from me at arms' length, smiled down into her serious, concerned face and said, as lightly as I could, 'I think we could do with a long, long time together, just you and me, away from everything. I know just the place, will you come, Anne? Two or three days more should be all that's needed of me here and then we'll go. Miles and miles from everyone where not a soul will know us. Will you come?'

Her eyes searched mine momentarily with a questing, roving expression that was both childlike, wanting assurance, and at the same time full womanly knowing—and then she was back in my arms agreeing, laughing, crying and planning, all in a flurry of small half-gasped phrases. We sat holding hands and time seemed to lose any meaning in the joy and wonderment we found in each other.

When at last she left, about noon, I watched her taxi until it turned a corner out of sight and all the while gazed at her, her contented smile as she waved through the rear window. For the first time in such a long time I had hope and a feeling of joy about the future. I went inside again and suddenly felt a feeling of loss and strange loneliness when I looked at where she had sat. In my imagination I could almost hear her voice superimposed on the subdued noise of the traffic in the street outside.

I began to think that I should never have let her go then, that we should have just acted on the impulse and left immediately, but I realised that I would not be perfectly happy until I had discharged my promise to Barrett. Even if I managed to slip out of London unnoticed, I would always feel that at any moment someone might find me and spoil the idyll that we had planned. After all it was little enough he'd asked really. It would be a tiresome day no doubt, having to go through all the details three times more, and no doubt the questioning would be exacting too, but nothing that would cause me any harm beyond the stomach-knotting fear and dread I felt whenever I let my mind dwell on it.

So the very fine edge of euphoria that Anne had raised in my mind was somewhat blinded when Tom's call came through. I took the call in Mari's office. Nothing seemed to have changed her mood through the morning. She carried on with her work as if I didn't exist. The line was perfectly clear, and for a moment I thought Tom might be calling from just around the corner and not across thousands of miles of the Atlantic. After the usual pleasantries and a lot of oblique references I was able to gather that his experience with some department of the Intelligence Agency had been similar to mine, except that he roused a lot more sympathy with his first attempt than I had—perhaps Americans are more imaginative! The report of the earthquake at Ladong had of course been the final factor to convince them, but, just like London, there had been an impasse when it came to any definite action being taken. I suppose it must have been even more difficult for the Service in America to work out any plan of interference because their activities in Africa are watched with even greater suspicion than Britain's.

Without saying it in so many words, I hinted that something was going to be attempted from London. It was not easy to communicate this at first, but we gradually managed by reference and inference so that a casual listener would have no idea what we were talking about. Even Mari, used as she was to oblique telephone calls, gave me a look that suggested I'd finally blown my head!

Much of what Tom was telling me I expected anyway, and didn't really have all my mind on what he was saying until towards the end of what seemed to be a pointless and, at £1 a minute, expensive account of his latest sexual exploit, I suddenly became very attentive to what he was saying.

... 'so after all the fancy come on she screwed just like any other dame—hell, I'd thought that at last I was on to something different. But the big thing is that it was right there that it came to me—just as I gave it to her you might say. Gary boy, there's somethin' been starin' us in the face ever since we went up to Fort Portal, and we just never saw it. Now I ask you—how in all hell did those punks who did for Mike get on to us in the first place? Eh? I want you to give this all you've got, boy, 'cause you and me we're goin' calling on a certain Mr Fletcher in Kampala. Remember the guy? Boozed-up, cheery sort of bugger? I reckon he'll be able to help us 'cause somebody in that lunch party must have called out the hounds.'

'Now wait a minute, Tom . . . ' I started but he cut me off.

'Just listen, boy, you can do all the talking you like a couple o' hours from now. I'm at Kennedy Airport right now and reckon on being in London early evening your time. Just sit tight there till I show up and tell that cookie Mari to get on her crumble outfit.'

'Now listen here, Tom, if you think that you're getting me back into that bloody . . .'

I was talking to a piece of dead plastic in my hand—I felt furious! Now that Tom was coming, I supposed he could be a great help at the briefings scheduled for the next day, but as for the stupid simpleton thinking that he could get me involved any further into the mess . . .! I was just about out of it now and nothing he could say or do was going to change my mind. There was Anne and me and the future—just that. I was about to become one of Barrett's ignorant millions and if ignorance was the price to pay for content-ment then I was prepared to swop all the discomfort, pain—excitement and thrill?—of my last few years, to get a piece of it.

I turned to Mari who had dropped her pose of detachment long enough to give me an inquiring look.

'He's coming back here,' I said. 'He's due to arrive this evening.'

She seemed to simmer with anger then and said sharply, 'Well, you can tell the Lone Ranger from me that he had better not bring his horse anywhere near my paddock—I'll—I'll nobble it if he does. He's ridden his last rough ride over my fair acres!'

In spite of her cynical words, there was something very poignant in the way she spoke. I could see Mari had been hurt. I felt that she'd taken a fall somewhere and I guessed Tom's 'lay 'em and leave 'em' approach to life had a lot to do with it. I visualised her for a mo-ment, so sensitive in love in spite of her detachment. I could under-stand her although I knew that I had never really got to the real raw woman in her. I looked long and thoughtfully at the visible acres of her that she had mentioned and it came to me suddenly that life could never be easy. There I was within inches, you might say, of taking fate by the forelock and getting some order and sanity into my life. I loved Anne more than any woman alive I could think of—and she loved me too, of that I was sure. Why was it then that I felt my stomach contract and a fullness in my throat that made me want to swallow as I saw Mari return my look with a frank eye-locking stare? Why was it that I felt the warm upward surge of thrusting desire when she walked slowly towards me?

She came like a sloop, port quarter to the wind, cleared for action under full sail, trembling, it seemed, with restraint as the helm held her—and then somehow the images got all mixed in my mind. She was rolling acres, and sailing ships, and soft cuddly bunnies, and svelte, silky pussy cat mewing and moist against my mouth. We seemed to float to the couch under the window, and I found myself beneath her. This was a new Mari somehow—who was not waiting for anybody or anything. No dramatic pause for my Mari now as I met her pounding hips with mine and put my hands to her breasts that were suspended above me.

Through a shimmering haze of burning urgency I heard her cry out and she arched in triumph. She was Diana the huntress, the goddess. Her own body was the bow that drove the shaft deeply and true into the quivering gold of herself—and I, the willing dart, felt myself sink into the throbbing, pulsing mystery of her, lost in the trembling taste of her mouth, the animal smell of her skin, the sound of her gasping breath and in the sucking violence of her tense, taut body.

Afterwards, lying somewhere between sleep and waking, I thought of her. She had used me—perhaps to balm the hurt she was feeling, perhaps to revenge herself on an insensitive Tom, or perhaps, feeling that she could not beat the widespread cult of hedonism, she had decided to experiment in sensual abandon. Whatever the reason, I did not resent it. In fact, I was grateful to serve her as she must so often have helped me. Her need was a desperate human loneliness, a desire to unite and thus share the burden that loneliness and sadness sometimes brought. Thus thought the altruistic Ashe as he tried to adjust his shortcomings and still come out of it all as a splendid chap! The other part of me sighed deeply. She'd been wonderful, spontaneous, exciting and so thoroughly unpredictable, better than ever before . . . ever? Well, aye, all right the hunter is going home from the hill. Too much hill you've had, boy! But I never did get to the top. There's still a chance though, fifty per cent chance did Barrett say? Good odds is that. What the hell do you want anyway—jam on it? And I slipped into a sleep, troubled, I remember, with dreams.

CHAPTER TWENTY-TWO

No one likes to feel that he's weak-willed. There is something satisfying about making a decision and sticking to it. It gives people a sense of control in their lives, without which they just wouldn't go on living.

So, thousands of feet above the Sahara desert, as I looked down from the window of the plane relentlessly moving south, I tried to convince myself once again that it was by my own decision that I was there, on my way back to Uganda and scheduled to arrive in another three hours. I like to think that I made the choice.

The briefing of the three teams had gone as planned, in fact rather more smoothly than planned for Barrett, surprisingly enough, had welcomed the addition of Tom's views. After the usual preliminaries of secrecy and a very concentrated few hours with some prominent vulcanologists, we both faced the three groups who were contracted to fulfil the mission that Barrett had planned. I gathered that they would have about a week to prepare and then would become operational, spreading out from the three East African capitals, Nairobi, Dar-Es-Salaam and Entebbe. It was a lot easier to deal with the Entebbe group because naturally we knew more about the Uganda set-up, but the other two had the advantage of a local knowledge about the countries they were to operate in. It was a tiring day, however, although Barrett had done a supreme job of organising it all. I had been labouring with the disadvantage of a supreme hangover—the result of the previous evening with Tom. He'd done some great talking trying to convince me to accompany him back to Uganda though I had remained unmoved all through the evening. However, it had taken a lot of beer to convince him, on my part, that it was all better left in the hands of the professionals.

It's a great place to think in—an aeroplane, I mean. I could feel the slight vibration of the huge jet engines through my forehead, touching the glass of the windows, and the subdued hum of them in the pressurised cabin was making people sleepy. Lunch had been cleared away, the cabin staff were taking a momentary break after the brisk activity of the lunch hour and Tom was somewhere up back with them, developing a theme he had started earlier with one of the hostesses. I could see the vast veinous system of the Nile below me, looking just like rain runnels in a pile of sand. There was a light ochre tinge in the air that seemed to spread right up to the rarefied atmosphere we were flying in. The sky was a wash of virgin blue.

I knew that there were several incidents in the past week that had helped to change my mind about going to Africa. The first breach in my resolve to stay out of it all was during the meeting we'd had with the vulcanologists. I did not know then why Barrett had convened the meeting. I was surprised to be included because he'd given me to understand that all he needed from me was help with the briefing. However, both Tom and I started that day with the meeting. Much of the time was devoted to the discussion of technical data which, though interesting, was hardly captivating. Towards the end I began to get the feeling that it was all unreal. There was something so casual about the way in which they were discussing it. I butted into their theorising with my opinion that no amount of seismic activity could produce the sort of result that would wreck the whole economy and devastate the whole area. The reply that came jolted me back to a sense of reality and to a feeling of belief and fear.

I think his name was Valinados—a visiting professor at London. Although Greek, he spoke English with a precise accuracy. My question must have given him the opening he'd been seeking, and an opportunity to expound on the area in which he was a recognised authority. He started dryly.

'In the Aegean there is an island called Santorin and known also as Thera, it is the most southerly of the Cyclades. After a long history of volcanic activity it erupted violently about 1470 BC and probably destroyed the Minoan civilisation in Crete some 175 kilometres distant. It is probably too long ago now to be absolutely certain of the facts. It is sure, however, that forces were released during the eruption that raised millions of tons of tephra and deposited it relentlessly over a vast area in a fiery rain of pumice and ash which charred and petrified all living vegetation.'

He looked at me directly—a man not given to letting his imagination run wild, I thought. He continued, stating facts without emotion, but conveying an intense atmosphere of conviction.

'In 1815 the eruption of Tambora, in the East Indies, was responsible for the death of 80,000 people. They died, not as a direct result, but because of the disease and starvation which followed the destruction of plants and animals by the deposition of volcanic ash. You see, productive land is put out of action for years after a coating of only 10 centimetres of acidic ash. I think this is the critical figure mentioned by Ninkovitch and Heezen . . .' He looked for confirmation from his colleagues. They nodded agreement.

'The island of Thera itself, some ten miles in diameter, was overlayed with deposits which are still evident, 60 metres thick! The whole centre of the island collapsed into an exhausted Magma chamber to produce a caldera—something like Crater Lake in Oregon. It is too long ago now to really appreciate how that cataclysm affected human society, but the race memory of man still carries it in his legends and myths.

'All major volcanic outbreaks of this nature are preceded and followed by serious earthquakes and they become the locus of explosive eruptions of devastating violence. An eruption very similar but much smaller than that of Thera occurred in Krakatoa in 1883—recently enough to have very well documented evidence about it. On the days of climax, the 26th and 27th of August of that year, sounds of the explosion were audible for over 200 kilometres. As far distant as Java, people could not sleep at night for the noise. The final explosion was heard at the Island of Rodriquez 4,800 kilometres away in the Indian Ocean. Over thirty-six thousand people lost their lives, and some three hundred towns and villages were destroyed in the great tidal waves which followed.'

He stopped and looked seriously around the room and then continued in an atmosphere of stark silence.

'I am convinced that it is possible to duplicate such eruptions on a vast, terrifying scale by the induction of artificially created earthquakes. There is enough evidence from these gentlemen—all experts on African vulcanology—to satisfy me that we are faced with a threat to the whole temporary physical stability of the earth's crust, and a disaster of such tremendous size that it will remain in the race memory of man for ever. I am no historian or archaeologist but I would like to point out that it is highly likely that the ancient mainland Greeks took advantage of the effects of the Thera eruption on Crete and quite quickly moved in to occupy that panic-stricken, starving land. A whole thriving cultural and commercial empire was reduced to nothing with one crippling overnight blow by the blind fury of nature and it never rose again.'

He sat down amid an oppressive silence broken only by a nervous cough from one of his colleagues. The quiet hung like a pall and then someone, to relieve nervous tension, broke the silence—I think it was Barrett.

'Those Ancient Greeks were opportunists. It seems that man has progressed anyway—he can now make his own opportunities.'

No one commented on this. We were all lost in a confusion of thoughts. At that moment, having had the facts stated in such a plain, convincing way, I was more aware and afraid than at any time since we had discovered the plot. I did not want to know anymore. I felt a compelling urge to ask these men where they thought the safest place to be was when such an event happened, but I just couldn't. Tom asked a question which took the tension out of the air and put the whole thing onto a practical level.

'How can these people calculate just how much force they're going to let loose? Surely they won't be able to control it? Yet, I reckon they must be fairly confident if they've got all those people already in ships in the Indian Ocean, just waiting to converge on the East African Coast!'

I could see some hope in this, I backed him up.

'They've got their beachhead forces in those ships, it's the whole key to success that they land as quickly as it's safe to do so. If any tidal waves resulted they would destroy the ships and the whole plan would abort.'

We were answered by a quiet, thoughtful man who up until then had not contributed much to the discussion: 'I estimate that there would be tidal waves in the Indian Ocean up to eighty metres high!'

I tried to picture a vast wall of water that high tearing across the ocean. No ship could possibly live in it. Everyone there must have thought the same because sounds of astonishment came from all round the room.

'But I would like to remind you gentlemen that there were many ships in the vicinity of Krakatoa, some only 40 kilometres away. The *Charles Bal*, the *Norham Castle*, the *Robert Sale*, the *London*—to mention but a few—and all, with the exception of closely moored vessels, reported no damage and were hardly aware that they were riding such momentous waves. You see the waves move with a speed relative to the depth of ocean, any boat in deep ocean would feel only a vast rounded hump of water undulating swiftly and silently below her. The frightful wall would only become apparent when it reached the shallower seas or crashed onto unprotected coasts. It will not only be disaster for mainland East Africa, gentleman—every country in the path of the tidal waves will suffer untold destruction along its coasts.'

The meeting went on a while after that, ideas, theories and examples were tossed about without reserve, but lively as it got I was left with no doubt. These men, experts in their line of work, were convinced that the threat of the Third World in Africa was a real one and very, very practical given the right amount of nuclear material to trigger it off.

My greatest shock, however, came right at the end, when Valinados said that he hoped with all his heart that it could be prevented, but that he was going to East Africa anyway because such an opportunity for knowledge and study could not be missed! And what is worse, many of those present agreed with him, while others only expressed regret that they could not do the same!

It set me thinking. Valinados could not possibly organise himself to be there in time, but the very coolness of it all! A new line in casuistry that left me dumbfounded yet envious. A lifetime opportunity, an excitement, a dicing with danger and a chance to do something good for all humanity—well, Ashe?

But it was no altruism that made me finally decide to go back to Africa—it is difficult to explain now, but somehow I knew after Valinados had spoken that the only peace I would ever find from the haunting sense of guilt about Fona would be in a trial of myself in circumstances of such magnitude that the memory of her death would diminish and shrink from its prominence in my mind. The whole memory had to be obliterated and purged with fire. Perhaps it was with some sense of finality—the trial had gone on a long time—I had lived through years accusing myself, defending myself and judging myself over my inability to shoot down a vicious terrorist who meant less than nothing to me. Fona had died because of my squeamishness. Now recrimination was done with and sentence was passed—trial by ordeal!

Tom eased his long legs under the seat as he came back to join me. He had a smirk on his face and a whisky in his hand. He gave me a 'we're the boys' wink and then picked up the book that he'd been reading off and on since leaving Heathrow. It was the paperback edition of *Atlantis Exploded*—an account of the research that had taken place on and around Thera, with the accent on submarine core sampling. It was dreadfully convincing about the effects of the eruption with facts that made my stomach lurch when I applied them to Africa. He started to quote some more at me.

'Look, Tom, I've got the picture now, spare me any more details—I've got some thinking to do! We're on our way. You don't have to flog it anymore—I'll see it through to the end now.'

'Right on, boy—you and me both!' He went back to reading, a fascinated look on his face.

The time droned by and I got to thinking again. Valinados, Thera, Krakatoa—it all seemed so pat somehow. I took out a cigarette and offered one to Tom. He accepted, putting his book aside to take a light from the match I offered. He looked at me thoughtfully a moment and then said, 'I want to level with you about something that's been on my mind since you decided to come.' I nodded encouragement and he continued. 'You know the way you've been trying to figure out this set-up—the vulcanologists, that meeting and everything? Well, it was rigged, Gareth, I gotta tell you now. The International Agency back home have been in touch with Barrett all along over this thing—they work closer than a flea on a dog's arse.'

'How do you mean rigged?' I asked.

'It was set up, that's what. Didn't you think it strange that he welcomed me in with open arms? I'm sorry it had to be like that, but I contacted Barrett before I got to your place that night— and we had a long discussion on it.'

'Why didn't you tell me this before—and what's that got to do with the meeting, anyway?' I asked.

'Well, now, that's just it. Back home, they didn't quite see eye to eye with London and when I came up with this Fletcher lead they were all for it. They got right on the ball and got the Embassy in Kampala to work on it. I've got all their support, and backing to follow up the Fletcher lead, provided I don't get them involved. They made it pretty clear that if I get caught with my hand in the cookie jar, they just don't want to know. So all right, I can see their point of view, but I tell them it'll cost them more that way.'

'Cost? What do you mean?' I was getting a bit confused.

'I mean we're hired, that's what, to follow it up as far as we can—and then turn over what we get to the team working in Uganda. Payment by result, but expenses anyway.'

'I still don't understand, what's all this got to do with . . .'

'Now hold it, son, just listen. Barrett didn't like the set-up one bit—he was pressurised I guess, and then he agreed. After all, can they really afford not to follow up every little chance they get?'

'No, I suppose not,' I said.

'But there was one snag. The night I met him he knew that you wouldn't play ball—even before you laid it on the line yourself to me, this Barrett guy had told me that you wouldn't go. I don't figure how he knew that, but he sure as hell was right. You were stubborn—boy were you stubborn! So he rigged that meeting to get you involved, I think he mentioned conditioning your responses. Does that sound right? Anyway, he reckoned he had you figured.'

I must have looked pretty disgusted for he became very crestfallen.

'Aw hell, Gareth, he made me promise about this thing, pulled "the good of humanity" line on me, I just had to back him up after you turned me down flat. If you'd agreed to come when I asked, I'd have just told him to go screw himself and see what sort of response he got from his condition, but as it was I had no choice!'

But I wasn't looking disgusted—I was just thinking how wrong Barrett had been. It's true, the meeting had made a big impression on me and had started me thinking, but it was not that, not even the earthquakes around Aringot that finally changed my mind. It was my own decision. That I did know! For certain!

They had wasted no time. Seven days after the 'quake at Ladong, minor tremors had been reported from Tanzania and the centre had been estimated at about fifteen miles from Aringot. The tremors had been very slight with practically no damage nor any loss of life, but for us it was worse news than if there had been a major natural earthquake. It had meant that there was a tremendous decrease in the chances to interrupt the plan. Everything had to be speeded up—even as we were travelling to Uganda I knew that the three teams would already be on the move. For all I knew, one of them might have been on the same plane. Time was really against us—Spencer had reckoned on well over five days. They had already proved the experts wrong in getting the data from Ladong processed. Now it was just anybody's guess—but certainly we could not count for sure on Spencer's estimate. That meant seven days at the very outside, and one practically gone already on the daylight flight to Entebbe.

Tom still looked a bit hangdog, so I said to him, 'Barrett and his bloody contriving had nothing to do with it—I just changed my mind that's all, and for God's sake don't look so sheepish. I'd have pulled this same sort of thing on you—probably worse, if I'd been in the same position.'

Tom looked at me and grinned.

'Yes, I believe you would, you crafty Celtic bastard, yes, by all hell I think you would've got your way too—damned if I don't! All the same, I felt pretty bad about it at the time—getting you set up like that. Wouldn't have done it, though, but that I reckoned there was no one 'cept us had a hope of getting anywhere with this lead and I felt that it was right somehow for you, too!'

He left it at that so I didn't press him further. One way or another, I hadn't got a lot of sleep during that last week and so I let myself doze off with confused images flitting through my mind, in a half-way state between reality and illusion.

We took a long low sweep across the papyrus swamps by the edge of Lake Victoria and then came in along the new international runway. Entebbe Airport looked the same as always—tired and jaded, with the tattered flags of a few airlines trying their best to give a touch of colour and gaiety to the scene. The steady decline that had been going on since independence seemed to have taken a sharp plunge downwards. The buildings and rooms, even the staff, looked unkempt and soiled, as if they had all just woken from a long afternoon siesta. There was an air of despondency somehow, contrasting sharply with the way it had once been, gay, exciting and welcoming. Uganda, like so many other emergent free nations of the world, was beginning to pay the price of freedom, the bewildering range of responsibilities that no one was prepared to accept.

We were met in the foyer by a man who identified himself to Tom and were soon speeding along the twenty odd miles to Kampala in the back of an undistinguished-looking Peugeot which we were told was to be made available for us during our stay. I must say that I was impressed with the efficiency of it all. Briefly, Tom's compatriot outlined a few basic facts, and then passed a plain manilla file over to us.

The file contained varying amounts of information on some of the people who had been present at the Fletchers' lunch party. Although incomplete, it was a good start and one which would save us a lot of time. We started into it straight away. It didn't take long, and we were through it just as we reached the city.

Rounding the Queen's Clock, the driver said, 'I've got you both fixed up with accommodation at the Nakasero Club. It's a bit more private than the hotels in town, and has another advantage. All the people in that file are members. It's the biggest club in town, residential, tennis, swimming, et cetera, and was the old colonial water hole in the old days—it still has a large European membership. The chances are that any of those'—he indicated the file with a backward jab of his thumb—'who are still around will turn up there in the next day or so. It's Thursday today and that's the most popular night. I think that by the time you've got yourselves installed, had a shower and a bit of a rest, you'll see just about everyone who's around town in there tonight.'

The club stood on the crest of one of Kampala's hills. The early tropical sunset threw a rosy glow over the whole city and the lights of the suburbs began to stand out like threads of jewels, stretching away between the hills. The air was warm and balmy, without any hint of the chill one would expect at four thousand feet. Quite a number of tables on the open bar verandah were occupied with tennis players just off the courts, their murmuring sometimes broken with an outburst of laughter. Stewards moved between the tables and the long polished mahogany bar at which I sat, waiting for Tom to come down. The half-litre bottles of beer before me looked strangely dumpy in reflection in the timeworn patina on the polished surface. I looked across the room and appraised the long, flanky thighs of one of the women players. She sat with easy grace, long dark hair drawn into a ribbon at the nape of her neck, and moved her shoulders in a little tremble beneath the baby pink cardigan. There was a momentary glance of understanding as our eyes met, but I looked away purposefully into the distance where a last, long ray of the setting sun flashed on Lake Victoria like a fiery ruby in a dull silver setting.

There was such a gulf separating ordinary things like tennis, women's thighs and lovers' sighs from the serious thoughts that were running through my mind. Right then I was visualising the two thousand miles of lake shore—the most densely populated part of the country—and imagining the twenty-six thousand square miles of the lake slopping about and spilling like water being carried jerkily in a gigantic tin tub. Only three hundred feet at its greatest depth, lying in the plateau between the eastern and western branches of the Great Rift Valley, it was a feature of vast potential destruction. It was known as Nnalubale locally and was the locus of the god-like spirits of creation in the old Kiganda mythology. If anyone remained alive to remember it after the cataclysm it would surely be renamed in honour of a god of destruction.

Tom slipped on to the stool beside me and leaned back, elbows on the bar, while I wrote out a slip ordering him a beer. I noticed that his view was confined to what was in the room, but he must have had his mind on other things, too, for he spoke in a low confidential tone.

'I've just been reading that file again and I got an idea. Do you remember the fact that Fletcher's wife and kids have left on vacation to Europe?'

'Yes, and the families of two of the other men as well,' I answered. 'That's quite usual out here. You notice Fletcher's tour is up in about a week anyway. He'll be off himself then. Quite a lot of wives and kids go home earlier than the husbands. It's not quite as happy a place as it was, there's a lot of robbery and violence about now, a new type of criminal called Kondo seems to be on everybody's mind—black, white and brown. Two years is about as much of Uganda as anyone can take at a stretch. There's a lot of racial tension building up too.'

'A hell of a pity that,' said Tom. 'This little country has a reputation, unique in the world I reckon, for happy co-existence of different races. Still, I reckon Firaz and his crowd are fixing to change it all, anyway.' He took a long pull at the beer. 'What I was saying about Fletcher though is this. He's staying right here in the club, the floor above us, room 27. Hardly been to bed sober for a couple of weeks. Comes from work, gets into the men's bar, round back of the club, leaves when it closes around ten—straight up to his room, blotto till morning.'

'How do you know all this?' I asked.

'Couple o' dollars and a lot of Afro-American diplomacy—and I guess his room steward hates his guts.'

'You mean, if we're to get any sense out of him it'd better be now?'

'Right on, man, pick up your glass and follow me.'

We walked down a long covered verandah along one side of the building, overhearing a hum of subdued talk in the club library as we passed the sign that informed women they were allowed no further. And then we entered the sacred precincts where the sound of clicking billiard balls and the occasional forced belly laugh of lonely men assured us that God was in his heaven and all was right in the world of the stag male.

The men's bar was smaller and more enclosed than the 'popsi bar', large comfortable chairs were scattered about the room, and an imposing roll of past club presidents in gilt and mahogany dominated an entire wall. Three or four small groups of men stood at the bar, in various states of dress ranging from the *de rigueur*, light tropical suit of the commercial world down to the wrinkled shorts and sport shirt of the less chair-bound members. We were only barely noticed as we entered. The conversation level had slight overtones of alcoholic confidence. We stood sipping awhile and talking softly while the ripples of disturbance that our entry had caused settled. There were no familiar faces in the room—I thought we might have been a bit early for the main sundown rush so we ordered a couple more beers and when I judged it an opportune moment I caught the eye of one man whose interest seemed to be wandering and asked, 'Has Fletcher been in yet?'

'Den? Couldn't say, really, just got here. Hey! Malcolm, have you seen Den?'

A slightly built man detached himself from a group further up the bar, and hobbled across, one leg in a plaster cast to the knee. He smiled, stuck out his hand and introduced himself.

'Wayle,' he said.

We shook hands.

'You looking for Den? Friends of his? Then come on over and join us, he should be in soon. What are you drinking? Never mind that!' He waved aside our half-full glasses. 'Bring them over and have another. Nothing else to do in this bloody place after dark, especially when you're nobbled like this.' He tapped his stick against the cast. 'Got it water-skiing down at the lake. I wasn't exactly skiing at the time though—fell down the steps of the club at Murchison Bay, only there are no steps to the club; I found that out the hard way! Ha!' He laughed loudly, tugging nervously at a rather straggling beard.

We declined his offer, saying that we were in a hurry and couldn't wait long. 'That's where Den went this afternoon, come to think of it,' he continued. 'He's bar member there and had some handing over to do—so he said, but if there's anyone else there he won't move until the beer runs out or else he'll be pissed out of his mind by ten o'clock.'

'Murchison Bay?' I asked. 'Where's that?'

'The Boat Club just off the Ggaba road,' he answered.

'Is it far?' asked Tom.

'Far? Good God, no! Only about six miles out of town as a matter of fact—fifteen minutes at most.'

'Could you give us some directions?' I asked.

Wayle took the pink booklet of bar chits and drew a neat directional map on the back.

'You can't miss it; the road doesn't go anywhere else!'

The directions he gave led us out of town about four miles along a main road and then we took a murram road through the papyrus swamps towards the lake shore. It was a bright moonlit evening and we had no difficulty finding our way. As we neared the lake we could see a solitary light burning ahead of us and made our way towards it.

The club was a grass-thatched building, quite unimposing even in the moonlight, and obviously only a temporary structure. Only one car was parked outside and not a sound came from within. Just visible in the moonlight we could see the silent shapes of the moored boats in the bay all lying bow-on to the slight off-shore breeze. We went to the open door. It was a large room, a bar occupied one corner and the rest of the space was taken up with light outdoor tables and chairs. One side was fenced off with expanded metal mesh, and a motley of fuel cans, skiis and outboard motors seemed to be dropped haphazardly everywhere.

Fletcher was sitting on a high stool behind the bar swaying slightly and almost soundlessly singing to himself. A mournful group of empty glasses was scattered around the bar. Even when we approached him he didn't look up. As we got closer I fancied that the song he was singing to himself was familiar. We reached the bar just in time for me to join in the last line: 'Went nine times around and the poor dog was drowned, I'm the last of the Irish Ro . . . vers.'

He looked up owlishly. Recognition was long in coming; he struggled for quite some time, and then we could see it dawn on him. We'd counted on the pleasant surprise of seeing us alive being a favourable factor which would encourage him to help us in our search, but we never expected the look of fright and horror

that came to his face. He began to blubber in a mixture of drunken
incoherence and abject fear. But he did not have to say a word—we
both knew that the search was over almost as soon as it had begun.
Fletcher himself had obviously been involved in the attempt to
kill us.

'It wassn' my fault, Mike, it wassn' me!' he shouted. 'It was
that bloody arsehole that done it. I didn' know, Mike—I didn'
know, I tell yer,' he screamed.

A sharp clean swipe to the point of his jaw from Tom lifted
Fletcher clean off the stool and sent him staggering against the
wall to collapse in a mute heap on the floor.

'Come on,' Tom said, 'let's get this rubbish out of here. We're
taking Mr Fletcher where he's goin' to sober up and then he's
got some more singing to do!'

We both took hold of one of his arms, each around our shoulders,
and dragged him towards the door. We went sideways through it
in an awkward shuffle and, being last, I reached up and flicked the
light switch. There was a moment of temporary blindness as we
went out into the darkness which was suddenly split by a series of
short flashes and the crackle of an automatic weapon from the lake
shore. I saw Tom dive to the ground and in the sudden change of
balance, I toppled over backwards, letting Fletcher's inert weight
slip away from me. I heard Tom's hoarse whisper, 'Don't move a
muscle!'

As my eyes gradually got used to the darkness, I could see that
he lay prone behind the scant cover of one of the troughs of
flowers that marked the edge of the concrete apron in front of the
building. Myself, I was in a sitting position against the door,
terribly exposed to the direction from which the firing had come.
The limp form of Fletcher lay between us, snoring heavily. It
seemed that the silence was tangible and then the croaking of the
anvil frogs started again—and all the night sounds of Africa were
cued in once more. Whether it was the breaking of the silence
affecting him or the subconscious mind of the drunk prompting
consciousness I don't know, but quite suddenly Fletcher sat bolt
upright, got to his hands and knees and then lurched into a
standing position. He had barely reached upright when a blinding
light bathed us all in baleful glare and three crisp single shots
ripped through the night, ending with a series of sickening thumps
into Fletcher's lurching body. He was bowled over backwards
with the impact, to collapse in a heap of certain death on the

ground. Almost immediately, there was a roar of outboard motors which shattered the night—and I could see the creaming, iridescent wake of a boat move from the shore with a terrific thrust of power. We must have remained immobile for another couple of minutes and then I tentatively made a move, expecting every moment to be blinded by the glare and shot down without a chance. I stood up. Nothing but the distant sound of the outboard, barely a murmur now in the cool clear moonlight.

'Come on, Tom, let's get out of here!' I whispered.

'I'm with you—too unhealthy here, I reckon.'

It took only one glance at Fletcher's inert body to see that he was very dead indeed. Three ominous dark holes had been punched into his fleshy body, one through the middle of his forehead, one at the base of his throat and the other in the centre of his chest—deadly accurate marksmanship that made me tremble to think that if we had made the slightest move after going down, it would have been our last.

The worst thing about it was that after being so close to finding out something from Fletcher our hopes had died with him. If I am any judge of men I would say that he had been in no condition to resist us; he would have told us everything he knew, and thus perhaps have given us some further leads to follow. But that hope had been smashed. We discussed it as we drove away and decided that we would go back to the club and, if possible, see Wayle and tell him that we'd lost our way and had never got to the Boat Club.

When we arrived back at the club we went into the men's bar again. Wayle and his group were still at it, the tempo of the drinking had reached full cruising speed and our story was accepted without question. The talk centred on Fletcher for a few minutes after we arrived. He was very popular among the group and some really funny anecdotes were being related about him. It seemed so macabre to visualise him in some of the situations they related, knowing that he now had three gaping holes through him. I pictured his over-fat face, drawn into a mask of fear when he had recognised us, and heard again the last words he'd screamed before Tom had silenced him—a slurred, drunken appeal to poor Mike, whom I gathered had been a great friend of his for years.

'It wasn' my fault, Mike, it was that bloody arsehole that done it—I didn' know, Mike! I didn' know! I didn' know!'

It suddenly dawned on me there was the faintest possibility that I had misheard him. I looked across to Tom and caught his eye, and inclined my head over to the door leading to the men's room. I started towards the door and he joined me. Once outside, I said to him as we walked towards a pair of red swinging doors, 'Do you remember what Fletcher was saying just when you hit him?'

'Sure I do, the lousy bastard was carping on about it not being his fault,' answered Tom with some disgust.

'No, I mean the actual words he used,' I urged.

'Well now, let's think a minute—yeah—I guess it was something like "I didn' know . . . I didn' know, it was that bloody hustle that did it not me" or something like that. Why?' He looked inquiringly at me.

'Bloody hustle—what do you make of that?' I continued.

'I dunno, I guess it's some sort of a limey thing, is it? Hell, Gareth, why ask me? There's half of what you bloody British say makes no sense, anyway. I guess it could be a rush or something like that, you know, a hurry.'

'I thought he said arsehole not hustle,' I said.

'Arsehole, sparse hole, hustle, spustle—what's the difference, anyway?'

'Well, I was thinking that it didn't really sound right somehow, and wondered if you'd heard it any different. You did obviously, but your version doesn't sound any better!'

We started on our way back, but I stopped short with a sudden idea.

'You go back in there,' I said. 'There's just something I want to check out—I'll join you in a moment.'

I went back through the popsi bar. It had filled up considerably, but the thighs were still there. Again we exchanged a thoughtful glance, but no time now. I went on through to the club office where we had first booked in. I asked to see the manager and almost immediately was shown into an inner office. The manager turned out to be a woman, late middle-aged and saw-faced with an expression that would frighten a bulldog. A ghastly slash of orange red framed itself around a tirade of whining complaint about the inefficiency all around her, so it took a lot of cool nerve to try to charm the old bag into giving me the information I wanted and more time than I'd thought, too, but eventually I got back to the men's bar.

The crowd there had thinned considerably—gone to eat I supposed—so it was not easy to draw Tom aside immediately to tell

him what I'd found out. I listened to the end of a story that Wayle
was recounting and then, amid the guffaws of appreciation that
followed, I said, 'I've been looking at the club membership list.
There is only one name on it which could be anything like what
Fletcher said.' I passed him a slip of paper on which I had written
'Hassel—Robert—Radio Engineer, PO Box 7231, Kampala'.

'What do you think?'

'Certainly worth a try!' He folded the paper and put it into his
pocket, turned to the three that he'd been drinking with and
asked, 'Any of you bums know a guy called Hassel—Bob Hassel?'
His question was greeted by three embarrassed grimaces and an
answer from Wayle.

'Yes, we all know Robbie—friend of yours?'

'No, can't say that he is really, just supposed to look him up this
trip, that's all. I wondered where I might find him.'

Two of the group finished off the beer in their glasses and made a
pointed departure, leaving Wayle, Tom and I alone in the bar,
except for two rather young-looking men absorbed with the dart-
board.

'Robbie's all right really, you know,' said Wayle. 'Get on quite
well with him myself—after all everybody's got a right to their
own point of view, haven't they? I mean to say, that's what I
think—I dunno about you chaps.' He looked cannily at us both.
Although he'd drunk a fair amount he wasn't at the point where it
had him by the tongue. I tried my best to look as if I were the
soul of discretion and put on my 'I inspire confidences' look. I
didn't get a chance to see if it worked because Tom took a different
line.

'What's so different about his point of view—he queer or
somethin'?'

'No, no, no—nothing like that, but . . . well look, I'll tell you.'
He dropped his voice to a low nasal monotone and spoke
through the side of his mouth. I don't know what the secrecy was
about, for it merely turned out that Hassel was a strange type who,
after working for the Colonial Service in some minor capacity,
came in very strongly with the new African Government and had
lent his support to a lot of anti-British propaganda in the press.
He was obviously an opportunist who had managed to secure a
well-paid post and, so rumour had it, got mixed up with a lot of
shady deals. He had fallen out of favour after a year or so and
now was between two stools as it were, having antagonised most

of the non-African communities, and lost popularity with the Africans who had any say in the running of things. He was sacked from his job and had taken to living on his farm somewhere—and having little to do with Kampala or anyone any more.

Much later, when we had had supper and the club was empty except for a few residents, we sat around talking over a last drink. We now had what might prove to be a further lead. Two things about Hassel made it worthwhile visiting him. The first was a very tenuous hope, based on the idea that he might be the type who'd get mixed up with the alternatives of the Third World. The second looked a bit more hopeful. When we had asked Wayle where Hassel's farm was he had taken us to the large wall map in the billiard room. It was an interesting thing in itself, being a copy of the first survey made for the Admiralty. The section showed the north-east corner of Lake Victoria.

'You see,' said Wayle, 'to get to Hassel's place by road would take three or four hours from here, but across the lake, especially with the twin Pentas he's got, Robbie can make it in half an hour—less if there's a flat calm on.'

CHAPTER TWENTY-THREE

The next morning was overcast and dull, threatening rain, with a hazy humid atmosphere that seemed to sit on the whole country-side, and yet it was so warm that we had to open all the windows of the car to get any relief from a feeling of sticky discomfort. Under the pretence of wanting to go fishing, we'd managed to hire a small outboard runabout for the day, together with all the necessary gear, from a firm called Yusef who had a marina enter-prise on the lake shore close to the Murchison Bay Boating Club.

Even though we travelled partly over the same road as the previous evening it looked totally unfamiliar and it was not until we'd actually reached Yusef's marina and I could see the distant shape of the club house, did I get any sense of orientation. While Tom went down to the jetty to check if our telephoned booking was okay, I walked up on to the rise of ground to get a better view of Murchison Bay Club through the binoculars that I had brought.

There was considerable activity going on there, several police cars parked outside and a white-painted Volkswagen that I assumed to be an ambulance. I focused on the concrete apron in front of the club house—no sign of the body—and then slowly followed the pathway down to a floating jetty that stretched out like a dog leg into the water. Sixty yards at most—even so the shooting had been good. I imagined again the creaming wake of the boat as it had leapt away from the shore, and tracked an imaginary course for it. On the horizon was the faint smudged outline that was the peninsula where Hassel lived. But quite a few small islands could be seen much clearer in the middle distance about six to nine miles away. From where I looked they seemed to be covered in forest, right down to the water's edge, and then ringed with a bright green belt of papyrus growing right out into the water. I heard Tom hail me from the jetty and went down to join him.

The little runabout looked fairly serviceable, fibreglass, about twelve foot, with a 10-hp Yamaha to push it along. I dropped the two haversacks, one containing the club picnic lunch we'd brought

along, my binoculars and a few other odds and ends, into the
bottom of the boat. It was cable steered, having two seats up
front balancing the weight of fuel in the back; there were four
bright red tanks. Tom was busy signing for the gear we were
taking—a miscellany of rods, nets and lines, and a couple of boxes
of bait and lures. Going fishing was not such a bad idea really
either. Victoria had been stocked with Nile perch a few years
back, and they were beginning to come in big now. Not a good
game fish but certainly big enough to give anybody a thrill when
they hooked one. The tilapia were a snip and if nothing else came
of the day we might try to land on one of the smaller islands and
lunch off a couple of them.

We left at a fairly brisk pace, the motor sounded good and there
was hardly a ripple on the flat, leaden surface of the water. It was a
lot cooler away from the shore, but still the only breeze was what
we made ourselves. I began to think that we would soon be needing
the rain capes we'd brought. Just over two hours out, we came
close to the peninsula. Having crossed the bay, we turned to
follow the coast line, at a slower speed, trolling, but studying the
shore closely. We expected to come up to Hassel's jetty in about
half an hour, and had judged it best to approach from the east
where we would be easily visible. The last thing we wanted was
to scare anybody off or create any suspicion. With a great deal of
luck, the weather might help us. If it started raining we could
have a perfect excuse for landing.

As soon as the jetty came into view—perhaps a mile from us—
I crouched low in the boat and took a look through the binoculars.
Tom shut off the motor and baited a rod with a white waxy
squirmy grub from the tin we'd been given. A boat, Hassel's I
guessed, was moored alongside. She was a beauty indeed, powered
by twin 55 Pentas. Their blue and orange colour stood out sharply
against the sleek white stern. Even at rest she looked like a panther
poised for a spring. The only other craft at the jetty was a big
awkward raft made of oil drums and used possibly for swimming.
I searched the track up from the water's edge to a low white
bungalow on the side of the hill, and then blessed the caution that
had made me crouch to do my observing. I just caught a quick
blurred view of a man on the verandah in the action of bringing
some field-glasses up to his face and I was up and baiting a hook in
the wink of an eye. Tom never budged—he just went on fishing
as if I'd never moved.

'Guess we're being observed! Good thing you got up out a' there, 'cause it was in my mind to just push that big fat arse of yours—you know just to break the monotony—'cause these fish just ain't thrillin' me one little bit.'

As if in response to a cue we both got a bite simultaneously and hauled in a couple of fairly reasonable tilapia, not a bit of struggle, just like pulling a tin of sardines out of the water on the end of a string. They didn't even need netting.

'Bit of luck that,' I said. 'Now all we need is the rain.'

But rain it didn't. The sky got lighter and lighter and a breeze came from the south. The water ruffled a bit, and then there was no excuse at all. I went back to the motor and kicked it over—a sweet little engine, no more trouble than pulling at some knicker elastic. I told Tom so. 'Knicker elastic!' he groaned. 'Where the hell you been for the last twenty years? Haven't even seen those things since my mother used to do Monday washing.'

'Make for the lee of that island,' I said, as we got moving.

Directly off shore from the jetty were a number of small islands, some of them only rocks. The nearest was perhaps a mile and the furthest maybe five miles off. 'We might get a better look from one of those and it'll give us the advantage in that he'll think we've gone.'

'Yeah, let's try and land anyway. I've got such an appetite, I could eat these raw. We'll give it another try later in the afternoon.'

We found a fairly good landing spot around the lee. The island was maybe a hundred yards long with a few wild mango trees growing in a grove near the top. The fish were delicious, and we were lying down in the late afternoon sunshine, just about having decided to call on Hassel anyway, when the low throbbing sound of a boat came from down the lake. We watched a while and then saw the high bow wave of a fast boat come curving from behind one of the larger islands further out. We were sitting up then and I brought the glasses to bear on it. She was going fast across the front of us—something about the size of a Coronet, with inboard-outboards. Right opposite us she changed course with a flourish of wake and then came straight towards us on the plane, topping the gentle swell and giving the impression of a much larger craft.

The idle curiosity with which we watched her was very soon satisfied, and only five minutes after that we were putting back to the mainland with a sharp rebuke ringing in our ears. Tom was swearing loudly above the full-pitched roar of our little Yamaha.

'Of all the saw-faced, fat-assed bastards! The jumped-up, swine-mannered paid pigs—I just don't believe it! I never realised what a filthy rotten bottom there is in people. Black fascist mother-kicking bastards. . . .' and a further wealth of epithets whose finer shades of meaning escaped me, but all of which I agreed with heartily.

The boat had nosed up to the small strip of sand we were sitting on, and six scruffy-looking men had scrambled over the side and sauntered up to us. Dressed in crumpled dirty khaki, reeking with the sweet sickly smell of banana beer, they were armed with automatic weapons—cheap mass-produced things, rusty and ill-kept but nasty nevertheless. The man in charge came at an even more leisurely pace. A fat slobby-looking individual whose belly was draped with a webbing belt and holster, he held a bottle of white spirit by the neck and approached with a vaguely military precision, swig from the bottle, spit, put right index finger in right nostril, explore, swig from bottle, spit, put right index finger in left nostril, explore. It was some of the most insulting officialdom I'd ever encountered. The fact that they were all drunk did nothing to relieve the tension they created, because they were mean, nasty, spiteful drunk, bloated, gluttonous drunk. Considering the fury that we both felt it was a miracle that we left there without getting involved any further.

Luckily though, none of them spoke anything but the most basic English, nor indeed did they have any thorough grasp of Swahili. From the way they spoke it, using it as a *lingua franca* between themselves, I judged them to be Congolese. Mercenaries for the new army that was being developed in the country? Deserters from the dissident units of the old one? I couldn't guess, but I could imagine the vicious, warped mentality of them.

In a light casual tone that concealed the intention of my words— for I could hear the sounds of two-way radio contact from the boat, and there was at least one other man aboard—I started to reason Tom out of the sort of action I imagined he was contemplating.

'I know we can take them, and there's nothing I'd like better now than to put my foot into the face of this bladder-faced gentleman here, but swallow it, take it all, let's get out of here. We've got a job to do and we can't risk any involvement with authority.'

And it worked. I saw him visibly screw the cap down on to the fury that was fizzing up inside him—and we left with nothing worse than broken fishing rods and the loss of the half dozen remaining cans of beer we'd brought with us.

We took as direct a course as we could for Murchison Bay. About a half mile from the little island I risked a look back through the binoculars. They were pushing their boat off and clambering aboard. Our way took us past the east point of the larger island where we had first spotted them. And then we saw how wise our decision had been. Another boat of the same type was moored just around the point—we passed within a couple of hundred yards of it. A loud hailer echoed across the water. '*Kwenda! Kwenda!*' and the side was lined with men menacing us with weapons—but what was worse, a light cannon mounted on the bow turned purposefully in our direction.

Tom swung away immediately and gave the motor full throttle. I thought it wiser not to look back, but just before we had changed course to avoid them, I'd got a view of a fresh-cut belt of papyrus that surrounded the island. Like most of the little islands, it was obviously uninhabitable. It was almost bare rock with thick tangled bush and papyrus crowned with a stunted grove of wild fig trees clinging to the only bit of soil it supported. I was almost convinced then that these men were not carrying out any official duties. There was the sloppy, dirty dress of them, the blatant drunkenness, and one final factor that decided me. I was willing to swear that at least two of the men on the boat which had warned us off were not Africans. Even at that distance I had no doubt in my mind about it. Then why was that wide channel cut through the reeds?

We returned to Yusef's marina by about half-past five, but only stayed long enough to refuel the boat and take on another few hours' charter. While the jetty staff were checking over the engine and refilling two of the tanks, we walked up to the small club house that commanded a splendid view of the bay, in search of a chart of the area, and were lucky enough to find a very large rally board, copied from the official chart. It represented the whole of the bay right out to the peninsula, and showed all the islands and reefs.

We spent a while studying and copying this and then went back to our boat. We had decided to go back to that island in the first few hours of darkness before moonrise and planned to paddle in the last mile to avoid being heard. So, having the last hour of daylight left to kill, we went west along the coast, staying close to the shore and nosing into the dense papyrus to see what it was like. It was impenetrable. Sounding with the paddle revealed a bottom of thick black mud and rotted reeds. Clouds of mosquitoes rose into the air when we shook the reeds and quite frequently we saw the bright flashing green of reed snakes as, disturbed, they slithered away. That, together with my conviction that the water was infected with bilharzia and crawling with water leeches, made the prospect of our evening's entertainment far from attractive.

Tom was quite confident about making an accurate landfall in the darkness, using the speedometer, the dash compass and a watch. The compass, though cheap and gimmicky, seemed reasonably accurate and over a distance of about ten miles wouldn't put us far out, particularly with so many other small islands and reefs to take bearings from and no tide or current to cope with.

By nine o'clock we had the boat tied to a small weathered rock encrusted with bird lime and affording only one or two square yards of foothold out of the water. We were crouched beneath the small fore-decking of our boat, making a last minute calculation by the light of a small torch. We had abandoned the idea of paddling right in, and had decided to swim in the last four hundred yards because we could see the unmistakable glow of firelight coming from the island. Twice between cutting our engine and choosing the small rock to tie up to, we had heard the sound of a boat going by between us and our destination. With this activity, the risk of paddling was too great. The first light of the moon began to lift the darkness as we took to the water, fully dressed, and armed with our guns wrapped carefully in plastic covering. We took a bearing and then moved as silently as possible towards the island.

Once more before we reached it we heard the sound of a boat. The noise grew louder and the boat drew closer until it cruised by barely fifty yards from us as we stayed motionless in the water hardly daring to breathe. Low down as we were, it was difficult to see where it went in the darkness, but it had surely not come from the island and had not stopped there either. Tom was of the opinion that it was the same boat as before making a wide circular patrol. If that were the case then we would be sure of arriving undetected, for there seemed to be an interval of about twenty minutes between our hearing it last time and this.

I felt the black mud sucking at my shoes as we reached shallower water. I laced my fingers through the reeds and lay there, waiting for Tom to come alongside. A channel certainly had been cut into the papyrus; the white triangular stumps of the reeds showed up quite clearly along the edges. It was about ten yards wide and the water seemed to be deeper in the middle. As far as we could see in the moonlight, it went inland at an oblique angle to the shore line. We decided to follow it, keeping as close as we could to one side. After about fifty yards, it turned almost at a right angle and then opened out into a wide lagoon—a natural deep basin where the reeds had failed to get a hold. Obviously the channel was natural, too, having only been widened at one or two places, and the reason was easy to see, for right ahead of us, silhouetted against the light of a fire was a boat, nothing like the one we' had seen earlier. This was a steamer.

We stopped and edged our way into the cover of the reeds. All fear of mosquitoes, bilharzia and snakes had gone in the excitement of the discovery. This could not be any peaceful, legitimate exercise by some government department. The steamer had been hidden most cleverly on a small deserted island. And the question 'Why?' screamed for an answer.

As far as we could make out there was no papyrus on the shore side beyond the steamer. It was moored stern on to the shore and had a bow anchor quite a long way out in the lagoon. A wise precaution, for if the wind got up—and the sudden storms on the lake were notorious—the boat could be winched out to ride safely and swing freely at anchor.

The night was warm and balmy with only the faintest of breezes. We felt no cold or discomfort amongst the reeds, half in, half out of the water, but it was obvious that we could not stay there all night. To return without finding out anything further would be equally pointless. So we decided to get a closer look and board the boat if possible. The stout hawser to the anchor seemed the only way without risking discovery. It looked a nasty exercise to me but Tom seemed to think nothing of it. Okay for him, I thought, who could count on the help of both legs, but I realised that for me it would have to be a hand-over-hand venture. Fortunately the hawser was quite long so the angle was not too steep.

'We'll go up one at a time,' Tom said, 'then we'll always have someone on look-out. I don't fancy arriving after that climb just to meet a hostile welcome on deck. If anything goes wrong, head for the reeds and we'll try to cut back to our boat.'

As silent as a couple of fish, we reached the anchor hawser and
Tom started his long climb upwards. He seemed to ascend quickly
though. He stood on the cable at the hawse hole and then disappeared with a nimble leap over the edge of the bow. There was
only one thankful thought in my head as I started my arm-
wrenching climb: that the same indolence that kept men from
oiling their weapons also made them neglect to grease the anchor
cable. So just by grim determination to start with and then by
lack of an alternative, I kept on until I thankfully felt Tom's arm
as he reached down to help me over the bow.

The boat was in darkness, but all the while we had been climbing
we could hear occasional noises and the sound of indistinct voices
coming from the shore. There was a slight tremble in the deck
beneath our feet and the low hum of a generator. There were
probably people below and, no doubt, lights too, but not a glimmer
showed above deck. She was an old boat: one of the old East
African Railways fleet that had once plied all round the lake
linking up the railheads for cotton, coffee and maize, and she had
probably seen more years of service on the lake than I'd had
birthdays. There were not many of these boats left now; most were
rotting, forgotten, in some derelict lake port. The new rail links
had made them obsolete. They had been designed to pay their
way with cargo, but all had had a few deck cabins set well aft of
midships, leaving a very long fore deck as valuable space for deck
cargo. She was well loaded with such cargo now. A bulky mass
rose perhaps five feet above the deck level.

Crouching below the rail, we unpacked the guns from their
plastic covering, loaded a magazine and then crept forward to
examine the piece of cargo more closely. It consisted of a large
number of long pipes about nine inches in diameter. They were
cradled and supported by wooden frames about every six feet of
their length, in bundles of nine, each bundle having an end
section of about a yard square. We examined them by touch and
the dim light of the risen moon, and then moved back to the bow
where, crouching low with heads together, we discussed what to
do. It was a difficult decision to make, but we had to move. The
longer we stayed the greater were the chances that something
would be revealed. We determined to stick it out, and looked
around for some place to hide. We crept along the narrow starboard deck that went the whole length of the ship. Above the
cabins was a false roof of sheet metal, serving as an insulation

against the fierce tropical sun. It was raised well above the top of the cabins and the space between seemed an ideal place to conceal ourselves.

The spot was warm and yet the gap fore and aft allowed a bit of breeze to come through and also gave us the advantage of being able to watch both the main companionways. With this in mind we stretched ourselves out head to foot. I was thankful of the rest, and felt that if I could have a smoke my night would be complete. It was out of the question, of course, though I whispered as much to Tom. I heard him chuckle quietly in the dark and then felt a sodden mass being thrust into my hand followed by a lighter. 'I forgot to take them from my pocket,' he said. 'Help yourself!'

There were a few bits and pieces of things pushed up there, so we had to be a little careful as our exploring fingers moved about our immediate surroundings. I was grateful for the lump of what felt like amorphous old blanket, and manœuvred it under my head for a pillow. Tom had to make do with the doubtful comfort of a plastic jerry can. Still an' all, we settled down quietly for a long wait. We hoped that at first light we would be able to see more and then perhaps slip away unnoticed before anyone really was up and about.

The sounds ashore grew a little more noisy and bursts of conversation occasionally reached audible level, but nothing comprehensible reached us. About eleven o'clock we were frozen into silence and immobility by the sounds of men coming aboard. There was a brief, glaring flash of light as the forward hatchway was opened, and then, almost immediately, darkness again in response to some shouted admonishment. After that I think I must have slept, because I was aware of Tom nudging me and in reaction my holding the luminous dial of my watch close to my face. It was one thirty. 'Gareth, listen!' There was the sound of an outboard, throttled down, thrumming in the silence. It grew nearer, but quieter as it was throttled back even further. I looked forward to where the sound was coming from. The moon had risen high now and over the deck loads I could see the lagoon quite distinctly and make out the deep shadow that marked the banks of papyrus reeds. Then I saw the boat appear first as a floodlight as it sought its way along the channel and then, as it crossed the bow, as a twin-engined power boat, followed by a deeper darker mass—a raft—low-loaded and awkward in contrast to the speedy craft that towed it, a strange pair that were never meant for each other.

They went out of sight as they came under our lea, moving aft.

A number of men came tumbling up from the forward companionway busily buckling on side arms, or carrying light machine guns already slung across the shoulder, and then, quite abruptly, all attempt at secrecy and concealment was abandoned. There was an increase in the sound of engines, two powerful spotlights blazed down from somewhere above us and the whole foredeck was bathed in their light. Busy sounds of activity seemed to fill the air. Tom wriggled himself around and we both lay flat on our stomachs watching. There was not the slightest chance of our being seen. The two bright lights would blind anyone to our presence if they looked aft—even in daylight it would have been difficult. The noise of the forward winches as they came into operation made it possible for us to talk quite audibly without fear of discovery. This was lucky, for as four men came down the narrow deck from behind us and entered the pool of light, I could not help letting out a cry of surprise.

I would have known that blunt block of a head anywhere. Without needing to see the face, I was sure it was Kopft. Every shuffling, lumbering step he took away from us towards the winches convinced me, and there could be little doubt that the straight upright figure with a walking stick was Sloeder. Of the other two, I imagined one could be Hassel; I felt sure that it had been his boat I had seen come alongside, towing the bulky raft. It did not require a lot of guesswork either to pick him out from the other, for he carried a rifle loosely on the crook of his arm with all the ease and grace of an expert marksman. Tom had recognised Sloeder and Kopft almost at the same moment as I had and now he confirmed my suspicion.

'That's the guy that paid Fletcher off last night, I'd bet my last dime on it—couple o' thousand dollars and three neat ounces o' lead—and his sidekick's the one who tried to give us the haircut with the automatic.'

'Highly likely—he must be Hassel, so it looks as if our Fletcher lead has given us something big after all. What I wouldn't give now for that rifle—from here I could get them all, and damn the consequences. In fact, I've a good mind to . . .' I reached for the Biretta but felt Tom's hand come down firmly on my arm.

'Now steady, boy, don't let's get all riled up. We'll let it ride a while.'

'But Sloeder's a key man in this operation. It's his job to get the charges distributed, I'm sure. If we knock him out, and the other three, there's a chance that the whole operation will fold, and we stand a good chance of making a break afterwards in the confusion.'

But I realised that it was only a momentary temptation triggered by the sight of those two again—and with something like self-consciousness too, I realised that I could never have used that Biretta.

One of the forward winches came into operation and the loading boom swung out over the side. It wound up slowly with lots of shouting and advice from everyone. Then the load came into view and swivelled across in front of us, so close that we could have reached out to touch it. There was a clamour of shouting as it seemed as if it would crash into the superstructure, and then the winch stopped suddenly. All eyes were turned in our direction. It was very unnerving for a moment as the load swung dangerously towards us, even though I told myself it was impossible for us to be seen, and then the donkey man, using a bit of initiative, started his motor again and lifted the load clear. There was an audible sigh of relief from the men gathered on the deck. I felt like joining in.

'Did you see it?' said Tom excitedly. 'Did you see the brand mark on the wooden frame?'

The load had been similar to the items already loaded as deck cargo—nine long sections of pipe nesting in a wooden framework. I hadn't noticed anything on the wooden cradles.

'It was there, stamped all over it!'

'What was?' I asked.

'E.A.A.C.,' he said. 'East African Artesian Company.'

Then suddenly it started falling into place like the pieces of a Chinese puzzle. Why would nine light alloy pipes require such an effort to get aboard? Why would they be loaded secretly in the dead of night miles from anywhere in the middle of the lake on a deserted island? Why would Sloeder and Kopft be present? And what was it that Barrett had said about the system of transportation of the nuclear charges? Long loads wasn't it! This was it! This was 'the goods' that had arrived from Beirut, and been taken from Entebbe under 'military' escort. Doubtless they had been taken directly by road to Hassel's place and now were being moved again.

The winches were screaming loudly as the load was lowered

on to the deck. It went into place with a dead weight certainty and a resounding thud. I could hardly suppress my excitement. I felt as if my whole stomach had turned to jelly and was quivering inside me.

'What you reckon those pipes are made of, Tom?'

'Felt like some sort of aluminium—an alloy, I guess.'

'Light, would you say?'

'Yeah, I guess so—no! the hell I would, not the way that lot just sounded! They must be filled with something.'

'Something heavy? Heavy as all hell I'd say—heavy as lead . . .'

'Shielding!' We both said the word together, and then the whole thing dawned on him too. This was it.

'Good God, Gareth! You realise what this is—we've probably got the whole lot right here. How many loads do you reckon there is out there?'

It was easy to count them, they were stacked quite neatly.

'Twelve,' I said, 'counting the one just put on board.'

'I wonder is there any more out there.'

But if there were, we were not to know about it because with the lashing down of the last load, it became quite apparent that the steamer was about to get under way. The bridge above and aft of us was lit up. The engines took up a steady thrumming beat, and with the clang of telegraph, she inched forward with anchor windless winding as she moved on to her anchor.

Soon she was under way, following the lights of the Coronet that was waiting at the channel end of the lagoon. The papyrus almost touched her sides as she edged down the channel, and then there was a change in her rhythm as she steamed out into the lake, crisping up the dark waters in a lively wake behind her.

The ship was lit now. No further concealment was necessary— she was a lake steamer peacefully working on the lake. Even if patrols were maintained on the lake, nothing would be suspected. Who would ever guess that this venerable old thing carried a load so deadly and ominous that it could devastate the whole territory. The Coronet still cruised ahead anyway and its armament could silence any embarrassing inquiry.

After about half an hour of cruising almost due east in comparative silence—the deep peaceful quiet that settles on a ship at night in tropical waters—there was some activity around the bridge. Voices were raised and footsteps rang out loudly as men hurried to some task up forward. The smaller boat escorting us eased up and we gradually drew level with her. There was a brisk ringing of telegraph and we came to a gliding graceful stop. We wondered what the stop was for. As far as we could judge we were well away from any land by then and then it became apparent by the cursing and shouting in broken English and Swahili that the Coronet was low on fuel and could not make the rendezvous. Engines were stopped altogether and soon a couple of stout lines went over to moor the smaller boat close alongside. Again, the foredeck was lit by one of the bright spotlights. Hassel, who must have been piloting the smaller boat, climbed aboard with a degree of trepidation but arguing violently with someone, his arms gesticulating wildly. It was an argument that he had a fair chance of winning until Kopft sauntered up to him and silenced him with a swiping backhand that left him twitching in the scuppers.

It was not a serious setback, however, for in next to no time a hose was passed down to the boat below and in a few minutes she was refuelled from one of the large drums lashed securely in the well just below us. The only difference it seemed to make was that, when finally the Coronet resumed station ahead and we were underway again, she was under the command of Kopft—or at least he was now aboard to prevent any more inefficiency on the part of the chastened Hassel.

Almost immediately on starting off again the course was changed and both boats swung due south. Ahead lay the open water with no land for over a hundred miles. My theory that we were bound for western Uganda had to be revised. If this course was maintained the next landfall would be the Tanzania shore. There was a general settling down over the whole ship then, all but the riding lights were put out and except for the dim glow from the bridge the decks were in darkness. I heard Tom shuffle about beside me, trying to get some change in the cramped position of his limbs. I knew just how he felt.

'How long will it be, you reckon, before we reach the Tanzania side?' he asked.

'About ten hours,' I guessed, roughly estimating the speed we were making.

'Sometime before then we've got to do something. If we wait till daylight, we'll lose the only chance we've got.'

'What chance?' I asked.

'Well now, not really a chance I guess, but an advantage anyway —the darkness I mean—surprise—that sort of thing.'

He didn't sound too sanguine about it, but he was right of course. We'd had this chance presented to us on a plate. Never in all the time that we'd been planning and worrying in London, had we ever thought that this opportunity would arise. To find all the charges still together under the command of Sloeder was something we'd never even thought of. If only there was some way we could take over the boat, then we could scotch the whole thing. I said as much, continuing:

'After all, you hear of hijacking now where two or three people take over an aircraft and practically nothing can be done to prevent them. All they have usually are a few simple weapons, even less sometimes.'

'There you've got decent people involved, and that's what the hijackers count on, isn't it? The fact that there are people who care about moral values and human life—though I don't know how much longer anyone will be able to afford to go on caring about these things—the turning point is bound to come soon and do you know what it's going to be? It'll be when western man stops kidding himself that he's the goody goody who's got to lead the rest of the world along the path of peace and harmony. If this world is going to take that path, it's got to be booted up every painful inch of the way. We're soft, Gareth boy, we've got a soft belly of morality and conscience and honesty and everyone knows it and keeps hitting us there every chance they get, not only these enemies abroad but even our own people at home. But you can bet there's no soft underbelly to this lot.' He jabbed his finger downwards. 'You're up against people who don't care a damn about anything except fulfilling their power-crazed ambitions, and you and I know it. So if anything's got to be done it's got to be hard, it's got to be powerful and it's got to be big. We've got to finish this thing now, tonight, even if it means the both of us going out with it!'

His whispered words hung on the air for a few moments. I could see he was right. Anything could happen after this stuff was delivered. Barrett's plan was all right up to a point, but what if it failed? What if they'd calculated this and held some charges in reserve against such a loss as a blockade would ensure? How trustworthy anyway were the hired teams that were supposed to pull the thing off? One leak or one man among them devoted to the Third World cause could negate the whole plan. His last few words were not nice to think about. To die in an attempt to stop them sounded very noble, but I just don't have too much stomach for that sort of thing though I agreed with him, anyway.

'Fine, Tom, fine. Like you say it's got to be soon, but what? and how?'

'That's just it, boy. I just don't know!'

We lay in the dark for hours with nothing but the monotonous throb of the engines and the lights of the Coronet up ahead to fix our attention on. Many times we came up with ideas, brainstorming the problem in an attempt to work out a plan of action, but each time the slender chances of success could never quite justify the throwing away of this advantage we had. Each hour that passed diminished that advantage and we were no nearer a solution. Then about five in the early hours of the morning, sometime after the moon had set and the pitch-black hours before dawn dominated the sky and the water, there was a change in the pattern of lights ahead of us. The Coronet was signalling and soon this was taken up from both of the wings of the bridge above us.

'Looks like we're expecting company,' said Tom, and indeed, as our engines stopped, we could distinctly hear the sounds of others, moving towards us. But we could see nothing. A boat or boats were approaching from the beam and our view was cut off completely. Short of sticking a head out of cover there was no way of knowing who or what they were. Up front where we could see, though, there were signs of activity that dismayed us. The lights came on and men got busy with the lashings that held the deck cargo secure. It seemed certain that they were getting ready to unload right out there, bang in the centre of the lake—that could only mean transhipping.

Sloeder came forward from the bridge to superintend the business and soon we saw the boat that had just met with us. It was much smaller than I had expected from the noise of the engines, but it was big enough. It looked like the sort of excursion boat that is used for pleasure trips in the game reserves—about thirty-five feet long and wide in the beam. All the awnings and seats had been removed, thus making it an ideal craft for transporting the long bundles of pipes. And then another came up on the other bow and they proceeded to tie alongside.

'They're going to split the load three ways,' said Tom.

I thought he was right. It would make more sense than the steamer making the complete journey to three places to serve the three main sites. From here each of the boats would have at most ten hours' steaming and then Ladong, Aringot and Kaluli could receive their quota of nuclear explosive within a couple of hours of the final decision to put the plan into operation. The more I thought about it the more convinced I was that Barrett's blockade stood very little chance indeed.

'Once this load is split up, it'd take months to try to trace it again,' I said, 'even if we ever get off this boat alive to do it.'

'Right, so it's got to be now before any of the stuff is moved. There's no more time to kick it around. We've got to work in two areas here. One, the unloading's got to be delayed. Two, something's got to be done to make sure that that nuclear explosive travels no further than the bottom of this lake. Right?'

'There's a third, Tom,' I said thoughtfully.

'And that is?'

I felt sick as I put the thought into words. 'No one's got to be left alive to tell the story. If we're going to give Barrett the time he needs to clear up those sites with the help of the three African governments, then the more mystery we make for these people the better his chances will be. There must be no questions, no repercussions and not the slightest proof of any aggressive activity in this area. Firaz, his counterparts at Ladong and Aringot, and whoever else is behind this, must get no information at all. As far as they are concerned, these nuclear charges must just disappear without trace and so must everyone who knows anything about them.'

'Wrong, Gareth! There's two people going to get away from all this and that's you and me! Right?'

'Right!' I said, and I wished there was as much conviction in my heart as I tried to put into my voice.

'Now then, this is what we're going to do. Stage one—and this we've got to do right soon, 'cause they'll be starting unloading any moment. We've got to make a diversion. I've got it figured. Listen, see those drums of fuel down there in the well among the other stuff? We're going to fire them. One of them should open easy enough after that refuelling they did. It'll make a hell of a blaze if it gets going, but not enough for the whole job. Now, I want you to cover me while I go down there and get it started. We'll wait for the right moment and then go—pass me that heap of stuff you're lying on and the lighter. I'll try and fix it so that I get a few seconds to get out of there before the big blaze starts.'

I started to protest but he shut me up.

'Gary boy, just listen, we got no time for discussion now, it's action right the way through—okay?' I nodded, he tore three or four long shreds from the material and then dropped the rest on to the deck below to cushion his drop.

'So, once I get clear I want you to join me round the rear side of this cabin block . . .'

'And then?'

'Well, let's just wait and see.'

We waited for the right moment when we judged that his movement would cause no attention. There was not much danger that he would be seen, masked by the blinding glare of the lights, and everyone down there concentrating on the work in hand. He slipped down noiselessly and I gave him an encouraging sign that everything was okay. He moved forward, bent low so that he would be concealed by the drums themselves and the miscellany of objects that the well-deck held. From then on he had to work trusting that I would cover him for he, too, would be unable to see aft, from his position, though from my point of view I could see him as clearly as I could see the others and I realised suddenly that if he moved any further forward he would be visible from the bridge.

He removed the screw plug from the drum without any trouble and then started to feed the shreds of material into the hole. He withdrew them, dripping wet with fuel, and squeezed them over the remaining bundle. He did this several times and then seemed to be searching for something. He came back to the bulkhead of the cabins, just below where I lay and whispered urgently, 'Quick! pass down that jerry can, the big plastic one.'

'But it's empty,' I said, fumbling about in the darkness.

He gestured his urgency so I pushed it over the edge and it dropped into his waiting arms. He went back, placed the can on top of the sodden mass of oil-soaked material, and then heaved the half-empty drum on to a tilt, resting it on top of the plastic can. For one mad moment I thought it would fall and go clattering down on to the deck, but it held, the plastic sagging and giving it some stability. He then knotted the shredded lengths together and lay them down on the deck, paying them out as he went around the side of the cabin block.

I took one last look up forward and then slithered away towards the rear where I could drop off the cabin roof to join him. Already

the donkey engines had started to rattle into action and although
Tom had worked very quickly it seemed that I had been watching
for ages. I could just barely see him in the deep shadow of the
narrow passageway between the base of the bridge and the rear
of the cabins.

'All clear?' he asked.

'Yes,' I whispered, 'but for God's sake hurry! They've begun
the unloading.'

'Right, come on. Immediately I light this strip we've got to go
over the side with as little noise as possible. So wait for the racket
that will start when they see the blaze and then over.'

My mind was in a whirl. Over the side! Where did he think we
were going? We were over a hundred miles from the nearest land,
far from any traffic lanes, in the middle of a pitch black night. I
could hear him fumbling in his pocket for the lighter. It sparked
once or twice without any result. I heard him coaxing it in a
whisper of curses as he adjusted the gas jet to high. He tried again.
It lit. He doused it.

'You ready? Get to the rail, hang overboard and, as soon as I say,
let go and drop.'

'And what the hell then?' I asked. My heart was hammering
with excitement and fear, but I'd be damned if I was going on any
further without knowing.

'We're going to hijack one of the smaller boats that's what. Now
go!' I clambered over the rail and saw the fire go snaking along
the strip before my head went below deck level. Just as Tom
joined me there was a dull whump as the flame reached the
bundle, and a momentary pause before the shouting started. There
was an absolute chaos of sound which was soon joined by the
clang of the fire alarm from the bridge.

'Now!' said Tom, and I felt the side of the ship graze my knees
and hands as I dropped into a seemingly bottomless pit of blackness. Even though the night had been warm, hitting the water sent
a sudden shock of chill right through me. I seemed to be going
down endlessly before I was able to get my sense of balance and
kick up towards the surface. I drew a breath gratefully and lay
over on my back. The whole night seemed to be lit as by a gigantic
flame torch. I looked around for Tom and saw him coming towards me.

'Quick now,' he said. 'They'll cast those two boats off as soon as
they recover from the shock.' He led the way, swimming silently

through the blood-red water. The ship looked like an inferno and the clamour and shouting made the whole air tense with fear, as black oily clouds crested the flames. But I think we had under-estimated Sloeder's efficiency. I heard a voice whipping through the night on a loud hailer as he took command of the situation. An oil fire is serious on board any ship, but if panic can be controlled and measures taken to contain it then it need not be a disaster. I saw him lean over the side and give orders to the waiting boat below, his magnified voice echoing above the roar of flames.

'Send all available men aboard here, then cast off and wait at a safe distance.' He disappeared—probably to give the same order to the boat on the port side.

We were some ten yards from the smaller boat then and had made a wide circle to come in on the blind side of it when a bright blade of light cut suddenly through the shadows. The Coronet approached unheard in the noise and clamour. Instinctively, we both submerged in the instant of seeing the light and recognising it for what it was. I don't know how long Tom had been able to stay under, but when I felt that I could stand it no longer I struggled with bursting lungs to the surface. The strain had been intolerable and the sound of the Coronet's engines below the water was torture. She must have passed right over us. The bright white light was somewhere between me and the ship. I looked about for Tom, and saw no sign of him. Only yards away I could see the churning wake of the Coronet as she manœuvred to hold station and keep her spotlight on the ship—it was like blood frothing in the light of the fire. I noticed ruefully that the con-flagration was already much less than it had been. I had hoped that the other drums would have burst and made it worse.

Then suddenly I felt something with my legs and in one of my few moments of quick reaction, gulped air and did a duck dive deep beyond where my legs had been. My outstretched fingertips barely touched something, and with a frantic kick I went deeper and took a firm hold. It was a body and I knew it had to be Tom. Once more I broke surface, holding him beneath the arms. There was utter nothingness in my ears; it was not silence, but the deep beat of engines below the water had deadened my hearing so that I could not distinguish one sound from another. With the limp dead weight of Tom in my arms, I made for the only place within immediate reach—the swaying, frothing stern of the Coronet. There was a small foot-platform on these boats outboard of the stern. I tried desperately to avoid the thrashing of the propeller blades and attempted vainly to push Tom's inert body on to the ledge.

Just at the moment of exhaustion when I would have had to admit defeat, he became conscious and, coughing violently, grabbed and scrambled himself out of the water in some instinctive panic for survival. He retched and choked helplessly, but, seeing me in the water, managed somehow to grasp reality in an instant. I clambered up beside him but there was no need to caution him not to try to get up. He couldn't anyway. So we crouched there. I hung on to a cleat and grimly tried to support him until he became sufficiently aware to hold on himself. He was a strong man and as I've said before, in very good condition, but even so it must have required a tremendous act of will for him to stay there with barely sufficient room, and the stern backing and swaying as it was. His coughing seemed to shake his whole body. Water poured from his mouth and nostrils and an ooze of blood crept down from his forehead. The Coronet must have hit him before he went deep enough.

With a terrible sinking feeling of failure, I noticed the red glow die away to nothing. They had beaten the fire—and us. I felt an anguish of pain in my ears and then all the sound came back, assaulting my senses. I clearly heard the voice that I had come to hate echoing out from the loud hailer. 'Fire under control. Resume loading stations.' It was repeated over and over until I thought my head would burst with despair.

The Coronet reversed and swung away from the ship taking us away from all hope of intervening and placing us in a vulnerable state of weakness and dejection. The only favourable factor was that we were still hidden and safe from discovery, at least till someone looked over the stern.

The boat resumed her duty making a wide patrolling circle around the other vessels. She kept to a low cruising speed, and thus we were able to hang on without too much difficulty. It took a good ten minutes for Tom to recover sufficiently to reassure me that he'd be all right. Thankfully, the dreadful retching and coughing were over before we were out of earshot of the big ship. But he was in no condition to do anything much. Daylight could not be very far off and our chances of remaining undiscovered would be absolutely nil then, for we would be clearly seen from the other ships by anyone who happened to look our way.

So it was up to me to do something. It came to a very simple choice really: clamber aboard now and risk being killed outright or wait another half hour or so and be killed outright for certain. I felt for my gun in the waistband of my trousers. Lost of course! I mimed the fact to Tom and asked in the same way for his. He felt and then shook his head. Great, Ashe, all you've got to do now is climb over the stern and seize the boat single-handed —after all there'll only be about six people aboard. Nothing to it!

Impossible or not I had to go, so I carefully eased my way into an upright position so that I could get a look at whatever was in store for me. There was no one on the small afterdeck, but through the latch-back double door of the control cabin, I could make out at least three men, dimly lit by the glow from the console. I ducked back down quickly and gestured to Tom to rise and follow me. With a series of hand movements I told him what I wanted him to do, and in a couple of seconds we'd slithered on-board like a couple of undulating worms, to lie flat on the small deck, one each side as far away from midships and the line of sight from the cabin as possible.

I rose to a crouch, partly to get a better view and partly to be ready to meet any opposition. The main saloon was situated half below and half above the water line. The entrance to this was by a pair of double hatch doors that would swing up and out. These were closed, so I thought that the best thing to do first would be to ensure that they remained so and then, if there was anyone below, they would be prevented from interfering. I prayed that there was no other way out. The control cabin was built above the saloon and this was what I wanted to reach. I looked again at the double hatch doors. I noticed they were fitted with a pair of locking levers for storm conditions, and then, just while I was thinking how effectively these could be used to secure the main saloon, I suddenly realised how visible they were. I looked up and right enough, the ghostly light of pre-dawn was beginning to show in the sky. I would have to hurry. I slithered across to Tom and whispered my instructions about the doors. He nodded with half-closed eyes, hardly moving his head, but I could not wait for any other confirmation. If he passed out now—well, that was just one other complication. I already had enough to make one more seem trivial. I stood up and crept stealthily forward and mounted the small companionway that led to the control cabin.

There was only one advantage in my favour. I was alone, I was unarmed and I was outnumbered, but I had the slight edge that they were completely unaware of my presence and would be completely unsuspicious.

I stood as near to the doorway as I dared just around the starboard side of the cabin, but not far enough forward that I would be seen from the windscreen that swept from the front right around the sides. My preoccupation with silence and secrecy made the next stage very difficult. I had almost to force myself to start a regular rhythmic tapping with my foot against the side of the cabin. I was counting on someone coming out to investigate. Power boats are like motor cars; any knocking sound makes the driver sensitive and curious. I felt the boat slow down slightly as he throttled back a bit. I heard a grunting and mumbling as someone got up to come to see what the noise was about, and my throat went dry as I prepared to meet him. If two men appeared I was going to be in trouble, but I didn't dare think about it. I sensed his coming towards the sound of my tapping foot, and when I judged it right, moved out from behind the corner with both fists clenched together aiming for the angle at the base of the neck. He went down before the blow with a question half forming on his lips and a surprised startled look in his eyes, but he was far from out.

I could imagine the sickening, nerve-jarring sensations he was feeling as his brain struggled with waves of blackness, but there was no time for sympathy. I took the gun from his side holster with thick, fumbling fingers, hefted it in one hand and took a handful of his woolly black hair with the other. Turning his head, I delivered a hard follow-through blow to the base of his skull, and he went limp like a rag doll. I felt the beginnings of a nausea in the pit of my stomach and leaned a moment against the angle of the cabin. I felt the motors pick up slightly and a muffled, shouted enquiry.

'*Tayari?*' I slapped the side of the cabin hard with my open hand and shouted back.

'*Yari sasa!*' My voice came out hoarse with the tension I was feeling, but it was accepted and the motors picked up their beat to cruising speed once more.

I glanced back to where Tom crouched, gave him the sign to come on, slipped off the safety catch of the gun and moved in through the door. They didn't even look around! Sitting in the two high cockpit seats, they kept looking to the windscreen. They were the only others there. The one at the wheel only half turned his head as he enquired, '*Shauri nini?*' but he started with alarm as he saw me. 'How? What the . . .'

'Keep your hands on the wheel,' I barked. The other turned on the sound of my voice and looked askance at the man at the wheel.

'*Mikono Joo!*' I gestured upward with the gun. He hesitated. '*Sasa!*' I warned sharply but he swivelled quickly in the chair and made a move to go for the pistol at his hip. It was surprisingly easy really. My finger on the trigger and it was all over. No recriminations, no guilt.

My bullet had a double effect, it skittled him out of the seat to crash lifeless on the floor and it convinced the other—Hassel I guessed—by now that I meant business.

'All right, all right,' he said, 'take it easy—what is it you want?'

I heard a sound behind me and backed off into the corner where I could keep him covered and watch the door. Tom came through —I was so nervous that I could easily have put a bullet through him, but his voice whipped through the air sharply and I acted in reaction to it without thinking.

'Look out, Gareth, up front.' I turned and fired at the figure I could see through the windscreen. I missed, but it must have been close enough to make Mr Kopft dive for cover behind the mounting that held the gun on the foredeck. Hassel took advantage of the confusion and reached for the rifle that stood upright in the corner beside him. The boat lurched as he let go of the wheel and I was thrown off balance as I tried to shoot. My bullet went wide and made another hole through the windscreen. He was good with that rifle. In that confined space I wouldn't have been able to handle it, but he had it up and pointed at my chest in the split second that I took to recover my balance. Had it not been for the heavy object which Tom threw into his face I would surely have felt his bullet slam into me. My next shot was a lot more careful. As he bent over, holding his face, it went into the top of his head with a splattering thud. I saw the blood ooze through the grey of his hair and my gaze riveted on it. I began to tremble, my arm dropped to my side and I could feel my fingers slacken on the pistol. Waves of nausea began deep down in my stomach, but hardly had he hit the deck when Tom had seized the rifle and took up a position covering the forward deck. He sent a volley of shots to keep Kopft pinned down while I crouched down low and eased the twin throttle controls back to an idle slow.

'Any more of them about?' I spluttered, choking back my vomit.

'I don't think so, can't be sure though, but when I slammed the bolts on that saloon door it didn't seem to phase anybody. Take the wheel, Gareth, I'll keep Mr Kopft down.'

I pushed the body of Hassel aside with a shudder of sick self-loathing, and slid into his place uneasily. I didn't very much like the idea of being exposed like that, but there wasn't much choice. We were making a course that would take us right past the big ship. I swung away again and as soon as I'd done so, the radio burst into voice with a startling suddenness.

'Report in, two—report in, two—what is the shooting?'

I flipped the switch over and it grew silent again.

'I don't like it,' I said to Tom. 'Kopft is too quiet up there. Is there any way he could get through to the main saloon from up there? He could come up behind us.' I looked over my shoulder nervously and kept one hand free of the wheel, holding the gun at the ready.

'No, by God, there can't be,' shouted Tom. 'Look out! get down.'

I looked forward again just in time to see the muzzle of the big recoilless rifle up front swinging aft to bear on us. Tom poured lead as fast as he could, but the gun was well shielded with armour plate. One of his shots must have got home though for we heard Kopft scream with pain and then curse in a blind furious anger before all other noise and sound was lost in a deafening roar as the small shell tore through the control cabin in a whirl of spinning debris and choking smoke. The engines were still turning. That was the first sound that crystallised out of the confusion; I must have lost consciousness for a few seconds. I looked up and forward from the floor where I had flung myself. A great jagged space was all that remained of the forward bulkhead of the control cabin—and there was no sign of Tom.

The smoke was swirling away rapidly and then I saw them up on the forward deck locked in an almost statuesque pose. One large ham-sized arm of Kopft's was locked around Tom's throat, the other hung bloody and useless by his side. I fumbled about, but could not find any weapon in the debris. Tom's practically unconscious body was held in front of Kopft, hanging there with heels barely touching the floor, draped like a shield in the purple-faced paroxysm that precedes death by strangulation. And Kopft was coming forward. I felt a helpless sense of panic and almost turned to run, but then Tom must have summoned one last ounce of strength from somewhere. He swung his legs up against the remains of the superstructure and then pushed backwards. Kopft must have instinctively put out his wounded arm to break the fall, the shattered bone and torn muscles of his wound as they touched ground causing him to scream in pain and fury—but he let go his stranglehold on Tom and went slithering backwards beyond the gun towards the bow.

Two things seared through the confusion in my mind. One, the bulk of one of the smaller vessels moored to the side of the steamer lay dead ahead about fifty yards in front; and the other, that if I threw the engines into reverse abruptly it might give an extra momentum to Kopft and put him overboard. I don't know which was a priority in my mind, to avoid collision or to dislodge Kopft, but I acted instantly and jerked the dual controls right back through neutral into full throttle reverse. It had the desired effect in helping him on his way, but it did not dislodge him. I could still see the upper part of his body as he lay across the bow—like a grotesque figurehead clinging on to a forward fairlead with his only good arm.

He would have got back aboard, I'm sure, and he would have had no trouble dealing with the prostrate and helpless Tom who lay gasping for air on the deck, or the jelly-spined Ashe who felt so terrified. So, I did the only thing I could, I pushed the controls again to forward and pushed hard and deliberately. The boat leapt in answer as all the hundreds of horse power thrust her forward with proud, rising bow. She hurtled into a certain crash course with the other boat. I heard the chatter of machine guns and was aware of the splinters that went flying all around me, but I held the wheel steady, fascinated by one small square yard of the ship's side and oblivious to the helpless screaming of Kopft, who either didn't have the sense to let go or couldn't in his terror. We struck with a terrible impact and I swear I heard nothing of the strident crash of steel on steel—only the squelching, screaming sound of Kopft as he was sliced to instant death by our sharp bow striking deep into the side of the other boat.

I gave all the power I could again to the engines in reverse and swung the wheel over hard, determined to put as much distance between us and that scene of horror as I could.

Tom came stumbling to join me in the shattered cockpit. He had seen the last of Kopft, and now his face was blanched, contrasting vividly with the last time I'd seen it. I didn't ease up on our speed until we were a good mile from the steamer. Our departure was accompanied by random volleys of shots, but the partial cover of the cockpit sheltered us from sight and so we got away unscathed. Not so the Coronet, however. It was well down in the water and must have been leaking steadily by the bow. We rummaged about among the debris and eventually found the rifle and two pistols. The two bodies were all but buried where they had fallen. In a locker below deck level we discovered some binoculars and a partly full bottle of whisky and gratefully took a couple of long pulls at it. The bite of the spirit did much to help me pull myself together. The unnatural cold that had come upon me making my hands tremble gradually went away.

Leaving the boat to drift in the flat leaden calm of early dawn, I took the binoculars and stepped out on to the foredeck to examine the damage. Tom went below through the saloon to explore the galley hoping to find some coffee. I could not speak then, it was as if all the emotion and feeling were drained out of me. I lay down on the deck to look over the bow. It was steel re-inforced, aluminium moulded, and had crumbled badly under the impact, but did not seem as bad as I had first thought. With some pumping it would probably last us back, if we could raise the bow out of the water a little by getting some weight aft. Lying there, I looked back at the steamer. They had cast the damaged boat off and moved a little away from it. I got hardly any satisfaction from noting the frantic activity to get a cable round the cargo before it sank. It was going down for sure and was almost awash even as I looked. I focused on the dark hole in her side and shuddered as I remembered the impact, cushioned only by the terrified body of Kopft.

I went aft to look at the fuel tanks. There was just under a half still unused—enough to make the return journey at an economical speed. Tom came up out of the saloon with a couple of mugs of coffee and some biscuits. At first my stomach revolted at the thought, but as I sipped at the coffee I realised how hungry I was. We sat awhile chewing, each in our own thoughts.

'There's probably enough fuel to get us back,' I said flatly.

Tom did not answer for a while, but took the glasses from me and looked long and steadily.

'She's gone down,' he said with a deep sigh, 'but it looks as if they've saved the pipes—they're there hanging from the boom now.'

I looked out across the flat, calm water, reddening now as the sun rose above the horizon in rosy cloud-rimmed aura.

'Let's get out of here,' I said. 'There's no more we can do now. Give me a hand with the bodies—I don't fancy their company for the journey. That one may be still alive though!' I gestured to the inert form lying against the rail.

Tom just shook his head and I knew he was feeling much as I was. God! the enormity of it! When I thought about the killing, the mad senseless slaughtering . . . and all for what? It was no use me trying to convince myself that I'd done it out of any sense of righteousness—it was all to save my own miserable skin. I think I was on the point then of breaking up altogether; I went into the cockpit and just sat in the middle of all the debris and destruction. I heard Tom come in behind me.

'It's no good, Gareth! We've got to finish it, we've got to go back and sink the damned boats, we can't leave it like this, it'll make a mockery of everything we've tried to do!'

I looked at him with disbelief. Was he mad!

'No!' I shouted. 'I've had enough, I'm finished, Sloeder can go and blow the whole world to hell for all I care, it's not worth a damn anyway. There's nothing to choose either way. I'm having no more to do with it. I'm getting out of here! So what if we do stop it—is that any guarantee that some other maniac in your country or mine or somewhere else won't go and split the whole bloody world apart in a nuclear war for the very same reasons that Firaz and the like are doing? For some sort of national glory or to gain or maintain a homeland. Well, is there?' I shouted.

'Yes, I reckon there is—the guarantee is that there's still some people around who are prepared to do something about it. The minute you throw your hand in it's finished, but up till then we've still got a chance. Remember what I said earlier about having to get tough? Hell! do you think it's easy—don't you think I got some feelings, too, about this?' He gestured to the bodies on either side of him. 'But it's got to be and this is only the start.' He looked grimly at the foredeck. 'Up there there's eleven more rounds for that thing—and we're going right back in there to finish this whole bloody mess, and like you said before—nobody gets home to tell the story.'

I looked long and hard at him. 'You could do that?' I asked.

'I don't know, I don't know—God, I don't know, Gareth, but we've got to try!' He looked as miserable and confused as I felt.

Perhaps it was harder for him, he seemed to have lived his life with clean-cut issues. What is good, what is bad—and now for the first time probably, the whole thing had become doubtful for him. It takes a long lifetime's training in casuistry to believe in a cause, or wage a crusade. It needs absolute faith and confidence in yourself and your opinions. I have never had any of these things, issues have always been clouded for me by the nagging suspicion that the other point of view might be right.

I felt I had to be alone to think, so I went up forward and sat on the crumpled bow, and strangely the image of Kopft was not there any more. I did a lot of hard thinking then and made a decision: that this was a time for me to face up to myself and the world. It was a time when the comfort of vacillation was denied me, and the soft cosy mantle of self-deception had to be torn aside. It was late in life for me to try to work out what was establishment, what was revolution and what was stark mad murder, but I decided and even now cannot really say that I was convinced.

I lived in a cold frightened daze that started from the moment I decided to help him. The eleven rounds from the recoilless rifle on our bow had sunk the remaining two boats and we'd moved in to finish off the survivors who had leapt clear of the vessels as they sank. Hours and hours of recrimination were to remain with me long after it was all over and nothing remained but the memory of ships torn and broken, flying apart in the shattering destruction of men gone mad; the ear-splitting shrieks of men who screamed in burning pain for mercy, their mouths full of fire and blood and curses, and the deep, deep stains on the surface of the water black beneath the innocent blue of the sky with the charred stumpy remains of hopeless resistance still red beneath the harsh forenoon sun with the blood of men slaughtered in blind execution.

The rifle dropped from my hands into the water—and I watched the ripples spread out like a glowing ring of fire.